"Where is this mortal that I might reward their loyalty?"

She hesitated to answer. If this god was a wrathful sort, he might not take the news well.

Thunder cracked as he impatiently waited for her response.

She said, "You sort of…well…you kind of…ate him."

The god writhed. "Ah, damn. That is embarrassing. If I had cheeks, they'd be red right now." He scanned the room. "Are you the only ones then?"

"Yes, sir," said Helen.

"And neither of you worships me?"

"No, sir," she replied.

A shudder ran through the god's flesh. "Get banished for a few thousand years and the whole operation falls apart. Damn the gods and our petty feuds."

"We're terribly sorry for the mix-up," said Troy, as they edged toward the door, "but we'll just be on our way—"

"No need to apologize. Not your fault. But you can help me just the same. A couple of strong young mortal specimens."

The god focused his gaze on them, and they were immobilized by his supernatural power.

"You'll do."

By A. Lee Martinez

Orbit
Hachette Book Group
237 Park Avenue, New York, NY 10017
HachetteBookGroup.com

First Edition: July 2013

Orbit is an imprint of Hachette Book Group, Inc. The Orbit name and logo
are trademarks of Little, Brown Book Group Limited.

The Hachette Speakers Bureau provides a wide range of authors for speaking
events. To find out more, go to www.hachettespeakersbureau.com or call
(866) 376-6591.

The publisher is not responsible for websites (or their content) that are not
owned by the publisher.

The characters and events in this book are fictitious. Any similarity to real
persons, living or dead, is coincidental and not intended by the author.

Library of Congress Cataloging-in-Publication Data
Martinez, A. Lee.
Helen and Troy's epic road quest / A. Lee Martinez. — First Edition.
  pages cm
ISBN 978-0-316-22643-1 (trade pbk.) — ISBN 978-0-316-22644-8 (ebook)
1. Fantasy fiction. 2. Humorous fiction. 3. Road fiction. I. Title.
PS3613.A78638H45 2013
813'.6—dc23
  2012046116

10 9 8 7 6 5 4 3 2 1

RRD-C

Printed in the United States of America

Helen & Troy's EPIC ROAD QUEST

A. LEE MARTINEZ

orbit

www.orbitbooks.net

For Janet, a mother-in-law a guy is lucky to have.

For Aunt Peggy, because I know she'd be really excited to see her name on a dedication.

And for Stinkor, Evil Master of Odors. You stink, buddy, but in the good way.

ACKNOWLEDGMENTS

The tenth book. How did this happen? How did I get here? It's a rhetorical question. I know how I got here. Hard work. A whole lot of luck. The support of a bunch of great people. While I usually abhor a long acknowledgments list, I think I'm due. If you don't like it, feel free to skip it. Won't hurt my feelings. Thanks for buying the book. Or at least borrowing it from your local library, friend, or kind stranger and giving it a read.

Once I was a normal man. Though it's been a while, I still remember what it was like to be a regular joe. The simpler days, back before I had my own solid-gold robot butler. Yesterday, as I put the down payment on my weather machine, I thought back to those days, and I realize that my fame and fortune came because of the hard work of a lot of fine folks.

As always, I'd like to thank Mom, who always believed in me. She's the foundation of everything I've accomplished. I don't say that in some cheap bid for good-son points. It's absolutely true, and while most everyone thinks their mom is special, mine really is. So deal with it.

Being an aspiring writer is a journey through a long, confounding wilderness. That journey was made a lot less harrowing thanks to the fine folks at the DFW Writer's Workshop. They made the difficult times easier, and the easy times even more enjoyable. Thanks for everything you've done and everything you will do.

I'd be remiss if I didn't mention Paul Stevens, my first editor and the guy who was willing to take that first chance. If a writing career is a fortress city where all aspiring authors pound on the front gates (and it pretty much is), Paul was the guard who sneaked me into its walls and told everyone else I belonged on this side. And he did so for no other reason than that he believed people would want to read a book where a vampire and a werewolf fight zombie cows. So thanks.

Then there's my agent, Sally Harding, a heck of a cool lady and someone who makes my life run a lot smoother.

There's my Sally, my beautiful wife. I love you, baby. Promise you won't forget me when you make your first million-dollar book deal.

Or at least be sure to leave me with half the moola.

And there are all the readers, the dedicated fans, the not-so-dedicated fans, and everyone else who has ever enabled my particular career by buying, reading, recommending, or even criticizing my books. At the heart of it all, this doesn't happen without you.

And the list goes on. My friends, my enemies, people whom I like and admire, others whom I seek to crush and destroy. This acknowledgment could go on for pages, and I'd probably still forget to thank somebody. Who are we fooling anyway? You don't want to read this stuff. You want to read about a couple of crazy young kids making their way on this journey we call life, but with more cyclops punching and orc fighting. Come to think of it, so do I.

So thanks, everybody.

Now on to the monster battles...

1

The strangeness of a minotaur working at a burger joint wasn't lost on Helen, but she'd needed a summer job. If she'd applied herself, she probably could've found something better, but it was only a few months until she started college, so why bother?

Fortunately Mr. Whiteleaf had been pretty cool about it. He didn't make her flip burgers, and he didn't make her stand out on the curb with a sandwich board as she'd feared he might. She usually ran the register, and while some customers might give her funny looks before placing their orders, that was their problem, not hers.

Full-blown minotaurism was rare in this day and age. Last time she'd checked, there had been thirteen recorded cases in the last hundred years. All the others were male. The enchantment or curse or whatever you wanted to call it usually didn't take with girls. Not all the way.

The last full female minotaur, Gladys Hoffman, aka Minotaur Minnie, had made a name for herself as a strongwoman touring with P. T. Barnum's Traveling Museum, Menagerie, Caravan, and Hippodrome. Gladys had made the best of her circumstances, but that was 1880. The world was different now, and Helen had more options. Or so she liked to believe.

She was still a seven-foot girl with horns and hooves, dozens of case studies in various medical journals, and her very own Wikipedia page. But she'd learned to roll with the punches.

The family waiting to be rung up right now was giving her the Look. A lot of people didn't know what to do with Helen, what category to throw her in. Civil rights had made a lot of progress for the orcs, ratlings, ogres, and other "monstrous" races. But minotaurs didn't have numbers. There had been no protests, no sit-ins, no grand moment in history when the rest of the world saw them as anything other than anomalies, victims of lingering curses from the days of yore carried along rare family bloodlines.

The father squinted at her as if she were a traitor to her kind. She didn't even eat meat. Not that it was any of his business.

Helen rubbed her bracelet. She did that whenever she felt self-conscious. Jewelry wasn't allowed on the job, but Mr. Whiteleaf had made an exception since hers was prescription to deal with her condition.

The little girl stared. Kids couldn't help it.

"Are you a monster?" she asked.

Helen smiled. "No, sweetie. I'm just an Enchanted American."

The mother pulled the girl away. Helen was going to say she didn't mind, that kids were only curious, and that she preferred it when people talked to her directly about her condition rather than pretend they didn't notice.

"I'm sorry," said the father.

"It's OK," replied Helen. "Kids, huh?"

He placed his order. She rang him up, gave him back his change and his number.

"We'll call you when your order is ready, sir," she said with a forced smile. "Thank you for eating at Magic Burger. And we hope you have a magical day."

Helen leaned against the counter, but she didn't allow herself to slouch. Working the register was, from a fast-food perspective, a dignified job, but it also came with responsibilities. Mr. Whiteleaf didn't expect much. Look as if she were happy to be there. Or, if not happy, at least not ready to clock out and go home.

"Helen."

She jumped. Mr. Whiteleaf was like a ghost sometimes. The small, pale elf was past his prime by a few hundred years. Middle age wasn't a pretty thing for elves, who went from tall, regal figures to short, potbellied creatures with astigmatism in a very short time. And then they were stuck with another six or seven centuries walking this earth as creaky old men with tufts of green hair growing out of their drooping ears. But Mr. Whiteleaf was a good boss.

If only he wouldn't sneak up on her like that.

She craned her neck to peer down at him. As she was very tall and he was short, he only came to her lower abdomen.

"Hello, sir," she said.

He adjusted his glasses. "Quitting time."

She made a show of glancing at the clock on the wall, as if she had just noticed it and hadn't been counting the minutes. "Yes, sir."

Whiteleaf said, "I hate to trouble you, Helen, but would you mind working late tonight? I need some help giving the place a thorough cleaning. Word through the grapevine is that there's a surprise health inspection tomorrow. It won't be a problem, will it?"

"No," she replied.

"Excellent. I'll see you around ten thirty, then?"

"Sure thing, Mr. Whiteleaf."

The sudden obligation left her with a ninety-minute block. It was just long enough to be inconvenient but not long enough to make it worth her while to go home, change out of her work clothes, goof off for a bit, then come back. She grabbed an expired salad (they were free) and went to the break room.

Troy was there. She liked him. He was easygoing, smart, handsome, physically gifted. These qualities should have made him annoying, but whereas most people with Troy's gifts would've considered them a license for arrogance, he seemed to know how good he had it. He was always pleasant, always friendly and helpful. Nice to everyone. He was too good to be true, but with billions of people out there, there were bound to be one or two perfect ones.

Smiling, he nodded to her.

She nodded back. She wondered how many girls would go mad for a chance like this. One-on-one with Him. Him with a capital *H*, though not in a blasphemous way. Although there were whispers of demigod in his family tree.

Helen was never nervous around boys. One of the advantages of her condition was that she knew where she stood from the beginning. She liked to think of her figure as curvaceous. Like Marilyn Monroe's. Except gentlemen preferred blondes, not brown fur with white speckles. She had yet to find a pair of heels that fit her hooves. Troy was tall, with wide shoulders. She was taller, with shoulders just a smidge wider. And then there was the whole cow-head thing.

In short, she avoided butterflies in her stomach by knowing she had absolutely no chance with Troy, especially since he was rarely single in the first place.

"Hey, did Mr. Whiteleaf ask you to work late too?" she asked.

Troy looked up from his book. "Didn't mention it. Why? Does he need help?"

She sat, popped open the plastic salad container, and jammed her plastic fork at the wilted lettuce with little success. Either the fork needed to be sharper or the lettuce crisper.

"Guess not," she said.

"Shoot." (He didn't swear either.) "I really could use the money."

"Since when do you need money?" she asked. "I thought your parents were loaded."

"I'm saving for a car. Dad won't buy it for me because he says I need to learn responsibility."

"Don't you volunteer at the homeless shelter? And the senior center? And the animal shelter? And weren't you valedictorian and prom king?"

"Dad thinks I can do better."

"Well, if that's what Dad says, who am I to argue? I can see now that you're a young man in serious need of personal discipline." She stuffed a few leaves and a cherry tomato in her mouth. "What'cha reading there?"

"T. S. Eliot," he said.

That he read poetry was almost comical to Helen. It was as if he were trying to spontaneously ascend to some higher plane of perfect boyness, some sacred dimension birthed from the philosophical union of Aristotle and *Tiger Beat* editors.

He caught her smile.

"What? Don't like him?"

"Haven't read him," she replied.

"You haven't read him? One of the preeminent poets of the twentieth century, and you haven't read him?"

"He isn't that guy who doesn't capitalize, is he?"

"That's E. E. Cummings."

"My mistake."

He slid the book across the table. "Do you want to borrow my copy?"

She slid it back. "No, thanks."

He pretended to gape.

"I don't like poetry," she said. "I know I'm supposed to because I'm a girl and all that. I tried. I really did. But outside of Dr. Seuss, it doesn't do much for me."

"I've always found *The Lorax* to be a little preachy."

"'Don't burn the earth to the ground' always struck me as more common sense than preachy," she replied.

Troy chuckled. "Well, I'd love to stick around and chat about all the metaphorical implications of *Hop on Pop* with you, but I've got stuff to do."

"Giving blood, saving kittens, running from throngs of adoring young ladies," said Helen.

"I'll have you know I only save kittens on the weekend. Later, Hel."

He bounded from the room like Adonis in jeans. She was glad

she hadn't been born five thousand years before, when, instead of being friends, they would've probably had to fight to the death in an arena.

She tried reading the poetry book, but it didn't do anything for her. She hid out in the break room, watching its tiny television, because she didn't want to get stuck helping to lock up. Whiteleaf would get her when it was time to clean up. Or so she thought, but everything was quiet at eleven fifteen.

Helen poked her head into the kitchen. The lights were on, but it was all shut down. No sign of the other employees. Her hooves clomped on the tile. They seemed especially loud with the Magic Burger so quiet. The silence was eerie.

The tables and chairs in the dining area, the ones that weren't bolted down, had been pushed to one side, and boxes of frozen hamburger patties sat in their place.

Whiteleaf spoke from behind her. "Hello, Helen."

She jumped.

"Oh, hi, sir. Should those burgers be out like that?"

He smiled, adjusted his glasses. "They'll be fine."

"Are we cleaning the freezer?" she asked.

He held up a small wand with a chunk of blue stone on the end. "Stand over there."

"By the meat?"

Whiteleaf frowned. "Damn it, this thing must be wearing out. It's barely two hundred years old, but once the warranty expires..." He shook the wand until the barest hint of a glow flashed in its stone.

"Are you feeling OK, Mr. Whiteleaf?"

"Look at the wand," he said. "Feel its power wash over your mind, numbing your will, robbing you of all resistance."

Helen stepped back. "This is getting kind of weird. I think maybe I should go."

He threw the wand aside. "Fine. We'll do it the less subtle way." He reached under the counter and removed a sword. She wasn't familiar with weapons, but it looked like an ornate broadsword with runes carved in the blade. It didn't glow, but it did sort of shimmer.

She didn't freak out. An advantage of being taller and stronger than nearly everyone was that she'd developed confidence in her ability to handle physical violence. She'd never been in a fight precisely *because* she was bigger and stronger than everyone. If someone ever did attack her, she'd probably freeze. She wasn't sword-proof. And the blade could do some damage in the right hands. But Whiteleaf was a frail little creature who was barely able to hold the weapon. He certainly couldn't raise it above her knee, which meant he might be able to nick her shins, which would probably hurt but wouldn't be particularly life-threatening.

"I'm very sorry about this, Helen." His arms trembled, and he sounded exhausted already. "But when the Lost God manifests in this world, he must be offered a sacrifice. Preferably an innately magical virgin. And you're the only one I could find who fit the—"

"What makes you think I'm a virgin?" she asked.

Whiteleaf lowered the blade. The tip scraped a gash in the tile floor.

"Ah, damn. Wait. You're not a virgin?"

"I didn't say that. I just asked why you thought I was one."

"It's just...I guess I just...assumed you were."

"Why would you assume that?"

8

He chewed on his lip for a moment. "Well, you're a very responsible young lady. It's one of the things I respect about you."

She glared. "It's because of the way I look, isn't it?"

Whiteleaf shook his head. "No, no. You're a very attractive young lady. You are!"

She moved toward him. He lifted his sword a few inches off the floor.

"I don't need this," she said. "I quit."

"You can't quit," he replied. "I need you. For the sacrifice."

She removed her name tag and set it on the counter. "I've never gored anyone before, Mr. Whiteleaf. But in your case, I'm considering it."

The Magic Burger's lights flickered and a low, guttural cry echoed from the center of the room. The aroma of sizzling meat filled the restaurant as the boxes of hamburger patties burst into flames. The ground chuck collapsed in a mound of brown-and-pink cow flesh, and it formed a giant gnashing mouth.

"At last, at last!" shouted Whiteleaf. "He has returned to us!"

Helen studied the twisted meat deity.

"You worship a hamburger god?"

Whiteleaf sighed. "He is not a hamburger god. He is a god currently manifested in an avatar of flesh that just happens to be made up of, for convenience, hamburger. Now, we haven't much time. So I'm going to need you to throw yourself into his jaws. I assure you it will be fast and quite painless."

"No."

"I'm afraid you don't have a choice, Helen." He advanced on her. "In my youth, I was a warrior to be reckoned with."

She used one hand to push him down. He fell on his ass. His

sword clattered to the ground. The noise drew the attention of the hamburger god. It probed the floor in their direction with its twisted limbs.

Helen immediately regretted knocking the old elf down. He was intent on sacrificing her, and that was a pretty lousy thing to do to a girl. But his lack of ability rendered him harmless, and she could've handled it better.

He struggled to stand. His knees weren't very good, though, and it was painful to watch. "Please, you must do it. If the god isn't given his sacrifice, he'll never be able to focus and he'll never give me the sacred command. I've waited too long to blow this opportunity."

"I'm sorry, Mr. Whiteleaf. I'm not going to let a monster eat me for minimum wage."

She moved to help him up. He slashed at her with a butcher knife he'd had hidden behind his back. The blade sliced across her forearm. The cut was shallow, but it triggered a rage within her. Perhaps it was the wound. Or perhaps it was something buried in her minotaur id, the collective memory of untold billions of bovine in pain and fear.

She seized him by the collar and lifted him in the air.

"Drop. The. Knife."

He did. It clanked against the floor beside the broadsword.

"You crazy old man," she said. "It would serve you right if I offered you to your own hamburger god."

He trembled. His feet dangled limply. "It isn't personal. It's just that my god only appears once every three hundred years, and this is very important to me."

The Lost God lurched slowly around the dining area. If this blind and clumsy thing was any indication of the gods of yore, no wonder they'd mostly been forgotten. It gnawed on the corner of a table.

The glass door swung open and Troy entered. It took only one glance for him to see something was wrong.

"Hel?"

She had yet to figure out how the god perceived the world, but there was something about Troy that drew its attention. The mound of meat squished its way in his direction.

"Troy, get out of here," said Helen.

But it was too late. The god opened its mouth, and out shot a tongue of the same flesh. It wrapped around Troy's leg and pulled him toward its jaws. Yelping, he latched onto a table bolted to the floor.

She didn't think. She didn't have time. She certainly hadn't rehearsed this scenario in her mind. But by instinct she dropped Whiteleaf and grabbed the sword. A leaping blow chopped the tentacle. The god shrieked and leaned backward.

The meat coiled around Troy's leg whipped and writhed. They pulled at it, and the greasy flesh broke apart in their hands. But it kept moving, crawling on their arms like living snot.

The god charged. Helen drove the sword into the monster's lumpy body. The blade flashed and the thing recoiled. It sputtered and bubbled and squealed, swaying erratically through the room until it fell apart into a smoking pile in the middle of the room.

"What the hell was that?" asked Troy.

"A god of yore," she replied. "But I think it's dead now."

Whiteleaf ran to his broken god's corporeal remains. "What did you do? You destroyed it. Now I have to wait another three hundred years. Do you have any idea how annoying this is?" He stuck his hands in the hamburger, pulled them out, and scowled at the rancid meat. "You're fired. Both of you."

"I already quit," said Helen.

Troy grabbed some napkins from a dispenser and cleaned the burger from his hands. "What the heck is going on here?"

"I'll explain later. But we should probably call the police or something. I'm sure it's against the law to sacrifice employees."

Whiteleaf screamed as his not-quite-dead god grumbled. It surged up his arms and swallowed his torso. His short legs kicked as they were drawn into the mass. Whether or not Helen would've tried to save him given a chance was unimportant, because his god devoured him whole in a matter of seconds. He struggled within the fleshy thing. A limb would break the surface, only to be drawn back in. At one point his face appeared. Half the skin had been eaten away, and he screamed, his cries muffled by mouthfuls of ground beef, before vanishing within.

"Quick and painless, my ass," said Helen.

"I think I'm going to throw up," said Troy.

The Lost God sprouted a skull. Most likely Mr. Whiteleaf's skull. Though the flesh had all been eaten away, the eyes remained. It turned those eyes on Helen and Troy, and its jaws parted.

"Ah, that hit the spot. Nothing like a little ritual sacrifice to get the juices flowing. Your god is pleased."

"I'm afraid there's been a mistake," said Helen. "We aren't your worshippers."

The god scanned the room. "Well, you're the only ones here. Someone summoned me, didn't they?"

"Yes, sir. Someone did."

"Where is this mortal that I might reward their loyalty?"

She hesitated to answer. If this god was a wrathful sort, he might not take the news well.

Thunder cracked as he impatiently waited for her response.

She said, "You sort of...well...you kind of...ate him."

The god writhed. "Ah, damn. That is embarrassing. If I had cheeks, they'd be red right now." He scanned the room. "Are you the only ones then?"

"Yes, sir," said Helen.

"And neither of you worships me?"

"No, sir," she replied.

A shudder ran through the god's flesh. "Get banished for a few thousand years and the whole operation falls apart. Damn the gods and our petty feuds."

"We're terribly sorry for the mix-up," said Troy, as they edged toward the door, "but we'll just be on our way—"

"No need to apologize. Not your fault. But you can help me just the same. A couple of strong young mortal specimens."

The god focused his gaze on them, and they were immobilized by his supernatural power.

"You'll do."

The god asked them to sit. It was only a formality. Their bodies surrendered to his impulses.

"What do you want?" asked Helen.

"What does any banished god want? To return to my rightful place in the heavens above. You're going to help me do that."

"How?"

"A quest," he replied.

Troy and Helen shared a glance.

"What?" asked the god. "Don't tell me people don't quest anymore."

"It just seems a bit arbitrary," said Helen. "You pop out of…wherever you popped out of…and give us a quest, just like that."

"Of course it's arbitrary," said the god. "Quests are always arbitrary. Why does the knight have to slay the dragon to get his princess? Why does the magic knickknack have to be stored away in some faraway mountain? Why do gods and the Fates themselves ask mortals to undertake perilous missions and face impossible odds in the vague promise of fabled reward? Because that's the way it is."

"That's your answer?" she said. "It's stupid, but that's the way it is?"

The god snarled. "I don't make the rules. If you want me to smite you, I can just do that."

Helen sighed. "No, I guess not. Go ahead."

The god chuckled. "Look at it this way. You can still kill and terrorize. You'll just be doing it in my service."

Helen frowned. "I don't kill and terrorize."

He slunk back. "Really? But you're a monster, aren't you? A curse inflicted on the mortal world for its sins. A beast made to torment and bedevil."

Helen scowled. Whatever transgression her ancestors had committed to earn their horns had been lost to history. If anyone in the family knew, he hadn't told her. It was something they'd put behind them.

"Look, guy—" It seemed the wrong term, but she didn't care. She would be damned if she'd allow this god to assume the worst about her simply because she had hooves and a tail. "We don't do that anymore. Anyone with any sense will tell you that enchanteds were the terrorized, not the terrorizing, more often than not throughout history.

"Furthermore, judging someone by the size of their horns fell out of fashion a while ago. Just because you gods cursed my family line, it doesn't give you a right to assume I'm a monster. I don't know what my family did to deserve this. Maybe they committed some horrible crime. Maybe they just ate turkey on

Tuesday or caught the attention of the gods on a bad day. Regardless, the way I look has nothing to do with anything I or anyone in my family for untold generations has done. So I'd appreciate it if you didn't assume so."

The god shrugged. "All right, all right. I didn't mean to insult you."

"But you managed to just the same."

He slumped low. "You're right. It was rude of me to make assumptions, but I've been away a long time."

"Well, aren't you a god?" asked Troy. "Shouldn't you know these things?"

"It's easier when you're looking down from above. Like watching fish through a glass-bottomed boat. Although even that has its problems. Try keeping up with the politics of bacteria while studying them through a microscope and see how well you do. Also, have I mentioned I've been banished to a lower plane? I've been stuck watching you from beneath for the last thousand years. Aside from your taste in shoes, I'm not really up on much."

Helen imagined the Lost God lurking, unseen, below her. She was glad she avoided dresses.

He must've read her face. Or possibly her mind.

"I was speaking metaphorically," he said. "I have more important concerns than sneaking peeks at naughty bits. And, if I may be honest, I've always found those bits rather disconcerting." The skull trembled. The mound of flesh shuddered. "If I'd had my way, we'd have stuck with asexual reproduction. But I was outvoted."

He slunk close to Helen's and Troy's immobile bodies.

"But we're getting off topic." The face studied Troy. "You're a fine specimen, aren't you? Strong jaw. Good teeth. Nice hair. Sturdy, athletic body. Plus you've got that heroic glint in your eyes."

Helen snorted. Owing to her enchanted nature, she was very good at it.

"Would you two like to be alone?"

The god clicked his teeth together. "I like you. You've got moxie. Those mortals who dare defy the gods are the ones who usually end up most useful to us. The sycophants, the toadies, they're good for assembling a crowd, but at the end of the age, it's the defiant souls who get things done.

"Not always to our liking, though. That's the catch, isn't it? This universe does so love making fools of mortal and immortal alike. It's why the gods of irony rarely get invited to any of the cool parties."

"Is there a point to this?" she asked.

Troy whispered, "It might not be a good idea to antagonize the skull god."

The god chuckled. "I don't mind. Really. The best champions are fearless, even in the dread presence of the gods themselves."

"Up yours," said Helen.

"Oh, now you're just forcing it."

A clap of thunder shook the restaurant.

The god shouted to the heavens, "Oh, shut up. I'm almost done here."

Lightning struck the roof, causing the lights to flicker. In the moments of darkness, the god's true form could be glimpsed around the edges, a shadow in the emptiness, a strange shape from the primordial beginnings of time. But it was only a reflection of a thing not meant for mortal eyes and not really what he looked like at all. Just as close as either mortal could grasp.

It looked like a turnip on legs to Helen. A dragon made of sausage links to Troy. Both viewpoints were closer to the truth than either knew, though not really close at all.

"Haven't much time," said the god. "The last time I stayed too long, they sent down a meteor strike. Thousands of mortals dead because the gods above couldn't give me five more minutes. And I'm the bad guy."

Thunder cracked.

"Yes, yes, I'm finishing up now."

Grumbling, he slithered before Helen and Troy.

"Your quest is this. You must gather the relics and bring them to the place of power at the appointed time."

"What kind of relics?" asked Troy.

"I'm not sure," he replied.

"How many?" asked Helen.

"Somewhere between two and six, I think. Possibly seven. No more than eight, I feel confident in saying."

"Where is the place of power?" asked Helen.

"I don't know."

"When's the appointed time?" asked Helen.

The god rolled his eyes. "Soonish."

"That's a bit vague for a quest, isn't it?" asked Troy.

"Heck, maybe we already did it," said Helen with a smirk.

The god heaved a sigh. "It's details. Just details. I don't concern myself with them."

"But how do we complete a quest we don't even understand?"

"If I could give you a diagram, photographs, and sextant coordinates, I would. You still use sextants, right?"

They shook their heads.

"No matter. The more help I give you, the more the other gods are allowed to intervene on their end. Since I'm at a serious disadvantage, what with me being trapped in the lower dimensions and all, I can't win the game that way. My best shot is to give you your quest, push you out into the world, and hope for the best. It's bound to work one of these times."

Helen said, "You've done this before?"

"Once or twice," he replied. "Or nine or ten times."

"What happened to the others?" asked Troy.

"You really should stop worrying about the details. It'll only stress you. They failed. They died. Those are the terms of the quest. Either accomplish the task or perish. That reminds me…"

Both mortals felt a sharp sting on the back of their right hand. A swirling pattern burned itself into their flesh.

"There," said the god. "You are now officially and irreversibly bound to your quest. Succeed and I shall reward you most bountifully."

"A vague promise of fabled reward," said Helen.

"You're catching on. I like that. You're a bright pair, I can see. So I'll be straight with you. The big reward at the end of this quest is that you get to keep on living, which is exceptionally generous on my part. Fail and oblivion awaits."

"You can't just do this," said Helen. "It has to be against some rule somewhere."

"You could try appealing to the mercy of the gods," said the leering skull, "but in my opinion, you're better off on your own. In any case, it's done."

"What's done?" asked Troy. "You haven't told us what to do or how to do it."

"Do you really want me to? Would you find it comforting if I told you that every action is planned and that I know exactly what I'm doing?"

They nodded.

"OK, then it is and I do."

"You're lying," said Helen.

He laughed. "Moxie."

Mr. Whiteleaf's sword and wand floated in the air and hovered over the god. "Tell you what I'll do. Since you seem like nice mortals in a bad situation, I'll give you just a smidge of extra help. I'll charge these items with magic power to help you on your quest."

His eyes flashed, and the wand and sword flared with an inner light.

"It's not much, but it's the best I can do."

The Magic Burger rattled as if it might shake apart.

"All right already. I'm leaving. Sorry, kids. No more time for questions."

The mound of hamburger fell apart, and the skull bounced to a stop at their feet. The sword and wand clattered to the floor. Troy very carefully nudged the skull with his toe. The eyes fell out and rolled across the floor like marbles.

"What now?" he asked.

Thunder rumbled far, far in the distance.

They called the police. Then they called their parents. Eventually, after much hullabaloo, Helen and Troy found themselves sitting in a sparsely decorated room with a table and four chairs. They were there for a little over an hour until a man in a gray suit entered.

He had the crisp suit and stone-faced demeanor of a government agent. Or rather the image of one television and movies had given Helen. But his tie was bright yellow, and his hair was a bit shaggy. And not in that pretending-to-be-messy way. It was actually messy. There was his soul patch and his wire-framed spectacles. It was as if someone had taken an all-business bureaucrat and a beatnik, and dropped them in a blender to create a not-entirely-convincing mix.

He smiled.

"Hi, kids. How's it going?"

"Could be better," replied Troy.

The man chuckled. "I'm sure it could be." He took a seat across the table from them, loosened his tie, and removed his glasses, holding them between his long index fingers and delicate thumbs as if the spectacles might explode.

"Helen Nicolaides and Troy Kawakami, I presume."

They nodded.

"Well, haven't you two had an exciting night?" said the man. "My name is Waechter. Neil Waechter. National Questing Bureau." He held up a badge. He didn't flash it, but allowed them a good long look at it.

"What's that?" asked Helen.

"Your tax dollars at work. We're a small agency. Not very well-known. We were the ones to throw Hitler's cursed ring into the fires of Mt. Heidelstein. We were the people who harvested and planted the last seed of the dying yax imix che tree to finally end the dust bowl. We found the magic arrow that ended General Sherman's rampage before he could gather enough sacrifices to...well, perhaps I've said too much." He smiled. "The point is that we take care of problems that arise that can't be solved by politics, wars, or wishful thinking. We're the people behind the pages of history."

"You know about these, then?" Helen pointed to the mark burned into the back of her hand.

"Indeed I do. It's a divine brand, a form of motivational magic a god might place upon a mortal. They can be fairly complex, but this one's very simple. It marks you as compelled to complete a certain task. And if you don't"—Waechter frowned, tapped his glasses against the table—"well, I'm afraid that's the bad news."

Helen rubbed her thumb across the back of her hand, hoping

she could just brush off the mark. "Can't you do something about that?"

Waechter sighed. "I wish I could, Miss Nicolaides. But this is some very potent magic here. If this were just something placed on you by a wizard, I have an ointment in my coat pocket that could erase it with a few drops. But this is divine, and divine magic trumps anything I have at my disposal. I'm sorry."

"So what does this mean?" asked Troy. "Are you telling us we're going to die?"

"I won't lie to you. It's a definite possibility." Waechter leaned back in his chair. "I'm sorry. Perhaps that was a bit too honest."

"Actually, I'm glad you just said it," replied Helen.

"Me too," said Troy. "No point in tiptoeing around it. But you said it was a possibility. Does that mean there's a way to avoid it?"

Waechter smiled slightly. "There's no guarantees, of course, but I'm authorized to help you out."

"You mean you can help us with our quest," said Helen.

He nodded. "You're quick on the uptake."

"You're with the National Questing Bureau. We've been given a quest," she said. "It's obvious, isn't it?"

"So it is." Waechter leaned forward and steepled his fingers. "But there's a certain procedure to these things. So before I can help you, I need you to commit to this course of action. Questing isn't an easy business."

"What choice do we have?" asked Troy.

"There is always a choice, Troy. Always. When most people are called to adventure, they elect to stay in their nice, ordinary lives. It's not a judgment on their character. If questing were easy, everyone would be doing it."

He removed some papers from his pocket, unfolded them neatly, and slid them across the table. He handed them each a ballpoint pen.

"I'll need you to sign these."

"I'm not signing anything until I talk to my mom," said Helen.

"Nor should you. I'm not here to prevent you from speaking to anyone. But I find that it's easiest to discuss these affairs directly and without a lot of unnecessary people around. They only confuse the matter, even if they are usually well-meaning. The point is that you have been called. You have taken the first steps into a new world, a realm of wonder and peril, where the laws of nature take a backseat to the rules of adventure."

"We didn't ask to be called," she said.

"That's a common occurrence. We've tried having trained questers in the NQB, but it never really worked out. Even if you put them in the right place at the right time, they never get picked. It's always some poor sap who happens to be walking by, some unfortunate farm kid, a bank teller, a reluctant rogue. It's never the guy or gal who should be saddled with the burden. It's always the one you don't expect."

"If it's always the one you least suspect," asked Helen, "shouldn't it sometimes end up being the one you suspect by virtue of not suspecting them?"

"Oh, that happens too," he replied. "We have an agent who has undertaken fifteen separate quests. The hell of it is that never once was he on official NQB business when chosen for them. We keep him on the payroll and just leave him to his own devices. It seems to work better than anything else we tried. But he's the exception, not the rule. Most of the time it's people like you who end up called."

"So what are these?" Helen asked. "Permission slips?"

Waechter shook his head. "You don't need our permission to quest. It's a free country, isn't it? You are guaranteed the right to life, liberty, and the pursuit of glory. It's in the Constitution. These are just a formality. Signing them will grant you all the rights and privileges of a questing government agent for the duration of your adventure. I'm afraid our lawyers insist upon them."

Troy asked, "If we sign these, we get to be secret agents?"

Waechter waggled his hand. "Of a sort. Yes."

Troy grabbed his pen, but Helen covered his form with her hand. "You can't just sign that."

He grinned. "But come on, Hel. We're talking secret agents here. That's kind of awesome."

She grinned back. "OK, that is kind of awesome. But we should still read it before signing it."

It didn't take long. The forms were only a page long and avoided extensive legalese.

"Do we get magic amulets?" asked Troy. "Or maybe a helmet of invisibility?"

"No helmets," said Waechter, "but you do get travel expenses, questing permits, and decoder rings."

"You're kidding, right?" asked Helen.

"There are no decoder rings," he admitted. "Budget cuts."

Troy signed his form, but Helen was still reluctant.

"Secret agents, Hel," he said. "When are we going to get this kind of chance again?"

Against her better judgment, she signed.

Waechter tucked the forms back into his pocket. He dropped two manila envelopes onto the table. "These are yours."

They tore open the envelopes, finding their own National

Questing Bureau IDs, credit cards, and Waechter's business card.

Helen frowned. The ID used her driver's license photo. The one where her nostrils seemed especially flared and her eyes were half-closed. And she should've polished her horns that day.

She wasn't surprised Troy looked perfect in his.

"This is it?" she asked.

Waechter nodded. "For now. I'll need to clear the sword and wand through our artifact division before returning them to you."

"Those weren't ours," said Helen.

He stood, put his glasses back on. "They are now."

"Wait a second. I thought you were going to help us complete our quest."

"And I am."

"But where's the map? The directions?"

"Questing is not a video game. There are no walk-through guides, no maps, no checkpoints, no big X that says, 'Slay giants here.'"

"Then what are we supposed to do?" asked Troy.

Waechter smiled. "There will be time for questions tomorrow. I suggest you pack for a trip and drop by my office around eleven. We'll work out the details then."

He exited before they could say anything else.

Helen noticed that Agent Waechter's business card had an address printed on it. There was also the phrase "The answer is destiny" handwritten in pen.

4

Nigel Skullgnasher's midlife crisis hadn't been much different from any other. He'd gotten a tattoo and some piercings, started working out, begun dressing inappropriately for his age, had his tusks sharpened. His wife had been tolerant of these new habits. Just as long as he didn't try trading her in for a younger model, which he never would have done because, by orc tradition, divorce could come only after a duel to the death, and he wasn't at all certain he could take her in a fight.

He wasn't unhappy with his wife or his marriage. He just wanted to feel young again, to tap into his ancestral spirit, to feel the wind in his black hair, to ride as part of the horde, to plunder and pillage and be feared and respected. He ended up settling for the next best thing and joining a motorcycle club.

There wasn't any pillaging. His Harley-Dragonson Twin Cam parked in the heated garage saw the open road only on the weekends.

But he traveled the open road in his nightly dreams, barreled down the endless highway where his hideous gods waited to reward anyone who could make the final journey across the broken plains where every orc soul met its final reward.

He brought his motorcycle to a sudden stop. The cloud of dust and sweet exhaust in his wake swept over him. He wiped the grime from his face, pulled off his obscured goggles, and used his tongue to loosen a fly stuck in his teeth, which he swallowed.

He'd reached the foot of the Gray Mountain. No orc ever saw the mountain and lived. So he must've been dead. He didn't remember dying, but it was the only explanation. Perhaps in his sleep. He'd just gone in for his checkup and the doctor had mentioned it would be good to cut his cholesterol but hadn't made it seem like a big deal.

He was most mad that he'd skipped dessert tonight. Death he could deal with. But it would've been nice to have a slice of cherry pie before bleaching under the Cruel Skies for eternity.

He opened the cooler beside the Mound of Unworthy Bones. The selection of beers was limited, but at least they were only slightly warm.

The ground rattled as a giant motorcycle came roaring down the mountain. It spewed clouds of screaming smoke and its wheels split the earth in its wake. It could've crushed Nigel without slowing down, and he half expected that. The gods of the orcs were a merciless lot. Even making it to the mountain didn't earn you a place at their table. Not until one strangled the life from them with one's bare hands did one earn that privilege.

The motorcycle came to a sudden stop, kicking up clouds of dust and smoke. When it cleared, the great god Grog stood before Nigel. Grog towered thirteen feet high and wore armor made out of thorns. Each of his five heads had a giant maw and one eye. His pale skin carried the scars of 1,003 battles with the other gods.

Nigel nodded to his ancient god. "'Sup?"

Grog said, "Not much. Toss me a brew, would you?"

Nigel threw a six-pack to his god.

Grog shoved it into his jaws, cans and all, and swallowed. "Thanks."

"Another?"

"No thanks. I'm driving." Grog cleared his throat and spat up a wad of acidic phlegm that burned its way into the ground. "Nigel Skullgnasher, you have been called."

"Right." Nigel chugged the last of his beer, tossed it onto a pile of cans and the bones of all the previous challengers. The pile was about twice as tall as the Gray Mountain.

"So how do we do this?" he asked. "Bare-knuckle? Axes? I have a tire iron. Or is that against the rules?"

Grog chuckled. "There are no rules."

"Right. OK then, I'll get the tire iron, if that's OK with you."

"Go ahead."

Nigel found his weapon. He swung it a few times to get the feel for it. He knew he couldn't win this fight. According to history, even the legendary orc warlord Rork Orabrork had only put a crack in Grog's toenail before ending up on the unworthy mound, though that had earned his skull the honored position of the very summit, which was more than any orc could honestly hope for.

"Ready when you are," said Grog.

Nigel charged and with a mighty roar he smacked the god across the armored shins. The air filled with a steady clang as he pounded on that one spot until his arms grew heavy. Only until he was thoroughly exhausted, until he could no longer hold the iron, did he fall to his knees. Wheezing, he wiped the sweat from his brow.

"How was that?" he asked. "Anything?"

Grog shrugged. "Not particularly impressive."

"Go to hell."

His god laughed. It was the closest thing he'd give to a nod of approval. "Get yourself together. Have another beer."

"Another? I thought I was only allowed one."

"That's only if you were dead," said Grog.

"I'm not?"

"Did I say you were?"

Nigel stood. He was still out of breath. "But the Gray Mountain..."

Grog spoke with a booming voice that knocked Nigel off his feet. "No orc may see it and live!"

Nigel sat up. "Yeah. That."

"You're still going to die. Just not tonight."

Nigel stood, grabbed another beer from the cooler. "Then why have you appeared to me? No offense, but I didn't think I'd have to see your ugly mug more than once before going on to oblivion."

"Nor I yours, but I need you to kill someone for me."

"Uh-huh." Nigel took a drink, belched. "You do know I'm an accountant, right?"

"I was not aware of that," admitted Grog.

"I've never killed anyone before."

"It's not that hard. Just find something sufficiently sharp or heavy and do what comes naturally."

Nigel scoffed.

"What?" asked Grog.

"I don't know if you've been paying attention or not, but I live in a more civilized age. Just because my ancestors were barbaric hordes that doesn't mean I'm a natural-born killer. I think it's a bit racist that you assume that."

"That's uncalled-for."

"Isn't it, though?" said Nigel. "You appear to me in a vision and demand I kill someone. Surely there must be more qualified souls for the job."

"I am the greatest god of the orcs," said Grog. "I work with what fate has given me."

"I have to imagine there are one or two orc killers out there who you could appear to."

Grog stomped the ground with his foot and the Gray Mountain rumbled. "Enough! I don't have to explain myself to you. I am your god, whether we like it or not. I'm here to charge you with a holy mission. So shut the hell up and just accept it."

"All right, all right. Don't get your panties in a bunch. Although why me?"

"Because you have sworn the oath to serve me, have you not?"

Nigel said, "I don't remember that."

Grog cleared his throat. "'I, Nigel Skullgnasher, vow to honor the spirit of the wilderness.' Sound familiar?"

It did. It was the oath he'd taken when joining his motorcycle club. He hadn't thought much of it at the time.

"So that counts?" he asked.

"Am I also not known as the Spirit of the Wilderness?"

"I don't know. Are you?"

"I am."

"I didn't know that," said Nigel.

"Still counts."

It was Nigel's own damned fault. Orc religion mostly involved ignoring the gods and having them ignore you in turn. But the hideous gods had a wealth of nicknames—mostly, Nigel suspected, for situations like this. Some he suspected were made up on the spot, but since there was no way to prove that, it was pointless to argue.

"Fine. Who am I killing?"

The sands swirled and formed into two statues of Helen and Troy.

"Wow. She's a big 'un," said Nigel. "And the human, he's Asian. Does he know karate?"

Grog rolled his eyes. "You called me racist."

"Hey, if this kid has a kung fu grip, it's probably something I should know."

"Your fear brings shame to your ancestors," said Grog.

"My ancestors can kiss my ass. They didn't have to figure out a way to kill someone after already using up all their personal days at the office. I have a performance review at the end of the month, by the way. Not that I expect you to care."

"Good. Because I don't."

"So where do I find these two?" asked Nigel.

"You will be sent a seer, a guide to show you the way."

"You can't just give me their names and addresses?"

Grog said, "There are rules we must all follow."

"I thought you said there were no rules."

"I may have been exaggerating." Grog mounted his monstrous motorcycle. "Be seeing you, Nigel."

He revved his engine, and the screaming black smoke enveloped Nigel.

He snapped awake, and for a moment he thought it might all have been just an ordinary dream. Then the phone rang. He answered in the middle of the second ring. His wife stirred in the bed but didn't wake.

It was Peggy Truthstalker from the club. She'd had the dream too and had been chosen to be his guide. After they both grumbled about the situation, he hung up and made plans to see her the next day.

The phone rang again. It was another club member. Nigel hadn't been the only one called upon by Grog. The entire club had been charged with the mission. It seemed like overkill for two people, even if one of them was seven feet tall and the other might possibly know kung fu. But he was in no position to question anything.

After the fourth call he left the phone off the hook and crept up to his attic to find his grandfather's old battle-ax. He wiped away some of the dust. His grandfather had killed over thirty Nazis with this ax during the war, and slain the last Axis ice dragon at the Battle of the Bulge. Nigel had the medals stashed somewhere.

He swung the ax a few times. Then sliced a steamer trunk in half with one stroke. Grinning, he picked at the pieces of frost along the edges of the cut. The enchantment from the dragon's final breath still clung to the weapon. Though Nigel wasn't keen on killing anyone, he was excited about getting a chance to break it out, to test himself in real battle and make his grandfather proud.

Although a minotaur and a kid probably weren't up there with a dragon. But beggars couldn't be choosers.

His wife shouted from below. "Nigel, what the hell are you doing up there at this time of night?"

He said something about hearing rats.

"We better call the exterminator tomorrow," she shouted. "I don't want those things chewing up my mother's quilts."

Nigel picked a thread clinging to the ax's blade. The halved steamer trunk and its sheared quilted contents stared back at him.

"Ah, damn."

"What's that? Did you say something?"

Nigel set the ax down. "Nothing, dear."

5

"I can't believe you signed anything, Helen," said Roxanne. "After everything I've taught you."

Helen had seriously considered leaving her mom in the dark about her discussion with Waechter.

Helen had been a good kid, never in any real trouble, and her mother had given her the respect that came with that. But Roxanne was also innately distrusting of authority figures. Helen had to admit that distrust of a mysterious government agent from a mysterious government agency wasn't unwarranted.

Now Helen was trapped in the passenger seat of a minivan on the long ride home from the police station with her mother.

They didn't say much for the first ten minutes. Helen's minotaurism came from her mother's side, though nobody in the family had suffered from a full-blown case in centuries. Roxanne had the ears. One of Helen's older brothers had fur. And her younger brother had a tail. But only Helen suffered *enchantment regression.* Luck of the draw, she often thought. Or whim of the gods. She wasn't sure which idea bothered her more.

Roxanne's ears twitched when she was upset.

"What did this man look like?" she asked.

"Like a guy, Mom," said Helen. "He didn't look weird or anything."

"Of course he didn't. He's trained to be invisible, unidentifiable. He walks in the shadows, screwing with people's lives for some *greater good*." She released the steering wheel just long enough to mime quotation marks.

"I've never even heard of this National Questing Bureau," said Roxanne. "I doubt it even exists."

"Troy Googled it with his phone, Mom. It seemed legitimate."

"Oh, I'm sure it *looked* legitimate." Air quotes. "It always looks *legitimate*." Air quotes. "Always looks *harmless*." Air quotes.

"Uh, Mom, do you want me to hold the wheel while you make your point?"

"Don't sass me."

Helen shrugged. "Sorry, Mom. Guess I learned to question authority. Wonder where I got that from?"

Roxanne shook her head. "So you pick this up from me but you're perfectly willing to sign any random paper pushed your way."

"Mom..."

Silence passed between them.

"Mom what?" asked Roxanne.

"Nothing," replied Helen. "You're right. It was probably a dumb thing to do, but I did it."

She flipped open her government-issued questing permit. She still hated the photo, but the ID was growing on her. The credit card seemed legitimate, though she hadn't had a chance to charge anything on it. Still, it all seemed very official, very important. Although she wasn't sure what her powers as an NQB agent were at this point. She doubted it was a license to kill, which vaguely disappointed her even though she had no plans to kill anyone.

But she had thought about it because quests usually involved some level of violence. She'd already been almost fed to a hamburger god, and that was before officially starting the damn thing. It might get worse.

Or maybe her quest would be as simple as driving across the country, picking up a few packages, and dropping them off. Agent Waechter hadn't seemed too concerned for her safety, though he had been difficult to read.

"I wouldn't be surprised if he was a Black Knight," said Roxanne, and Helen realized her mom had been talking even if Helen hadn't quite been paying attention.

"I don't think the Black Knights actually exist, Mom."

"That's what they want you to believe."

There weren't many conspiracy theories Roxanne didn't believe in. At the center of it all, the Black Knights sat like spiders spinning a giant web. There wasn't a mysterious celebrity death (or many non-mysterious ones) that didn't have some whispered connection to the Knights, and, supposedly, the only reason flying carpets had been rejected as an eco-friendly alternative to automobiles was the Knights' nefarious intent to create smog. Helen wasn't clear on the reason, but it seemed to change every week anyway.

She'd always suspected that the sinister machinations of the Black Knights were based on how many books and magazines those machinations could sell. Judging from her mother's impressive collection, this was a surprisingly large amount.

"Do you know what your problem has always been?" asked Roxanne. "You're too trusting. Like your father."

"Did you call him?" asked Helen.

"Of course I did. He almost canceled his business trip to come home, but I told him it wasn't necessary."

"Maybe it is, Mom." She pointed to her hand. "I have been cursed by the gods."

"I'm not worried about that," said Roxanne. "And you shouldn't be either. Haven't I always told you that you can handle anything?"

"Yes, Mom, but—"

"Don't give me any buts, Helen. You're a very capable young woman."

"Yes, Mom, but—"

"You are as strong and able as anyone. Don't let anyone tell you otherwise."

The minivan pulled into their driveway, and they exited.

"Actually, I'm stronger than most everyone, Mom." Helen slammed the door shut to make the point.

"You know what I mean, Helen."

They hugged.

"We'll get through this." Roxanne tried to hide her nervousness behind a smile, and she almost succeeded. "Now let's call your father and tell him everything is OK."

"Thanks, Mom."

"You're welcome. For what?"

"For believing in me."

"You've never given me any reason not to." Roxanne's ears

perked up. "It's only the gods, after all. And if they know what's good for them, they won't harm a hair on my girl's head. Otherwise I'll storm the heavens myself and show them what wrath really is."

She went inside.

Helen lingered, staring into the sky and the few stars she could see through the city's light pollution. She smiled.

"She'll do it too."

The constellations dimmed in fear of the notion.

Troy got home late from the police station. His parents went to bed while he slapped together a sandwich and ate it over the sink.

Lights flashed in the window. He heard the front door open slowly and the click of heels on the hardwood floors. Imogen cautiously poked her head into the kitchen.

"You can relax," he said. "Mom and Dad went to bed."

His older sister entered. She removed her jacket and draped it across a chair. "We have anything to drink?"

"There's juice," he said.

She smiled, put a hand to his cheek. "You're cute, little brother." She opened the fridge and pulled out a pair of beers. "Can't Dad buy imported, like any good upper-middle-class family?"

"You know Dad," said Troy. "Buy American. I didn't know you were in town."

Imogen shrugged. "You know how it is. I don't like giving the folks a lot of notice. Better to slip in and out, like a thief in the night."

"Uh-hmm."

Troy and Imogen had always gotten along, though their parents had a bad habit of pitting them against each other, dangling approval like a maiden before a hungry dragon. She'd always been smart and beautiful. In any other family she'd have been too good to be true. Then he'd come along and wrecked the grading curve. Imogen had elected to stop competing and become the black sheep. Though being the bad daughter mostly involved wearing tight jeans, bumming around Europe for a few months to "find herself," and dating a few hippies and a beatnik. Troy had always been impressed she'd found a beatnik in this day and age.

He handed her half his sandwich. She took it, sniffed it. "What is this? Bologna?"

"Yeah."

"I don't eat meat."

He laughed. "Since when?"

"I'm vegan now."

Troy said, "Not even dairy or eggs."

Imogen frowned. "I still eat eggs."

"That's not vegan then."

"I'm pretty sure it is."

"Next you'll tell me you're still eating seafood."

She bit her lip. "Fish aren't vegan?"

Troy said, "Some are. Not sharks, of course."

Imogen smiled insincerely. "You know what I mean, smart-ass."

"So why are you vaguely vegan?"

"I'm not allowed to try new things?" she asked. "Anyway, we shouldn't be talking about me. You're the one who is in trouble. Quest, huh?"

He nodded.

"Mom couldn't wait to tell me," she said. "Couldn't wait to

brag about her popular, smart, and now officially *chosen-by-the-gods* son. You just can't stop overachieving, can you?"

"It's not as impressive as it sounds," he replied. "It was a hamburger god."

"Sounds gross."

"It was." He nodded to a sketch of the god on the kitchen table.

"Ewww." She flipped through the sketchpad. "I didn't know you could draw."

"Just a hobby, Sis."

She dropped the pad on the table and shook her head. "Maybe if you'd stop excelling so much, Mom and Dad wouldn't think of me as the bad child."

"I think you were stuck with that label once you got that tattoo. I'm pretty sure they think that butterfly on your ankle means you're in a gang."

Imogen handed a beer to Troy.

"Don't argue with me," she said. "Just drink it. You've had a rough day."

They twisted off the tops, clinked the bottles together, and took a drink.

Troy grimaced. "Stuff tastes terrible."

"You get used to it. Sit with me, little brother. We should talk."

They sat at the table.

"So how are you holding up?" she asked.

"I'm good."

She tapped her fingernail against her bottle.

"What?" he asked.

"It's OK to admit you're nervous," she said.

"Why should I be nervous?"

She pointed to the mark on the back of his hand.

"Oh, I've got this under control," he said.

"So we're playing it that way?"

"What way?"

"You might get away with the *I'm awesome* attitude with everybody else, but not with me."

Troy smiled. "But I am awesome."

"Yes, and I acknowledge your awesomeness. But it doesn't change things. This is big stuff. Even for you."

He took another sip. "Yes, but I've got it under control. And it's not like I'm facing this alone. A friend of mine carries the curse too."

"Have I met this friend?"

"Maybe. She dropped by my birthday party. You'd probably remember her."

Imogen raised an eyebrow. "That pretty?"

"Distinctive." He paused. "And pretty in a unique way."

"What's that mean?"

Troy said, "She's tall. Brown eyes. Wide shoulders and hips. A bit…meaty, but not in a bad way. Brown hair with white spots."

She stopped halfway through a swallow. "Spots?"

"On her neck," he said.

Imogen nodded to herself. "The minotaur chick?"

"That's her."

"Well, why didn't you just say that in the first place?" asked Imogen.

He picked at the bottle label. "Whenever someone describes me, the first thing that comes up is *Asian*. And I hate that. And don't tell me you don't hate it too."

Imogen said, "That's a fair point, though minotaurs are a little more distinctive in the grand scheme."

"Doesn't change the fact that she shouldn't be defined by the fact that she has horns."

"Maybe," she said, "but that doesn't change the fact that it'll be the first thing someone notices about her."

"Doesn't make it right," he said softly.

"So do you like this girl?"

He stared blankly at her.

"What?" she asked. "It's a legitimate question. If you're going to be questing with this girl, you're going to be spending a lot of time together, right?"

"We're just friends. Casual ones. We didn't even really talk to each other until she started working at Magic Burger. It's not like we've hung out a lot."

Imogen said, "Yes, but do you like her?"

"She's like a foot taller than me and has hooves. I haven't even thought of her in that way."

"I gotta say, little brother, I'm surprised you're so superficial."

"Haven't the last four guys you dated all had washboard abs?"

She laughed. "Hey, I know I'm superficial."

"You just want me to date a minotaur so Mom will forgive you for bringing that Belgian guy home last year."

"He was French," she corrected.

"No, he was Belgian."

"I'm fairly positive he was French."

"He came from the French-speaking southern region of Wallonia," said Troy. "But he was most certainly Belgian."

"But he had that flag on his backpack."

"Yes, the Belgian one."

"OK, don't pretend that you know all about flags. Because I'm not buying that."

"I know next to nothing about the subject," admitted Troy. "Other than he and his flag patch were Belgian because he told me so. At least a dozen times. He also mentioned how much he hated being mistaken for French."

She nodded. "OK, now that's ringing a bell."

"Mom is still convinced you did that just to irritate her."

"Back on topic." Imogen rapped the table. "So how does one quest anyway?"

"I haven't had a lot of time to research it yet," he replied. "But from what I've read, it's about time for some sort of supernatural aid to appear to point me on my way. I'm hoping it's some form of talking animal."

A white cat meowed as it rubbed against his legs.

"What's that, Mister Scraps?" asked Imogen. "You want Troy to journey across the river of fire to the land of the forgotten dead and kick the lord of the underworld in the shins?"

Mister Scraps looked up at her with wide blue eyes and mewed insistently.

"Well, I'll be damned," she said. "I'd get on that if I were you, little brother."

Troy fed the cat a sliver of bologna. The cat gulped it down and licked his lips.

"Seriously, Troy. I know you've always been able to do . . . anything. But it's OK to admit maybe this is a tough situation."

"I can handle it."

"I didn't say you couldn't. I just said you don't have to be perfect. Not in front of me. You can admit you're human."

He smiled. "Thanks. That's always nice to hear."

She leaned forward. "So is there anything you want to confide then?"

"No, I've got this. But it's still nice to hear."

Troy took a sip of his beer, stuck out his tongue, and pushed it across the table.

"I should get to bed. Have to start my quest tomorrow."

She stood, gave him a hug. "Watch yourself, Troy. The gods love ruining a hero's life."

"I'm no hero. Just an overachiever."

She smiled, tousled his hair. "Close enough."

He turned to leave but stopped.

"I liked that Belgian guy. Why did you break up again?"

"Once Mom started liking him, he stopped being interesting. Some of us have issues, oats to sow. Not that I'd expect you to understand, Mr. Perfect."

"I hope you broke it to him gently."

"Oh, he took it just fine. Turned out he was just dating me to piss off his father."

Troy said, "And Mom and Dad wonder why you aren't married yet."

"It is a mystery." She tapped her two beers together and opened the fridge. "Do we have any bologna left?"

6

Helen slept in.

She hadn't planned on it, but she'd forgotten to set her alarm. She'd assumed she'd wake up early because she didn't think she'd be able to sleep well. But she did, and it was only when someone knocked on her bedroom door that she awoke.

She opened the door a crack. It was her little brother.

"You have a visitor," said Will.

"Who?" She was still struggling toward alertness.

"It's that Troy guy. He said you were expecting him."

Then she remembered that they'd made plans to go to the NQB together. She was supposed to be packed and ready by ten. It was ten till ten now. She could have a suitcase packed in a few minutes, but her morning preparations, owing to her minotaurism, took at least fifteen.

"Tell him I'm running behind," she said.

"I'll tell him you're making yourself pretty," replied Will with a sly grin.

She almost told him not to say that, but that would only have ensured he would. Probably even embellish it with kissy noises and a girlish dance. She tried her best defense: feigned indifference.

"Whatever, squirt."

Will walked away, swishing his tail. "Mom is making pancakes, if you want any."

Helen didn't have time to be annoyed. She grumbled to herself, but even this was halfhearted. The first thing she did was slap on her bracelet. The prescription magic within sent a tingle up her arm as it always did. This was followed by a sharp sting in the curse mark burned on the back of her hand. The magics didn't seem to get along, and while the cold prickle was easy to ignore at first, it would get worse. She'd had to take off her bracelet just to get some sleep, and it'd been months since she'd done that.

She'd had some bad dreams without it. Not exactly nightmares, but unpleasant visions of herself stalking a maze like a trapped wild beast. She didn't know if they were the result of her curse or her own subconscious fears, but either way the restless night hadn't helped her mood.

She didn't even consider not wearing the bracelet. She could live with the irritation if she had to. Her curse didn't give her much choice.

She threw on some clothes. It was at times like this that she hated having to wear button-up shirts. But her horns, slight as they were, tore holes when she tried putting on T's. Tank tops could work in a pinch, but they rarely fit properly. Her breasts were always threatening to spill out of those. The fashion industry had long neglected the needs of the young minotaur on the go.

She had to button up twice because the first time the shirt ended up lopsided.

She fussed with her hair, giving it a quick brush, then deciding today was a ponytail day. Although she wasn't fond of ponytails, because they did nothing to de-emphasize her ears.

She frowned at her reflection. It bothered her that she had body issues. It seemed so typically *young woman* to have them.

In her rush to get ready, she'd done things in the wrong order. She usually brushed herself down before getting dressed. It was easier that way. More thorough. Kept the shedding in check. She didn't need to do it every night, but it was her habit. She'd skipped last night. She debated stripping down and starting the process over again.

Will knocked on the door again. "You ready or not?"

"I'm coming, I'm coming."

There was no time. She brushed down what was visible and took another five minutes to throw stuff in her suitcase. In her hurry, she didn't bother folding the clothes. This only made them more difficult to fit, taking longer, but she managed to zip the damn thing closed. She paused to consider if she was forgetting anything, deciding she most definitely was but that she'd wasted enough time already and would deal with it later. As long as she had clean underwear and a good brush, everything else could be worked around.

Downstairs, she found Troy eating breakfast with Will and Roxanne in the kitchen.

"These are delicious, Mrs. Nicolaides," Troy said. "You have to tell me your secret."

"It's Bisquick."

"I'll pass that along to my mother."

From anyone else the comment might have seemed sarcastic, but he managed to sound sincere.

"How's your hand?" asked Helen.

"A little itchy. Yours?"

"Same."

She was relieved to hear it. Maybe itchiness came with the curse and had nothing to do with an interaction with her bracelet.

Roxanne said, "Troy tells me you're starting your quest today."

"I don't know," replied Helen. "We're going to the NQB. They didn't say anything more than that. Speaking of which, we're running kind of late."

"So we're a little behind." Troy smiled at her, pulled out a chair. "There is always time for pancakes, Hel."

"Listen to the young man," said Roxanne. "He knows of what he speaks."

Helen shook her head and chuckled to herself. She allowed herself to enjoy her breakfast, and while she couldn't forget the curse hanging over her head, she could at least spare fifteen minutes to sit with her family and pretend it didn't matter. And it didn't. Not right now. All that mattered were her plate of pancakes, her glass of juice, and people she cared about.

After breakfast Helen loaded her suitcase in the back of the electric-blue Ford Chimera parked in her driveway. It had all the hallmarks of a classic fifties car: chrome, fins, leather, and monstrous proportions.

"I thought you didn't have a car," she said.

"It's my dad's," he replied. "He thought if I'm going questing, I should do it in style."

"Not very inconspicuous, is it?"

"Every knight needs his fire-breathing steed. If we're going to be stuck on the road, you'll be happy for the extra legroom."

The soft-top roof was folded down, and she leaned over, studying the cavernous interior. She could probably have lain down in the backseat and taken a nap. Though she wouldn't actually do that. Her horns might rip the flawless leather seats.

"What if we get a scratch on it?" she asked.

"You worry too much," he said.

It was easy for him. He didn't have horns or hooves. No hard pointy bits to scrape paint or slash open the Chimera's soft top. Even if she managed to go the whole trip without an accident, there was always the shedding to deal with.

More than any other problem of her condition, it was the shedding that bothered her. She brushed herself, top to bottom, every night. Almost obsessively. It kept the problem mostly in check. But there was always going to be some incidental fur left here and there. And, of course, the Chimera's seats couldn't be a compatible shade of brown to hide the problem. No, they just had to be a flawless white.

"It should be out on the road," said Troy. "It should be allowed to feel the asphalt beneath its whitewalls, to get bugs on its windshield, cracks in its upholstery."

"It's just a car," she said.

He jumped behind the wheel without opening the door. He started the engine and revved it.

"Hear that? That's not a collection of pistons and tubes. That's a beast. She's spent the last fifteen years under a tarp, sitting in a heated garage. Once a year Dad takes her out to a car show, where she's gawked at and gaped at and caressed, like some kind of museum piece, like a spoiled show pony. Oh, sure, her engine might get to rev a bit to allow a glimpse of the raging spark in her plugs, but it's a sham, a mock drama. Because people are afraid of her, afraid of what she can do, afraid to let her out on the road where she was meant to be, to prowl, to hunt, to remind every other car on the road that there is only one queen of this jungle. And this is she."

Troy let the engine roar, and try as she might, Helen couldn't think of that sound as anything else now.

He said, "She wants to live. She wants to feel her oil pump, to draw the air through her radiator, to sear her burning rubber footprint on the highway so that, even when she's gone, the gods themselves will celebrate her life rather than mourn her death."

He leaned back in the seat, adjusted the rearview mirror, and flashed a wicked smile.

"Let her live, Hel."

She shook her head. "That is either the biggest load of crap I've ever heard or the most beautiful thing ever said. You rehearsed that, didn't you?"

"Maybe a little bit. On the ride over here."

"If you don't go with him," said Roxanne, "we will."

"I call backseat," said Will.

Helen gave her mom and brother a hug. "I love you, guys."

Will made no jokes at her expense. He only squeezed her tighter.

She said, "Tell Dad I love him."

"You'll tell him when you get back," said Roxanne.

"Mom..."

Roxanne put a finger to Helen's lips.

"You'll tell him when you get back."

Her mother wiped away the beginning of a tear she was fighting. She gave Helen another hug.

"Go on. Get out of here. Go show the gods above and below what a strong young woman my little girl has grown into. Come home victorious, covered in glory." She gave Helen another hug. "Just come home."

Helen reluctantly slipped out of the embrace. She climbed into the car, settling into the plush seat. Gently at first, but then she leaned back. Troy had been right. It was nice to have the legroom.

"I register my distaste for the leather," she said.

"Duly noted," replied Troy.

"Take care of Mom, squirt," said Helen. "And yourself."

Will nodded back to her. "You too."

She tapped the door with her knuckles. "So are we questing or not?"

Troy pulled into the street. He didn't roar away in a cloud of dust and exhaust. This was the suburbs, after all. The Chimera's engine purred under the hood like a chained monster. Helen watched Roxanne and Will shrink in the side-view mirror until Troy turned a corner, and they were gone.

7

The National Questing Bureau's offices were located in a sleepy business district. There were a few small office buildings, but for the most part it was just row upon row of warehouses. Most of the traffic was eighteen-wheelers carrying cargo to or from the neighborhood. Helen and Troy nearly missed the NQB sign, a nondescript placard with the initials and the address. From the outside it looked like an old warehouse, but it was the only building on the block with a fence.

They pulled up to the front gate. A gargoyle in a security guard outfit came trudging out of the booth. An unlit cigarette dangled from the creature's beak, and he pulled his sunglasses down, peered at them with piercing green eyes, and pushed the glasses back up.

Helen did her best not to stare. Gargoyles weren't quite as rare as minotaurs, but they weren't common. They were relatively easy to make with magic, but security cameras had rendered them mostly obsolete. They took their job more seriously than most rent-a-cops, but that dedication could be a double-edged sword. You could always fire a guard, but once a gargoyle was on the job, he was on for life. For beings made of stone, that could be a very long time.

"We have an appointment with Agent Waechter," said Troy. "Troy Kawakami and Helen Nicolaides."

The gargoyle moved his cigarette around his mouth, checked his clipboard. "You're late."

"Pancake emergency." Troy grinned slyly.

The gargoyle did not.

"You got ID, Mr. Kawakami?"

Troy and Helen held up their NQB-issued badges. The gargoyle adjusted his hat and gave them a very thorough inspection.

"All right. You check out. But you must answer the riddle first."

Helen said, "But we have an appointment."

"And I have a riddle I have to ask because when some stupid wizard created me five hundred years ago, he put this requirement in my stone. So just listen and answer. If you can.

"Men seek me out, yet fear what I have to say. I am unavoidable yet always surprising. All travelers meet me, regardless of which road they travel, and even if they choose not to travel at all. I am a burden to many, a joy to a very few, and something only a fool thinks he can know. What am I?"

The gargoyle paused.

"Well. Do you have the answer or do I kill you now?"

"You didn't mention anything about killing us," said Troy.

"It's assumed."

"Isn't that a bit excessive?"

"Don't blame me. You can blame the stupid wizard, but he's been dead for a few hundred years now, so it's not going to do you much good."

"Can you repeat it?" asked Helen as she dug through her pocket.

By the time he'd finished asking the riddle again, she'd found Waechter's card with the answer scribbled on the back.

"You're destiny," she said.

"Did someone give you the answer?" The gargoyle leaned forward. "What's written on that card?"

"Nothing." She quickly tucked it back in her pocket.

The suspicious gargoyle flapped his wings with a snarl. "Whatever." He lifted the gate and let them pass.

They found a space marked VISITOR near the entrance and walked right in. There weren't any other guards. Not even a receptionist. Just some old furniture arranged around a sword in a stone that was the centerpiece of the lobby. Agent Waechter sat on a worn blue couch with another agent. Waechter didn't have a jacket on, though the other agent was a more expected button-down type. She had the government-issued black suit and stone-cold demeanor of a Secret Service agent, and when Waechter stood to greet them, the agent rose, clasped her hands behind her back, and remained unreadable.

"Sorry we're late," said Helen.

"Nothing to worry about," replied Waechter. "These things proceed at their own pace. And we're very casual around here. Isn't that right, Agent Campbell?"

Campbell nodded, smiled very, very slightly.

Waechter offered them a tour, starting with the sword in the stone.

"Feel free to give it a try. We all have. Campbell here usually does it twice a day. Isn't that right, Campbell?"

"Yes, sir. I did get it to wiggle once."

Helen tried to remove the sword without success. Troy did manage to get it to wobble a bit. Agent Campbell frowned in a barely noticeable way.

"Shouldn't you have this locked away?" asked Helen.

"You wouldn't believe how common these things are," said Waechter. "Magic weapons just waiting for the right person to come along. We have a warehouse in Hoboken full of the damn things. Completely useless otherwise. We give tours. Very boring, really. Once you've seen one ax or spear or halberd stuck in something, you've seen them all. But people still try it because...well...you never know. Three years ago, a plumber from North Dakota discovered he was king of the Morlocks when he pulled a mace from a piece of granite."

"King of the djinn, sir," corrected Campbell. "Morlocks are fictitious."

"Right, right. Shall we get on with it?"

"You don't have much security," said Troy.

"Don't really need it," said Waechter. "One of the peculiar things about the NQB is that no one finds us unless they need us. We're not a secret agency. We only tend to slip through the cracks of the everyday world. Might be magic. Might be fate. Or maybe people are too busy with their lives to worry about us. We get our funding and nobody pays us much attention. Nor should they. We're merely facilitators and support. It's fine citizens such as yourselves who do most of the heavy lifting. We're just here to see that things stay on the right path."

He led them down a long hall. Agent Campbell followed a few steps behind. They passed a sphinx in a tie.

"Hey, Akil, are you going to make it to the poker game tonight?" asked Waechter.

The sphinx kept walking. "Wouldn't miss it. Gotta get even from last week. These the two you were talking about earlier?"

"Yes."

"Good luck then." Akil flapped his wings and disappeared through a door.

Along the way they passed more employees. Most were human, orc, or elf. But there were an unusual number of enchanted and thaumaturgical creatures prowling these halls. A six-armed woman with a serpent tail instead of legs chatted at a water cooler with a pudgy bald man and some manner of giant talking mushroom. A pair of gremlins from tech support were either fixing a computer or taking it apart. It was hard to tell which. And a hulking, scaly creature hunched over a row of cabinets, alphabetizing files.

Helen was used to being the monster in the room. Not just one of many. In a weird way, the situation made her more uncomfortable.

"We provide gainful employment for those in need." He nodded to the filing creature. "Yorick used to guard a bridge until they tore it down to build a shopping mall."

Yorick shrugged. "The hours are better here."

Waechter led them to his office. Compared to the drabness of the rest of the NQB, it was lively. He had one of those executive office toys with the clacking metal spheres, and a desk that was made out of imitation wood, not plain plastic. Behind the desk a framed watercolor poster of a French art film was hung. He sat on his desk and gestured to the two chairs in front of it. They sat. Agent Campbell stood.

"Now then, what's important for you to understand is that the NQB is here to help, but we can't actually do anything beyond a support role. Most of what we do is guidance and easing your transition into questing. If you were in school, for example, we could get you excused. If you needed time off from work or a good car or someone to look after your kids while you were off on your road to adventure, that's all part of our services. Campbell here is great with kids. Isn't that right, Campbell?"

She remained expressionless. "Kids love me."

Waechter said, "Now, you don't need any of that, so our job is considerably easier. We're basically here to ensure you're properly prepared for what's coming."

"You know the future?" asked Troy.

"No, not exactly. But there's a tradition to these things. We've been at this a very long time. Long before there was even an official NQB. Our records go way back, and after a while patterns emerge. Now where the heck is that report?"

He sorted through the scrolls and tomes on his desk.

Someone knocked on the office door hard enough to shake it loose on its hinges. Campbell opened the door to reveal a tremendous ogress in a crisp pantsuit.

She was far too big to fit through the door, so she stuck in one giant arm. She opened her massive hand to reveal a dusty book. "Jenkins in Tomes and Records said you asked for this."

"Thanks, Valerie."

"Don't mention it." She deposited the book in his arms and lumbered away.

Waechter flipped through the tome's worn pages. "Yes, here

we are. According to this, it's a fairly typical fetch quest. The Lost God appears, compels two to four mortals to seek out magical objects. Operates on a three-hundred-year cycle."

"This keeps happening," said Helen.

"Like clockwork," replied Waechter.

"And you haven't stopped it."

He thumbed through the book, half-reading, half-talking. "It's not that easy. These cycles can't just be stopped. They have to run their course. The metaphysics are a bit complicated, but it all comes down to cause and effect. You can't simply change one fundamental aspect of reality without altering everything else."

"So your job isn't to help us with this quest," said Helen. "You're just here to maintain the status quo."

Waechter shut the book and smiled at her. "You're a very astute young woman, Helen. Yes, we spend the bulk of our time ensuring things run smoothly. It's not that we don't accomplish positive results. It's just that most of those results are in the aversion of earthshaking kabooms, and it's hard to measure success against things that haven't happened."

Troy said, "If you've done this before, and you know how it usually goes, then what happens to us at the end of this? The hamburger god said he'd sent people on this quest before, and that they'd all died."

Waechter's smile dropped. "I could lie to you and say it's all going to be fine, but this isn't an easy quest. But our records indicate it isn't quite as dire as the Lost God made it sound. Our guys in statistics say odds of survival are somewhere around 27 percent."

"In other words, 73 percent chance we're going to die," said Helen.

"Not the best odds," agreed Waechter. "But I've seen questers with worse odds triumph. In fact, in this business, the lower your odds of survival, the better chance you've got."

Helen said, "That's contradictory."

"Only mathematically. But the quests that look easy, the ones with a ninety-plus percentage of success, those are the ones that can sneak up on you. If the Fates ask you to deliver a package across the street, you're practically guaranteed to fail that one. But if they pick the unlikeliest farmhand to journey across a desert full of monsters and bandit hordes, then he makes it more often than not."

Helen tried to wrap her head around the idea. "You're saying your records, the ones that you've been meticulously keeping for ages, say that this quest is so dangerous that we're bound to succeed."

"It helps not to think about it very much," said Waechter. "But when it comes to quests, statistics often take a backseat to other requirements. Irony. Drama. Triumph. Tragedy. Deus ex machina."

"You make it sound like a story."

"Every life is a story," replied Waechter.

"So what now? You tell us where to find these objects?"

"Not really our department, I'm afraid."

"Then you give us special training?" she asked.

"Given the time frame of the quest, we'll probably have to skip that."

"Why even call us agents then? We're just ordinary people without any special skills stuck in a lousy situation."

"You are hardly ordinary citizens. Mr. Kawakami here is an exceptional young man. And you, Ms. Nicolaides, well, your exceptional nature is as obvious as the horns on your head. You have, in my experience, the perfect combination of the unassuming and the extraordinary. If there's a better pair of candidates for a quest, I haven't seen them. What do you think, Campbell?"

Agent Campbell said, "An excellent quest success quotient, according to our analysts."

"But you just said the better the odds, the worse our chances of..." Helen lowered her head, covered her eyes. "Forget it. There's no point in trying to understand it. But why are we here, then? We don't need any of the support services you provide. You already gave us our badges. You can't tell us anything. The whole thing seems like a waste of time."

Waechter smiled brightly.

"You're here because you choose to be."

He said it as if it answered everything.

"Walking through our doors was the first step. Every hero who has ever dreamed of glory has had to cross that threshold. Not that threshold specifically, but one like it. It's the signal to the universe, the moment when you agree to begin your journey into unknown worlds."

She couldn't decide if Waechter believed what he said or was pushing pseudo-intellectual nonsense. She wasn't sure she cared anymore.

"Can we at least see that book?" asked Troy.

"I'm afraid that's against the rules. It wouldn't do you any good to read it anyway. It's not like quests follow a road map. They work in broad strokes, not paint-by-numbers. There are certainly similarities, established patterns, but they avoid being too predictable."

"The gods above love irony," added Campbell.

"The more we know, the less we know," said Helen.

"Now you're getting it," said Waechter.

She didn't get it, but she decided that she didn't care anymore. As for Troy, he only sat there, smiling too. As if he were in on some joke that everyone got but her. Even Campbell sported the barest hint of a grin.

Waechter and Campbell escorted them back to the lobby. They were met there by a pair of agents who presented them with the confiscated sword and wand the Lost God had given them. Helen was given the wand, Troy the sword. The sword was sheathed in a scabbard. Not too fancy, but more heroic than the old shoebox the wand came in.

"We get these back now?" she asked.

"We had to make sure they weren't too dangerous," said Waechter. "They checked out. They're dangerous. Just not too dangerous."

Troy tested the weight of the sword. "Do we need licenses for these?"

"Comes with your NQB agent status."

"We aren't agents," mumbled Helen. "Agents have training."

"Now, there's one more thing," said Waechter. "After you leave here, you're going to want to get on the freeway, take Exit 42. Look for a sign. The rest is up to you."

"Is that it, then?" asked Helen. "We're not going to see you again?"

"Oh, we'll be in touch. Somewhere down the road."

Helen and Troy drove away.

"She seemed annoyed," said Agent Campbell.

"She had every right to be," replied Waechter.

"I think she suspects we aren't exactly on their side. The young man too, even if he was less obvious about it."

"We don't take sides, Campbell. You know that. We just help them on their journey. Reaching the right destination, that's up to them. Cleaning up the mess if they take a wrong turn, that's our job."

"Does that last part ever bother you, sir?" she asked.

"Every day. But greater good and all that, right?"

She frowned.

"Yes, sir. All that."

8

Their briefing at the NQB hadn't filled Helen with confidence.

"They're hiding something."

"Probably," agreed Troy.

"And doesn't that bother you?"

"Hel, they're the government. They hide stuff all the time. But it's not like they forced this quest on us. And they did give us the sword and wand."

"Yeah, and that's another thing. Why did I get stuck with the wand?"

He shrugged.

"It's because I'm the girl," she said.

"Do you want the sword?"

"Waechter gave it to you."

"Who cares?" he replied. "You said it yourself. You don't trust the guy. Just because he handed me the sword doesn't mean we have to stick with that arrangement."

"I didn't know you had such a rebellious streak."

"I have my moments. I used to sneak grapes to feed my pet turtle, even though Mom told me not to."

"Ne'er-do-well."

"I prefer the term *scofflaw*, thank you very much." He ran his fingers along the flat of the blade of the sword beside him. "But I'm thinking they gave me the sword because, in our pairing, I'm the little guy, and the NQB thought I'd need something to keep up with you."

She grinned. "You always know the right thing to say, don't you?"

"Not always. But usually."

She waved the wand around. "Alakazam! Presto! For the honor of Grayskull! It's clobberin' time!"

Nothing happened.

"Careful where you point that thing," said Troy. "You don't know what it does."

"Would've been nice if it came with instructions." She shoved it back in its box, leaned back, and decided to enjoy the ride. The situation wasn't ideal. She was probably going to die on this quest. But maybe not. If she did have only a few days to live, it would be foolish to waste them being grouchy. She gave herself permission to enjoy the ride.

There was an incredible sense of freedom and adventure that came with riding in the Chimera, the top down, the wind blowing in her hair, the freeway open before her like a doorway to the world beyond.

That faded a bit when they were caught in a traffic jam five minutes later. The road that had seemed so welcoming before now only felt like a sizzling, sucking slab of asphalt doing its best to keep them from leaving town. That was only her imagination, though she was on a quest, so maybe a wizard had used a curse to close the two left lanes and bottleneck the flow of traffic. Or maybe it was just the regularly scheduled construction that had been going on for weeks now. But she couldn't dismiss the evil wizard idea. Wizards were tricky like that.

She stifled her annoyance. Troy didn't seem to have any annoyance to stifle. He signaled a car ahead of them that it was safe to merge.

"You don't have to keep doing that," said Helen.

"Doing what?" he asked.

"Letting everyone in."

"It's called being a courteous driver, Hel."

"One or two cars is being courteous," she replied. "That's your seventh."

"You're counting?"

"I'm estimating."

"Seven's pretty specific for an estimate."

"So I was counting," she said, "and maybe you don't care, but the people behind us are probably getting a touch irritated."

Troy nodded. "Good point."

He pulled ahead. The car moved a few feet before having to stop again.

"There. Happy now?" he asked.

She laid her head back on her seat and stared at the blue sky above. "Ecstatic."

"Is something wrong, Helen?" he asked.

"Just seems like a lousy way to start a quest," she said. "Being swallowed alive by traffic."

Troy chuckled. "And they were never heard from again."

She closed her eyes. "Wake me when the dragons show up."

Once Troy got serious about it, he guided the Chimera through clogged traffic like a ship in choppy waters. They didn't get above thirty miles an hour, but given the circumstances, it seemed as if they were soaring. The strangest part was that Troy managed to do this while remaining a courteous driver. He didn't cut anyone off. He didn't ride anyone's tailgate. It was proof to Helen that he'd been born under an anti-curse, chosen by the gods above to do great things, and while she was just along for the ride, she wasn't complaining.

He worked his way across two lanes of traffic to their exit ramp. By all logic the Chimera should've come out with a few bumps and scrapes. But the ride had been effortlessly smooth, almost as if the other cars weren't even there. If morning traffic was the first beast encountered on their legendary journey, Troy slipped from its jaws with such skill and grace, it was probably worth a sonnet or two.

They pulled off the exit ramp and into a downtown neighborhood that she couldn't tell much about except that it was gray and dingy.

"Waechter said there would be a sign," he said.

She pointed to a street sign reading AUGURY AVENUE. "Does that count?"

"It's a little literal, isn't it?"

Helen said, "Depends. How many people do you think know the definition of the word *augury*?"

"Well, there's the two of us, obviously."

"Obviously. So either we're just two people who took Honors English together or it's our sign."

He drove down Augury Avenue. In the space of a few blocks,

a subtle shift transformed the neighborhood around them. They couldn't say exactly when the transition had happened. It wasn't as if they had felt the crackle of electricity down their spines or noticed all the people disappearing one by one. However it had happened, it had happened unnoticed, and they found themselves driving through an empty neighborhood.

Their curse marks stopped itching.

Cars were parked on the streets, but none moved down the road. The brisk pedestrian traffic had vanished. While the sounds of a bustling city could be heard, they didn't have any visible source. The brick buildings all looked several decades old but in pristine condition. There was a smattering of graffiti, and a few scraps of litter blew through the streets, but it all seemed meticulously placed.

Troy rolled the Chimera to a slow stop. "Weird."

Helen stepped out of the car. When her hoof hit the street, a tingle ran up her leg, the sense that they weren't in the world they knew anymore.

"I'd call this a sign," she said.

"Yeah, but of what?" asked Troy.

A breeze kicked up, blowing a piece of wrinkled paper past Helen's face. It snagged on her right horn. She pulled it off and read it. It was a crude photocopied advertisement for a lunch truck: "The Meat Wagon. We got what you need."

She handed the paper to Troy. "What do you think it means?"

"Probably means we should find this thing."

Helen sighed. "Great. So the first leg of our quest is all about finding a lunch truck. Where do we start?"

"How about over there?" Troy pointed to a lunch wagon parked just down the block.

Helen hopped back in the car. "That was easier than I expected."

As they approached the Meat Wagon, they spotted the first people they'd seen since entering this mystical street. The single customer was a woman, perhaps forty, dressed in a bathrobe and disheveled. The guy behind the counter was a hairy, thick fellow in a fez.

The truck itself sparkled like a polished diamond. If that diamond were made of aluminum and smelled of grease.

Helen and Troy parked beside it and approached. They kept their distance, but still caught the tail end of the current customer's conversation.

"What you're going to need to do," said the truck operator, "is get on the first flight to Galveston you can book. Then you're going to check into the hotel at this address..." He scribbled something on a napkin. "Tell them Castor sent you and they'll give you a discount rate. Then, on the night of the next full moon, take a swim in the pool. Enjoy yourself. Eventually, you'll notice some flowers on the bottom. Take one—and only one— and get out of the pool and walk back to your room without looking back."

She reached for the napkin, but he pulled it away.

"This is very important now. Because you'll be tempted to take more than one flower. And you'll definitely be tempted to look back. If you look back, then it's done. The flower will disappear. Your journey will be over. There won't be any second chances here. Do you understand what I'm trying to tell you?"

She nodded vigorously.

He looked unconvinced but handed the napkin to her. "I'm serious about this, Jillian. Game over."

She mumbled something before turning and jogging down the street.

"Good luck with...all that," shouted the cook insincerely.

Troy and Helen stepped up to the counter.

"She'll look back," said the cook.

They glanced to see the woman looking over her shoulder at them.

"Everybody looks back. Welcome to the Meat Wagon," said the cook. "What can I get you? Might I recommend the brisket? Got a pretty good ham sandwich too."

"Agent Waechter sent us," said Troy.

"Never heard of him."

Helen and Troy flashed their badges.

"Put those things away," said the cook. "Never could stand those NQB suits. Did they give you the Greater Good speech yet? If they haven't, they will. Biggest load of bull you're going to hear. Mortals who think they're smarter than the gods above. Not that the gods are any better. Bunch of clueless morons, every single one of them."

Helen and Troy were unsure of what to say, so said nothing.

"Ah, hell. Sorry for the rant. I've been on this job too long. You can only gaze into the future and all its possibilities for so long before it gets to you. Now why don't you give me a minute to fix up an order of brisket. And some French fries for the lady. Sorry, but it's about the only thing I got suitable for vegetarians."

"How'd you know I'm a vegetarian?" she asked.

"Knowing things is my thing," he said. "Pollux Castor is the name. Seeing is my burden. I see what even the gods cannot see, know what even the Fates are uncertain of. I've also mastered the art of barbeque, but nobody ever seems as excited about that."

"Where are we?" asked Troy.

Pollux disappeared into the shadowy regions of his vehicle, but they could hear his voice. "We are currently in a sacred glen, a hidden place where neither mortal nor immortal treads lightly. Many years ago, civilization succeeded in doing what the gods never could and paved over it. But you can't destroy something like that. So it returned as this hallowed city block, this perfect realm between."

"Between what?"

"You name it." Pollux shuffled into the light and dropped a paper plate of meat. "But it's lousy for business, so I'm going to have to charge you for the meal. That'll be three bucks. Also, you might want to remember that the future of your entire quest depends on what I say in about four minutes when you consider the tip."

Troy was worried Pollux might not take their NQB credit card, but money was money. The oracle didn't discriminate. He informed them it would be a few minutes on the fries, and that while they waited they should get their sword and wand out so that he could explain how to use them. They had no place to sit and leaned against the Chimera while Troy ate his late breakfast.

"How is it?" Helen asked.

"Good. Kind of greasy."

A three-legged dog trotted up and sat before them. The fluffy brown-and-gray mongrel lowered its floppy ears and whined.

Troy put down his plate, and the dog wolfed down the meat.

The back door to the Meat Wagon opened, and Pollux exited. He was a short, hirsute man. Not fat but certainly stout. He thrust a cardboard tray of fries at Helen. "No charge, miss. They aren't very good."

"Uh, thanks?" Helen looked at the soggy planks of under-cooked potatoes but didn't take a bite.

Pollux wiped his hands on his stained apron and studied the dog eating brisket.

"I had a big breakfast," said Troy.

"You paid for it. You can throw it in the garbage for all I care." Pollux held out his hand. "OK, let me see the sword."

Troy gave him the weapon.

"What you got here is a standard enchanted weapon. Super-natural sharpness, of course. That's a given." He took a mighty swing at a lamppost and felled it with one stroke.

"Also, if you're holding it and both your feet are on the earth, nothing can hurt you. But pay close attention to that sentence because it'll matter later on."

He gave the sword back to Troy.

"Finally, if you tap the point of the blade against the ground three times, you can summon an animating elemental spirit that will obey a single command. But—"

Troy smacked the sidewalk three times rapidly. The ground quaked, and chunks of concrete and asphalt ripped free and shaped themselves into a ten-foot hulking humanoid shape. Two lights glimmered in its approximation of a head.

"But you can only do it once a day, so you should probably think ahead," said Pollux.

The elemental spoke with a slow, rumbling voice. "What is your first command, master?"

Troy sucked a breath through his teeth. "Oh, sorry. I was just testing it."

The elemental shook its head. "You realize that you called me away from my kid's birthday party for this?"

"Elementals have birthdays?" asked Troy.

"No, but I'm trying to put it in terms you understand. I've got better things to do than a twelve-hour commute across the cosmic void just so you can see if your magic sword works."

"Aren't elementals timeless?"

The elemental shut its glowing eyes and rubbed its face. "Human terms. Again."

Pollux stepped between Troy and the creature. "You can yell at the kid later. We're in the middle of something."

The elemental stalked away, grumbling to itself.

"What's the wand do?" asked Helen.

"Nothing right now," replied Pollux. "It's an unharnessed battery of magic. Technically it can do almost anything, with one caveat. It can't harm or heal any living thing. Not even indirectly. So don't think you can beat the system by opening a pit beneath someone or conjuring a safe to drop on their head because that won't work."

"How do you turn it on?" She shook it. "I tried using it earlier, and it didn't do anything."

"Did you have anything in mind? You can't just point it at something, shout some magic words, and expect it to know what you want. You don't pick up a phone and just expect it to dial the number for you, do you?"

When he put it like that, it made her feel silly.

"You have to program it," he said. "Teach it to do things. However, and here's the other caveat, you have to be absolutely focused when you do. If you aren't, it's just as likely to screw up as get it right. Like if you wanted to conjure some ketchup for those fries. You have to have the amount of ketchup in your head when you do the conjuring. And if you want a bottle, you should probably decide if you want an old-fashioned glass one or squeeze. It wouldn't hurt to know the brand. When you've got all that figured out and clear in your mind's eye, only then would it be safe to try and summon your ketchup. Even then, you'd probably screw something up, end up with ketchup that's expired or making a giant ketchup monster that would only slither around and growl at people.

"If I were you, I'd put the wand back in the box and just forget about it."

Helen dropped the wand in its box. "Want to trade?"

Troy said, "No thanks. Think I'll stick with the magic sword of invincibility."

Pollux bent down and petted the dog. "You're going to want to head east down the interstate and drive until you reach the land of the setting sun. That'll be your first stop. Hopefully not your last. After that . . ." He pulled a paper placemat from his back pocket. He put it on the hood, smoothed it with his thick fingers. The wrinkled mat had a simple child's maze on it with a grinning knight at the entrance and a princess at the exit. The maze was already solved. "It'll just be easier if I draw you a map."

He scribbled some crude doodles on the maze, then handed it to Helen.

"What kind of map is this?" She pointed to a stick figure of a monster. "And is that supposed to be a giant?"

"Cyclops."

"That's its eye?" she asked. "I thought that was its mouth."

"I flunked out of art school. What do you want from me? And it's the best map you're going to get on this journey. You don't quest by following conventional landmarks. Your road is shown by a different method."

He paused, chewed on his pen.

"And don't think just because I'm drawing this that I'm guaranteeing anything. There are no guarantees. This is only the path you'll take if things go smoothly. And even then, there will be bumps. Lots of them. But keep moving, and you might just make it to the end in one piece."

"And what's this?" asked Helen. "Like a swamp or something?"

"Just a grease stain. Hazard of my secondary profession."

He wiped his hands on his dirty apron, shook their hands. Helen hated getting grease in her fur, but she didn't want to risk offending the oracle.

"Good luck." He waddled his way back to his truck.

"Hey, so do you know what's going to happen to us?" called Helen.

"Kid, there are things I know and things I don't know. Things I think I don't know that I do. Things I think I know that I don't. And then there are things that nobody knows. Not me. Not nobody."

"Which thing are we?" she asked.

"Doesn't really matter, does it?" he replied. "Because even if I know, or even if I think I know, I'm not allowed to tell you. That's the rules. Anyway, you don't really want to know. Nobody does. Trust me on that. It's one of the things I know. I think."

"Mr. Castor," said Troy.

"Yeah?"

"You do know that *meat wagon* is slang for a vehicle that carries away dead bodies, right?"

"I'm not an idiot," said Pollux. "It's supposed to be kitschy."

"I'm not sure associating your food with corpses is good marketing."

Pollux nodded to himself. "Think so, eh? Truth be told, I've been thinking about changing it. Thanks, kid. For that, I'll throw in a little extra advice. Take the dog with you. Might come in handy. All I'm saying."

The mutt's ears perked up, and it barked once.

Troy looked into the dog's big brown eyes. The canine wagged its tail.

"Absolutely not," he said.

The dog's tail fell flat.

Troy jumped into the Chimera. The lumbering earth elemental stepped in front of the car. "Aren't you forgetting something? I don't go home until I complete my command."

"Sorry. Can I just give you one order? Go home."

The elemental shrugged. "It's your dime." It fell apart into a mound of stone.

"You ready, Hel?"

She narrowed her eyes. Her ears pushed forward. "We have to take the dog."

"It'll shed all over the car," said Troy.

"So will I."

"C'mon. That's different." He drummed his fingers on the steering wheel. "It's dangerous for animals to ride in an open convertible."

"We'll put the roof up then."

He drew in a long breath.

"Don't you like dogs?" asked Helen.

Troy neither nodded nor shook his head, but instead kind of waggled it loosely. "I like dogs fine. I mean, I've got nothing against them."

"What's that mean?"

"It means that I respect dogs as living creatures, but I don't see the appeal."

Helen scooped up the mutt in her arms. "Our spirit guide told us to take the dog, so we should probably take it. And if you get the super invincible sword, I get this."

"Might come in handy," shouted Pollux from the Meat Wagon.

Helen dropped the dog in the backseat. It promptly curled up in a ball and yipped.

Troy glared at their new passenger.

"Whatever."

9

The Wild Hunt motorcycle club met at Dan's Donut Delights, a small store set in a failing strip mall. The doughnuts weren't as delightful as advertised, but the coffee wasn't bad and there was plenty of room in the parking lot for all the club's cycles.

The Wild Hunt motorcycle club wasn't an orcs-only organization. It just had worked out that way. Originally there had been an elf and several humans. But they'd gradually stopped coming to weekend gatherings, and eventually the orcs were the mainstay. They still had one human among their membership, and while Franklin was tall and skinny and stood out among the orange-, green-, and blue-skinned club members, most everyone had to give him points for enthusiasm.

A thousand years of civilization hadn't knocked out the orcish tendency to be thick-limbed and hardy. Even though none of the members held jobs more dangerous than sous-chef, they tended to intimidate decked out in their leathers.

Franklin, though, even wearing his leather jacket and with his pierced ears and traditional orc haircut (which orcs didn't even wear anymore), still looked as if he belonged behind a desk, sniffling and being vaguely passive-aggressive to his coworkers.

Nigel assumed that while his own orc ancestors were sacking and pillaging, Franklin's forerunners had been sitting behind civil servant counters, directing farmers to Line B because that was where the licenses to grow carrots were issued while Line A was for paying wagon parking tickets and while Franklin's great-great-great-grandfather could empathize with the inconvenience, he couldn't really do anything about it even though the farmer had just wasted three hours standing in the wrong line because he'd missed a small sign under a larger sign where the line began. And even if Franklin's nameless ancestor wanted to help, his hands were tied, so there was no use in complaining to him.

Perhaps it was those countless generations of middle management encoded in Franklin's DNA that finally pushed him over the edge, because Franklin might not have been an orc, but he really, really, really wanted to be one. Apparently he'd succeeded too, because he'd gotten the call from Grog like the rest of them.

The only difference was that he was excited about it.

"Hey, Nigel!" said Franklin in his faux-gruff voice. "Check this out!"

He pulled a flail from his bike's saddlebag. The weapon was old-school, complete with a heavy iron ball at the chain's end.

"Sweet, right?"

He fixed Nigel with an eager puppy stare. For some reason Franklin thought of Nigel as the orc to look up to. Perhaps because Nigel was tall and stout. Or perhaps because Nigel had been a touch rude to Franklin when the human first joined the club, and Franklin had mistaken this gruff dismissal as a challenge to win Nigel over.

"What the hell are you going to do with that?" asked Nigel.

Franklin appeared perplexed by the question. "I thought I'd smash in some heads with it."

"You do know that murder is illegal, right?"

"But we've got divine orders. That means it's not murder."

"You try telling that to the judge when the time comes," said Nigel.

Franklin whirled the flail around lightly, though he was obviously afraid of the weapon. For good reason. He didn't appear to have any idea how to use it.

"You really think we'll go to prison for this?" asked Franklin.

Nigel nodded.

"Cool." The flail smacked him in the thigh, and he yelped. "Do you think I can join an orc gang in jail?"

Nigel took a bite of his jelly-filled powdered doughnut and shrugged. "If you kill someone for our gods, you're a lock."

Franklin grinned, envisioning prowling the halls of a penitentiary like a warrior chieftain. Nigel grinned, envisioning Franklin getting shanked before even getting off the prison bus.

"Where did you get that anyway?" asked Nigel.

"Oh this?" Franklin rattled the flail. "I bought it. The guy said it has stopping power."

"Nobody ever used those things in real life," said Nigel. "Too unpredictable. Too clumsy. You're more likely to take your own head off than your opponent's."

"I've been practicing."

Franklin whipped the weapon forward. The iron ball at the

end of the chain rushed at Nigel's skull, but he caught it in one hand.

"Cute." Nigel frowned. "Now put it away before you hurt yourself."

Grumbling, Franklin did so. Nigel walked away and checked on Peggy Truthstalker, the seer appointed by Grog. She stood hunched over a pool of spilled motor oil.

Peggy was a tough old orc. Orc skin tightened with age rather than wrinkling, and either darkened to a deep black or paled to a ghostly white. Peggy's had gone pale and in the right light she could've been mistaken for a ghostly revenant risen from her grave. Her eyes were two yellow slits, and her face was stretched in a permanent grimace.

"Surprised you didn't hurt your hand," she said.

"I think I broke a bone or two," he replied. "But they're little ones, so I choose to ignore them." He bent down and looked into the black pool. "See anything yet?"

Peggy shook her head.

"Are you sure you're doing it right?" he asked.

"I didn't become the most feared trader on Wall Street by not knowing how to read omens," she replied.

"Can I get you anything to speed this up? If this takes longer than the weekend, my wife is going to kill me."

Peggy said, "In the old days, a little blood could help."

They glanced to Franklin.

"We should probably save him for an emergency," said Peggy.

Nigel grunted. He ran his knife across his hand and let the blood drip into the oil. She mixed it with her fingers and leaned down to give the puddle a deep sniff. Her eyes rolled back in her head, and she spit out a string of unintelligible syllables.

He sipped his coffee and waited for her to finish. The rest of the club milled about paying her little mind as she swayed and chanted to herself.

A crash drew Nigel's attention. Franklin stood over his bike, having knocked it over with one of his careless flail practice swings.

Peggy snapped out of her trance. "Grog damn it, Franklin. Now I have to start over."

Nigel snatched away the weapon.

"Hey, that's mine!" Franklin protested.

"You can have it back when you're ready for it."

"But I'm going to need a weapon, aren't I?"

"Someone arm him with something he can make less noise with," said Nigel.

Franklin accepted a short sword offered him, but he wasn't happy about it. "It's kind of small, isn't it?"

"I'm sure you can still manage to find a way to poke your eye out with it," replied Nigel.

Peggy started the ritual again. She was nearly ready to say something useful when another crash broke her trance.

"Sorry." Franklin struggled to right his motorcycle, having knocked it over with his new sword. The blade had drawn a long scratch across its paint job. "Ah, man."

Nigel nodded to Harold Marrowmaw, fattest orc in the club. "Sit on him until we're done with this."

Harold smiled. He was a dentist in Pasadena, so his teeth were perfectly aligned, his tusks sharpened in a way normally only seen in movies.

"That really isn't necessary," said Franklin.

Harold pointed to the ground, and Franklin reluctantly lay

down. Then Harold plopped down on top of him. Franklin's expression of discomfort was mixed with a half-smile. He liked being mistreated, usually mistaking it for orcish camaraderie. It made him difficult to discourage.

Peggy started her third attempt. This time no clatter disturbed her, and she completed her ritual. The motor oil and blood exploded in a small ball of fire, engulfing her face. Fortunately she didn't have any eyebrows to burn, having lost them to years of soothsaying. She tried to wipe the smudge from her pale face, though she succeeded only in smearing it around.

"South," she said.

"That's it?" asked Nigel.

"What do you want from me? I go where the spirits tell me. And the spirits say south."

"Can I get up now?" wheezed Franklin.

Harold stood, though it took several rocking attempts and some help from others.

The club climbed onto their motorcycles, and their engines rumbled and roared. The Wild Hunt left behind only the smell of burning grease and exhaust at Dan's Donut Delights.

10

The electric-blue Chimera skimmed across the highway with the relentless pace of a beast on a mission. The ride was smooth, but Helen still felt as if she held a wild animal by the steering wheel. She didn't fear losing control of the Chimera. She didn't have much control to begin with. The car had a will of her own, a desire to prowl imbued in her four tons of classic Detroit steel.

It was surely the car's own will that caused Helen to push a few miles above the speed limit when she normally abhorred speeding. She might have been envisioning the Chimera as a hungry monster, eager to devour as many miles as she could before sunset. The thrill that surged through Helen when she passed a slower vehicle surely came from her own primitive impulses, not some overpowering alluring spirit originating within the engine.

Try as she might, she couldn't shake the feeling that the Chimera was driving her.

She hadn't wanted to get behind the wheel at first, but Troy had convinced her to give it a try. If they were going to be on the road for a while, she might as well get used to the idea. Troy was bound to need a break every now and then.

"Maybe fifteen minutes," she'd said.

That had been five hours ago.

They'd left the urban sprawl behind a while before, and now drove through an endless desert. Civilization was ever present in the form of billboards, rest stops, truck stops, and a string of small towns that came with the miles. The Chimera barely noticed, and she was mostly annoyed whenever her passengers had to stop for a bathroom break or to grab a snack.

The dog in the backseat put his head on the seat and whined.

"I think he needs to relieve himself," said Helen.

"Again?" Troy groaned. "You didn't even eat or drink anything since the last time."

The dog whimpered.

Helen forced her hoof off the accelerator, though she couldn't make herself hit the brakes. The Chimera rolled to a slow stop, and she was honestly surprised by that.

The dog jumped out of the car and sniffed the dirt.

"I told you he'd slow us down." Troy frowned. "Just do it already, dog. It's all the same. Not like you're going to run into anyone you know here."

The dog raised his head and yawned.

"By all means, take your time," said Troy.

The dog returned to his search for the ideal spot.

"I still can't believe you don't like dogs," said Helen.

"I'm allowed, aren't I?"

"No," she said. "Actually, you aren't."

The sun hung low in the red desert sky, only twenty or thirty minutes from dipping below the horizon.

Troy said, "Guess we're almost there. Land of the setting sun, right?"

"That's a bit literal. And don't think I didn't notice you trying to change the subject."

The dog sniffed a yellow bush, but it didn't pass inspection.

"So what if I don't like dogs? I don't hate them. I'm not mean to them. I just don't see the appeal."

"Don't you volunteer at the animal shelter?" she asked.

He nodded. "Yes, and I take very good care of the dogs. I'm not afraid of them. And I don't begrudge them the right to exist."

She smiled. "How very noble of you."

Troy threw his hands in the air. "See? This is why I don't tell people. The moment you suggest that maybe dogs aren't awesome everyone looks at you funny."

"You have to admit it's a bit unexpected," said Helen. "You're so...*you*. And liking dogs seems like it should be part of the package."

"Well, it isn't."

Helen grinned. "That's what makes it so strange. And I don't think I've ever seen you so irritated."

"And this amuses you?"

"Nice to see you having a sore spot." She bumped her fist against his shoulder. "Makes you seem almost mortal."

Troy smiled, despite himself. "I'm not a big fan of apple pie either."

She put a finger to her lips. "I'll take your dark secret to my grave."

She rubbed her curse mark. She had the willpower to avoid

scratching it, but it itched. Troy either had more self-control or his was less irritating. Her enchanted bracelet felt constricting, as if it were cutting off her circulation. But running her fingers along the edge, she could tell it wasn't any tighter.

Troy noticed her fiddling with the rune-scrolled band. "So what's that for?"

She covered it with her hand. "It's just something I wear."

"But you always wear it. I've never seen you without it."

She put her hand behind her back. "It's nothing."

She tried, and failed, to hide her discomfort with the subject. He was too nice a guy to push it, and she was thankful for that. She pulled out the map (in the broadest sense of the word) the lunch wagon oracle had given them.

He'd drawn doodles along the solution traced through the child's maze. First was the cyclops, though it still didn't look like much of one. Next he'd doodled three faces. After that some kind of squiggle. It could've been a snake. Or a winding road. Or maybe just a part of the map where the oracle's pen had run out of ink and he'd had to scribble to get it working again.

She rotated the map and took a closer look. "This thing is unreadable." She pointed to a house on two sticks. "Are those stilts?"

"Look like stilts to me," agreed Troy.

The final doodle on the maze, just before the exit, was a big question mark. It wasn't comforting. Either destiny was holding out on them, or it didn't know. She folded the map, stuck it in her back pocket.

The dog finally located the proper patch of land to pee on, then trotted over and jumped into the car without prodding.

"What are you going to name him?" asked Troy.

"I'm surprised you care."

"If he's going to stick around, you have to name him something."

"I'm still working on it."

He hopped in the driver's seat, and Helen was simultaneously annoyed to have her position taken and grateful to be free of the responsibility that came with it. The Chimera tore down the road, and within the half-hour Troy pulled off the interstate as the sun touched the horizon.

As luck or fate would have it, there was a rural town located just off the exit. It appeared like a shimmering heat mirage, a few dozen buildings. It didn't look like much. Maybe only two or three miles across at its widest. Only the main road was paved.

WELCOME TO GATEWAY, NEVADA declared a wooden sign. YOUR ROAD TO ADVENTURE BEGINS HERE.

"This has got to be the place." He called to an old man sitting in a rocking chair, "Beg your pardon, sir, but is there a hotel here?"

The old man nodded, pointed down the road. "Can't miss it, young man."

Troy thanked him, and they drove on. The people sitting on their front porches seemed a quaint mistake in the space/time continuum. Or would have if all of Gateway hadn't seemed a refuge from another world, a place that had never existed outside of the imagined Good Ol' Days. It was surely a trick of the dusky twilight that made everything appear black and white, and even with the shadows stretching across the town, it never seemed ominous. Only friendly and welcoming. Not in that unsettling too-friendly way either. People smiled and waved at them, and they had the distinct impression that they were expected.

The Noble Wanderer Inn was a two-story building where

the paved road ended. They parked and went inside. The lobby looked more like a den than an office. A man and a woman sat on a pair of recliners watching television.

The man nodded to them. "Customers, Billi!" he shouted.

A short-haired brunette girl, maybe fourteen years old, came down the stairs. She smiled somewhat sincerely.

"Passing through? Or are you questers?" she asked.

"Questers," said Helen.

"You looked like questers. Have a seat. I'll be right with you." She ran upstairs.

The only seats available were on the couch between the couple. Helen and Troy sat. The couple were too engrossed in their *Have Sword, Will Travel* rerun to say anything else.

Billi came halfway down the staircase. "Are you going to need two solo licenses or one group?"

"Licenses for what?" asked Troy.

"The cyclops. That's why you're here, isn't it? You're questers, right?"

"We're on a quest," he replied.

"And we are looking for a cyclops," said Helen.

"Well, you can't face the cyclops without first purchasing a license. It's against the law. All I'm finding are the solo licenses, though. Most groups prefer to fight the cyclops together. But if you'd be willing to take the solo licenses, I've got plenty of those."

They didn't reply quickly enough, and Billi said, "Don't worry about it. I'm sure I can find some group licenses around here somewhere. If you want, you can come up here and help me look."

She ran upstairs. They followed her, finding her in a room that seemed to be half bathroom, half storage area. Billi sat on the rim of the bathtub, rifling through a filing cabinet. She instructed Troy to check a different cabinet while Helen stood outside the room and watched.

"I'm not sure we're here to fight," said Helen. "Maybe we're just here to talk to him."

Billi shook her head. "That's not how it works. You don't talk to the cyclops. You fight him. Because if you're on a quest, the only other reason you'd be here would be to get the chalice at the bottom of Garvey Cavern, and someone finally managed to kill the giant spider that guarded it last year."

"And why do we need licenses?"

Billi said, "Because Gateway's economy relies on four things. We have our truck stop. We have our hotel. And we've got the people who come to fight the cyclops. I guess that's only three things now that the spider is dead.

"You used to be able to face Cliff's challenge without a license, but then the city council passed a law. It's only a way to squeeze a few extra bucks out of questers, but there's nothing you can do about it. Cliff won't fight you if you don't have a license."

"The cyclops is named Cliff?" asked Helen.

Billi winced. "I wouldn't call him that to his face. Only his friends can get away with that. If you want to stand a chance, call him Clifford."

Troy pulled a couple of sheets of paper from a drawer and showed them to Billi.

"Nope. Those are monster-spider-hunting permits. Now the cave just has bats in it. We've been trying to get people excited about that, but we still mostly rely on the truck stop and Cliff right now."

Billi slammed the drawer shut.

HELEN AND TROY'S EPIC ROAD QUEST

"Oh, forget it. I'll get some new forms in the morning. Let's just check you in."

"We have a dog," said Helen. "I hope that's OK."

"What's its name?" asked Billi.

"He doesn't have one yet. We just got him."

"Mom doesn't like dogs in the rooms, but I'll take care of it."

"Thanks."

"I'm a dog person," said Billi.

"Who isn't?" replied Helen with a sly smile.

Troy rolled his eyes.

They paid for two rooms. The Noble Wanderer's rooms were an addition built onto the back of the house. They were well kept and came with vouchers for free drinks from the local restaurant. The wallpaper was a bright-blue rubber duck motif more suited to a bathroom, but the beds were comfortable.

Helen left the three-legged dog in her room. The pooch hopped on the bed and promptly fell asleep.

Billi gave them their two eating options. They could dine at the local Magic Burger franchise. Even before getting nearly sacrificed to a hamburger god, their time as employees had soured them to the chain. That left the truck stop, where someone had opened a Mexican restaurant on one end.

The place wasn't terribly fancy, and the only attempts at ambience were a few sombreros hanging on the walls and some mariachi music playing from the speakers. But the food smelled good.

They found a table, tucked between busy groups of truckers and locals. The waitress took their orders. A tall, lean man sat a few tables away. He wasn't especially noteworthy, except that he had only one eye where he should've had two. Helen pointed the guy out to Troy, then stopped him from turning and looking.

"Do you think that's the cyclops?" she asked. "He's a bit small."

Troy turned his head to get a glimpse from his peripheral vision. "He is a cyclops."

"There could be more than one."

He nodded, took a moment to enjoy the complimentary chips and salsa. "I'm just going to ask him."

She grabbed Troy's arm. "Don't do that."

"Why not?"

"He's eating."

"I'm just going to ask him if he's Cliff the cyclops."

"You aren't supposed to call him Cliff," she reminded him.

"I remember." He slipped out of her grasp and walked up to the cyclops's table.

"Hi, sorry to disturb you," said Troy, "but we've been told that we have to fight a cyclops in town, and I hope it's not too rude to ask—"

"That's me," said Clifford. "I'm the town cyclops."

"I hope it's not considered impolite to introduce myself then."

Clifford set down his fork and smiled. "Not at all. I'm Clifford."

"Troy." He pointed to Helen, who sank into her chair. "That's Helen."

Clifford offered Troy a firm, friendly handshake.

"Would you care to join me?" asked Clifford.

"We'd be delighted."

Troy waved Helen over. Helen shook her head.

"Don't mind her," he said. "She's shy."

"Most people are," said Clifford. "They seem to think this is personal. But it's just business. I like most of the questers who pass through. Decent folks, most of them."

Troy waved to Helen again. She pushed away from their table and approached.

"Clifford said we can sit with him," said Troy.

Helen forced a smile and sat. "Wonderful."

"Always a pleasure to meet another Enchanted American," said Clifford.

"So tomorrow we're supposed to fight?" asked Troy.

"Provided you buy the proper permits," answered Clifford.

"It's a bit barbaric, isn't it?" said Helen.

"Agreed." Clifford shrugged. "But that's the way it's done."

"Isn't there an alternative?"

"Technically, our contest doesn't have to be a violent one. You only have to best me. A quester challenged me to a riddle contest once." He took a bite of his enchiladas and chuckled. "That was when I discovered I'm lousy at riddles. Another challenged me to a game of checkers. Lost that one too. And there was this one guy who wanted to flip a coin. Can you believe that? Just leaving everything up to blind chance. What's the point of going on a quest if you're going to just let luck decide the outcome?"

"Did he win?" asked Troy.

Clifford grunted. "He had a magic coin that always came out in his favor, so yes. But if you ask me that's a bit underhanded. It's one thing to be a clever hero. It's another to rig the game.

"Eventually I realized that the only thing I'm good at is beating the snot out of people. It's my strength. Why fight it? No tricky contests, no cunning stratagems. Just a straight-up brawl. It's much simpler.

"You two look like you've got some fight in you. How much do you bench?" he asked Helen.

"I don't know. I've never benched."

Their food was brought to the table. Helen only took a few bites of her vegetarian tacos.

"You should eat," said Clifford. "You'll need your strength."

"I don't get it," she replied. "This all seems so—"

"Retro? Yes, I guess it is in a way. All I know is that I answered an ad in a newspaper, and here I am."

"Can't you just let us pass through?" asked Helen.

Clifford choked on his rice.

"If I do that then I cease to be a guardian. I'll be out of a job, and Gateway risks losing its place along the road to legends. Just two exits down there's a town that's already built a deadly maze of booby traps. If they ever find anything worthwhile to hide in it, then we could lose a healthy chunk of our quest dollars.

"No, these people depend on me. I can't allow you to walk on by without besting me. And I can't hold back either, so please, don't ask."

"We understand," said Troy.

"Don't worry, though," added Clifford. "I'll only beat the crap out of you. I won't kill you."

"Thanks," said Helen. "But we're under a divine curse. If we don't complete our quest, we'll die anyway."

As if the curse was listening and excited to be mentioned, it poked her hand like needles gently pressed against her skin.

"That's unfortunate." Clifford wiped his mouth, stood. "But it doesn't change anything. This is my job, and I'm not qualified for anything else since I dropped out of nursing school. But I'll go ahead and buy your dinner, since you seem like good kids."

"Oh, you don't have to do that," said Troy.

"Think nothing of it. Just so you know, I haven't lost a challenge in four years, and I had walking pneumonia then. I look forward to facing you on the field of battle tomorrow. Should be fun. Good luck."

He shook Troy's hand.

"You too."

Clifford walked away.

"Seems like a nice guy," said Troy.

"Seems like," Helen agreed.

"Hey, Hel, are you going to finish your tacos?" he asked.

She pushed the plate toward him.

11

"The field of battle" wasn't merely an expression. Gateway had an actual clearing reserved for the event. It was only a patch of dirt, but it did have stands for the locals to come and watch. A small crowd occupied the bleachers. There was also a shady awning under which challengers waited their turn.

A broad, scarred man was already there. He balanced a huge war hammer across his shoulders.

Clifford the cyclops wasn't there yet, so Troy passed the time chatting with his fellow challenger, who introduced himself as Smith.

"Nice sword," said Smith.

"Nice hammer," said Troy.

"Gets the job done."

"Do this kind of thing often?" asked Troy.

"The gods have decreed that if I defeat seventy-seven monsters, I can join them in the heavens above as one of their own," replied

Smith. "This will be my forty-first." He glanced at Helen. "Don't suppose your friend would be interested in being number forty-two."

"She's not a monster."

Smith sucked on his teeth. "I'll give you twenty bucks if she wins."

Troy excused himself. "Wow, that guy is an ass."

"What'd he say?" she asked.

"It's not important."

They sat in the folding chairs available. Billi brought them some lemonade.

"How does this work?" asked Helen as she petted her dog. "What are the rules?"

"There's only one rule," said Billi. "The first to yield loses. Or the first to lose consciousness. Although technically that's not counted as a victory and those challengers are allowed to try again once they get out of the hospital. Most don't. Those that do, don't ever try a third time.

"I haven't seen this many people come out to the field in a while. Folks seem to be more excited by this fight than normal. Must be because of your condition, miss. Not often we get questers of your persuasion. Promises to be a good fight."

She went over to offer a glass to Smith.

"Have you ever been in a fight before?" asked Helen. "I mean, like a real fight?"

Troy shook his head. "I've done some wrestling and boxing, studied some Jeet Kune Do, but no, I haven't been in a fight fight. You?"

"No."

They sipped their lemonade.

"Are you nervous?" she asked.

"A little bit."

"I'm surprised to hear you admit that."

"Why?" he said. "Because I'm always so confident? Confidence doesn't mean I'm an idiot, Hel. I know what's at stake here."

"I know you know. Just surprised that you would admit to any doubts."

Troy said, "Do you think I never have doubts? I have them. Maybe not as much as your average person, but I have my moments. The problem with being perfect, though, is that I'm not supposed to say it out loud."

He caught Helen smiling at him.

"I know it's stupid to complain about being awesome."

"No, it's not," she said. "If you didn't have complaints, you wouldn't be human."

"Maybe, but it's obnoxious. Especially complaining to you about it."

Helen's smile dropped.

Troy bit his lip. "That was a stupid thing to say. I'm sorry, Hel."

"Don't do that," she said. "You don't have to tiptoe around the minotaur thing. I know what I am. Not like I'm going to forget. But it's not like we don't have a lot in common that way. We're both stuck with the expectations people put on us. Whether we like it or not. Funny thing is, we may be the two people who can most relate to what the other is going through."

Troy laughed. "Hadn't thought about it that way."

They tapped their divinely cursed fists together.

Someone in the stands blew a horn.

"He's coming," said Billi.

Clifford approached the battlefield, a scrawny figure in bike shorts and sandals. An accompanying drummer punctuated Clifford's every step, thumping as if the earth were shaking beneath his feet.

Smith spat in the dirt, smacked the ground twice with his giant hammer. Each blow sounded a clap of thunder. "I'll go first, if you don't mind."

"Be our guest," said Troy.

Smith marched out into the field to meet Clifford. The cyclops drank some Gatorade and slipped out of his sandals while Smith loosened up with some practice swings. The combatants exchanged a few words, but they were too far away to be heard.

The cyclops grew into a tremendous twelve-foot giant. He nodded to the horn blower, who sounded the start of battle.

Smith charged. His hammer crackled with magic lightning. He didn't get a chance to use it. Clifford knocked Smith off his feet with one swift punch. Smith bounced across the field. The woozy warrior struggled to his feet. He stumbled in a clumsy zigzag to recover his weapon.

Clifford calmly walked over and tripped Smith. The cyclops then stomped him into the dirt. Clifford appeared bored by the act. He stopped occasionally to check if Smith yielded, which he didn't until the third pause.

Clifford shrank to his scrawny proportions and used a towel to wipe the sweat from his bald head, which was more likely to have been caused by the heat of the morning than by any strain on his part. Smith was carried out on a stretcher.

"You're up," said Billi. "Good luck."

She stopped Helen.

"Oh, and I came up with a name for your dog. Achilles."

"That's not bad. Why don't you keep an eye on him while we try not to get our butts kicked?"

Achilles whined. Helen scratched him under the chin. "Don't worry, little buddy. We've got this."

Billi said, "Miss, I don't normally give questers hints, but just so you know, Cliff's father was an air spirit and his mother was an earth goddess. I can't tell you more than that, but it might prove helpful."

"Thanks."

Helen caught up with Troy.

"Did you hear that? She gave us a hint because we have a dog."

"I heard, but we don't need it," he replied. "I think I know how to beat this guy."

Clifford stretched. "That guy was a good warm-up. Now, before we start, I like to give everyone one last chance to back out. There's no shame in it."

"Is it all right if I use this sword?" asked Troy. "It's magic, just to be up-front."

"It's all right." Clifford nodded to the horn player, who sounded the start of the fight.

Troy tapped his sword on the ground three times. A rumbling monster of hard-packed dirt rose before them. "What is your command, master?"

Troy pointed to Clifford. "Beat him up for us."

The dirt elemental lumbered toward the cyclops, stopped in front of him, and spoke with its deep, dry voice.

"Hi, Cliff. How's it going?"

"Can't complain."

The elemental said, "Sorry, kids, but I can't fight Cliff."

"But I command you," said Troy.

"Yes, but the magic of your sword is inferior to his birthright. I can't attack him. Even if I could, against an earth godling I wouldn't stand a chance." The monster shrugged. Clouds of dust fell off its shoulders and blew into their faces. "But I'll be happy to help you with anything else if you survive this." It walked over to the stands to watch the fight.

"Was that your master plan?" asked Helen.

Troy said, "I'm working on a backup."

Clifford inhaled and expanded into his monstrous form. Helen didn't even see his punch as she was knocked across the field to lie in a heap. Clifford followed it with a fist smash meant to flatten Troy, but Troy's athletic reflexes kicked in. He dodged to one side, though the concussion of the blow nearly knocked him off his feet.

Troy sidestepped another strike and another. Clifford was powerful and fast, but he telegraphed his attacks. Troy had always been good at reading body language and years of sports had honed that talent to a fine point. He was able to stay one step ahead of the giant.

Though Clifford was easy to read, he was also too skilled to give Troy an opening. Even if he had, Troy wasn't sure he'd have been willing to take it. The sword was a lousy weapon because it was designed to kill. Intellectually, Troy understood he was fighting for his life. And for Helen's. But it was a big jump from never being in a fight to slaying a monster. Especially a monster that seemed as if he was just doing his job.

After a minute of cat and mouse, Clifford paused, blew out his breath, and shrank. "You're a fast one."

Troy held up his sword as if he might actually use it. "Do you surrender, then?"

"Nice try. But you'll have to do better than that."

Clifford expanded and rushed at Troy. Troy was too slow, and the cyclops plowed into him. And bounced away harmlessly.

Both Troy and Clifford were surprised by that.

Clifford threw a punch. Troy stood his ground, and the huge fist hit him without effect. He didn't feel it, though to judge by the way Clifford held his reddened knuckles, he had.

Troy whirled his weapon. "Magic sword of invincibility."

Clifford exhaled and became scrawny. "Why the hell were you dodging so much?"

"Instinct. Also, I kind of forgot."

"This is a surprise," said Clifford. "I thought your minotaur friend would be the challenging one."

Behind him Helen stirred. Troy kept Clifford's attention focused away from her.

"I don't want to stab you, but I will if I have to. And since you can't hurt me, you might as well surrender."

"That's very kind of you, but I can't just give up. Usually enchanted weapons have a catch to them."

"There's no catch. I'm invulnerable. You're not."

"Would you like some advice? If you're going to go on a quest, you have to commit to it. Now, I'm not suggesting that I want you to stick me with that magic sword of yours, but that's part of my job. I can't walk away every time some ambitious person waves a blade in my direction."

"So it's a standoff?" asked Troy.

"Only until I figure out the flaw in your weapon."

"What if it doesn't have one?"

"There's always a flaw. That's how magic works."

"That must mean there's a flaw in your magic too," said Troy.

"I didn't say that."

"Yes you did."

They smiled.

"All right then. That's the challenge, is it? First to find the other's kryptonite."

Helen was on her knees. She was dizzy, but Troy couldn't tell if she was hurt.

"I've already found yours," said Troy. "You're the child of an earth goddess and an air spirit. You grow when you inhale, but only for as long as you're holding your breath. And since you are barefoot, I bet it only works for as long as you're touching the ground."

Clifford's brow furrowed. "Ah, damn it, Billi, what did I tell you about giving hints?"

"Sorry, Cliff," called Billi from the tent. "But you know I'm a dog person."

"You got me," said Clifford. "But I've got you too. You haven't moved from that spot. I'm betting that your invulnerability only lasts so long as you stay put."

Helen stood. Troy nodded subtly to her not to interfere.

"It's a stalemate?" asked Troy. "We just stand here until one of us gets exhausted?"

"Not quite."

Clifford inflated. He grabbed Troy in his two giant hands and lifted him off the ground. Clifford, holding his breath, couldn't speak, but his smug grin said it all. Troy's sword arm was pinned to his side. He couldn't do anything about it.

"I can't yield," said Troy.

Clifford nodded as if he understood. He cocked his arm back, preparing to hurl Troy like a football. A fleshy, crunchy football that would end up a shattered sack of bones.

Helen charged from behind and knocked Clifford's legs out from under him. He tumbled into the air, deflating. Troy hit the ground hard but not nearly as hard as Clifford had intended. Relief overwhelmed any pain.

Clifford stood. "OK, that was a bit of a cheap shot, but I have to give you credit. Not many people can—"

Troy heard the steady thump-thump-thump of hooves and Helen crashing into Clifford again. It was followed by his yelp and the light thud of a shrunken cyclops hitting the ground.

Troy sat up. His eyes followed the trail of dust left in Helen's wake. She was fast. Really fast. She swung around for another charge, her head held low.

"I knew she'd be trouble. But nobody knocks me off my feet three times in a row." Clifford adopted a linebacker stance and grew.

The two Enchanted Americans crashed together. Clifford reeled from the collision and for a moment it looked as if he might fall over. But he held steady. He twisted and threw Helen off balance, and she landed on her face, choking on the dust in the air.

The crowd cheered. Clifford bowed.

"Can I say how much fun this has been? I haven't had a genuine challenge in such a long time, I forgot what it felt like. You did good, but you're only mortals in the end."

He expanded, lifted Helen off the ground, and prepared to lay her out with his strongest punch.

"Hey, you forgot about me." Troy stood with his enchanted sword at the ready.

Clifford grinned and shook his head. He couldn't say it aloud, but he didn't need to. Troy was next.

Helen undid the clasp on her bracelet. It fell to earth, and a bristling mix of her family curse and adrenaline surged through her.

She kicked Clifford in the gut with both hooves. He exhaled painfully and dropped her. He gasped, struggling to draw in a suitably deep breath. She laid a punch across his jaw. Her form was sloppy, but it was her first. It still knocked him to the ground.

"Stay down," she said.

"It doesn't work like that, Hel," said Troy. "He recovers from anything as long as he can touch the earth. If you want to beat him, just throw him over your shoulder before he catches his breath."

She did. The cyclops squirmed and writhed, but she held firm.

"Game over, Clifford," she said.

12

Victory over the Gateway guardian had earned Helen and Troy more than permission to carry on their quest. They'd also earned a special reward from the town's prize cache, rare and unusual items of interest that had made their way into Gateway's possession. They were kept in a shack behind Clifford's house.

"You get one thing," he said as he slipped the key into the padlock.

"But there are two of us," said Troy.

"You fought as a team. That means only one item. That's the rules."

"Who makes these rules?" asked Helen. "Everyone keeps acting like they're written down somewhere. Is there a manual we should have?"

"They're just the damn rules. Everyone has to follow them. Don't ask me where they come from."

He pushed open the door and walked away, scowling.

"What's wrong with him?" asked Helen.

"You kicked his ass," said Troy.

"Oh yeah. I did, didn't I?"

Smiling, she unfolded their map and used a pen to mark out the scowling cyclops' face with an X. It felt very satisfying.

"That was amazing, Hel. I didn't know you could take a punch like that."

"Neither did I. Nobody ever punched me before."

"How are you feeling?"

She rubbed her chin, stretched her right arm out. "Little sore. But considering I just wrestled a godling, I can't complain."

They entered the shack. Knickknacks and collectibles lined its shelves. Troy picked up one golden chalice among many. "Do you think some of this stuff is magic?"

Helen shrugged. She held up a Gilgamesh Pez dispenser. "Behold the awesome gifts of the gods: chalk-based candy."

"Does it come with Pez?" asked Troy. "Or would that count as two things?"

She put the dispenser back on the shelf. "Good question."

They picked through the various items. Troy tried on a rubber mask of the Creature from the Black Lagoon. "Here's a serious question, Hel. Just how strong are you?"

She tapped a plastic skull. "Too strong."

"How can you be too strong?"

She hesitated.

He said, "It's cool. You don't have to talk about it. It's none of my business."

She sat in an old rocking chair. "No, it is. We are questing together. You should probably know."

"I wasn't trying to pry, Hel."

"Forget it. It's cool."

She picked up a banjo.

"Until I was seven, I was only a little stronger than kids my age. Then the full enchantment kicked in, and I got stronger. It started slowly at first. I even got a kick out of it. And so did my friends."

She strummed the banjo.

"Until I started breaking bones."

"Jeez," said Troy. "How did that happen?"

"Accidents. Kids just being kids. Except roughhousing can be a little... rough when you're a little girl who is stronger every day. I broke an arm, two legs, and cracked some ribs in the space of three days. After that, parents stopped letting their kids play with me. Not that any of my friends were eager.

"I took it hard. I'd always known I was different. Not like I couldn't know. But the way my folks raised me, they always made it seem unimportant. Horns? Tail? Those were just things I was born with. Superficial stuff. I'd be lying if I said it didn't bother me sometimes. Or that I didn't sometimes have fantasies about a handsome prince kissing me and making me normal. Not even beautiful. Just normal. But for the most part, I was OK with my condition."

She rocked in the chair, drumming her fingers on the instrument's neck.

Troy said, "Hel, you don't have to—"

"That day," she continued, "with me sitting in my room, playing with dolls and action figures because they were all I had, it's the first time I felt alone. And even Mom and Dad couldn't change that. I was afraid to even touch them. The whole world seemed like this delicate, special place, and I was a monster stomping my way through it."

Troy prided himself on his ability to know the right thing to say, and in a moment like this, saying nothing was exactly the right thing to say.

"They called in specialists who were able to make an enchanted bracelet that eventually reduced my strength to acceptable levels and kept it in check." She held up her wrist to show the band of silver around it. "It works. Although the prescription needs to be increased every few years. The doctors say that one day it might not be enough or the counterspell might eventually cause a severe allergic reaction. But it works, even if it gives me hives during equinoxes and solstices."

She scratched around it. It'd been insistently pricking her arms since she'd put it back on after the cyclops battle. It was as if her enchantment had been given the chance to run loose, and was unhappy to be chained again. The Lost God's curse had something to do with it too. Troy had been scratching his hand as well, and if he was like her, entering the shack had triggered something, causing their marks to throb.

He said, "Wow, Hel. That's...I don't..." He shook his head. "I mean...jeez."

She chuckled. "I've never seen you speechless before."

He shrugged. "It happens. Not very often, but it happens."

"They tell me it's OK to take it off now and then. I don't. I know it's dumb because it's not like I'm going to Hulk out the second it leaves my wrist."

"But you took it off when you were fighting Clifford," said Troy.

Helen rubbed the bracelet. "I didn't have a choice. We were fighting for our lives."

"But you didn't hurt anyone either," he said.

"He's a godling. I don't know if that counts."

"It counts. You were in control."

"Next you'll tell me I don't need this."

"I wouldn't tell you that. If you need it, you need it. But let me ask you this. If you wore glasses would you be self-conscious?"

She smirked. "It's not the same."

"Sure it is."

"The nearsighted can't accidentally kill people."

Troy turned around, thick spectacles on his face. "Why do you think the *Titanic* hit that iceberg? Hundreds dead. All because the captain thought he looked old in glasses. That's a historical fact."

"Oh really?"

"Yes, I read about it in the book *Tragic Tales of Reckless Astigmatism*."

Helen said, "No matter what else I take away from this conversation, I can at least be glad I'm unlikely to drown hundreds of innocent people."

"Not my original point, but you can take that away if you like."

They wasted another few minutes looking through the shack until Helen found something special in a pile of old shields. She knew she was on the right track when the divine throb became a sharp tingle in her fingertips. It subsided the second she touched the relic.

"I found it." She held up the small circular shield made of dented, tarnished silver. There was no doubt it was what they were looking for. If the vanishing pain wasn't enough of a clue, the swirling pattern etched into its surface matched the symbol burned into their hands by the Lost God.

"Should we take this as a sign that we're on the right path?" she asked.

Troy ran his fingers across the cold metal. A slight tingle ran up his arm as his own ache faded. "I'd say yes."

They exited the shack. Thunder rumbled. The skies darkened, though there wasn't a cloud in the sky, only a supernatural inky void. A gale kicked up with hurricane force, but somehow they remained anchored to the earth. The shack wasn't so lucky. It collapsed. Half of it was carried away by a tiny tornado. Drops of darkness fell from the sky to strike the ground as slithering black liquid creatures. The things howled an earsplitting dirge before evaporating along with the darkness and the wind, leaving only the heap of aluminum and plywood to mark their passing.

"Now that's a sign," said Troy.

"Yes, but of what?" asked Helen.

Clifford came running up. "What the hell did you do?"

"Act of gods," said Troy.

While Clifford was sorting through the broken shack, they quietly slipped away.

13

Billi helped Helen load her luggage into the Chimera.

"Thanks for your help," said Helen. "I don't know if we could've beaten Clifford without it."

Billi patted Achilles's back. "If I can be honest with you, it's good to see Cliff get his ass handed to him sometimes. Keeps him from getting overconfident. As much as I like him, everyone needs to lose every so often so they don't forget what it's like."

Helen gave Billi a ten-dollar tip. "Just my way of saying thanks for everything."

"Thanks." Billi shoved the money into her pocket. "Were you born like you are?"

"Yes."

"That's cool. I wish I was special like that."

"I'm not special. I'm just hairy."

"Is that why Troy isn't your boyfriend?"

Helen bit her lip. "It's complicated."

"No, it's not," said Billi. "You should grab him before some-one else does."

"It's not really up to me."

"You do like him then."

"I didn't say that."

"You didn't have to. People say too much. They're always talk-ing like it means something. But one of the things I've learned from living in Gateway is that the questers who talk the most do the least. It's not what you say that matters. It's what you do."

Helen laughed to herself. "You're pretty smart, but Troy and I are just friends."

"If you say so." Billi sounded unconvinced.

Troy, having settled their hotel bill, came over. "Are we ready to go?"

Helen shut the trunk. "Ready when you are."

He shook Billi's hand and bowed to her in a way that should've been corny but somehow wasn't. "Thanks for every-thing."

Billi nodded knowingly at Helen, who wiped the smile from her face.

"We should get going."

Billi pointed down the road. "What you're going to want to do is take this road out of town and follow it all the way. It gets a little bumpy in places, but keep to it until you get to the cross-roads. You'll pass about a dozen crossroads before you get to the one you're looking for, but you'll know it when you see it. There will be a sign."

They jumped in the Chimera. Billi gave Achilles one last scratch behind the ears and then they were off.

* * *

They drove all day along the dusty road. Patches of broken pavement sometimes eased the ride. Some stretches of lumpy asphalt were worse than others. They endured the unpleasant miles, assuming this was yet another trial on their road to glory.

They reached the crossroads they were looking for as the sun was setting. Troy pulled off the road and parked the Chimera in front of a store. The old wooden structure was quaint in a decidedly deliberate way. Strings of multicolored lights ran along its porch and traced its outline in the shadows, while a soft glow came from its many windows.

"How do we know this is the place?" asked Helen.

He pointed to the neon sign attached to the roof, which read THREE SISTERS DRY GOODS AND NOVELTIES. Beneath that, in smaller letters, was written DIRECTIONS GIVEN AS NEEDED.

She unfolded the map under the Chimera's interior light. He pointed to the three crude faces drawn as their next destination.

"Why are we always arriving at these places at dusk?" asked Helen.

"Twilight is the time of transition," replied Troy. "The moment the previous day ends and the new one begins. It's sacred, and even the gods above respect its power."

She shook her head. "Sounds like metaphysical nonsense to me."

Troy said, "Probably. But it does set a nice mood."

Helen let Achilles out. The dog wandered off to find a bush worthy of his mark.

A bell rang as they entered. The interior matched the impression given by the facade. The cluttered shelves were filled with merchandise, equally divided between traditional groceries and novelty items aimed at tourists.

Helen's hooves clonked loudly against the wooden floors. "Hello? Anyone here?"

A dark-haired girl, tiny and perhaps ten years old, spoke up from behind them. They'd only taken a few steps into the store, and there'd been no way for the girl to get into that position without being spotted.

"Hello," said the girl. "And welcome, noble questers."

"Thanks," said Troy. "We're here to see the sisters, we think."

The girl brushed her long bangs from her eyes, but the hair just fell back into place. "You are."

"Are you one of them?" he asked.

She nodded. "I am."

Troy and Helen took their eyes off the girl for a moment. When they looked back, she was gone.

"Where'd she go?" asked Helen.

The girl cleared her throat. She was behind them again.

"I'm always with you," she said. "For some people, I'm always by their side. For others, I'm far in their rearview mirror. But regardless of how far away you might think I am, I usually catch up to you. Usually at the most inopportune times."

"You're the anthropomorphic manifestation of the past," said Helen.

"I'm *an* anthropomorphic manifestation," said the girl with a slight grin. She was behind them again, though neither of them remembered looking away from her.

Helen was tall enough to glance over the shelves and saw no other signs of life, no tops of heads. Aside from the sound of her own heavy footsteps, she heard only a radio playing "Que Sera, Sera" by Doris Day.

"Are you alone here?" asked Helen.

"We're never alone," replied the girl, with a grin so coy and enigmatic it had to be rehearsed. "Do you need directions?"

Helen nodded.

"Why do you think I'm the one to give them to you?" asked the girl.

"You have a sign out front that specifically says you give directions. A great big one. It lights up and everything."

The girl said, "We do that. But what I'm really asking is why do you assume you need directions at all?"

Helen said, "Terrific. You're going to be vague and inscrutable, aren't you? Because really, all we need are directions. You can skip the Zen."

A new voice spoke up from beside Helen. "You'll have to excuse my sister. She's young."

Helen jumped.

"Oh, I'm sorry," said the middle-aged woman with brown hair. Except for the color of her hair, she could've been the young girl's twin, aged an additional thirty years. "Did I sneak up on you? People tend to ignore me. They're too busy with my sisters to bother with me."

"You must be the present," said Helen.

"I must be," answered the sister as she rearranged a display of clams with googly eyes glued to them.

"Where's your third sister?" asked Helen.

A voice called from an aisle in the back of the store. "I'm here. Stocking some canned goods. We have peas, buy two get one free."

Helen saw the top of a dark-haired head and a wrinkled hand waved at her.

"You never get a clear glimpse of the future," explained Helen.

Troy chuckled. "And you said you weren't interested in Zen. So are you really the Fates?"

Present replied, "We are fates, though we aren't necessarily *the* Fates, with a capital *F*. There are many of us on these old roads. Wherever monsters still roam and heroes seek their destinies."

"It's a franchise thing," added Past. "Like Stuckey's, but with more prognostication. Speaking of which, if you're here for directions, you need to buy something first."

"Does every oracle of the road sell junk?" asked Helen.

"We have to pay the bills some way," replied Present.

Troy scanned the shelves. "This isn't one of those things where we buy some seemingly unimportant items that end up being essential to completing our quest, is it? Like we purchase one of these vanity mirrors and then we end up facing a monster that turns us into stone if we look at it directly? Or we cross paths with a giant who collects novelty postcards?"

"A touch clichéd," said Present, "but not beyond the realm of possibility."

Future chuckled from the shadows. "Don't listen to her. She's just trying to sell you something."

"You're saying that won't happen?" asked Troy.

"Oh, it probably will. Or something like it. Though whether it's fate or your own resourcefulness that allows you to defeat a dragon with a teapot is anyone's guess."

Helen and Troy exchanged glances.

He asked, "You're saying to buy a teapot?"

"If you're so inclined," said Future. "But you didn't hear it from me."

Helen and Troy grabbed a few items from the shelves: a bumper sticker, a Lucille Ball bobblehead, some beef jerky for him, some dried apricots for her, a teapot, a bottle of hot sauce, a snow globe of the Library of Alexandria, and a handful of postcards with photos of adorable kittens romping with equally adorable puppies.

They dropped the purchases onto the counter and Present rang them up and dropped the items in a bag.

Troy grabbed several balls of yarn out of a bin marked TEN FOR A DOLLAR.

"That's a good price."

"We have tons of it," said Present. "Too much. We tried to stop delivery after we gave up weaving, but they just keep sending the stuff to us. If you like it, just take it. Take as much as you want. We don't need it."

"Leave us a purple," said Future. "I'm finishing a sweater."

He sorted through the balls of yarn.

"What do you need yarn for?" asked Helen.

"I knit."

"And you never shared this information before?" she asked.

"You didn't ask." He tucked a bright blue ball under his arm. "I find it relaxing. And it's the closest I'll ever come to doing magic."

"Magic, huh?"

"If someone came up to you on the street and gave you a ball of thread and two sticks, and asked you to make them a scarf, wouldn't your first reaction be to call them a nut?"

She decided he had a point.

"So you aren't weaving anymore?" she asked the sisters. "Isn't that your job?"

"Destiny has ever been a complicated business," said Past. "Back when we tried to weave the threads into something sensible, everything still always managed to get tangled together into a great big mess. Eventually we determined that the kings and the peasants, the heroes and the villains, the winners and the losers, they all end tied together in one giant knot. If we worked very hard, we might be able to direct the course of a single mortal life. But as a cosmic profession, it seemed like a lot of effort to ensure that John ends up where he's supposed to be when, really, Jill or Jerry or Jacob will do just as well in the end. Chaos and fate are mostly indistinguishable. Their end results are basically the same."

"That's depressing," said Helen.

"Is it?" asked Future from over Helen's shoulder. When Helen turned, she caught only a fleeting glimpse of Future's skirt disappearing around a corner. "What's more depressing from a mortal perspective? To believe that there is no grand plan and that all is random chance? Or that all is by a single unified design and that you are nothing more than the dancing puppets of a universe that merely sees you as a means to an end?"

Helen did find each equally unsettling.

Present said, "But you aren't interested in existential discussion, are you? You're here for directions. And considering the distance you must still travel on your journey, we've wasted enough of your time."

"But you just said you don't bother with fate," said Troy.

"Oh, we dabble still. More of a hobby at this point. As to your ultimate destiny, we can't say anything for certain."

"I can," said Future. "But I won't."

Present whispered, "And she wonders why nobody likes her."

Helen said, "I don't want to sound ungrateful, but we really only stopped in for directions, not existential dilemmas."

"You haven't earned your directions quite yet."

"We're buying your"—she almost said *junk* again—"your souvenirs."

Present laughed. "It's not as simple as that. You can't just purchase wisdom on an expense account."

Past said, "You have to face the storeroom. The place where your worst fears are made manifest, where you will confront that which terrifies you most. Only after you have overcome that last spiritual hurdle, when you have looked into the maw of your inner self, will you have proven yourself worthy of the next stage of your journey."

"We beat a cyclops," said Helen. "Isn't that enough?"

"You would think so," said Present. "But apparently not."

Helen uttered a noncommittal grunt. "Fine. Let's get on with it."

The sisters led Helen and Troy to the back of the store and an unmarked door. Blue mist swirled under the frame, and something big and shadowy stomped behind it.

"My worst fear, huh?"

Helen paused before the door.

"I hate to ask this, but this isn't one of those things where I go inside and discover a horrible monster in the dark. Then I fight it, and just as it looks as if it's about to overcome me, I end up killing it. And then I look at it and see that the monster was me all along?"

The sisters hesitated.

"That's it?" asked Helen. "That's what it really is?"

"Well, I must say," said Present, "you're a very wise young woman."

"Not really. I saw it already in *The Empire Strikes Back*. Kind of a big movie. Maybe you've heard of it."

"Maybe you shouldn't sass the fates," whispered Troy.

She shrugged.

"I keep telling you we should update the test," said Past.

"But it's a classic," said Present.

"There's a fine line between classic and uninspired."

Helen pointed to the door. "Do I still have to go in?"

"Hardly seems worth doing now," said Future from a shadowy corner. "Only going through the motions at this point."

"What about me?" asked Troy. "Do I face the trial now?"

Present shook her head. "You have no fears to exploit."

Helen held up her hands. "I don't believe you. I know Troy's practically perfect, but he can't be fearless."

He nodded. "Gerbils creep me out."

Behind the door something squealed with bestial vigor.

"As much as we might enjoy watching you wrestle with a monstrous rodent," said Past, "the point of this passage is to test your willingness to surrender yourself to the unknowable and accept your own limitations. You've already done this, Troy. She hasn't."

Helen scowled. "Wait a second. I'm on the journey. I fought the cyclops. I think I've demonstrated a willingness to venture into the unknown."

"Have you?" asked Past. "Troy has been the leader of this journey so far. Without him, can you honestly say you would be here now?"

"I don't know. But I'm here. Isn't that enough?"

"If only it could be," said Past. "But to complete your quest, you'll need to be more than merely present. This is about more than attendance. Unless you're content with playing the hero's stalwart companion. That can work."

"Though I wouldn't recommend it," said Future from the shadows. "Sidekicks usually end up dying at the most inopportune times to give the quest a little tragedy."

"Is that what will happen to me?" asked Helen.

"I'm not allowed to say, but I wouldn't rule it out."

"Fine. I'll go into the storeroom and face my fear." Helen grabbed the handle, but the door didn't open.

"Too late for that," said Future. "But if you're determined to be more than the sidekick, we need something."

The three sisters turned their backs and discussed it. Future hid behind Past and Present, though there was also some supernatural darkness wrapped around her to keep her obscured.

Helen tapped her hoof on the floor, aware of the steady clomping but annoyed enough not to care. She glared at Troy. None of this was his fault, but she resented him, though she had no specific resentment in mind.

"You are not a sidekick," he said.

She turned her back on him. Not because he'd done anything to deserve it, but because she needed to turn her back on something. Because she wasn't sure she believed him. Troy had gotten them here. He had been the first to sign up with the NQB. He had been the one who started their journey. The Chimera was his car. Aside from punching a cyclops, she hadn't done anything but follow. Even that had only been because she'd followed Troy onto the battlefield.

She wasn't a timid person by nature. She wasn't a follower. Or so she'd always believed. But Troy was a natural leader, a guy who just seemed as if he should be in charge. He didn't seize control. It just came to him by cosmic expectation. Imagining them standing side by side, even she saw him as the one in charge. She was Watson to his Holmes. Iolaus to his Hercules. Rick Jones to his Rom the Space Knight.

The sisters spoke up.

"We want your bracelet," said Past.

Helen covered it with her hand. "You don't understand. It's not a regular bracelet."

The sisters smiled, showing they understood all too well.

"I don't take this off," said Helen.

"You took it off when fighting the cyclops," said Past.

Present stepped forward and held out her hands. "Sometimes the only way forward is to abandon old limitations."

"You just said I have to accept my limitations."

"What makes you think those are two different things?"

"You don't have to do this, Hel." Troy put his hand on her shoulder. "You are not my sidekick. I don't care what the fates say."

He was only looking out for her, and she realized he always would. It was who he was. But if she listened to him, if she allowed him to talk her out of this, then she might as well turn the entire quest over to him and pick up her official boon companion badge on the way out the door.

She removed the bracelet. A heat ran through her body. Her fur bristled. Her ears swished. Her horns itched. She tightened her fingers around the bracelet.

"OK, but I want something else in addition to directions for this."

Present half-smiled. "You dare barter with the fates?"

"*The* Fates? No, probably not. But you're just *some* fates. Little *F*."

"Such foolhardy bravado," said Present.

Past nodded. "I like it."

"I want something useful, something that will come in handy at some point in the future at a vital moment."

"Is that all?" asked Future.

"You didn't let me finish. I don't want something dumb like toilet paper or good advice. I want something that will turn the tide in a life-or-death situation."

From behind Helen, Future slipped something cold into Helen's hand. It was a small rusted key.

Future was behind a shelf again in the blink of an eye. Faster. "I thought you might ask for something like that. And now for your end of the bargain."

Helen handed her bracelet to Present before she could talk herself out of it. Her fingers let go reluctantly. Her heart thumped louder in her chest. So loudly, she believed everyone else had to hear it too.

"Hel, are you sure about that?" Troy asked.

She swallowed hard, willed her body calm, her ears flat against her neck. She lied through an unconvincing smile. "I'm sure."

Present gave the bracelet to Past, who wore it like a crown because it was far too big for her wrists. The youngest sister skipped away.

"Thank you for shopping with us," said Present. "Please do stop by again."

"What about those directions?" asked Helen.

"Pick a road," shouted Future from several aisles away. "You'll get where you're going."

Helen grumbled. "Those aren't directions."

"Aren't they?" said Future.

Helen's hand clenched into fists.

"Forget it, Hel," said Troy. "Let's get out of here."

14

The Wild Hunt rolled into Gateway a little before midnight with all the subtlety one would expect from two dozen orcs atop raging mounts. Even if the town hadn't mostly been asleep by ten, they still would've made a heck of an impression. As they tore down the main street, lights snapped on in the houses along the way.

Nigel smiled. He felt like Johnny Strabler riding into Wrightsville to stir up fear and disquiet among the locals. He knew he wasn't much of an outlaw. The club didn't even break the speed limit on their weekend cruises. But it was at times like this that he could connect with his ancestors, sense the smallest portion of the fear the horde had once stirred in the old world.

It was a rush he rarely experienced in his normal life. The closest he'd come in any other situation was when he thought he'd discovered an embezzler. But that turned out only to be a misplaced decimal point.

They pulled into the local truck stop. The club left their bikes running, kicking up exhaust fumes and rumbling as if the pavement itself might shake apart under their feet.

He shouted at Peggy above the din, "Are you sure this is the place?"

"The spirits never lie," she yelled. The pale orcess picked a bug out of her pointed teeth and flicked it away. "Well, they rarely lie."

She tilted her head to one side and nodded as if listening to a faraway voice.

"They say the minotaur and the boy were here. Not long ago."

"They say where they went?" asked Nigel.

She shrugged. "To quote a great sage…answer unclear, try again later."

"You'd think our gods would send more helpful spirits," he shouted.

She cupped a hand to her ear.

He grumbled, revved his engine. The club followed his lead, pouring decibels into the air until the windows rattled. When Nigel felt he'd stirred enough terror in the hearts of these frail mortals, he gave the signal to kill the noise. The Wild Hunt fell silent in a moment. All except Franklin, who sputtered to a halt, ending with a loud backfire.

He smiled sheepishly.

Nigel thought about killing Franklin. Whenever the miles became too tedious, his mind would wander to the many ways he could slaughter the would-be orc, and the notion never failed to bring a smile to his face. But every horde needed an omega, and it was the will of the orc gods that their lives ever be filled with annoyance and strife. Killing Franklin might make Nigel happy for a day, but he was fairly certain Grog would send a more terrible annoyance. Nature abhorred a vacuum.

Nigel, for all his barbaric ancestry, wasn't a killer. Some part of him, deep down, might yearn for the old ways, but another part knew that it was a romantic fantasy. Under the old ways, Franklin would've suffered more humiliation, but orcs enjoyed their omegas. Nigel, on the other hand, would most likely have died at the hands of one of his ambitious lieutenants.

That was the advantage of a civilized world. Where once he could've relied on being stabbed in the heart by a treacherous ally, in this day and age he had to deal with a few passive-aggressive asides from Alan Spleenspearer, the self-proclaimed Plumbing Fixture King of Northeastern California.

Nigel didn't even like killing spiders if he could help it. He'd do it when required, but only if they refused to climb into his hand and be taken outside.

Yet here he was, tasked with assassination. While the dragon-blood ax strapped to his back thrilled him, he was less keen on his mission the more he thought about it. But it wasn't his choice to make.

The club barged their way into the restaurant and grabbed all the free tables and booths they could find. Nigel was disappointed that the staff and patrons didn't seem as unnerved as he'd hoped. What little malevolent aura the club had quickly faded when Carl Heartchewer ordered a salad and Becky Bonebreaker asked for egg substitute. Orc physiology, particularly orc digestion, became troublesome after thirty. Not a problem when the average lifespan was fifteen to nineteen years, but in the modern world an orc could live well past a hundred.

It wasn't as if cholesterol or heart disease could do them in easily. They were far too stubborn to allow those things to kill them without a fight, but they took their toll. To modern orcs the greatest battle wasn't against opposing armies or their indifferent gods, but against their own bodies. It was a battle they were destined to lose, but picking losing battles was tradition.

Nigel ordered the oatmeal. No sugar. No honey. No milk. Riding the open road for too long always made him a bit urpy.

"I'll take a steak," said Franklin, who had somehow ended up at the same table as Nigel. "Rare. Bloody."

Nigel glared at the wannabe.

"We're looking for a couple of young people," he asked the server. "Good-looking Asian human and a minotaur girl. Seen them around?"

"Oh, they came through a little while ago. Left a few hours ago."

He smiled. There were certain advantages to chasing after such a distinctive pair.

"Which way did they go?" he asked.

She opened her mouth but reconsidered. "You aren't on a quest, are you?"

"No."

"Because if you're on a quest," she said, "you have to defeat the cyclops to get to the next stage."

He grunted. "We're not on a quest. We're just looking for these two kids."

She appeared unconvinced. "I'd love to help you out, but this is an important business in our town. I'd rather play it safe. Anyway, I don't know which way they went, so I can't help you."

Nigel ground his teeth together. The noise reverberated through the restaurant and quieted all conversation.

He stood, stared down the woman. She held her ground.

"I don't make the rules, honey."

"I'm pretty sure we're the bad guys," said Nigel. "I don't think we have to follow the same rules."

A glance around the room showed that nobody cared.

"Maybe you're intimidating wherever you come from," she said, "but here in Gateway we're used to folks like you. At least half the heroes that pass through are arrogant schmucks. If they aren't, they tend to be preceded by schmucks they're chasing or followed by schmucks that are chasing them. Either way, if I didn't help the giant talking wolf or that lich with his army of mummies—surprisingly generous tippers by the way—that came through here last week, I'm not going to be bothered by you."

Nigel unslung the ax on his back and with a mighty roar cut a table in two with one stroke, leaving the ax embedded in the floor.

"Oatmeal, plain." The woman scribbled in her notebook. "You want anything to drink with that?"

"Yes!" shouted Franklin. "Your warm blood, pumped into our glasses by the last beatings of your heart!"

He jumped from his seat and threw his laminated menu to the floor. It slapped softly against the tile. When that didn't achieve the desired effect, Franklin swept his hand across the table and sent the aluminum napkin dispenser clattering across the room. He seized a bottle of ketchup and was moments away from dashing it to the ground when he noticed everyone was staring at him with mixtures of perplexity and irritation.

With an embarrassed smile he returned the bottle to the table. "Sorry. I thought we were all supposed to be breaking stuff now."

He retrieved the napkin dispenser.

Nigel plopped back into his seat. "I'll take a ginger ale."

She left to place the order.

"What do we do now?" asked Franklin.

"We eat," replied Nigel. "Any news on the spirit front, Peggy?"

"I'm working on it. The spirits get pissy sometimes." She unscrewed the salt shaker and poured its contents onto the table. She sifted through the grains for an omen, a portent, anything really.

The orcs settled down and waited for their food, which was delivered shortly.

The server set a steaming bowl of plain oatmeal before Nigel. "Sure you don't want something on that?"

He snarled as he stirred the brown paste. "I'm good."

The bell on the door chimed, and a thin, one-eyed man entered the restaurant.

"Hey, Clifford," said the server. "You're in here late tonight."

"Couldn't sleep," Clifford replied. "Thought I'd get some waffles." He sat at the booth behind Nigel.

"Sorry about your record," said the server. "You had a good run, though."

"Rather not talk about it, if it's all the same to you."

Nigel pivoted in his seat. "Excuse me, but are you the cyclops? The one we're supposed to fight for information?"

Clifford waved Nigel away without looking at him. "I've had a hell of a day, pal. Talk to me tomorrow."

Nigel grabbed his oatmeal and sat, uninvited, at Clifford's table.

"We're looking for a couple of kids. Maybe you know them. Young Asian male and a minotaur woman."

"I know them," replied the cyclops. "And believe me, I'd be

happy to tell you which way they went. But that's not how it works. First you have to defeat me."

Nigel nodded to the club. The orcs (and Franklin) stood and encircled the table.

"There are rules," said Clifford. "You have to do it the right way."

Nigel grabbed Clifford by the collar.

"Now wait just a minute—" said Clifford.

Nigel threw the guardian of Gateway to the mob. The orcs proceeded to deliver a beat-down to the godling, who had several feet of concrete foundation between him and the empowering earth.

Franklin, unable to push through the mob, sat with Nigel.

The server and customers gaped at the one-sided battle.

"I told you." Nigel grinned. "We're the bad guys."

Franklin picked up Nigel's bowl and hurled it to the floor. The shattering dish brought everything to a standstill.

"Oh, sorry. I thought that was the part where we were supposed to break stuff."

Nigel yanked away Franklin's steak. He took it in his bare hands and bit off a hunk of meat that he swallowed without bothering to chew. His colon would pay for it in about an hour, but right now he was feeling too orcish to care.

And it felt good.

15

Helen and Troy drove for a few more hours, but around one they found a motel in the middle of the desert. Considering its location, it was surprisingly busy. The parking lot was full. Not just with automobiles. A giant bird was tethered in one space. A woolly mammoth occupied another. A minivan parked between them kept them from fighting. Entering the office, Troy and Helen had to wait for the clerk to check in a fully geared samurai. The noble Asian warrior inquired about the location of the ice machine before taking his key and marching out the door.

The clerk was an ogre covered in shaggy gray hair, dressed in an equally gray suit. "Good news is that I got a room. Bad news is that I only got one. So you're going to have to share. Questing season is my busy time of year."

They were surprised to learn that questing had a season, but they didn't question it. It was his business. He should know.

"Want that room or not?" he asked. "It's a double, but you can push the beds together if you want."

"We're not together. Not like that," said Helen.

The clerk shrugged. "Didn't ask. Don't care. Running this place, I've seen plenty of weirder things than you two."

"We'll take it." Troy plunked his NQB card on the counter.

Helen immediately snatched it up. "Hold on. I'm not sure how comfortable I am with that."

He laughed. "Hel, we're mature adults."

"We're barely out of high school," she countered.

"Fine. We're legal adults."

"We can't even drink yet," she said.

He smiled in that way of his. That way that said she was worrying over nothing. Maybe she was. She wasn't certain why she disliked the idea, but she did. She wasn't interested in analyzing why. Or interested in analyzing why she wasn't interested.

"Do you allow dogs?" she asked, hoping to render the question moot.

"I've got a lady with a gargoyle in one room and a guy with a singing narwhal in another tonight. Dogs...no problem." The clerk's pointed ears fell flat. "Do you want the room or not?"

Troy nabbed the card from Helen and handed it to the clerk before she could protest. "We'll take it."

The clerk checked them in. He mumbled about a free continental breakfast at eight. They left, passing a regal woman with skin of polished wood and leaves for hair. The NO VACANCY sign flashed, and she groaned.

"Sorry," said Troy.

After bringing in their luggage, Helen sat on the edge of her bed while Troy took a shower. Achilles lay at the foot. The mangy dog studied her with his big brown eyes.

She held her cell phone in her hands. She'd meant to call her folks today to let them know everything was going all right so far. The day had gotten away from her, and now it was too late.

Only that wasn't what had happened at all. She'd thought about calling all day, but what was she going to say?

Yes, Mom, things are great. Fought a cyclops. Met some fates. Had a moment of self-realization that wasn't entirely to my liking. Now I'm sharing a motel room with a guy for the first time ever, and even though it isn't sexual or anything like that, it still feels wrong. Maybe because it isn't sexual.

Roxanne would say something that would be both frustrating and comforting at the same time.

Yes, Mom. You're right. It should be weird for me. I've never had to share a room with anyone ever. It's perfectly natural to be uncomfortable. Especially because I'm feeling a bit vulnerable without my bracelet.

Mom would reassure Helen that her strength wouldn't be super for a few days. It wouldn't be dangerous for at least a week or two.

I know that, but a security blanket would be nice to have right now.

That was where the imaginary conversation ended because Helen didn't know what Roxanne would say. Helen only knew it would make her feel a hell of a lot better. But it was too late to call.

She lay on the bed, turned on the television, and tried to ignore the howling gargoyle in the next room.

* * *

Troy stared into the bathroom mirror. He had a bit of fuzz on his chin. Nothing excessive, but more than he usually allowed. It didn't make him look scruffy, and that was disappointing.

It wasn't that he minded being attractive. He'd been attractive long enough to learn to live with it. Complaining that people had a tendency to like him right off the bat was akin to complaining about having too much money in the bank. It might be a problem, but you shouldn't expect much sympathy, even from yourself.

He tousled his hair, and it only came across as purposely disheveled.

Sighing, he gave up. He slid on his boxers and threw open the door. "You're up, Hel."

She barely glanced away from the television. "I think I'll skip tonight. I have trouble using regular drains. They can't handle all the fur."

After a shower, she also smelled exactly like a wet minotaur would. Keeping people from knowing that was one of her primary goals. It was why she stayed inside when it rained. Or when it looked as if it might rain. If she had to go out, she covered herself in rain gear. Her suitcase had a full set packed away. Just in case.

"Suit yourself." He stretched.

She avoided looking directly at him. His body belonged in a gym commercial. It wasn't surprising, given his athletic reputation, but this was more than being in great shape. This was being in ridiculously great shape. It was having a physique that belonged on a statue carved by Pygmalion. Or at the very least on an airbrushed model in a men's health magazine.

"Did you call your mom?" he asked.

"How did you know I wanted to call my mom?"

"I know you, Hel. And I've seen you with her."

She put her phone on the end table, picked it up, then put it down again. "I'll call tomorrow. What about you? I haven't seen you call your folks yet."

"I called earlier. After lunch. You were in the restroom."

"Must've been a short call."

"It was just a check-in. Let the family know I haven't been eaten by trolls or stepped on by a giant."

"That's it?" she asked.

He shrugged. "Dad was busy... with something. Mom was at her club, I think. Left a message."

Helen said, "Overachieving kid with distant, demanding parents. That's traditional."

"An oldie but a goodie. It's not really like that, though. I mean, it's like that, but..." He trailed off.

"But what?"

"Hey, is anything good on cable?" he asked.

"Oh, no, you aren't getting off that easy. You had a front-row seat to my psychological deconstruction by metaphysical forces of the universe. I think I'm entitled to a little payback."

Troy switched off the TV. He flopped into his bed, talked while staring at the ceiling.

"Remember that thing you said about us being alike? How we're both bound by expectations? It's like that. I was always good at stuff. I was always a good kid. Then I grew into a great one. Never caused any trouble. Always had solid grades. Natural leader. Likable. Smart. Capable."

He frowned.

"Now I sound like an ass. It's why I don't like talking about this stuff."

Achilles raised his head and whimpered.

"Nobody asked you," said Troy.

"Hey, I asked," said Helen. "It's cool. No judgment here."

He turned his head to smile at her. She smiled back.

"It's simple. My parents never had to worry about me. I never hung out with the wrong crowd. I never did anything reckless or stupid. I never ate paste or chased little Susie around the playground. Basically, once I was potty trained, their job was over."

"And that's not a good thing?"

"Probably was from their perspective. Gave them more time to work on their own lives. And deal with my sister, who really didn't take up much of their time either. They ended up having their lives. I ended up having mine. There's surprisingly little overlap. It's not that the folks wouldn't be there for me if I needed them. I just don't really need them. They know it. I know it."

Helen said, "My parents respect me too. It's not a bad thing."

"No, it's not," replied Troy. "Except mine respect me. They just don't particularly like me.

"I think if I'd been a bad kid, if I'd made mistakes along the way or needed some guidance now and then, then there'd have been some bonding. Or if I'd been perfect for them, for their approval, then they could feel connected. But I wasn't, and they know it.

"It's like we're less of a family than an organization. While I'm a valued member of the Kawakami organization, we're all busy with our own projects, and they trust me to take care of my own."

Helen frowned, understanding how often she took her own family for granted.

He said, "I know. It makes me sound like a jerk. What the hell am I complaining about?"

"No, I get it," she said. "It's a weird thing to deal with, but I can see how it could be annoying."

"You should call your family," he said. "I know it's late, but we both know they'd want you to."

She picked up her cell and went into the bathroom. Before she closed the door, she said, "Thanks, Troy."

"Anytime, Hel."

Achilles hopped off her bed and jumped onto Troy's. The dog laid his head on Troy's stomach.

"Just so you know," said Troy, "you're not fooling me. You're not an ordinary dog. You're some kind of magic dog, a spirit guide, a god in disguise. You can drop the act anytime now."

Achilles's ears flattened, and he whimpered.

"Have it your way. Either way, I still don't like you."

Troy's phone rang. It was Imogen. He sat up, and Achilles shifted his head to Troy's lap.

"Hey, Sis. Yes, everything's going great."

Troy petted Achilles, whose tail thumped against the mattress.

16

Helen woke up early and went outside in the hour of creeping dawn. As was her habit, she thoroughly brushed her neck, shoulders, and arms to keep shedding to a minimum. She usually did her whole body, but she wasn't going to leave telltale hair in the bathroom.

Troy wasn't dumb. He had to know that she shed. This was more for her than for anyone else. Much as she hated to admit it, there were plenty of things about minotaurism that bothered her.

She sneaked back into the room, went into the bathroom, brushed her teeth, polished her horns, and finished getting dressed. Troy was still asleep. Rather than wake him, she went for a walk. Since there was no place to walk to, she did a few laps around the motel. Out of sheer boredom she checked out the office.

The same shaggy clerk was at the desk. He raised his head and waited for her to say something.

"Uh...sorry," she said. "Just killing some time. Can't get back to sleep."

He leaned back in his chair and flipped through his magazine.

Helen studied a rack of brochures against the wall. There were two dozen of them, though no duplicates of any.

"It's so nobody follows anybody," said the clerk, anticipating her question.

She picked up a pamphlet on the Trial of the Seven Chalices and glanced through it. "Why would anyone care?"

"You're new to this questing business, aren't you?"

"Is it that obvious?"

The clerk said, "Everybody's gotta start somewhere. You must have heard stories about questing before, right?"

Helen nodded.

"Do you ever notice in those stories that some hero will come across the monster's lair or a castle of death or whatever, and there's usually a pile of corpses to indicate he's in a dangerous place?"

She nodded again.

"Where do you think those corpses come from? They're the bones of everyone who quested before but failed. Every sad sack who thought he was the hero of the journey, but actually was merely a nameless dumbass who got himself killed. Everybody wants to be a legend. Most people end up as set dressing.

"Questers started deciding the best way to be sure they didn't end up being the prologue to someone else's destiny was to be sure they weren't being followed by someone else. If there's no hero behind you, then it stands to reason that you must be the quester who triumphs. That's the reasoning, anyway."

"But that's a logical fallacy," said Helen. "Of course the person who completes the quest is the last to do it. No one needs to do it after that. It's like saying lost keys are in the last place you look, so why not just look there first? It sounds good, but it doesn't stand up."

The clerk set down his magazine. "You're a bright one. But when we're talking about questing, a lot of the rules of logic fall behind the laws of legend. So maybe it's just irrational superstition, but when you're dealing with these forces, a lot of people don't like taking chances.

"It got to the point that questers were spending all their time camping out, making sure they weren't being followed, and then fighting among themselves when they ran into each other. Even if that person was on an entirely different quest. Whole system went to hell for a while. Then someone finally got the idea to stick one pamphlet per slot in the stand. Every quester grabs one. Nobody follows anybody. And questing continues as it should."

"But—"

"You're overthinking it."

Helen browsed the rack of brochures. She assumed the motel was a questing nexus because there were an awful lot of places to go from here, lands of adventure and peril where ordinary people feared to tread.

It didn't make a whole lot of sense. In the days of yore there had been forsaken realms and vast acreage of untamed wilderness waiting for adventurers to appear. But this was the modern world.

"Are we still in Nevada?" she asked the clerk.

He lowered his magazine an inch and nodded without looking at her.

"Like Nevada Nevada?" she pressed.

He lowered his magazine another inch and fixed her with a curious stare.

"I mean, I'm just wondering if I fell into a parallel universe or something, where stuff like this is normal."

The clerk sighed very, very deeply.

"The Age of Legends never ended," he replied. "It just started hiding in different places."

"Places like Nevada?"

"And New Mexico. You didn't think they call it the Land of Enchantment for nothing, right?" The clerk tossed his magazine on his desk. "You're still in your world. You've just stepped into the part the gods pay special attention to, something to keep them preoccupied."

"We're the television of the gods?" she asked.

The clerk chuckled. "No, television is the television of the gods. You don't think they get that up there too? Quests are more like the live improvisational theater of the gods. They throw suggestions your way, monsters and trials, and then they watch how you cope with them."

Helen said, "Sounds sadistic."

"What can you expect from gods? But watching quests at least distracts them, limits the damage they can do. And if questers happen to destroy an evil artifact, slay evil monsters, or save the world now and then, that's a bonus too."

"But—"

"Look. You're clearly a smart young woman with a lot of deep questions. But I'm not here to answer them. I'm a guy who gets paid nine dollars an hour to run the place. If you want to know the best way to clean up gryphon crap or where's a convenient place to buy a good sword polish, that's me. Otherwise…"

The clerk stuck his nose in his magazine and turned his back on her to make it clear the conversation was over.

She picked through the brochures.

"Only one," he reminded her.

She considered her choices. The Cave of Seven Riddles looked intriguing, but the brochure itself was black and white and on cheap paper. Some of the ink came off on her fingers.

Seven was a very popular number among questing destinations. In addition to the cave, there was the Peril of the Seven Sisters, the Deadly Trail of the Seven Knights, the Deathly Lair of the Seven-Headed Ogre, and the Seven Perils of Deathly Doom.

She noted that the writers of these brochures would've benefited greatly from a good thesaurus.

Swamp Perilous had a terrific pamphlet. Full color. Well-written copy. Some nice photos that made the dark gray muck appear almost welcoming. But she avoided mud as resolutely as she avoided rain. Once it dried in her fur, it was hell to get out.

Not all quest destinations advertised themselves based on danger and glory, though. Some went a subtler route.

"HAVE YOU SEEN THE THING?" one asked in bold lettering. The pamphlet extolled the vague properties of the Thing without giving any concrete clues as to what it might actually be. Helen was intrigued, but at the same time she wasn't certain she was up to that level of adventure. She wanted to have some idea of what she was getting into, and if the Thing turned out to be a giant two-headed rat or a potato chip that looked like somebody famous, she'd kick herself.

Lake Hecate included details on the beautiful picnic grounds, the water park, and the antiquing opportunities. "Come for the Forbidden Temple of the Ancients. Stay for the fun of it!"

And then there were the pamphlets that went with reverse psychology.

"Ghast, Idaho, where only fools dare come."

"Norman County, where even immortals fear to tread."

"You're too much of a wimp to visit Amber Mound, Home of the Shrieking Bloodfiends."

If the crude painting of the fiend on the cover was any indication, she agreed.

Then she found it. The brochure she was looking for. Her curse mark prickled as she touched it. She took that as a sign from the Lost God. She plucked it from the stand, thanked the clerk for his time, and went back to the room. Troy was up and dressed. She wasn't surprised he was an early riser.

"I know where we're going." She handed him the pamphlet for the North American Wild Dragon Preserve.

He read it.

"Aren't dragons kind of high up on the questing scale, Hel?"

She laughed. "Wait. Are you actually trying to talk me out of doing something dangerous?"

Troy smiled. "No, it just seems a bit advanced."

"I've never seen a wild dragon," she said. "Have you?"

"Only seen them in zoos."

She started packing. "So let's do it then."

"We don't know if there's anything there for us," he said.

"Yes we do." She unfolded their map, pointed to the previously indecipherable scribble next on their journey. "It's not a squiggle or a snake. It's a dragon. Didn't realize it until I noticed these two triangles. They're wings."

He took a closer look. "I guess I can see it."

"Maybe I'm wrong, but the fates said I should be more decisive. I'm taking that as a sign, and so far following signs has been working for us. How's your mark feel?"

"Itchy." He scratched his hand. "Itchier now."

"That has to mean something, right? Like our curse is trying to point us in the right direction. And if I'm wrong, at least we'll get to see some dragons. You've got your magic sword. Those things are usually great at taking care of dragons, if we run into any problems."

They grabbed a couple of bagels and some mini-cartons of orange juice from the motel and headed to the preserve. The Nevada desert spread before them. It looked nothing like the lush forests pictured in the brochure.

"How far away is this place?" asked Troy.

"Says it's about thirty miles down the interstate."

"Are we still in Nevada?" he asked. "Like Nevada Nevada."

She smiled.

They followed the directions on the brochure because the GPS on their phones was stymied by any attempt to find the preserve. A search for an official website did pull up an informative page listing rules and regulations and giving contact information. But it didn't list any address. They considered calling the number on the site but decided to see if the directions on the pamphlet were correct first.

"Says here you aren't allowed to bring any weapons," said Helen.

"Isn't going in unarmed dangerous?" he asked.

"Visitors must sign a waiver before entering the preserve."

"That's comforting."

This was looking more and more like a dangerous undertaking. But they'd already committed, and she wasn't going back to the motel to grab another brochure. By now all the good ones were probably taken.

Danger was part of questing. Perhaps some quests were dull and safe affairs. Go to the store. Pick up some eggs. Return henceforth with said eggs and thou shalt be rewarded with the sacred omelet of justice.

Nobody wrote legends about that type of quest.

She wasn't interested in becoming a legend, but if she was going to be stuck on this journey, she might as well make the most of it. She doubted there'd be an epic poem in her future about that time they visited a preserve, had a picnic, and saw a dragon fly by. But at least it would be a day to remember.

They nearly missed the unmarked exit off the interstate, but the prickle in their hands flared up to alert them. It was an irritating form of guidance, but it did the trick.

From there they went down an old paved road. Then turned off onto a gravel one that transitioned into a dirt one before reaching their destination.

The preserve itself was marked with a wooden archway over the road. The sign declared, in hand-painted yellow letters, HERE BE DRAGONS.

"This must be the place," said Troy.

After they passed through the arch, that became obvious. On the other side a forest sprang into existence. The forbidding timberland was a sinister mix of dark greens and deep shadows. They parked the Chimera in a dirt lot and double-checked. On one side of the arch was nothing but desert. On the other, the forest.

They entered the visitors' center, a large blocky building made of stone with no windows and only one door, also carved of stone. The interior décor was dominated by a fearsome dragon skull on display. Its jaws were propped open, allowing one to imagine what it might be like to see the fleshy version bearing down on one.

Helen began to have second thoughts.

A tall, gangly ranger sitting behind a desk perked up at their entrance. She stood, shoved a last bite of a sandwich into her mouth, and held out her hand.

"Welcome, welcome," she said after finishing chewing. "Great to have you here. I'm Ranger Grainger. Yes, yes, I know. It does sound funny, but it's my name. There's nothing much I can do about it. And you are?"

They introduced themselves.

"Very nice to meet you," said Grainger. "Can I see your IDs, please?"

They gave her their badges. She cross-referenced them with a computer.

"Everything checks out. You're authorized for full access."

Helen said, "That's a hell of an enchantment hiding this place. Can't be easy to maintain."

"Easier with the dragons," said Grainger. "Their ambient magic powers it. And it doesn't just hide it. It actually displaces the entire preservation in a sub-dimensional flux. Unless you come through one of the authorized entry points, you'd pass through it without knowing. It's not so much to hide it as to head off any conflict. The dragons take up a lot of space, and they have a tendency to steal valuables, devour cattle, abduct virgins. And it's not like you can just fence them in. Not with an ordinary fence anyway."

"We went to the website," Troy said. "There weren't any directions."

"We try not to advertise," explained Grainger. "This is a public

148

park, and all citizens are allowed to visit it. But it is, first and foremost, a sanctuary for endangered species. Too many people tramping through these woods are bound to be trouble."

"If they go in, aren't they responsible for themselves?" asked Helen.

Grainger said, "You misunderstand. We're not concerned for the people. We're concerned for the dragons."

Helen reached out to touch one of the foot-long teeth of the giant skull.

"Don't touch that," said Grainger.

"Sorry."

Grainger paced around the skull. "This was a full-grown wyvern. Magnificent specimen. Pride of the park. Measured forty feet. The largest recorded wingspan of the breed. Do you want to know how she died?"

She sighed.

"She was chasing after some idiot, fell off a cliff, and ended up impaled on a very pointy tree."

"But couldn't it fly?" asked Helen.

"Of course it could fly. Just not while unexpectedly upside-down and plummeting. But that's not truly relevant. Dying in ironic or implausible ways is something dragons excel at, bred into them from the dawn of time by the gods above. It's why a thousand-to-one shot just happens to hit the one exposed scale next to their heart. Or they trip on something. Or they just decide to spontaneously explode with their own rage. It's in their DNA. Really, if you put a wandering idiot up against a dragon in a fair fight, well, the dragon will win most of the time. But all it takes is that one time, that one stumble, that one desperate stab with an enchanted dagger, that impossible moment of triumph, and the dragon ends up dead. And dragons are slow breeders. If even only one in a thousand mortal souls kills one now and then, then their numbers will continue to dwindle until they disappear.

"The fewer people wandering around, poking their noses in dragon territory, the better it is for everyone. But especially for the dragons."

"I'm surprised you'd allow us to go in at all," said Helen.

"I probably wouldn't," replied Grainger. "But I don't make the rules. But I do enforce them, and so I'm assuming you've read the disclaimer on the site."

"No weapons," said Troy.

"More importantly," she added, "no slaying. The weapon rule is just there to remind you. Failure to follow this rule will result in a serious fine, temporary suspension of your NQB agent status, pending review. Is that understood?"

They didn't reply.

Grainger straightened, narrowed her eyes. "Is that understood?"

"What if there's some incidental slaying?" asked Troy.

"Why are you so interested in slaying dragons?"

"I'm not." He aimed his most disarming smile at her. "But you said it yourself. Sometimes dragons die by accident."

"Give it to me straight," said Grainger. "You aren't poachers, are you? It's a federal offense to remove any part of a dragon, living or dead, from the park."

"Why would we poach?"

"Why wouldn't you? Dragons are made of magic. Their blood. Their teeth. Their scales. How do you think we ended up with that forest? Somebody killed a dragon, and trees sprang up where its blood hit the ground. Spread like wildfire. If we hadn't shunted the preserve to another dimension, the whole world might be covered right now. Or at least most of the continent.

"Dragons are an ecological disaster just waiting to happen. Two thousand years ago someone kills the last broodmother earth dragon and we end up with the Sahara. All because an idiot wants to drink dragon blood and understand the language of birds or bury some teeth to grow his invincible army. That's all well and good, but it's careless, shortsighted actions like that which cause and/or end ice ages."

"We're not poachers, ma'am," said Helen. "We swear."

"And we'll be careful," said Troy. "We don't want to kill anything."

Grainger said nothing. She appraised them for a moment before finally smiling slightly.

"Oh, you look like good folks. It's not like it's my call anyway. But if slaying does occur, accidental or not, the incident is brought up for review. Usually takes a week to a month for a ruling to be handed down. If you're cleared, you get your NQB agent status back."

"We're on a timetable," said Troy.

"Then I would recommend being careful," replied Grainger.

They went outside, and she inspected the Chimera, passing a weapon-detecting wand over it and all their possessions. The car passed, though Troy's magic sword was confiscated. He explained that he had no intention of drawing it, but Grainger was unmoved. She also suggested they hand over all their money and valuables. Including credit cards.

"You won't need these in there," she said. "Dragons can smell a high credit limit. And they love expense accounts. There's a speckled red serpent in the northeastern section of the park that has a mound of gift cards you'd have to see to believe."

Helen was allowed to keep her own wand because it explicitly couldn't harm anything, and their new shield was acceptable too. Grainger also issued them each a magic sword.

"They're enchanted to be supernaturally harmless," she explained. "But centuries of conditioning have taught most dragons to fear magic swords, so they'll most likely just smell the enchantment and run the other way. Mind you, it doesn't work all the time. Especially for the more aggressive breeds. Though it's not mating season, so you should be fine. Unless you dare to enter their lairs or steal their treasures. Which you will most certainly do because that's what questers do."

"We're sorry. We're not trying to cause any trouble," said Helen.

Grainger said, "It's fine. It's not your fault. You're just doing what you're supposed to be doing. Greater good and all that. Just do try to be careful."

"We will be," said Troy. "Is it safe for dogs in there?"

It was perhaps only Helen reading too much in Achilles's face, but he did appear to glare at Troy.

"Safe?" said Grainger. "No, but if you were interested in being safe, you wouldn't be going in there in the first place. Now the day's a little shorter in this place, the night a little longer. It'll be dark soon. And you don't want to be wandering around in the dead of night. There are sanctuary stones throughout the park. You can't miss them. They keep the dragons at bay for the most part." She circled a spot on a map with her pen. "You can reach this one in about an hour. I recommend you set up camp there. Wonderful view. Don't leave until morning."

With that done, she had them sign several waivers each, gave them the map of the park, and told them that they entered the preservation at their own risk, and that if they chose to wander off the trails, they did so at even greater personal risk.

"But you'll do it anyway," she said, "because that's what you questers do."

And they drove into the forest, leaving Ranger Grainger shaking her head and muttering to herself.

The Wild Hunt stayed the night in Gateway. The club was beginning to have some fun, and nobody was in much of a hurry to catch up with their divinely appointed prey. Once they did their job, they'd be going either to prison or back to their humdrum lives. Nigel wasn't sure which he preferred.

They dallied in Gateway, making a mess, breaking things, and acting like the vicious horde they usually pretended to be. The citizens of the town were tolerant of the intrusion, being used to destructive visitors, and after the club had their fun, Nigel wrote a check for the damages as a way of thanking the locals for their cooperation. It undercut the merciless-band-of-cutthroats vibe they were cultivating, but it was the polite thing to do. It was also appropriately reckless because his wife was likely to stab him in the face once she saw their new balance.

The Wild Hunt prowled the highway at a steady pace. Slow enough that they'd catch up with their prey later rather than sooner, but fast enough that their gods wouldn't have reason to complain.

Eventually the spirits started speaking to Peggy Truthstalker again. They directed her to a lonely archway in the desert, hiding behind some rocks.

"This is the place?" he asked.

"They're on the other side. This is a service entrance to a dragon preserve. Magically sealed." She knelt and scrawled symbols in the dirt. "Give me a moment, and I'll open it."

"Dragons?" said Franklin. His voice trembled.

The club laughed.

Becky Bonebreaker slapped Franklin hard on the back, nearly knocking him over. "You aren't afraid, are you?"

He straightened and puffed out his chest. "No. It's just dragons, right? Who's afraid of dragons?"

"Smart people," said Nigel, as he sharpened the edge of his dragonblood ax with a stone. The blade was supernaturally sharp, but he found the scraping sound it made soothing. Little flakes of frost spiraled to the ground where the stone sparked against the weapon.

Peggy did her shaman thing. She drew symbols. She chanted. She caught a tiny lizard, bit off its head. She had the club dance a strange jig. It was hot and uncomfortable and they all sweated in unpleasant places until the spirits were convinced they'd suffered enough and opened the doorway.

The arch cracked open with a flash of light, revealing a road leading into a dark and sinister forest. In the darkness, beasts of legend howled and shrieked.

"Don't worry, Franklin," said Nigel. "You're little. They probably won't even notice you."

"Or he'll get stuck between their teeth and at least take some small comfort in irritating the hell out of one of the beasts for a few days," said Carl Heartchewer.

They all chuckled. Even Franklin, though his was a bit half-hearted.

The Wild Hunt revved up their engines until the rumbling overwhelmed the creatures of the enchanted forest. They poured down the dirt road, kicking up dirt and bringing fear to even dragons themselves.

18

The dragons were hiding.

It was the only explanation. It wasn't as if Troy and Helen had been expecting the great winged beasts to come up to the Chimera and ask to be petted on the snout, but they had been expecting some sign of the great beasts. They drove through the thick woods with nary a wing or tail in sight and hearing only the predictable sounds of nature. Birdsong and insect chirping and an occasional owl hoot. Even before dusk fell, the woods beyond the road were dark and forbidding, so maybe the owls didn't know when day ended and night began. Maybe they lived in a perpetual night, a virtual owl paradise. Or possibly an owl hell, a never-ending darkness where the sun never shone to tell them it was cool to catch a few winks.

But dragons... there were none.

The forest's branches stretched overhead. Its thick canopy obscured the darkening sky. When it finally cleared, the silhouettes slipping across the stars belonged to clouds, not dragons.

A shriek would've been nice. Or a howl. Or something large knocking down a tree just out of sight. Anything.

Achilles sat between them in the front seat, his head on Helen's lap. He'd raise his head every so often, and his fluffy ears would swivel toward sounds they couldn't hear. Once he even growled very lightly, giving them the hope that a legendary monster would come charging out of the woods.

But it didn't.

After the lecture from Grainger, the waiver, and the fearsome dragon skull, they'd expected something more terrifying. Instead they reached the campsite clearing without so much as a brush with a dragon whelp. The sanctuary stone, a light blue smoothed oval, hovered a few feet off the ground, casting a soft glow.

Grainger hadn't been lying. The view was amazing. The campsite perched on the edge of a cliff, allowing them to see across the preserve below. The muted colors of twilight bathed everything in shades of blue and gray. Waning light shimmered across the surface of a faraway lake. The first stars sparkled at the edge of a red-and-cerulean night.

Helen said, "I was expecting less serenity, more forbidden terrors."

"You were?"

She picked up a rock, threw it at the setting sun. "I'm not complaining."

They set up camp as night fell on the preserve. In the darkened forest beyond the stone's protection, things lurked. But none of those things dared approach, though their eyes (sinister glints of red, yellow, and green) watched from the shadows. None of the dragons came close enough to be seen as more than silhouettes slinking around the camp. When Helen and Troy scouted the boundary's edge they would come across animal tracks, both large and small, they hadn't noticed before.

Helen had trouble setting up her pup tent. She'd wasted forty minutes with little to show for it but a misshapen lump of canvas.

"Need some help on that?" asked Troy.

"I can get it."

"It's OK to ask for help, Hel."

"I can set up a tent," she said through clenched teeth.

"Suit yourself." He sat beside his own standing tent and petted Achilles.

"You don't have to watch me."

Troy smiled but said nothing.

"I think there's something wrong with my instructions," she said. "I think the ranger gave me a defective pamphlet."

"There wasn't anything wrong with mine."

She untangled the ropes. She didn't know how they kept getting knotted up. "Don't you see? That's the insidious nature of it. If she gave us both bad instructions, then we'd know something was up. But if she gives them to only one of us, then that person ends up looking like a dummy who can't put up a tent."

"Let me see your instructions."

"No, it's OK. I got it."

Clouds, visible as a darkness crawling across the starry sky, had been moving in their direction. The threat might change direction before it reached them or pass overhead without leaving a drop of rain. But Helen could smell the humidity in the air, and she didn't take any chances when it came to rain.

"I don't know why you're being so stubborn about this, Hel."

She didn't know either, but somewhere along the way she'd decided this was a test of honor, of heroic endurance. If Hercules could drag Cerberus from the underworld, she could set up a stupid tent, and she could do it without any help.

She vowed to the gods above and below that, no matter what, she would make her own shelter. Nothing, no force of nature or supernatural curse, could stop her.

The plastic tent pole snapped in two in her hands.

To add insult to injury, thunder cracked the sky and a few tiny drops of rain fell on her face. Helen realized, as perhaps she never had before, that she was just an insignificant speck in a grand design and that her wishes and desires meant nothing.

"Well played, universe," she muttered.

A shadow soared overhead, kicking up a gust of wind that blew over her tent. It was followed by another. And another. The creatures sounded a warbling cry, more like birdsong than a dragon shriek. The monsters circled over the camp for a moment before soaring away to the lake in the distance.

Grumbling, Helen righted her tent and tried to figure out how to get around the broken pole. "Do we have any tape?"

"Hel, you have to see this."

She scanned the darkening sky, assessed the probability of a storm hitting them.

"Hel…"

She threw the pole pieces into the mess of her tent and joined him at the cliff's edge.

Below, the three dragons quenched their thirst at the lake. The clouds parted just enough to allow pale moonlight to reflect off their glittering red scales. They dipped their jaws in the water, scooping out gulps, swallowing by throwing their heads back like birds.

The creatures were long and lean, like snakes with elongated limbs. The forelimbs served as wings, and the dragons were a bit clumsy on land. The smallest one slipped, falling into the lake, shrieking and throwing a tantrum until the biggest gently wrapped her jaws around him and lifted him back on shore. The little dragon soon forgot his trauma as he wrestled with his sibling. The mother settled down, watching her hatchlings play.

"This was a great idea, Hel."

Thunder cracked. The dragons launched themselves, soaring with all the majesty they lacked on land. They passed overhead again, blowing Helen's tent out of the sanctuary's protection and into the dark.

The first few raindrops fell. She had only a few moments before the real storm began, and she knew it was going to be a hard rain, a thunderstorm worthy of the storm gods themselves. Her first instinct was to run for the car, but it was too far. She'd never make it.

Her only alternative was Troy's tent. If she'd had a few more seconds to think about it, she probably would've gone for the Chimera. But the years had honed her instincts so that she feared the rain more than anything, and those instincts drove her to dash for the tent. She dove in just as the deluge came, and in her haste she nearly trampled Troy and Achilles. But she made it.

Troy was only a second behind her, and his hair and face were wet. Achilles was right behind him. The scruffy moistened dog shook himself dry, and Helen turned away to avoid the deluge.

"Hel, it's OK," said Troy. "It's just a little rain."

A thunderclap belied his words. The storm beat down on

the tent with a steady staccato rhythm. Like thousands of little demons clawing at her shelter. She stifled her stupid panic. She knew it was stupid. She was cursed by an exiled god and in a forest full of dragons. She'd fought a cyclops. She was probably going to die on this quest.

But nothing filled her with dread like the sound of that rain.

The faint odor of wet fur filled the tent, but it wasn't her. It was Achilles. Her fur smelled muskier.

The tent was big enough for all of them but just barely. Helen lay on one side. Troy lay on the other. The blue light of the sanctuary stone was bright enough that they weren't completely in the dark, despite the storm. Though it probably sounded worse than it was, she was surprised at how well the tent was holding up. He'd even been smart enough to build it on the high ground so none of the water came in.

"Gone camping a lot?" she asked.

"No. First time," he replied. "Why do you ask?"

She snarled in the gloom. "No reason."

Helen's shoulder brushed against Troy. She was getting bigger. Not now, right this moment, but slowly over the hours since she'd given away her bracelet. She couldn't prove it, and she wanted to believe it was paranoia on her part. But she was convinced that she was half an inch taller and wider than she had been yesterday. She hadn't weighed herself, but she was willing to bet she was heavier too. The Chimera seemed to sink a little lower when she rode in it.

She wished she had something to take her mind off of this. Something, anything, to distract her from the rain outside and the cramped quarters.

"Why don't you like the rain?" asked Troy.

This was not a distraction.

"It frizzes my hair." It was her default excuse whenever she was asked the question.

A thunderclap shook the ground. In the darkness, something roared.

She shifted, and her right breast brushed against Troy. Maybe his shoulder. Maybe his arm.

"Sorry," she said.

"You don't have to keep apologizing."

"Yes, sorry about that."

She closed her eyes and willed herself to keep her mouth shut. She liked nothing about this situation. That made her tense. That made her likely to say stupid things.

"I meant I'm sorry about the apologizing," she said.

"Yes, I understood, Hel."

She concentrated on her breathing. She could feel herself growing even now. Not the sudden burst from Bruce Banner to Incredible Hulk. This was worse because it was something only she noticed. Something irreversible.

"Your hair always looks nice," said Troy.

She was caught unawares. It took her a moment to absorb the sentence.

"What?"

"I just said your hair always looks nice. You shouldn't be self-conscious about it."

Helen rubbed a few strands between her fingers. It was true. She did have nice hair. She might have had problems with the fur and the hooves, but she had no problem with her hair. She found the horns inconvenient, but they were easy to work around. But the fur was a pain in the ass, and the hooves robbed her of shoes. She couldn't imagine enjoying shopping for shoes, but she'd never had the chance to even try.

She actually kind of liked the tail. She'd always thought it cute. It did tend to swish whenever she was mad or nervous. As it did now. It made lying on her back for long periods difficult. This was why she was on her side, facing Troy to avoid smacking him with her flopping tail, brushing her chest against him whenever she drew in a deep breath.

"Troy…"

"Yes, Hel?"

The patter of the rain lightened.

"Never mind." She rolled onto her back. "It's nothing."

"No, what is it?" he asked. The faint blue light highlighted the left side of his face.

"When you told Ginger Cheney you were going on this quest with me, how did she react?"

"Why would I tell Ginger about this?"

"I thought you two were dating."

"We went out a couple of times. It wasn't serious."

"Oh. My mistake. I thought you two were an item."

"No. Not an item. She's cool, but we really don't click. Aside from being popular. But it was more like everyone expected us to be perfect together. It works good on paper, but none of the pieces match up."

"Like a bad instruction manual," she said.

"Like that. It's like you and Pablo Vasquez."

Helen groaned. "Don't remind me."

Pablo Vasquez had haunted Helen, in one form or another, for over a decade. Because Pablo Vasquez had antlers. He hadn't been born with them. Until the age of eight he'd been antler-free.

Then one year he'd returned from summer camp with two three-point projections growing out of the top of his head. The details were sketchy, and Pablo never talked about how it had happened. From then on, a lot of people had assumed Helen and Pablo belonged together. Heck, she'd even believed it herself for a little while.

Dating him had put an end to that.

"Don't get me wrong," said Troy. "Pablo is a good guy. But anyone could see you didn't have much in common."

"Not anyone. And we both liked comic books. Though he was more DC, and I was more Marvel."

"He didn't like the Hulk, huh?"

"Said he was stupid," she replied.

"Philistine."

They chuckled.

"How'd you know I like the Hulk?" she asked.

"You might have mentioned him once or twice. It's called paying attention, Hel."

Helen bit her lip. That urge to say something, anything, came to her. Otherwise, it was just the two of them stuck in tight quarters listening to each other breathe. He beat her to the punch.

"Why would you think Ginger would care?" he asked.

"It's not important."

He pushed himself up on his elbows, and there was just enough light that she could see his eyes. She wished she could turn away, but her tail was twitching under her leg. She couldn't afford to free it.

"Forget it, Troy. Don't even know why I brought it up. You wouldn't understand."

She almost got up and walked out into the rain. Better that

than to sit here in the dark, in the awkward silence. She closed her eyes to shut out what little light was coming in.

"Hel—"

"I said forget it."

He put his hand on her shoulder.

She sat up and pulled away. "Y'know what? Think I'll sleep in the car."

She was up and out of the tent before she had time to think it over. The shock of the rain hitting her face startled her back to her senses. Too late to turn back, though. The storm wasn't as bad as she'd imagined. It had only sounded like it from inside the tent, fed by her fear. It was less a storm, more a cool shower. It might have even been refreshing if she'd been a different girl.

Troy emerged from the tent, standing in the rain too. Achilles stuck his head outside, but with a whimper retreated to the dry sanctuary.

"Go back inside, Troy. I'll be fine. It's my problem. I'll deal with it."

He didn't move. "Hel, you're great. You know that, right?"

"Yeah, I'm great. I'm the greatest seven-foot-tall girl with horns in the world."

"You do that too often," he said.

"Excuse me if I have body issues." The rain soaked her, and she could smell her musky moist scent, somewhere between an odor and a stench but certainly not anywhere good within that range. "I was born with a tail."

"We all have issues, Hel."

She wanted to be annoyed, but he spoke with such sincerity.

"Do you want to know the real reason I stopped dating

Ginger? She was only dating me because she had a thing for Asians."

Helen cracked a smile despite herself. "Oh, come on…"

"It's true. Oh, it didn't hurt anything that I'm handsome and popular and generally an awesome guy. But the Asian thing was the topper. Except she liked China. Was into kung fu and warrior monks and Jackie Chan movies. But I guess a Japanese guy was the best she could do. Although, honestly, I'm not sure she understood the difference. It was all one big cultural heap to her."

He chuckled. She didn't. Not because she didn't find it amusing, but because it wasn't the same thing.

"I know it's not the same," he said, as if reading her mind. "But it is similar. It's still stuff we all have to deal with. You're great, Hel. And you're beautiful. And I don't mean that in a generic *everyone is beautiful* kind of way because what the hell does that even mean? No, you're smart and funny. You can punch a cyclops godling and get away with it. Maybe you've got fur, hooves, and a tail. But one day you're going to meet someone who sees past it. Or maybe you'll meet someone who is way into it. You'll know they're the right person because you won't care why they want to be with you. You'll just be glad they're there."

He came closer. Her first instinct was to retreat, but she was soaked. The stench of her minotaurism was unavoidable. He smiled, and she couldn't resist it even if she'd been trying.

"We should probably get out of the rain," she said.

"What's the point? We're not going to get any wetter."

They were soaked. Their clothes clung to them like second skins. In Troy's case, it only highlighted his chiseled physique. And his hair, even moist and flattened against his head, looked as if it'd been styled that way.

She sat on a rock and gazed into the dark sky. He sat beside her and put his hand on her arm. Just for a moment. And in the blue twilight, she could see the swirls in her wet fur left by his fingers.

"Sorry about the smell," she said.

"Hadn't even noticed."

He had to be lying. She believed him anyway.

"And for the record, Hel, I've always thought the tail was cute."

The rain fell harder, and she found she didn't care. She wondered why she ever had.

19

The Wild Hunt had neglected to bring camping gear, and this was just fine. Their ancestors had spent their nights under the sky. It wasn't that orcs hadn't known about tents. It was that seeking shelter against the elements had been deemed a sign of weakness in ancient orc society.

It was a very stupid thing to believe, as every modern-day orc knew. Many a great overlord and king had perished of pneumonia, frozen to death in the dead of winter, or perished from dehydration under the desert sun. Yet this had been their way, and most historians agreed it had worked out well for everyone else since orc machismo had kept them from achieving the numbers and organization to conquer the rest of the world in more savage times.

By the time common sense became an orc virtue, the time of conquest was mostly over. The world had been partitioned off into nations and the glory of war had become something ugly.

Nigel suspected it always had been, and that if he'd gotten the chance to know his ancestors, he would see them as a bunch of morons with not enough sense to put on a jacket when it snowed.

But tonight, in the dragon preserve, the brisk air did his lungs good. Just chill enough to cause the hair on his arms to stand up, but not life-endangering.

According to Peggy, it was too dangerous to hunt for their prey in the dark. They found a sanctuary stone. She used her shamanic gifts to summon a minor fire elemental, and the Wild Hunt sat around the flame and waited for the dawn. They played cards by the light of the fire and drank beers.

Nigel didn't participate. He found a spot off to the side, lay on his back, and studied the stars. Orcs had once believed that each star was a sun unto itself, and that the universe was filled with worlds, most of them lifeless failed experiments of the gods above. This world was fated for much the same destiny, as their prophets had foretold. Just a tiny, insignificant speck in a grand cosmos, doomed to inglorious death when the sun burned out.

Orcs had ever been a cheerful lot.

There were still those who rejected firmament theory. The world was full of nuts.

James Eyestabber sat in the dirt beside Nigel. "Nice night."

"Looks like rain," replied Nigel.

"Looks like."

Nigel said, "Something on your mind, James?"

"No. Just enjoying the night. Want a beer?"

"Got one." Nigel held up his bottle.

James sneered. "Don't know how you can drink domestic."

"Beer's beer."

"That's where you're wrong. You should try this. It'll change your life." He handed Nigel a bottle of something with a strange name written in glyphs. "It's brewed by Swiss gnomes. It's expensive as hell, but once you have a taste, you'll never go back to that swill you used to call beer."

Nigel had no interest, but James wasn't going to take no for an answer. Nigel popped the cap with his tusk and drank it all in one extended swig. He wiped his mouth, ran his tongue across his teeth.

"Plummy."

"You're supposed to savor it," said James.

He had always been a questionable orc, though everyone knew the answer to that question. Imported fruity beers and a splash of fuchsia on his bike's gas tank left little doubt in most club members' minds. It didn't help that Nigel knew it was fuchsia only because James had nearly throttled Travis Bladebiter for mistaking the color for purple.

It was an unfair assumption built on stereotypes, and even though Nigel knew better than to jump to those conclusions, he hadn't seen James so much as glance at a woman. He did have a lot of stories about his longtime roommate Gary.

It wasn't beyond the realm of possibility that two straight single men could go sofa shopping together, but it wasn't something Nigel would be willing to wager on.

"Try another," said James. "This time—"

Nigel bit the top off the bottle, chugged the whole thing, spit out the broken glass.

"Plummy."

Franklin walked up. "Hey, James, these imported beers are awesome."

A fuzziness crept around the edges of Nigel's senses. It started as a wobble in his ears. The stars grew incredibly bright, yet he still stared at them while they burned his eyes. He smelled chocolate.

"Hey, what's in this Swiss beer?" asked Franklin, his voice vibrating in Nigel's ears. "I feel weird."

Peggy Truthstalker spoke up from behind him. "It's not the beer. It's the vision weed I put in your sandwiches."

Their pale shaman smiled. Her face split in half and a rainbow of colors spilled forth, painting the sky like a canvas.

"Why would you do that?" asked Nigel. Or he hoped that was what he was asking. It felt as if his tongue was squirming against his will, and the words sounded like garbled radio signals. But Peggy seemed to understand it.

"We're in a magical land filled with dragons," she said. "It seemed like the right place for it."

Franklin and James stared off into space, drooling and mumbling to themselves.

Nigel tried sitting up, but his body refused to move. Peggy's headless specter bent over him and traced a symbol on his forehead with her finger and some red paint.

"Just go with it. Fighting will only make it worse."

Starlight devoured the world. He blinked, and it all faded. The fuzziness vanished, replaced by sensations so sharp he could hear the trees growing and count the stars, cataloguing them by brightness and their placement in the firmament.

He stood alone at the campsite or its closest spirit-realm equivalent. It was all so entrancing, marred only by his pessimistic assumption that he was really convulsing in the dirt right now, possibly eating rocks or about to walk off a cliff in his reverie. His face felt vaguely wet. Either it had started raining, or he was facedown in a puddle of water (or worse) and about to drown.

A figure stepped out of the forest. The plump orcess dressed in a burlap gown that hid very little, save for her face under the shadow of a hood, glided toward him. Freckles covered her bright orange skin, and her hands ended in blue claws.

She was the most beautiful thing he'd ever seen. Naturally he assumed she was here to devour his soul, and he grabbed his ax.

"There's no need for that." Her soft voice filled his body and melted away his paranoia.

She lowered her hood to reveal a face filled with golden eyes. So many eyes that her skull had to be four inches taller to fit them all.

"Oh, you're a goddess," he realized aloud.

She smiled. "What gave me away?"

"All our gods are hideous. So which one are you?"

It was understood by his people that they had more gods than they generally acknowledged. They didn't waste a lot of time keeping track, though there was probably a holy book somewhere that had the complete list.

"I am Thuzia, goddess of wisdom."

Nigel grabbed a beer and took a drink, wondering if he wasn't actually sucking on a stick in the physical world. "Wisdom? I didn't know we had one of those."

"I'm a relatively new addition to the pantheon," she admitted. "But I have been sent to offer you succor."

"Thanks for the offer, but I'm a married man."

Thuzia turned toward the woods. "Have it your way. It's your vision. If you want to waste it being a smart-ass, who am I to argue?"

"Do we kill these two?" he asked.

"I don't know. Wisdom is my specialty. Not prognostication."

Nigel said, "Can you at least tell me what they did to earn the wrath of Grog?"

"They've done nothing to anger your gods. Their only crime is being the unwilling servants of the Lost God, who was banished by the other gods above when your world was still young."

She sat on a log and gestured for him to join her.

"The reason for the banishment is a bit complex. The rivalries of the gods are as complicated as they are petty. Though the Lost God always was a bit of a dick. All deities see mortals and this world as their personal toy box, but they can usually share. But the Lost God got a bit too grabby, was a little too destructive. Earthquakes, floods, plagues, futile and bloody wars. These were his favorite things. Which didn't bother his brothers and sisters much at first, but when it became clear it was getting out of hand, something had to be done. Mortal suffering meant little to the gods above, but threaten their amusements with careless destruction, and they will act."

"Why banish?" asked Nigel. "Why not just kill the son of a bitch?"

"Where's the fun in that?"

Nigel used his hand to obscure the top of her hideous face. Her smile filled him with warmth. He wondered if it counted as cheating if it was a vision.

"It doesn't," said Thuzia. "But it isn't going to happen."

"Can't blame a guy for thinking about it."

"Can we return to the topic?"

He grunted.

"The real reason the gods didn't kill their especially destructive brother was that they couldn't. Gods cannot kill gods. Not as mortals kill mortals."

"Why not?"

"Metaphysics are complicated. Just accept my word on this. Gods can die, but it requires a specific alignment of circumstances. The most important element is the hand of a mortal, chosen not by the gods or the Fates, but by his or her own will. Such mortals are all too rare. But there is nothing in this world or any other that the gods fear more. They would be the greatest weapons for the gods to wield against one another, but by their nature, these mortals don't listen to the gods. Catch-22.

"Banishment was their best alternative, but it was an imperfect solution. The Lost God can't escape his punishment, but it doesn't stop him from trying. He succeeds, to varying degrees, every so often. And the clash of the gods shoving him back into his cage wreaks havoc upon the mortal world."

"How much havoc?"

"A few hundred thousand souls dead. Not much, in the grand scheme of things. Certainly nothing worth noticing by the gods above."

"Then why bother drafting us?"

"Because Grog is sick of the bullshit. If you think it's hard being an orc, you should try being an orc god. It's not any better for us up there. The way the other mortal races used to look down upon you, that's the way it still is up there. The other gods are polite enough, but they don't respect us. We orc gods can relate to you mortals in a way few other deities can. And Grog doesn't see the point in allowing thousands to perish for the amusement of the gods."

Nigel stared at the red moon. It stared back with its three eyes.

"You're telling me we're the good guys?"

"I wouldn't go that far. Whatever the future holds, mortals will live and die regardless of your actions. But many will die considerably less horrible deaths if you do your job.

"But to be clear, Grog's motives aren't entirely altruistic. He's also hoping to stick it to the other gods, deprive them of amusement. But benevolent spite is about the best one can hope for from the gods."

He could live with that.

Nigel took another drink. "Are you sure you don't want to take a tumble?"

Thuzia shrugged. "Oh, all right. But let's make it quick. I've got things to do."

She stood. Her dress fell away, revealing her in all her naked glory. She undid the clasp on her cape and hood. He stopped her, looked into her many bloodshot, yellow eyes.

"Leave the hood on."

20

Helen spent the night in Troy's tent, along with Troy and Achilles. She didn't sleep well. The quarters were tight. Some unidentified beast of legend stalked the edge of the camp for ninety minutes, shrieking as it did so. Her curse mark ached. And she was worried about rolling over on Troy and crushing him, even knowing the fear was ridiculous. She wasn't a giant, just a very big girl.

She awoke alone. Sitting up, she poked a hole in the tent with her right horn. There'd been just enough headroom the night before. She must've grown a fraction of an inch in the night. She hugged herself to take measure. She didn't feel bigger, but if the growth was uniform, the hug test wouldn't reveal it. She wished for a tape measure and a scale but changed her mind when she decided she'd rather not know.

She rolled a kink out of her shoulder as she exited the tent. Troy tossed her a granola bar.

"Coffee is almost ready." He stoked a small fire he'd built.

She wasn't much of a coffee drinker, but she had three cups that morning in an effort to keep up with Troy's energy. It annoyed her. As much as she liked him, she was beginning to find his sunniness irritating. It was as if he weren't even human, as if nothing bothered him. Even his professed dislike of dogs didn't keep him from petting Achilles.

A person without flaws sometimes didn't seem like much of a person at all. It was a petty thought, seeming all the more petty when she looked at Troy's smiling face. She wondered if he suffered from moments like this, if he ever was mad at someone merely for existing. Probably not, because he had no reason to feel inferior.

Also, he just wasn't like that.

It irritated her, but it wasn't his fault, so she did her best to ignore it. It helped that the qualities she resented about him were the same qualities that made him easy to forgive. It was practically impossible to stay angry in Troy's company because he made the world a much brighter place simply by existing within it.

Damn it. She was the sidekick.

Unseen dragons howled and warbled their morning cries. The clear blue skies and fresh scent of rain helped add a spring to her step. Not enough to keep up with Troy's enthusiasm, but who could?

She decided to have a good feeling about today despite standing in the middle of a wilderness full of monsters.

Troy scratched his hand. "The itching is getting more insistent."

Helen was glad it wasn't only hers. She rubbed her fingers over the mark carved into her furry flesh. "That's probably a good thing, right?"

"Probably," he agreed.

They packed his tent into the Chimera. Hers had blown out of the protective zone and been shredded by some creature of legend. The tatters hung on a tree branch, and it stank of acidic urine.

They drove down the road, trying to use their itching hands for guidance. Helen held her fist in front of her and moved it back and forth. The hope it would take them where they needed to go proved fruitless. It wasn't radar, and the prickles were too slight to be useful.

"This is a bust," said Helen.

"It's early yet," replied Troy. "I'm sure something interesting and/or dangerous will come along soon enough."

Achilles barked. Once.

"See? He agrees."

"Stop the car," said Helen.

Troy stopped. She got out, opened the trunk, and grabbed the box containing her magic wand.

"I've got an idea."

She removed the wand, closed her eyes, and envisioned her command in her mind. She waved the wand in a circle and mumbled the first magic word that came to her: "Huzzah."

A tingle ran through her hand and a pinpoint of light appeared at the wand's tip. The light shot off like a bullet into the forest.

"Damn it," said Helen.

"What was that?"

"I was trying to cast a dragon-finding spell. Create a ball of light to guide us toward the nearest dragon."

"It looked like it worked," he said.

"Maybe, except it was too fast to follow. I'm not even sure which direction it went."

"So try again."

Helen imagined the same spell, but adjusted the guide light's speed. She waved the wand in a circle. "Huzzah."

The result was the same. The light blasted into the forest.

"I don't think you can use the same magic word," said Troy. "It's like pushing the button for the windshield wipers and expecting it to start the car."

Helen frowned at the wand. "They could've included an instruction manual."

She repeated her modified spell, this time muttering, "Hocus pocus."

The summoned ball of light appeared. It crawled toward the woods, an inch at a time. Two minutes later, it had barely journeyed five feet.

"Fourth time's the charm," said Troy.

The new guide light sped off into the woods at a fair clip, but one they could keep up with. Except they weren't ready.

Troy put the roof up and grabbed the shield and non-dragon-slaying magic swords.

"We should leave Achilles," said Troy.

The dog whined, running between Helen's legs.

"You don't want to take the dog, but you have room for that?" She grabbed the novelty tin teapot from his hand. "How is this going to be helpful?"

"I don't know, but the fates practically said it would be good to use against a dragon. I assume we'll figure it out when the time comes." He snatched it, stuffed it in a backpack.

"The oracle said Achilles would come in handy."

"He already came in handy once. I don't think he gets to do it again. Not so soon after the last time."

"But what if he does?" she asked.

Troy pointed to the woods. "There are dragons in there. We shouldn't be dragging him with us."

Achilles barked and wagged his tail.

"If he gets eaten, it's on your head," said Troy.

She patted Achilles. "He's too smart for that."

Helen recast the spell, and they followed the light into the forest, toward whatever terrible beast it was leading them to.

"This is pretty crazy, isn't it?" said Troy. "We're looking for a dragon. We're actually doing this."

He was smiling.

"You're totally into this," she said.

"Aren't you? You're the one who brought us here. You're the one who cast the spell."

Helen nodded. "I know, but what if I'm wrong? What if all I end up doing is getting us killed?"

"But what if you're not?"

The guide light paused. Helen listened to the forest. Something warbled in the distance. It could've been a bird. She wished she'd spent more time camping. Or any time camping.

"This isn't like you, Hel," he said. "You're not an indecisive person."

"We can't all share your unshakable confidence." She was unable to suppress the edge in her voice. "Next to you, everyone's indecisive."

Troy said, "We're not talking about me."

The light bobbed away. She didn't follow.

"You don't know me, Troy. We're not even really friends."

"What are you talking about?" he said. "Of course we are."

She leaned against a tree. "No, we're two people who have spent a little time together because we share a job and went to the same high school. And now we're together because we're stuck on the same quest. It's not like we'd go out of our way to hang out without it."

"That's true," he admitted. "But I like you, Hel."

"So what? You like everybody."

"That's not true."

She folded her arms. "Name someone you don't like. Anyone."

"I wasn't crazy about Mr. Whiteleaf."

"Before or after he tried to feed us to an unholy meat monster?"

"That's not fair. Before that, he wasn't a bad boss."

"Barring attempted human sacrifice, is there anyone else?"

Troy said, "Well, no. I guess not."

"That's what I mean, Troy. You like everybody, and everybody likes you."

He said, "And why is that a bad thing?"

"Because it means that you really don't like anybody. Not if you like everyone."

He said, "First, I don't like everyone exactly the same amount. I like some people more than others. Second, I still think we're talking about me when we should be talking about you."

"You don't know me well enough to analyze me."

"But you know me well enough to analyze me?" he replied. "That's fair."

Helen glared. "I didn't start this conversation. You did."

Troy smiled. "Hel—"

"No. You don't get to do that. You don't get to say some cool, funny thing that makes everything better. Not this time. This time I wrestle with my inner demons on my own, thank you very much. I'm not the sidekick. And I'm not going to feel weird because I'm nervous walking around in a forest with dragons. Because that's the normal way to feel, the way a regular person should feel."

He nodded and put a finger to his lips.

"Now let me cast this stupid spell again so that we can get eaten by a monster and get this over with."

He bowed and made a sweeping "After you" gesture.

She resisted the urge to strangle him. He wasn't perfect. But he was close enough that it could be infuriating. "Thank you."

The new guide light led them farther. The forest grew darker and quieter, the foliage denser. It smelled of moss and humidity. Somehow the canopy caused the light to turn gray. And when they finally stepped into a clearing with an unobstructed view of the sky, it didn't brighten.

The clearing was full of broken and uprooted trees. Giant three-toed footprints marked the ground. At the opposite end a yawning, black cave swallowed up their guide light.

Neither said a word.

Achilles perked up and flattened his ears. He didn't make a sound.

The birds still sang, though. The bugs still chirped. A breeze blew across the clearing, bringing the scent of cut grass and wild-flowers.

Helen tucked her wand in her belt and took her magic sword. She didn't unsheathe it.

"I guess we should go in there," she finally dared whisper.

Troy nodded. "It's what questers do, right?"

They took a few cautious steps into the open.

She said, "Hey, I'm sorry about—"

"Don't be," he replied.

"But it's not right for me to—"

"Hel, it's fine. Really."

She said, "Troy, don't be a jerk. I'm trying to—"

"No, I was wrong and—"

She stopped, prodded him in the chest. "You were wrong, but you don't have to be so goddamn nice about it!"

She realized after she spoke that she hadn't whispered.

A harsh wind kicked up, adding something new to the smells of nature. The slight stench of rot. The wind came from the cave, and it pulsed with the steady rhythm of something breathing. Something big.

Achilles growled.

Without saying a word Helen grabbed Achilles, and Troy and she ran back to the concealment of the forest. They fell to the ground and peered out from under some bushes as a long blue dragon slunk out of the cave and into the light. It wasn't as big as they'd expected, only about the size of a bus. It was even built like one, with a square body and four short legs. Its belly scraped across the ground as its tail whipped back and forth. Its head was broad and flat, like a catfish's. It even had the whiskers. And its yellow eyes were set far back in its head and to the sides, like a rabbit's. A single sail ran down its back, catching the sunlight and reflecting it in shimmering gold. It didn't have wings.

The dragon turned its head from side to side. Because it didn't have a neck, that meant rotating its awkward body on its awkward legs. And just when they were sure the monster had spotted them, it quietly slunk into the woods in another direction. Despite its size, it slipped into the forest without knocking down a tree, without making much noise at all, except for a crack as it snapped its tail like a whip.

They waited a few moments to be sure it was gone.

Troy slung the shield over his back. "This is our chance."

If they were lucky they could get in, raid the dragon's lair, and leave before it came back. If they were unlucky there was more than one dragon in the lair, but it was still better to enter when one fewer dragon was about. If they were really unlucky it wouldn't matter, because without luck they weren't going to survive this quest anyway.

Helen was optimistic. She had the key the fates had given her still in her pocket. Until she needed it, it wasn't unreasonable to assume she wasn't going to die. The fates could be cruel, but even they couldn't be that lousy. Unless Helen's destiny was to carry the key here and get killed so that a later quester could find it on her skeletal corpse.

She wished she'd stop thinking of stuff like that.

"You don't think the shield has some special protection against dragons," she asked. "That'd probably be too convenient."

"Probably," he agreed. "But convenient coincidences aren't unheard of during quests."

The cave was quiet and while the stink of rot was still present, it was noticeably lesser. Helen used her wand to light the darkness. To her encouragement, it only took one try to get the spell right.

The cave went farther and deeper than they'd suspected. It was dark and damp, but there were no indications that a monster called it home. No piles of old bones. No claw marks dug into the walls. No heaps of treasure. Not even piles of dragon crap.

"Maybe it was just checking the place out," said Helen. "Maybe it doesn't actually live here."

Achilles barked. It echoed off the walls. Helen and Troy jumped.

They glared at the dog. His tail fell flat and he lowered his head by way of apology.

They reached the end of the cave, the edge of a dark hole cutting deep into the earth. Standing at the edge of the precipice, Helen used her wand to command a globe of light into the chasm. It sank down and down and down until it vanished.

"If the Fates want us to go down there," said Troy, "they can forget it."

Achilles barked. Again. They jumped at the sudden burst. Again.

"A cat wouldn't make so much noise," said Troy.

Helen replied, "If you want to pick up a cat to take on our quest, be my guest."

They found Achilles growling at a snake atop a small pile of treasure. It consisted almost entirely of coins. Quarters and dimes, and quite a few subway tokens. There were a couple of dollar bills as well. Altogether it added up to maybe thirty bucks.

"This is kind of sad," said Troy.

"Maybe it's just started nesting," said Helen. "We can't take any of it."

"Agreed. I thought we'd be grabbing a handful of treasure from a great big mountain of the stuff. But this just feels like stealing."

Achilles turned his head and growled toward the cave mouth. The unmistakable sound of the dragon scraping its belly across the rough stone came a second later. They ran behind a rocky outcropping.

"Damn it," said Helen. "Where's Achilles? Where'd he go?"

"The light," said Troy. "Turn out the light."

She shook the wand, hoping to extinguish it like a candle's flame. It didn't work. She stuffed it under her shirt, but it was still bright enough to see in the absolute dark. She got her wits about her and willed it off. The cave went black.

Something big slithered around in the dark with them. They couldn't see it. Or anything. But they could smell it, hear it breathing.

Something grabbed her arm. She stifled a shout, realizing it was only Troy's hand.

They stood still in the pitch-black cave, listening to the dragon move around. Its breath echoed off the walls, making the dragon impossible to pinpoint. It could've been anywhere. But it was big enough that odds were good it was nearby.

Helen had an idea. She fumbled with her wand. Magic was magic. She could conjure a new light, and maybe, if she was cautious and specific, she could make that light invisible to dragons. She didn't dare talk to explain to Troy. She only hoped he would follow her lead.

She thought about the spell, forming it carefully in her mind. She wouldn't get a second chance. "Presto," she whispered.

The wand flooded the cave with light, sudden and bright and blinding. Helen turned her head away and covered her eyes. She held tight to Troy's hand to make sure he didn't move.

After their eyes adjusted, it was as bright as day in the cave, though shadowy pools of darkness slid here and there. The glow bathed the blue dragon curled in a U shape.

It was staring right at them. One of its big black eyes was fixed on their location, but when they moved the eye didn't follow. Her first instinct was to assume the dragon was faking it. It had to see them. They were right in front of it. But the conjured light was doing exactly what she wanted it to do.

She took a step. Her hoof clomped on the ground. It sounded like a clap of thunder to her, but the monster's heavy breathing overwhelmed it. It didn't move its head in their direction, and its long ears stayed flat.

They sneaked toward the exit. The dragon took up a lot of space, but they were able to squeeze their way past. There was one close call when it shifted position and came very close to crushing them against a wall. Another when Helen almost stepped on its tail. But the creature seemed sluggish and dim, and it didn't notice them.

They said nothing until they got out of the cave and into the clearing.

"Holy crap," whispered Troy. "I thought we were done for."

Helen chuckled. "I can't believe it didn't sense us. We better get out of here before it does. Hey, where's Achilles?"

They looked around, but the dog was nowhere to be seen.

"Damn it," she said. "He must still be in the cave."

Troy drew his non-slaying magic sword and walked toward the dark cavern.

"What are you doing?" she asked.

"I'm saving your dog."

"I didn't think you liked him."

Troy said, "I don't. But I can't leave a dog to get eaten by a dragon. I told you we should've left him in the car."

Helen drew her own sword. "I'm going with you."

"There's no point in both of us getting eaten," he said.

"He's my dog. If anyone should get eaten trying to rescue him, it should be me."

Troy handed her the shield and stepped aside. "This might be helpful."

She stood there in shock.

"What's wrong?" he asked.

"I just thought you'd argue with me more."

"Why? You're right. He is your dog. And let's face facts. You beat the cyclops. If one of us has to fight a dragon, you're the smart bet."

"Thanks." His vote of confidence meant a lot to her. Even if it was sending her into the darkness to wrestle a monster. Because it was sincere.

"But if you're not out in five minutes, I'm coming in after you," he said.

"Fair enough." She adjusted the shield on her arm. It felt far too light and insubstantial to do much good against the creature's claws or teeth.

Achilles, tail wagging, appeared at the mouth of the cave. He ran over to them, and Helen picked him up. "Good boy."

An amulet was entangled around his hind leg. Troy pulled it off. It wasn't much to look at. A string of pearls and a big red jewel. It was less a treasure and more a piece of costume jewelry. He stuffed it in his pocket anyway.

"We should probably get out of here now," he said.

The earth shook as the dragon emerged from its lair without warning. No roar. No belching flame. Just the sound of its scraping belly, and even that was far too late to warn them.

The great beast moved toward them with slow, awkward steps.

They weren't certain it had seen them yet. The awkward placement of its eyes gave it a blind spot right in front of its snout. But it might be able to smell them. Its nostrils flared as it tested the air.

They took a cautious step backward, shifting their position to stay directly in front of it. For a few moments it looked as if this would work and they would make it to the forest where, if escape wasn't guaranteed, at least they wouldn't be so exposed.

Then Helen tripped over a branch. Her fall and the snap of wood caused the dragon to jerk its head to the side. It focused its pitiless eye on them.

A bird flitted by. It landed on the dragon's head as if to say there was nothing to be concerned about.

The dragon's green tongue darted out and snagged the bird. The monster swallowed it, then reared up on its long, awkward body and shrieked. It came crashing to the ground with earth-shaking force. Then it lunged at them.

Both Troy and Helen smashed the beast across the snout with their magic swords. The weapons shattered, but the dragon recoiled instinctively from the enchantments. It licked its snout and growled.

"That probably made things worse," said Helen.

The dragon lunged again. Helen laid a punch across its jaw. The dragon stumbled under the solid blow. It wobbled on its unsteady legs and probably would've fallen over if it hadn't already been so low to the ground.

"Holy crap, Hel," said Troy. "You are strong."

She smashed it on the snout, but the dragon was ready for her this time. The punch didn't stun it nearly as much this time. It shook its head clear. Its tail whipped like a lash and would've knocked Helen through a tree except that she had moved by the time it struck. She was instead standing a few feet to her left.

She didn't remember moving. She must've had superhuman reflexes in addition to superhuman strength.

The dragon snapped her up in its jaws, crushing the life from her. Only she was several feet away. Too far to have moved there on her own.

Enraged, the monster charged. Helen tripped, falling flat. She turned over and thrust her shield forward as if it would help her avoid being crushed beneath its bulk. But instead of being ground into a pulp, she was ten feet away. Still on her back.

"It's the shield!" said Troy. "It's a teleporting doodad!"

The dragon turned on him and hissed. Achilles rushed before the monster. The scruffy three-legged dog fearlessly barked from the dragon's blind spot. The confused creature swiveled its head.

The dragon drew in a deep breath. Flames licked around the edges of its mouth.

Helen ran over and grabbed Achilles. Afterward she'd say she had just been hoping she would be fast enough to get clear in time. But that was only afterward. At the time she wasn't thinking much at all.

She wasn't fast enough.

The dragon's hot breath washed over her and Achilles, clutched in her arms. Except for the shield, which once again whisked her out of harm's way, out of the clearing and into the forest.

The great blue reptile swept its flames several times across the clearing, setting the grass and tree stumps ablaze. Helen backed into the shadows where it couldn't see her. She saw no trace of Troy. Her first instinct was to look for a human-shaped scorch mark in the grass, like a Looney Tunes character death. Ridiculous, maybe, but better than being completely incinerated with nothing left behind.

Why had she grabbed the dog? Why hadn't she grabbed Troy? He'd been a bit farther, true, but she might have been able to save him. Her head swirled with images and questions. What would she tell his parents? What could she? Their son, their all-American boy, gone. Just gone. Like that. But at least she'd saved the dog.

The dog he hadn't even liked.

Something grabbed her shoulder and she jumped.

It was Troy.

She swept him up in one arm and hugged him perhaps a bit tighter than she should've. He exhaled painfully.

"Oh gods." She let go. Gasping, he fell to his knees. "Oh gods, I'm sorry. I didn't mean to—"

Choking, Troy put his fingers to his lips to remind her to keep her voice down. The dragon was still fuming in the clearing.

"I thought you were dead," she whispered.

He stood, his face flushed. "I anchored the track team. Remember? Getting out of the way of dragon breath is harder than hurdles, but I managed."

The monster ceased its clumsy rampage and scanned the forest for signs of its prey. They didn't dare move as it slunk in their direction.

Troy pulled the novelty teapot from his backpack and hurled it into the distance. It clattered among some trees, and the dragon, roaring, chased after it. They took advantage of the distraction to slip away in the other direction, not daring to move faster than a slow walk until the sounds of its rage faded into the songs of birds.

21

Nigel had never had much use for spirits, but for once the capricious forces had led them in the right direction. They found the electric-blue Chimera parked on the side of the road. No trace of the passengers, but Peggy assured him that the spirits assured her that their targets would be returning shortly.

The plan was simple. The club hid their cycles a mile down the road, came back, and waited patiently in the shadowy woods. Nigel found a good spot behind an old bent tree. He glimpsed a few other club members' hiding spots, but that was only because he was looking for them. Overall their dark leather allowed them to blend in quite naturally. Except for Peggy, who stood out like a white specter in a dark room, but she'd found a good bush that blocked the view from the road.

Franklin rustled through the underbrush.

"Hey, Nigel," he whispered. "Do you think they'll come?"

Nigel shushed him with a glare. It didn't stick.

"Why are we hiding, Nigel?"

"Because we don't want them to see us," Nigel replied.

"Yeah, but isn't that a bit...sneaky?" asked Franklin.

"It's an ambush. Ambushes are sneaky."

"Uh-huh."

Franklin nodded to himself.

"But they are only two people, right?" he said. "Do we really need to ambush them?"

"We don't want them getting away, now do we?"

"Oh, OK."

Franklin slunk away, disappearing into the shadows. He was surprisingly good at hiding, Nigel had to admit. Better than Nigel gave him credit for, because he failed to spot Franklin until he spoke up again.

"We're in the middle of a dragon preserve. If we surround their car, where are they going to get away to without it?"

"They might run for it," said Nigel.

"But where to? Peggy says we're miles from any civilized help. And it'd be stupid to run away from your only form of transportation in a dragon preserve. Wouldn't it?"

"People do stupid stuff all the time. And I am not going to waste my whole afternoon chasing someone down when I can jump out of the bushes and finish this quickly."

"But—"

"It's an ambush, Franklin. You're supposed to shut up now."

Franklin did shut up. For thirty seconds.

"It's kind of a shame, though."

Nigel closed his eyes, refusing to carry on the conversation. Franklin persisted.

"These last few days have been some of the best of my life. For the first time, it really felt like I was doing something important. My whole life, I've always been a pencil pusher, a nobody. But then I got the call from the gods, and everything was different. Air smelled sweeter. Felt like I belonged somewhere. Like I'm doing something that matters. Like for the first time, the gods above noticed me. You probably don't understand."

Nigel understood. More than Franklin could ever know.

"I know you guys don't like me, think of me as a wannabe," Franklin said, "but riding with you, being part of this, even if you all think I'm a joke..."

Nigel considered beheading Franklin with one clean stroke of his ax to end this awkward moment.

"Sorry, Nigel. I'll be quiet." Franklin vanished into the foliage.

Nigel ran his thumb along his ax's blade.

"Franklin," he whispered.

"Yes?" Franklin was right behind Nigel. He was very sneaky.

"You're not a joke," said Nigel.

Franklin's face lit up in a way that made Nigel want to punch the human's teeth in.

"You're weak and pathetic and you're a lousy orc, even for a human. In a sensible universe you'd be dead by now. But you're here, despite all that. And you try harder than any of us, even though you always look like a chump, falling flat on your face. You'll never amount to anything and if you're very, very lucky, you'll die alone and afraid, realizing just how miserable your life was and grateful for the promise of oblivion.

"I don't like you, Franklin. We're not friends. And you're deadweight on this mission, the weakest link. But you always try. If anyone's going to rush headlong into danger in some vain attempt to seize glory, it's you. And that makes you more orc than a lot of people I know. Including some orcs."

"Really?" Franklin's lip trembled. "Do you really mean that?"

"Yes, really," said Nigel. "But if you cry, I will cut you in half."

Franklin wiped his eyes. "No, no, it's my allergies acting up. Honest."

"Whatever. Now get out of my face."

Franklin vanished.

Peggy slid up beside Nigel.

"Not one word," he said. "Not one."

"Or what? You can't afford to kill me. I'm your shaman."

He grumbled.

"That was a decent thing you did," she said.

"Hell, he's not all useless," Nigel said. "Don't tell me the spirits approve."

"The spirits think you should've killed him." She smiled. "But the spirits are assholes."

"How much longer do we have to wait?"

She shrugged.

Nigel was torn. He wanted to get this over with, but he also hated to see it end, to go back to his old life, to trade the open road for the tiny cubicle. He wasn't keen on killing anyone. He wasn't as uncivilized as he liked to imagine. He saw it too in the others' faces. The struggle between the modern world and the exhilaration of tapping into the bloodlust bound in his DNA. Morality was a real bitch.

Things had been so much easier when it'd been orcs against the world. He envied his ancestors, who had the luxury of viewing everyone as an enemy. The ancient tribes might sign up with an ambitious wizard now and then, but even that was only for the hell of it, an extra excuse to march across the bloodied plains.

Today he saw his two victims as more than just notches in his ax handle. They were people with lives and dreams, friends and families. They weren't his enemies. Hadn't done a damn thing to him. Their only crime was being unwilling pawns of the gods above in their games. He had no problem relating, but there was no point in questioning the gods or their wishes. Mortal lives were offered up as playthings for powers beyond measure.

He hoped it wouldn't be too easy. He hoped these two would put up a decent fight. He even hoped that perhaps they'd win. It'd make things so much easier. He wouldn't have to live with guilt that way, and he much preferred the dark void of the orc afterlife to balancing ledgers.

Not that he could let them win. They had to earn it. He owed that much to himself, his ancestors, and his not-enemies.

Something roared overhead. A black shape blotted out what little sun came through the canopy. The speckled brown dragon came crashing into the forest, right in the middle of the club.

Charlie Liverchewer was crushed under one of the monster's feet. The dragon spread its wings and shrieked. It grabbed Harold Marrowmaw, the fattest, most tempting morsel, and chucked the orc into its jaws. Harold's girth saved him from instant death by preventing him from sliding easily down the dragon's throat. He latched onto its tongue. It gagged and choked before finally puking up Harold as well as copious buckets of drool and vomit.

Harold jumped to his feet, drew his sword, and charged the dragon. His charge was more of a trundle, and the monster watched him with fascination. Harold stabbed his blade into the monster's foot, and it howled bloody murder. His triumph was cut short when the dragon kicked him, sending him soaring off into the thicket.

The dragon spread its wings and roared. It toppled a tree with a swipe of its tail.

A deathly silence fell across the forest.

Harold pushed his way out of the underbrush. He limped forward, barely able to stand. His right arm was a mess of shattered meat. Coughing, he spat up a wad of blood and teeth.

The dragon's head danced on its long neck. It extended a hood and made a low rattling warble.

Harold used his good arm to wrench off a heavy tree branch. He raised it above his head and, with a bestial war cry, rushed forward again in his trademark loping manner. The Wild Hunt echoed his savage bellow and launched themselves at the magical beast.

It appeared this wasn't going to be so easy after all, thought Nigel, as he chopped off the tip of the dragon's tail with his ax.

In the heat of battle, he still took a moment to thank his gods for their blessings.

Troy and Helen jumped in the Chimera as a nearby dragon smashed and thumped its way through the forest. They didn't hear the howls of enraged orcs, and if they had heard them, they might easily have mistaken them for the bellows of other ferocious monsters better avoided.

They tore down the dirt road, leaving the temperamental beast behind.

A few miles down the road, Helen thought she saw a motorcycle parked behind a bush. She dismissed it as a figment of her imagination.

* * *

The dragon was bigger than the Wild Hunt. Stronger. Faster. Tougher. But it had picked the wrong fight. Civilization had deprived the orcs of their birthright, and while they hadn't been reluctant victims, they discovered a joy of battle in their very bones. Thousands of years of untapped bloodlust filled their heads with a red haze.

The dragon responded in kind, but it had been ages since it'd tried to eat anything that could put up a decent struggle. At first it thought these little blue, gray, and orange morsels would be easy prey, and it was pleasantly surprised when they weren't. It enjoyed playing with its food, but the food was supposed to stop fighting eventually.

Yet after several minutes the food still struggled. Though the dragon had swallowed many of the morsels, all had been too stubborn to slide all the way down its throat. Even after it chewed and gnawed on them. The dragon was always forced to spit them back out. The roof of its mouth hurt from all the knives and swords driven deep into its tender flesh. And its uvula was a bruised, purple punching bag.

The orcs climbed atop its back and wings as they stabbed and poked at the monster. Its brown scales repelled all but the most stubborn strikes, but they still irritated the beast. While the orcs would lose if the fight continued long enough, deep in its primitive brain the dragon seriously doubted they were worth the trouble.

Something landed on its head. Nigel grabbed a horn and held on as the dragon attempted to shake him loose. He couldn't even remember how he'd gotten up there. Perhaps he'd climbed a tree. Perhaps he'd run straight up its back. Or maybe he'd jumped, propelled by his lust for battle. Regardless, he swung his magic ax, aiming to split the monster's skull. At the last second he slipped and tumbled all the way to the ground. A sharp boulder broke his fall. His rage sputtered as the landing knocked the wind out of him.

The dragon made one last attempt to devour stunned Nigel. Before it could strike, Franklin (somehow still alive) jumped between the monster and its prey. He held his flail over his head, swinging it with wild abandon. He roared in the beast's face.

It wasn't a powerful roar. He'd already gone hoarse from screaming during the fight, and even at his best he still had fragile human lungs in a fragile human body. But as human roars went, it rated a solid six out of ten.

The winged reptile shook off the exhausted orcs pestering it, lowered its head so that its jaws were only a few inches from slurping down Franklin. It snorted, blasting him with hot breath from its nostrils.

Franklin smacked it across the snout with his flail. The spiked ball bounced harmlessly off the monster's hide and smashed him across the hands. He yelped, dropping his weapon.

The dragon grunted. It raised its head and licked its nose with its long, bloody tongue. It made a horrid gurgling sound and vomited black bile and red blood all over Nigel and Franklin. Then, with a curious grunt and an empty stomach, it launched itself into the air and flew away.

The Wild Hunt fell to their knees and on their backs. The forest was silent, save for their collective wheezing.

Nigel sat up. He tried to wipe the dragon vomit from his face but only ended up smearing it around. Franklin was on all fours, retching. Nigel limped his way back to the road. The Chimera was gone. If the Hunt ran back to their bikes, they might be able to catch up. But they were in no condition to run. Or to fight.

He dragged himself over to Franklin, who was retching and making a hell of a racket doing it.

"You all right, kid?"

"Oh gods, I swallowed it. It's in my mouth." Franklin dry-heaved. "It's in my mouth!"

The orcs laughed, then groaned at all the pain that came with laughing.

"You were right," said Franklin. "I am a terrible orc."

Nigel hefted Franklin to his feet. Franklin wobbled, but he didn't fall down. Peggy approached, handed him his flail. He took it, rubbing his bloody knuckles.

"You are a terrible orc," said Nigel.

He slapped Franklin across the back, hard enough that Franklin spit up a little of his own vomit along with the dragon bile he'd swallowed.

"But you're an orc," said Peggy.

The Wild Hunt raised their weapons and cheered. Then groaned.

Franklin smiled wider than he ever had in his life.

Then he fell to his knees and threw up for six straight minutes.

22

The Chimera zipped down the preserve road, kicking up clouds of dust. They didn't run across any more dragons, but they kept their eyes open. Just in case.

"I can't believe you punched a dragon in the face," said Troy.

Helen smiled, held up two fingers. "Twice. I punched it twice." She snorted, kissed her fist. "No big deal."

"You're lucky it didn't eat you. I think it was more surprised than hurt," he said. "Who would've guessed a dragon's weakness would be chutzpah? That's twice now you've saved our asses with that super-strength of yours."

"Maybe you're my sidekick."

Troy chuckled. "Maybe."

A monster cried out somewhere in the forest, but neither Helen nor Troy was afraid. They'd faced the beasts and come out the other side alive. The unknown didn't seem so terrifying right now.

"Don't you think you owe Achilles an apology?" she said. "He saved your life."

"He's a dog. Dogs don't care about apologies." Troy patted Achilles on the neck. "Although I still think he's not a dog, but something pretending to be a dog."

Helen looked into Achilles's dark-brown eyes. The dog licked her nose and wagged his tail.

She said, "If he's pretending, he's doing a great job. He has to be the method actor of pretend dogs."

"No point in arguing about it," said Troy. "It's not like he's just going to tell us if he's a helpful spirit or guiding gift from the gods above, right?"

They paused, giving Achilles the chance to speak up. He barked once and shoved his muzzle under Helen's hand.

"Have it your way," said Troy. "But when he does finally reveal himself to be a god in disguise, you're going to feel weird about all that time you spent rubbing his belly."

They might have imagined it, but Achilles did almost offer a coy smile.

"Any idea if that amulet is important?" asked Troy. "As if I have to ask?"

Helen checked the necklace they'd found wrapped around Achilles's leg. It wasn't much to look at. She might even have mistaken it for costume jewelry with its gaudy string of pearls and the bright red gem that appeared to be made of plastic. As treasures went, it was a bit disappointing.

"I don't know," she said. "It doesn't look magic. But the pricking in my hand is softer."

"Mine too."

Helen glanced at her curse mark. It didn't hurt much, and

she was getting used to the slight ache. The mark seemed burned deeper into her flesh. Perhaps only a fraction of a millimeter. Not enough that she could say for certain. Troy's mark was easier to see now, possibly because he didn't have fur to get in the way. Either way, it worried her.

She touched the necklace to the unholy symbol burned on the back of her hand. She touched it to the shield. She waved her magic wand over the amulet. There was no reaction. Not from the necklace. Or the other items. And the closest thing they got to an omen was when a horsefly splatted against the windshield.

"It can't just be an ordinary amulet," he said. "That's not the way it's supposed to work."

"Maybe that is how it works, though," she replied. "Maybe they just edit the pointless stuff out of legends and quests when they retell them. They leave out that part where Beowulf swam into the wrong cave and wasted a weekend wandering in the dark looking for the supernatural evil one cave over."

Troy frowned. "That won't do. They can't leave out the part where you punched a dragon." He held up two fingers. "Twice."

She leaned back in her seat and cracked her knuckles. "That would be a shame."

They exited the preserve without incident, though they did get a glimpse of a crimson serpent slithering across the road. Helen managed to snap a photo of the creature.

"Find what you were looking for?" asked Ranger Grainger.

"We don't know," replied Helen. "But we weren't sure what we were looking for in the first place."

Grainger returned their stuff to them, had them sign some forms.

While they were walking back to their car, the omen they were waiting for arrived. Maybe it was the interference of the preserve's sub-dimension that had prevented the gods from noticing their quest progress sooner. Or perhaps the gods above had been distracted by their own concerns. Whatever caused the delay, when the omen hit, it hit hard.

It started with a sudden heat in Helen's thigh. She yanked the tarnished amulet out of her pocket and threw it to the ground.

The ground trembled as an inky darkness spilled from the necklace. It spread like a living oil slick until it surrounded Helen, Troy, Grainger, Achilles, and the Chimera. Shapes shimmered on its surface until it became clear that they weren't points of light, but thousands of eyes looking up from the depths.

A blast of searing wind knocked them down as a giant of flame with magma for eyes and a mouth filled with teeth of pointed black stones burst from the chasm before them. The monstrous thing raised its fists and brought them crashing down on the Chimera. But the thing was only smoke, and its blow passed through the car. The mortals coughed and choked. Helen nearly stepped off the edge, but Troy caught her. She wondered what might have happened if he hadn't. Would she have gotten her hoof dirty? Would she have sunk into the muck, disappearing forever? Or would she have just plummeted into the abyss? She didn't know, and she was glad she hadn't found out.

The omen howled, an angry storm of divine fury and thunder. Its deafening rage ended with a whimper as it sputtered to a gasp, belched up a puffy gray cloud, and sank back into the void with a rumbling grumble.

The chasm dissolved, evaporating like an oily patch of mud. The ash and soot covering the Chimera drifted away into nothingness. The only signs any of it had happened were the ever-so-slight scent of burned minotaur fur and a scorch mark in Helen's jeans.

"Crap," she said. "I just bought these."

Troy bent down and touched the amulet. It was cool. "There's your sign, Hel," he said as he picked it up.

"That was a good one," said Grainger.

"Stuff like that happen often?" asked Troy.

"It's not unusual. Though that was one of the better omens. You two must be doing something big."

Helen said, "We don't really know. We're just playing it by ear."

"You wouldn't happen to know where we should go next?" asked Troy.

"If you want to know the dietary preferences of the South American cockatrice, I'm your gal. Interpreting the will of the gods, you should ask someone else. But I wouldn't worry if I were you. An omen like that probably means you're on the right track. The gods don't waste that level of pyrotechnics otherwise."

They thanked Grainger for her help. She wished them luck. And then they were off, following the road wherever it might take them.

Helen drove. She absently rubbed her leg where she'd been burned. She checked it at the first rest stop. The damage wasn't serious. Just some blackened fur and a patch of reddened skin. Her constant rubbing was more irritating than the injury.

"I've been thinking," she said. "Are we sure we should be doing this?"

Troy studied the necklace dangling from the rearview mirror. "We don't have a choice, Hel. Cursed by the gods." He held up the back of his marked hand.

"I know, but I can't help thinking that we're doing something wrong."

"I think we're making good progress."

"No, I don't mean we're not doing the questing correctly. I mean, maybe what we're doing is the wrong thing to do."

He tapped the amulet's jewel, swinging it back and forth. "You too, huh?"

"So we're both on the same page here," she said. "This banished hamburger god cursed us into doing his bidding. That can't be good, right?"

"Probably not."

"And gathering all these magic relics together, it's got to be for some purpose, right?"

"Maybe he's just working on his artifact collection," said Troy.

"Maybe, but it's no secret that the gods above aren't all that nice to begin with. They're capricious, unreliable, and they don't think twice about using mortals as playthings for their own unknowable purposes."

She wrung the steering wheel in tight fists and stared at the desert stretching into the horizon.

"Makes you wonder what terrible offense a god would have to commit for the others to banish him. This god, the god the other gods decided was too much of a jerk to hang around with them, is the god we're helping."

"That sums it up," he said.

They drove a little farther without saying much.

"And that doesn't make you nervous?" she asked.

"I don't know. I try not to think about it."

"But we have to think about it," she said. "We could be doing something terrible. We could be destroying the world."

Troy laughed. "That's a touch melodramatic."

"Is it? Did you see the smoke monster back there? Or the way that hamburger god slurped down Mr. Whiteleaf? And that was an accident. It could have just as easily been you or me."

"It's a big jump from human sacrifice to the end of the world."

"Maybe not for a renegade god," said Helen.

"Why would a god want to end the world anyway?" asked Troy. "What would be in it for him?"

"Why would he need a reason? Gods just do stuff. They don't worry about the consequences."

"I'll give you that," said Troy. "But if it was easy to destroy the world on a whim then wouldn't the gods have already done it?"

"So maybe it's not the end of the world."

He smirked.

"OK, it's highly unlikely it's the end of the world," she said, "but we agree that it's probably something bad. Something we shouldn't be doing."

Troy said, "You're overthinking it."

"No, I'm thinking about it just enough."

"Look at it this way. If we were doing something really dangerous, do you think the NQB would've issued us questing licenses? Agent Waechter seemed to know what he was doing, had a lot more experience at this sort of thing than we do. And he didn't seem worried."

"What if he's a bad guy? He could be a secret cultist, a worshipper of chaos. Or something."

"Now you are overthinking."

"Now…" She bit her lip and tapped her finger against her thigh. "Yes, I am. Probably."

She waited for him to say something, but he only unwrapped

the amulet from the rearview and pondered it in the palm of his hand.

"This is the part where you say something reassuring," she said.

"I didn't think I was allowed to do that anymore. I thought I was supposed to let you wrestle with your inner demons alone."

She shook her head.

He said, "We can sit here all day, wondering what we're doing and if we should be doing it, and it'll get us nowhere. Because we don't know how or why we're doing any of this. Except that we have to do it. That's all that matters. We have to keep going forward, do our best, and hope it all works out the way it should. What other choice do we have? Lie down and die?"

Helen huffed. "That wasn't very inspiring."

"They can't all be winners," he replied. "Did it make you feel better at least?"

"A little bit," she admitted.

Troy's cell rang. The caller ID labeled the call as coming from the NQB. The smooth, untroubled voice on the other end belonged to Agent Waechter.

"Hello, Mr. Kawakami. I trust everything is going well."

"Better than could be expected," said Troy.

"In eight miles you'll see an unmarked road on your left. You'll want to take that."

Troy didn't ask any questions. He'd gone past worrying about stuff like this. Their quest had been full of mysterious guides and so far following them had kept him and Helen on the right path. The pattern was obvious. Face some sort of challenge, collect an artifact, be pointed in the direction of the next challenge, repeat.

They would've missed the road if not for Waechter's warning.

It was hidden behind a grove of trees. Helen pulled onto it. It led to a small house.

Waechter sat on a rocking chair on the front porch, sipping a cup of tea. He wore black slacks, a white shirt, a lime-green tie. His soul patch was now accompanied by the stubble of a few days without shaving. Agent Campbell, dressed in her black suit and tie, stood behind him. She seemed incapable of sitting. Perhaps her legs didn't bend that way.

Helen and Troy joined him, taking a seat.

Waechter said, "Might I comment on the bang-up job you two fine young citizens have been doing?"

"You've been watching us," said Helen.

"We keep tabs," replied Waechter. "Do what we can when we can."

"You've been helping us?" she asked.

He smiled enigmatically. "Care for some tea?"

Troy took a cup. Helen didn't like tea.

"We've got some questions," said Troy.

"I'm sure you do. But I can't answer them. There are rules in place. Cosmic laws, set down by forces even more potent than the gods. A quest without mystery is like a wolverine wearing a carnation."

He took a sip of tea. They waited for him to finish the metaphor, but he simply smiled.

"OK, I give up," said Helen. "How is a quest without mystery like a wolverine wearing a carnation?"

Waechter shrugged. "Beats the hell out of me."

She stifled her irritation.

"That's the way of it, isn't it?" he said. "Always to be confounded by questions we can never answer. Such is our lot in this life. However, at this point, I am allowed to answer three questions."

"Just three?" asked Helen.

"Just three," he replied. "Well, two now."

"You didn't say we'd started," she said.

"You started before you were born. Before your parents or grandparents. Before even the gods above were birthed in the primordial dawn of time. You didn't think this was all a coincidence, did you? Your lives have led you to this moment. Everything you've done, everything you've never done, all the choices you've made, and all the choices others have made for you...your path started long ago, same as everyone's."

"We've met the fates," said Helen. "They didn't seem all that organized. And they admitted there's no such thing as destiny."

"Listening to metaphysical personifications of abstract concepts is a crapshoot at best," said Waechter. "Or so a personification of wisdom once told me. Of course, the very next day a personification of deceit told me the very same thing, so I guess it's a wash.

"I can't tell you there's a master plan at work. I can't tell you there isn't. Every quest is different. Certainly there tends to be an expected way for things to unfold, but that is less about predestination and more about the stories people like to tell.

"That's the secret, you see. The universe doesn't shape legends. People and storytellers do. So what if Odysseus wasn't cursed by the gods, but just having fun with the boys and lost track of time? Or that Momotaro wasn't born inside a peach and no one ever heard his dog talk but him? The details are just that: details. Things for the storytellers to clean up, after the fact. After a while the universe says, 'Sure, why not? That'll work.'"

Helen said, "That's all just double-talk and pseudo-intellectual nonsense."

"Most of it," admitted Waechter.

Troy asked, "Is our quest dangerous?"

"Dangerous to whom?" asked Waechter. "Don't worry. That's just clarification. Not an official third question."

"To the world?" asked Troy.

"Not the world, no. Just a substantial portion of it."

Helen's first instinct was to ask how big a portion, but she didn't want to use up their last question.

"But you're letting us do this anyway," she said. "That wasn't a question, by the way. It was a statement."

Waechter grinned. "Clever. I really shouldn't let that slide, but I will because I like the both of you. Yes, I'm letting you attempt your quest. Yes, it could bring terrible results to many innocent people. And, yes, it would probably be safer for everyone, including yourselves, if you were, as we say in the bureau, de-quested."

He took another sip.

"I won't force you to find a clever little way around your next question. Yes, we at the NQB do see that certain quests are never completed. It's a delicate art. You can't just kill a quester. Such actions usually just help them on their journey. If you want to de-quest someone, you have to manipulate things from the shadows in such a way that the gods and destiny don't notice. It isn't easy, but we are the NQB. And before that we were something else. And before that...you get the idea. There have always been those who stand in the darkness, unnoticed. By going unnoticed, they are allowed to break some of the universe's most sacred rules.

"Now, it bears mentioning that I, by merely being here, have become part of your quest. It makes me unable to de-quest you at this point, even if I wanted to do so. But the NQB has many operatives, and we operate with little interagency communication to ensure that there's always someone capable of handling things when they get messy. There might very well be someone attempting to de-quest you right now. I don't know. Not my end. My end is helping you complete your quest, which I shall do to the best of my ability."

"What happens when we get all the relics together?" asked Troy. "Don't tell us you don't know. We know you keep records."

"It varies. Sometimes faces melt as thousands of souls scream. Other times cataclysm. But it will be more than indigestion and a few burning cities, I can assure you."

"That sucks," said Helen. "You're basically telling us that we can either destroy the world or die."

"Not the world," he corrected.

"There has to be a way around it," said Troy.

Waechter offered no reply as he uncrossed his legs.

"Is there a way around it?" asked Helen.

He put a finger to his lips.

"Come on," she said. "You can't do this to us. You can't tell us we're going to destroy the world and then leave us hanging. Who came up with this three-question rule anyway?"

Waechter shrugged.

Helen jumped out of her chair and stomped her hoof. Her foot smashed through the wooden porch. Irritated, she extracted it, then grabbed her empty chair and hurled it. It sailed far into the distance.

"Take it easy, Hel," said Troy.

"Why are you always so cool?" she asked. "Why doesn't this bother you more?"

"Because I believe in us. I know we can do this."

"Do what? Unleash the wrath of the gods? Melt faces?"

He stood, put his hand on her arm. "We can do this."

Her rage burned. She tamped it down by closing her eyes and counting to ten. It still smoldered within her, but she could ignore it.

"Are you OK, Hel?" asked Troy.

"I'll be OK. It's just frustrating. That's all."

She rubbed her wrist where her anti-enchantment bracelet should have been. She didn't know if its absence had anything to do with how she felt, but she still wanted to smash something.

"What now, Agent Waechter?" asked Troy.

"He won't answer that," said Helen. "It's a question."

"No, I can answer that one," said Waechter. "You continue on your journey. You follow the road where it takes you. Same as any of us. And you hope that, if it's going to lead you someplace unpleasant, then at least it will be an interesting unpleasantness."

He petted Achilles.

"But if I were going to offer advice, I'd recommend checking out the Mystery Cottage. It's a fun place. Little touristy, but fun nonetheless."

Agent Campbell unfolded a road map from her inside jacket pocket and handed it to Troy. "I recommend the jerky," she said without expression.

Helen and Troy climbed into the Chimera and drove away.

"Think they'll finally be the ones to do it?" asked Campbell.

"Who knows? I've got a good feeling about those two. But I also had a good feeling about those other two, and we both remember how that turned out."

She frowned. "Still feel bad about those two."

"Questing is a dirty business," said Waechter. "You knew that when you signed up with the bureau."

"Maybe we should've given them more warning."

"If the story is to play out properly, we have to play our part. The rest is up to the gods above. And to them."

23

Waechter vanished from the rearview mirror. Helen waited until she couldn't see him before saying anything.

"I don't trust that guy."

"He's a secret agent," said Troy. "They're untrustworthy by nature. Hush-hush. Need-to-know. All that kind of stuff."

"So you don't trust him either?"

"I don't know. I don't not trust him. He hasn't steered us wrong so far."

"You and I have very different definitions of *wrong* then."

They cruised down the desert road in the Chimera. The ride felt bumpier than normal to Helen. She wondered if it was the road or if her increased weight put extra pressure on the shocks. She was getting bigger. She could sense herself expanding a quarter of an inch every day.

"Helen, maybe it's out of line for me to say this, but you seem a bit edgy lately," said Troy.

"I'm fine."

She wasn't. She didn't know if it was her minotaurism, unchecked by her bracelet. Or maybe it was the quest. Or him, so cool and smart and perfect and handsome and charming.

She'd liked Troy for a while, but they were just friends. It had been easy to be just friends when they saw each other for a few hours a week, and most of those hours were at the Magic Burger, where the smell of grease kept things in check. Now they were on this quest, trapped in a car together, fighting dragons and godlings together, sharing hotel rooms... together.

She had to remind herself that Troy was good with people, and that he had a talent for making everyone feel special. When he smiled at her, he wasn't smiling *at her*. When he demonstrated some intimate knowledge of her likes and dislikes, it wasn't because he was focused especially on her. He liked her because he liked people, and people liked him. It was his nature.

He was like a puppy. You couldn't resist him, and it was easy to believe there was some special connection. Then you caught him devoting as much attention to a rubber ball or a stuffed zebra.

But she was really, really starting to like him. And that smile. It sucked.

Troy watched the road. She glanced at him from the corner of her eye. She caught herself doing that more often lately.

"Hel, if you want to talk about something—" he said.

She closed her eyes. "I'm tired of talking, Troy."

"But if you ever want to talk—"

"I know where to find you."

Guided by their map, they crossed into northern Utah. The desert fell away and forest flanked the road. It wasn't the untamed wilderness of the dragon preserve. There were signs of civilization everywhere. Little towns. Houses. Signs advertising ski resorts. She welcomed the ordinariness of it. After the last few days, it seemed almost magical to return to the normal world. Although she was certain it was only a pit stop.

The Mystery Cottage wasn't hard to locate. There were billboards advertising it, and as they drew closer the signs grew more numerous.

VISIT THE MYSTERY COTTAGE, WHERE THE GODS OF YORE WAIT.

And THE MYSTERY COTTAGE, FREE BALLOONS FOR THE KIDS.

And WHAT MAKES THE MYSTERY COTTAGE SO MYSTERIOUS? STOP IN AND FIND OUT.

And finally, ALL QUESTERS WELCOME AT THE MYSTERY COTTAGE.

None of the billboards had any pictures. Perhaps it would've ruined the mystery.

Helen suspected what they'd find. There would be somebody there to guide them on their journey. Probably some sort of challenge, internal or external. Like a monster to fight or a boulder to be lifted. Or some sort of metaphysical revelation followed by an unpleasant confrontation of inner truth.

Gods above, she was hoping for the monster.

They reached the Mystery Cottage late in the afternoon. It was a giant wooden construction. It was as if someone had planted a cottage, given it plenty of sunlight and water, and grown it into a mansion. Coniferous trees wrapped around it. The highest were still only half as tall as the house itself, as if the house took the lion's share of the soil's nutrients and left the trees to fight over the scraps.

The sun hid behind the Mystery Cottage, and the house's chill shadow stretched across the parking lot. Helen shivered as they found a spot. She never shivered. Fur meant she was almost never cold.

Several families wandered around the manicured front lawn. They took photos or piled into cars. A brother and sister ran around, their balloons trailing behind them.

She stepped out of the Chimera. It squeaked and rocked. She compared the squeaking and rocking to her memory of yesterday, but there was no way of knowing if she was imagining that they were more pronounced today.

"Doesn't look very mysterious," said Troy.

"What would mysterious look like?" she asked.

"A figure in black, beckoning from the doorway. A fleeting shadow barely seen in a window. Ravens perched everywhere. Vines creeping up the walls. A peculiar statue out front."

"You've been thinking about this."

"We weren't talking. What else was I going to do?"

"Troy, I'm sorry. I'm not mad at you or anything like that."

"No need to apologize, Hel," he said. "It's a long ride. It's OK to want some quiet time."

There he went again. Being reasonable. Never offended. Never bothered. It troubled her that he wasn't quite human in that way. She'd decided it meant he was either shallow and overconfident *or* deep and Zen. She hadn't determined which.

Achilles wandered off to sniff around while they entered the cottage. The entrance room was festooned with touristy offerings. Bumper stickers, postcards, T-shirts, souvenir glasses. Helen glanced through the postcard rack while Troy talked to the elderly woman behind the front desk.

The woman sniffed the air. "You, young man, have the un-mistakable scent of a quester." She smiled. Her teeth were shiny white dentures. "Am I right?"

"Yes, ma'am."

"Always am." She tapped her nose. "Hasn't let me down yet. These old bones might not be what they used to be, but I can still smell a hero from a mile away."

He said, "I don't know if I'm a hero, ma'am."

"Call me Babs, Troy."

"You know my name?"

"A talent of mine," replied the old woman. "Comes in handy with so many people passing through. You most certainly are a hero, and a rare breed of hero indeed. One of genuine heroic mettle. I've seen many a strong young man come through here and few have what you have." She reached out with a long skinny arm and put a finger on his chest. "A fine soul you have there."

Helen cleared her throat to cover her groan.

"Ah, and I see this lovely young lady walks the journey beside you," said the woman. "Welcome to the both of you. The Mystery Cottage loves questers. We don't get quite so many as we once did."

"What's the deal here?" asked Helen. "What do you give us? Or cryptically warn us about? Or tell us we have to fight to carry on?"

The woman chuckled. "I can't tell you. That is the mystery of the cottage. It's late anyway. You probably want a room for the night. We can deal with the details tomorrow."

"Can't we just do what we have to do already?" asked Helen.

"You'll want to be refreshed. Trust me on this." Babs stood.

She was a tall, lanky figure of a woman with a bent back and hands like spiders. "Get your things, and I'll show you to your room."

"Rooms," said Helen. "We'd like two."

"As you wish." Babs smiled coyly in a way that Helen found suspicious. As if the old woman knew something Helen didn't. The thought didn't strike Helen as paranoid because it was most definitely true.

She showed them to their rooms. The second floor was for guests. It had a more homey feel, though its halls were cluttered with junk. Old suits of armor, odd oil paintings, stuffed animal heads, vases. Oh so many vases. Whether it was charming or claustrophobic remained uncertain, but it was an impressive collection. This was what a dragon's lair should've looked like.

They scanned the items, hoping to find their next relic. A sharp heat stung their hands, telling them they were close, but the sheer amount of odds and ends meant they could spend the better part of a day searching for it.

There were seven rooms on the floor. All of them were unoccupied.

"I apologize if they're a bit dusty," said Babs. "I do try to keep on top of things, but there's a lot to look after for a woman of my advancing years. Take your pick. Dinner is at seven."

She patted their cheeks. Helen had to bend down to accommodate the gesture. Babs excused herself to check on the other visitors.

"Kind of creepy," said Helen.

"I prefer to think of it as cozy, Hel."

"I wasn't talking about the cottage."

Troy laughed despite himself. "Oh, she's a bit strange, but that probably only means she's wise or something. It's not fair to judge her on first impressions."

"You're only saying that because she called you a hero."

"No, I'm saying it because she's a bit obvious to be a danger."

She slapped him on the back. "Aha, so you do think she's creepy."

"There is a certain uncanny valley factor," he admitted, "but we shouldn't hold that against her."

She agreed, but they decided not to unpack, just as a precaution, and they chose the two rooms closest to the stairs in case they needed to make a quick escape.

They spent the remaining hour and a half before dinnertime touring the cottage. Babs said nothing was off-limits, and that they were free to examine and handle the many antiques. It took them most of that time to explore a single room, picking through the knickknacks.

"Do you think all this stuff is magic?" asked Helen. "Just waiting for the right person to come along?"

"Good question. I have no idea." He held up a six-pack of Billy Beer. "But probably not. Then again, does it have to be magic? It's like that teapot the fates gave me. They said it would be helpful against a dragon and it was, even if it wasn't magic."

"No, they didn't say that. They said the teapot couldn't hurt."

"But it did help us escape."

"No, you helped us escape by using it as a distraction. You could've just as easily thrown a rock. There was nothing unique about the teapot that made it the right tool for that job. And the fates practically said that they get a lot of credit for stuff they don't do."

Troy played with an old marionette, making the wooden puppet dance a jig. "But I did use the teapot, so they do get credit for that one."

"Do they? What if you had used a rock? You'd still have that teapot, and if some day it came in handy, you'd think how fortuitous. And if you stuck it in the back of your closet and never thought about it again, you wouldn't say the fates were slacking on the job."

He made the puppet nod, cup its chin in a thoughtful pose. "I can't argue with you."

"Will you stop that?"

The simple wooden puppet held up its hands in mock innocence. "Stop what?"

She grinned at the puppet, then at him. "If you don't stop playing with that, I might have to reassess your cool factor."

"Really? What's my cool factor now, pray tell?"

The puppet cupped its face and looked eagerly at her. It had no eyes, but he somehow conveyed everything through body language.

She laughed. "Don't tell me you've never picked up a puppet before."

"Oh no. I love puppets. When I was a kid, I wanted to be a puppeteer for a while."

Helen feigned a shocked stagger. "Oh, gods above, please tell me that's not true. You're not cool at all. You're a dork!"

"Puppets aren't dorky. They're an ancient and venerated art."

Achilles, a Slinky wrapped around his head, whined at Helen's hooves. She bent down and untangled him.

"Whatever, dork."

"You're just jealous because you haven't mastered the art of ventriloquism."

"Ventriloquism? Well, I take it all back. You're clearly more awesome than I realized."

He handed her the crossbars. "Go on. Try it. It's a lot of fun."

She attempted to make the marionette dance, but it only looked as if it were having a spasm. It was fun watching the little wooden figure convulse.

"You're moving it too much, Hel. You need to use small gentle movements."

Troy put his hand on hers and guided her.

It felt weird, though not bad. Troy had touched her before, but this was different somehow. It might have been feelings she wasn't comfortable with or the strange intimacy of trying to bring a semblance of life to a block of wood. Her hands tingled, and it wasn't because of curses.

She stopped watching the puppet and looked at him as he intently focused not on the puppet, but on their hands.

"There you go, Hel. That's better. See, not so hard, right?"

"Yes," she said. "Dance, puppet, dance."

Troy looked into her eyes so suddenly she was too surprised to look away. She swallowed, though her mouth was terribly dry.

"Hel..."

Warmth ran up her thigh, and she jumped, breaking contact, destroying the moment. If there had been a moment. She wasn't so sure about that.

She rubbed her hands together. He did the same.

"Hel..."

Now this was a moment. She had no doubt about that. She was terrified of whatever he might say next.

Achilles barked, shattering the awkward pause. She didn't know if she should be grateful for that or not.

The puppet danced. No one was holding its strings. The warmth in Helen's pocket remained.

"I guess some things here are magic," he said.

She pulled the warm amulet from her pocket. She pointed it at the puppet.

"Stop."

The marionette halted its capering and stood still.

"It's not the puppet," she said. "It's the amulet."

She commanded the puppet to dance again, and it did so. Some simple experimentation with some of the other objects in the room showed that their relic could bestow animation to the inanimate. They made the Slinky slither, and an old boot hop. The orders couldn't be too elaborate, and only one object at a time could be animated. Attempts to bring a whole basket of golf balls to life worked only on one. Troy was better with the amulet, perhaps due to his puppeteer experience. Objects could twist and move in cartoonish ways under his command. He got an old wooden tabletop radio to sway and bob while playing a song.

"How fun," said Babs.

She was a quiet old lady, and they hadn't noticed her enter. Achilles growled.

"Dinner is ready," said Babs. "You'll find a nice orecchiette with broccoli and chickpeas on the table. Please help yourselves. Leave the dishes. I'll take care of them later."

"You aren't eating with us?" asked Troy.

"Oh, I'm afraid not. I must prepare things for you."

"Prepare what things?"

She smiled. Shadows pooled under her eyes and in dozens of wrinkles on her wizened face. "There's time to discuss such things later. Now eat. You'll need your strength."

The old woman slunk down the hall, gliding more than walking, swinging her long thin arms like pendulums.

Helen whispered, "Now tell me that isn't creepy."

24

After their battle with the dragon, the members of the Wild Hunt were too broken, battered, and beaten to chase after Helen and Troy. The orcs had just enough energy to ride out of the preserve. The spirits refused to give directions to a good bar, but where their spirits and gods failed them, GPS technology proved more helpful.

They found a run-down shack off the interstate that called itself a tavern. Under normal circumstances Nigel might have disagreed, but the place had four walls, cold-ish beer, and a jukebox, so the Wild Hunt called it close enough and settled in for a few hours of celebration, to treat their scrapes, their broken bones and lacerated flesh, with warm beer, classic rock, and hot wings. Medical care, the traditional orc way.

The orcs' biggest strength had always been their ability to recover from injury. It wasn't regeneration. They were still hurt. Nigel was fairly certain he'd broken a few ribs and maybe had a concussion. But he relished the aches and bouts of dizziness. They reminded him he was alive.

As the ancient orc saying went, "That which does not kill me can kiss my ass."

It was that legendary refusal to surrender to pain, to instead draw strength from it, that had given the orcs a reputation for stubbornness when meeting death. The more painful an orc's injuries, the more determined he was to keep going. It wasn't uncommon for an orc to recover completely from his injuries before being willing to die from them, a paradox they had no problem with.

The Wild Hunt packed in the nameless tavern and shared tales of bravery and adventure. Once they covered the dragon-fighting bit, they had to stretch the bounds of heroic triumph for this modern world. Jenny Gutspitter regaled them with her latest real estate sale, of a property that had long haunted her sales portfolio. Alan Spleenspearer told of the time, often told of before but it was somehow different now, when he bedded that drunken supermodel. Franklin, still covered in dried dragon blood and vomit, mentioned that time he noticed he had free cable but didn't let the cable company know about it. Nigel spoke of his greatest triumph (second-greatest now), that week when he spotted an accountancy error that would have cost the company millions, taught his son to ride a bicycle, and defeated that giant possum living in his attic, all while passing a kidney stone.

After each story the orcs would raise their mugs and cheer without concern for the other customers, and soon their boisterous celebration drove these few individuals from the darkened sanctuary. The staff, only three people, didn't mind. The Wild Hunt brought plenty of cash and tipped well.

The celebration passed into the evening. The only indication of the passing of time was in the dimming of the light in the tavern's two tiny windows. It might well have gone on into the next day if not for the arrival of Shoth, the avatar of death itself.

The avatar came through the front door and brought a hot wind with him. This was a positive sign, as orc tradition put hot death well above cold. No one had to be told who he was or why the pale figure was there. He wore a dapper crimson suit and fedora. Shadows covered his face. His eyes weren't visible, but his teeth were. The pointed white fangs formed a grim rictus.

The Wild Hunt continued their revelry. They didn't ignore death, but they refused to acknowledge Shoth with more than a glance or a nod. He strode quietly to the bar, ordered a fruity mixed drink that the bartender was unfamiliar with, then patiently instructed the bartender in how to make it before finding a seat at Nigel's table without waiting to be invited.

Shoth's voice was a smooth, sliding serpent that slipped from his unmoving grin and slithered into his listeners' ears.

"Having fun?"

Nigel said, "Yes."

"Good. Good." Shoth removed his hat, smoothed the brim. "You've certainly earned it."

"Am I dead?" asked Franklin.

"You? Oh, no, not you, dear boy," replied Shoth. "Though I must say I'm amazed you aren't. But death is full of surprises, isn't it? Even for me."

Nigel didn't ask about his own mortal state. If he was dead, he'd find out soon enough.

"Nice suit," he said.

"Just something I had sitting in the closet. I hope it's not too old-fashioned. It's been a few decades since I've been called down to the material plane."

Shoth was an avatar of death, but it was a very specific type of death he brought. He came for orcs who died in glorious battle, but this alone wasn't enough to make him manifest. His charges must also have been of such singular stubbornness that they refused to lie down and die when it was obvious they should, and, while true oblivion awaited all orc souls, anyone who earned Shoth's graces got a night of passion and carousing before being added to the Mound of Unworthy Bones.

Nigel checked himself for any fatal wounds he might have failed to notice. He noticed none, but if Shoth was here for Nigel, he wouldn't have. He would be surprised, though, because his Shoth should be a female.

"Grog sent me," said the avatar. "He's not happy you're wasting time."

"Then maybe he should get off his lazy ass and kill these mortals himself," said Nigel.

Shoth's smile widened. "Would that he could. Rules, y'know."

"He could do us a favor and back off then."

Shoth stirred his drink but didn't sip it. He hadn't taken a sip yet. Perhaps because his mouth couldn't open.

"I'm just the messenger."

Peggy, who was nearly as pale as the avatar of death, with a smile that was, truthfully, a touch more off-putting, said, "Was that the message?"

"Oh, there was something else. Something about ending the cycle. Something else about the most important tool at your disposal should the worst come to pass. Can't recall what it was, but he seemed to think it worth mention." He tapped his long white nails, clawlike, against the table. "I tried to pay attention, but you know how that guy is. What's the word I'm looking for?"

"An asshole," said Nigel.

Shoth chuckled, and every fly in the place died. The jukebox fell silent, cutting off the Journey playlist Becky Bonebreaker had selected. The bar fell silent.

"That's the word." Shoth ran his finger around the edge of his glass. "Regardless, it seemed important to him, so you might want to consider that."

"We'll do what we're supposed to do," said Nigel, "but we'll do it our way. The next time you see Grog tell him that."

"If it's just the same to you, I'd rather not. I try to avoid that guy. Not always easy. The orc portion of the heavens is rather small. And I'm not as busy as I once was, so we do run into each other more than I'd like. But such is our lot. He didn't ask to be your god. I didn't ask to be your avatar. And you didn't ask to be mortals. Yet we carry on, as we must."

Shoth stood. "But as much as I would enjoy dallying, I have a party to get to."

"Who are you here for?" asked Nigel. "It has to be one of the women. Or James."

James scoffed. "He can't be here for me. You're in male form."

The other orcs chuckled.

"What's so funny?" asked James.

Nigel punched James in the shoulder hard enough to knock him out of his chair.

"Buddy, we all know you're gay. We've known for a long time."

"You know?"

They murmured their positive replies.

"Your love of musical theater kind of gave it away," said Nigel.

"You can be straight and love musicals," said James.

"True, but when you get drunk, you won't shut up about Minnelli and Streisand."

"Your favorite movie is *Funny Girl*," added Franklin.

Peggy said, "You once punched me because I didn't know the difference between lavender and lilac."

James smashed his fist into the table, breaking the legs and spilling beer and pretzels across the floor.

"They're two different colors!"

He stifled his rage and took a moment to regain his composure.

"Wow. I can't believe I thought I was hiding it. Why didn't you say anything?"

"I always thought we should," said Franklin, "but I was overruled."

"It didn't seem important," added Nigel. "Although in retrospect, maybe it would've been easier on you if we'd put it out there. We weren't really sure about it."

"We figured you'd let us know when you were ready," said Peggy.

James grunted. "Gary always said I was being paranoid. Said you wouldn't care."

"Do we still have to call him your roommate?" asked Nigel. "Or is *life partner* the preferred term?"

"Funny. Hadn't really thought about it," said James.

Shoth said, "Though this is a touching scene of camaraderie, I should be going. Becky Bonebreaker, I hope you enjoy carrot cake and close-up magic because we must be off."

Becky, who had been quietly sitting by Nigel's side, said, "But I'm not dead."

The avatar of death pointed to a tree branch sticking through her chest.

"This? This is nothing," she said. "I've had paper cuts worse than this."

Shoth adjusted his hat. "Why do they always make this difficult? Becky, your wound is fatal. You died four hours ago, and it's time to admit this."

She stood, grabbed her leather jacket. She stuck her finger through the hole where she'd been impaled. In hindsight, the whole *being dead* thing was rather obvious.

The orcs raised their mugs and bottles and cheered.

Becky fell over, dead.

Shoth put his hat back on. The avatar of the stubborn dead shoved his hands in his pockets and walked out of the bar. He paused at the door and swept his eyeless gaze across the room, aiming at no one and everyone at the same time.

"See you around."

And then he was gone. His ghastly smile was the last thing to go, sticking around for a few seconds after his face was gone.

The Wild Hunt celebrated for a few hours more after his departure. Becky's corpse, with a beer taped in her hand and a cigar dangling from her lips, was propped in a place of honor at the bar, where the staff did their best to pretend they weren't put off by it. By the grace of Shoth, the jukebox returned to playing Becky's Journey compilation, and they sang a rousing rendition of every song from *Infinity* in Becky's memory.

If their gods had a problem with the delay, they wisely kept silent.

25

The Mystery Cottage's table was set with more than vegetarian pasta. It wasn't quite a feast, but there was plenty to eat. Breads, a selection of cheeses, and cake for dessert. Helen didn't eat any of it. Troy ate without hesitation. He tempted her with a plate of vegetarian pasta, but she passed.

"I've got a granola bar in my room," she said.

"Suit yourself, Hel, but you're missing out."

"I'm telling you it's a trap."

He buttered a hot roll. "You don't know that."

"You don't not know that," she said.

"I never thought you were the suspicious type."

"I wasn't. But then my boss tried to sacrifice me to his god."

Troy sighed. "You can't let one bad experience control your life." He threw a piece of bread to Achilles, who wolfed it down. "It passes the dog test."

"So does his own ass."

She picked up a fork, poked the pasta. It did smell delicious.

Helen set down her utensil, pushed away from the table. "All I know is that in all the legends I've heard there's no such thing as a free lunch. There's always some catch."

"You might be onto something there," he admitted. He'd already eaten enough that there seemed little point in stopping now.

"I'm going to bed," said Helen. "It was a long day, and I want to be ready for whatever challenge awaits us tomorrow. Just promise me you'll be careful, Troy."

"I'll keep an eye on that wheel of brie." He winked. "See you tomorrow, Hel."

She smiled, walked away with Achilles trailing behind. When she glanced over her shoulder she could've sworn she caught him checking her out. His gaze darted from her back to his pasta.

She wondered if that was a blush on his cheeks or the dim lighting of the old chandelier.

She said, "Just don't come running to me when that second helping of cursed salad transforms you into a pig."

He held up his hand in a Boy Scout salute. "Won't hear an oink from me."

Troy ate his fill and retired for the evening. He wasn't tired, but there wasn't much else to do in the Mystery Cottage. He played around with the amulet, bestowing life on random objects in his room. After getting bored with that, he read a book for an hour. Having exhausted his entertainment options, he tried to sleep.

He climbed into his nice comfy bed and closed his eyes. It didn't work.

This was unusual. So unusual, he could remember the last time he'd had trouble falling asleep. His mom had gone into the hospital with a burst appendix, and it'd been touch and go for a few hours. That had been nine years ago.

Since then he'd always slept like a baby. Untroubled. Relaxed. Not tonight.

He sat at the edge of the bed and flipped open his phone. It was barely eleven. Imogen would be up. He dialed her number.

"Hey, li'l bro," she said. "What's up?"

"Didn't wake you, did I?" he asked.

"You're kidding, right? How's the questing going?"

"Good," he replied. "Almost got eaten by a dragon earlier today."

"Cool."

He paced around the bed once, then again.

"Imogen, I think I need some advice."

Silence.

"Hello? Are you still there?" he asked.

"Yes."

More silence.

"Imogen?"

"Yes, I'm here. I'm just trying to absorb what you're telling me. You want advice. From me."

"Well, you're my sister. And a woman."

Silence again. Troy waited for her response. It didn't come.

"This call is about a woman? You're calling *me* for *advice* about *women*? You?"

He put the phone to his chest and shook his head. He placed the phone back to his ear. "It's not that weird."

"It's pretty weird," said Imogen. "If there's one thing you

don't need help with, it's women. And calculus. And athletics. And...hey, when have you ever needed my help?"

"When I was six you helped me get my kite out of a tree."

"Oh yeah."

She said nothing, but he could imagine the smile on her face. Imogen had rarely resented him for his talents, but he knew he could be irritating to live with. Especially for his big sister, who would've easily been the star in any other family.

"Is this about Helen?" she asked.

"How'd you know?"

"How hard is it to put that together? What's the problem?"

"I like her."

"Cool. And how is that a problem?"

"I mean I really like her."

"No shit," she replied with breathless sarcasm. "So tell her. Problem solved. You're welcome."

The phone beeped as she hung up. He stared at the phone as if it had betrayed him. Fifteen seconds later it rang, and he answered.

"Very funny," he said.

"I thought so," said Imogen.

"You don't have to enjoy this so much."

"I don't have to, but I will. So you like this young woman. How serious are we talking about?"

He thought about it. He'd been thinking about it for a few hours now, behind other thoughts, and the answer remained unclear.

"I don't know."

"OK. That's honest. We can work with that. You've liked girls before. You've dated plenty. And you've never been hurting for confidence with the fairer sex. The question is what makes this situation different?"

He lay on the bed and closed his eyes.

"Is it the minotaur thing?" asked Imogen.

"I don't know," he admitted. "I mean, I know it's not the way she looks. She's actually very pretty when you look at her. Not traditionally, of course. But she has a great smile, and knows how to handle herself. Did I tell you she punched a dragon?"

"You have always liked strong women," said Imogen. "And tall ones too, if I remember right."

"You do."

"Hey, I'm not judging anything here. I don't remember much of her from that one time we met, but she had a nice figure and she seemed cool enough. I thought the tail was kind of cute, honestly."

"Me too." He sat up. "But what if it is a problem?"

"What if you're shallow?" she said.

"Not the way I would've put it."

"Hey, you called me, little brother. No need to tiptoe around the question. To which I say relax. You aren't shallow. If you were shallow you'd be dating some empty-headed chick with big tits who was always telling you how awesome you are. It's not as if you'd have trouble finding one."

This was true. Troy had always been popular. He'd never hurt for dates. He'd never been in a serious relationship, but it hadn't been because there weren't any applicants for the position. He'd been too busy for the most part. People thought he was good at stuff without much work, but the truth was that he had to work. He picked things up fast, but he also had a habit of finding everything fascinating. He was always exploring something new, and women had been a pleasant diversion from his life, but he'd never pursued them seriously. Usually he enjoyed them as they passed through.

"Let's put aside the minotaur thing for a moment," said Imogen. "What else is bothering you?"

He didn't know, and that was what bothered him. Uncertainty was a foreign concept to Troy.

"You're worried because you like this girl," said Imogen.

"That's what I already said."

"No. Listen closely. You genuinely *like* this one. And not how you like everyone else. You're a people person, Troy. You get along with everyone. You find the bright side in everyone. You like people, and they like you. But this is different because this is someone you like specifically. This is someone who you want to like you back."

He was about to interrupt, but she knew him too well.

"Don't interrupt. There's a big difference between being liked and being *liked*. I'm not sure you've ever been liked like that. Everyone adores you, but it's a distant sort of adoration. It's like having good feelings about an actor or a pro athlete. It's less about who that person is than what they represent. You've always been this ideal, this great guy, perfect son, fun dude, boyfriend material. That's nothing to complain about, but it isn't the same as being liked in a personal way.

"If I had to guess, I'd say that's what's bothering you. If Helen was some chick who fell into your lap, you'd have no problems here. You don't want her to be that. You want to be liked for who you are. The problem is that you can't help but ask yourself if maybe who you are, under all the sheen and popularity, is maybe someone not worth liking. That's risky stuff. Especially when you like someone yourself and want them to return the favor."

Troy said nothing.

"Am I wrong?" she asked.

"No, I think you nailed it. When did you get so deep?"

"I've always been deep. You've just been too busy being handsome to notice."

"What do I do?"

"Seriously?" Imogen clicked her tongue into her phone. "You still don't know? Ask her out, you dope. Or at least tell her how you feel."

"But what if she doesn't—"

"She will."

"You don't know that."

"No, you're right. I don't. Not everyone goes for the good-looking, intelligent, athletic, fun type. She might be into bad boys or quiet, angry loners. She might be into guys who dress up like chickens and play jazz flute. But I'm willing to bet she's not."

"But what if—"

"I'm going to have to cut you off there, Troy. I'd love to sit here all night talking to you about what might happen, but in the end, the only way to find out is to just do it already. I can't guarantee it'll work out. I can't guarantee it won't blow up in your face, and you'll end up looking like a chump. For most of us, that's just the way life works. You take your chances, and you see what happens. Congratulations, little bro, you've stumbled into being a regular person."

"I don't think I like it," he admitted.

"Who does? I find it comforting that you can experience uncertainty, but talking to me is a waste of time. You should be talking to her."

"You're right. Thanks, Sis."

"Anytime, little bro. Good luck."

He hung up, screwed up his courage, and walked across the hall. He wiped the sweat from his palms. This thump in his chest, the way the hairs on his arms stood on end, this was all new stuff. He'd felt pressure before. He'd experienced all the adrenaline and edginess that came with it. Despite his many talents, he wasn't perfect. He failed more often than people gave him credit for. They tended to downplay the failures because his triumphs were so much more impressive. Nobody cared if you dropped a pass if you caught six interceptions.

He knocked on the door. Helen didn't answer.

"Hel," he said to the door. "I know it's late, but can we talk?"

No answer.

He knocked again. "It's important."

He opened the door a crack and stuck his head in.

"Hel?"

She wasn't there, but he heard something scratching from the closet door. He opened it, and Achilles slunk out. The dog's tail was flattened and his ears pressed low. He ran around the room, sniffing and growling.

"How'd you get in there?" asked Troy.

Achilles exited the room, then stuck his head back in and barked at Troy.

"What's wrong?"

Achilles barked again.

"Can't you just tell me? I know you're not an ordinary dog, so do we have to keep pretending? If you can talk, this'd be a lot simpler."

Achilles ducked into the hallway and barked. Troy followed the dog, already halfway toward the staircase.

"Should I get my sword?"

Achilles whined and wagged his fluffy tail.

"I'll take that as a yes."

Troy retrieved his enchanted weapon. He put on some pants too, since boxers weren't the best armor. He stuffed the amulet in his pocket. He added the shield. If he was wrong, if Helen was just down in the bathroom or kitchen, it might be hard to explain wandering around fully equipped, but better safe than sorry.

He followed Achilles downstairs. The Mystery Cottage was quiet. The lights were dimmed, and the place seemed like a renovated dungeon where all the skeletons had been removed and replaced with porcelain curios and motel-art oil paintings.

Achilles trotted back and forth before a closet door. Troy debated forgetting the entire business and going back upstairs. Helen could take care of herself. There was no reason to assume anything was awry. A dog was hardly a credible witness. Even a possibly magic dog.

"If there's a bag of kibble in there, I'm not opening it."

He threw open the door and readied himself for whatever might come charging at him.

It was only a closet, full of old clothes and shoes.

He lowered his sword and glared at Achilles.

"Very funny. Are you done wasting my time?"

Something stirred in the closet.

With a whine, Achilles scampered behind Troy.

A long brown tendril lashed out, grabbing the shield. He sliced the tentacle with one clean stroke of his sword. The thing in the closet withdrew.

He stepped back. The remnants of the closet thing were still draped over his arm. Brown fabric, like that of a cheap coat, on one side. On the other, a polyester lining.

The thing in the closet growled as it spilled into the room. It wasn't a monster hiding in the closet. It was the contents of the closet itself. Old coats and shoes, polka-dotted ties and tan slacks. They swirled and congealed into a hulking humanoid form, eight feet tall, with a dusty green bowling ball for an eye and a broken umbrella for a beak.

The monster struck. The magic shield zipped Troy to the side. A red feather boa wrapped around the shield and yanked it off his arm. It hurled the shield. Troy ducked beneath it. The metal disk embedded itself deep into the wall.

A loose coat fell over the creature's bowling ball eye, and it stumbled blindly. Its arms flailed. It smashed an antique mirror and crushed a writing desk. The monster groped, groaning and gurgling, as Troy and Achilles watched from the other side of the room.

Achilles looked up at Troy and barked softly.

"OK, so you were right," said Troy. "Something is wrong here."

The coat monster roared as it shook its body with such force that loose raincoats, hats, and an encyclopedia were flung across the room. The castoff bits squirmed and wriggled across the floor. Except for the encyclopedia. It fidgeted in a small hopping circle. The coat fell from the monster's eye, and it fixed Troy with a glare.

His choices were limited. He could run for it, but the monster was sure to give chase. Or he could stand his ground and hope that magic sword trumped fabric monster. In the brief moments he had to consider, he knew running wasn't a choice. He couldn't find Helen if he was fleeing.

Troy held his blade before him with his feet firmly planted in a wide stance, but most of his weight on his toes, ready to move. He looked the monster in its bowling ball without blinking.

"I've never had the opportunity to slay a monster before," he said. "Want to be my first?"

The monster tilted its head-like protrusion to one side and stepped back. He was amazed that had worked, but he was also smart enough not to let his surprise show.

"Where's Helen?" he asked.

The monster chuckled. It opened its jaws to reveal teeth made of brown loafers and ran a fuzzy yellow scarf across its lips.

"If you've hurt her—"

The monster charged. It expected Troy to attempt to avoid the attack, but he moved forward to meet it and thrust his sword deep in the center of its mass. The creature shrieked and came toppling down on him.

Troy swung his sword and struggled free of the mass of old clothes threatening to smother him. He jumped to his feet and stabbed at the pile of apparel covering the floor. Seven seconds later he noticed Achilles watching from the corner of the room.

The monster, whatever it was, however it had been animated, was dead. Or close enough. Troy stabbed it a few more times to be sure. He plucked the shredded remains of a fedora off the tip of his sword.

"Better safe than sorry. Right?"

Achilles hopped through the remains of the beast and ran into the closet. Without the monster in the way, the door now opened onto a spiral staircase winding downward.

"What were you guarding?" Troy prodded the bowling ball. "One way to find out."

He wasted a minute trying to free the shield embedded in the wall, but he wasn't strong enough. He gave up and descended the staircase. Achilles followed close behind. At the bottom a sitting room waited. It smelled of gingerbread and decay. Plastic covered the furniture. It was a sensible precaution to keep the mummified corpses from decomposing on the fabric. The five desiccated mummies (and the skeleton of their dog) caused Troy to retch.

Up to now the quest had had its dangerous moments, but aside from the death curse hanging over their heads, it had seemed like a grand adventure. The grim scene changed all that. The walls were adorned with portraits, some of them decades old and faded with age. The smiling families chilled him in a way the corpses hadn't.

His first thought was of Helen. He hadn't gotten the chance to tell her how he felt yet, and he wondered if he ever would. The thought bothered him more than the idea of dying.

He was getting ahead of himself. Helen could take care of herself. She was stronger and tougher than Troy. He wasn't dead yet.

A voice echoed from somewhere. Helen's voice. Achilles's ears perked up, and he scratched at an innocuous-looking door. Troy kicked it open and steeled himself for battle.

There weren't any monsters. Just a cozy kitchen with an art deco design straight from the thirties. Blue and white tile. Bright-green refrigerator and oven, both twice as large as ordinary appliances. A table and chairs made of chrome and vinyl. Babs stood over the sink in the middle of washing her hands. A large burlap bag writhed at her feet.

"Let me out of here, you crazy bitch!" screamed Helen.

Babs rinsed her spiderlike hands. "Oh dear, how inconvenient."

Troy pointed his sword at Babs. "Let her go."

The old woman cackled. "I can't do that, young man. It's been ages since I've enjoyed fresh minotaur. You don't expect me to deprive myself of such a delicacy, do you?"

The bag stopped twitching. "Troy?"

"I'm here, Hel! Don't worry. I'll take care of this."

"She's stronger than me!"

To demonstrate, Babs hefted Helen off the floor with one hand and threw the bag over her shoulder as if it were a bag of packing peanuts. Babs's spindly, withered form didn't as much as slouch under the weight. "How did you get past my monster?"

"Magic sword," said Troy. "And I'll use it on you unless you drop that bag right now."

Babs snickered. She twisted her head in his direction. The motion was too smooth, as if the old woman's neck operated on a well-oiled gear.

"You threaten me with magic, but I am magic. No enchantment of mortal or god can harm me. The sharpest blade cannot pierce my wicked flesh. The mightiest club cannot part the hairs on my gray head. And I cannot die because I do not live."

"Is that some kind of riddle?"

"No, it's merely the facts. You might as well put away your sword and go back to your room. I'll get to you soon enough."

"But I thought you were here to guide us."

"No, I'm here to eat you."

"Why?"

"That's a silly question. I'm hungry. I was polite enough to feed you. It's only fair that you return the favor. Your friend here seems like she'll be the finest meal I've had in ages."

"I didn't eat any of your food!" shouted Helen.

"You didn't? That's a fly in the ointment." Babs smacked her lips. "I suppose I'll eat you just the same. It's technically against the rules, but I don't mind if you don't."

"I mind!" Helen yelled.

"Can't say that I blame you, dear, but if I listened to every dinner's complaints, I'd never get anything to eat."

"Is this some kind of test?" asked Troy.

"No, it's a late-night snack," said Babs. "I don't know how I can be any clearer about this."

She opened the oven and started shoving Helen inside.

"Ow!" said Helen.

"You are a big one," said Babs.

"Hey!"

"No offense, young lady. I knew I should've torn you in half."

Troy raised his sword.

Babs kept shoving, not bothering to turn around. "I wouldn't do that if I were you. If you go to your room I'll bring you a nice ham sandwich and a Pepsi. Doesn't that sound more pleasant than having your heart ripped from your chest?"

He sprang, bringing the blade down where her neck and shoulder met. The sword clanged as if striking stone. It didn't so much as nick Babs's housecoat.

Her hand was wrapped around his throat. He hadn't seen her move. It was just there, strangling the life from him. She grinned with her perfect white dentures as she dropped him in one of the chairs.

"Courage makes a fine broth, but the aftertaste of stupidity can ruin a dish." Babs picked up his sword and handed it to him, hilt first. "Now be a good boy and wait your turn."

She turned her back on him as she wrestled Helen into the oven. He resisted the urge to attack her. It was possible she had a weak point, but he couldn't risk it. If he was going to stop Babs, he had to be smart about it.

He noticed a rusty old helmet among the cookie jars and cutlery on the countertops. The helmet was marked by the same design as the one on the back of his hand. They'd found the next relic, just sitting there, but he was too concerned with saving Helen to think much about it.

He moved slowly toward the exit. She made no move to stop him.

"There's no escape now," she said, "but you're free to amuse yourself trying."

He returned to the ghastly den. She might have been lying, but he doubted it. Even if he could escape and find help, he'd never get back in time to save Helen.

He ran through the magical items they'd collected on their quest so far. The sword hadn't worked on her. The shield might have protected him, but it was stuck in a wall. That left only the amulet in his pocket and its ability to animate the lifeless.

The mummies seemed an obvious target, but it only worked on one object at a time, and a single zombie probably wouldn't bother Babs.

He sat on the arm of the sofa, away from the corpses, and scanned the room for a suitable minion. The only remotely threatening object was a drooping houseplant. There was that old suit of armor in the foyer, but again, he doubted it would accomplish much. Brute force wasn't going to work. He had to be smart about this.

A plan came to him. Not so much a plan as an outline, but time was not on his side.

Troy tapped his sword in the dirt. The brown-and-red soil

climbed its way out of the pot with the houseplant still growing out of its head. It stretched its small form.

"Didn't give me much to work with, did you?"

"Circumstances beyond my control," said Troy.

"What is your command, master?"

"How are you at distracting evil witches?"

The elemental rolled its shoulders, causing the houseplant leaves to shake. "I'll do what I can, but don't expect much."

Troy pushed open the kitchen door. Helen was nearly all in the oven.

"I'm giving you one last chance," he said. "Let her go."

Babs's head twisted all the way around to smirk at him. "It's a generous offer, but I've already put far too much work into getting your friend in here."

He clutched the amulet in his pocket. He'd only get one shot at this.

"Get her."

The diminutive elemental hurled itself across the room to strike her in the face. He exploded in a choking cloud of dust. Babs clawed at the dirt wrapped around her head. She charged blindly at Troy. He anticipated her attack, moving to one side. As she bolted past him, he thrust his magic sword between her ankles. She tripped, scrambling across the linoleum like a wild cat with a bag over its head. Her shrieks were muffled by mouthfuls of dirt.

Troy pointed the amulet at the oven. "Spit her out."

The amulet warmed in his hand as the oven came to life. With a harsh, gurgling retch it vomited the burlap sack onto the floor. He knelt beside it, only to have Helen's flailing knee, elbow, or other body part smack him in the throat from the sack.

"Hel," he croaked. "It's me."

"Troy?"

"Don't move. I'm going to cut you out."

He sliced open the sack with the sword. She pulled herself free, sitting up.

"I'm going to kill that crazy bitch."

Babs stood. She'd pulled off enough dirt to expose the left side of her face. "You're more stubborn than I thought, children, but your tricks only forestall the inevitable."

She slunk forward with a liquid grace, as if she were nothing more than flesh wrapped around slithering oil.

"You caught me off guard last time," said Helen. "You won't be so lucky this time."

She unleashed a haymaker that would've crushed mortal bones but only put a stagger in Babs's step. The old lady backhanded Helen. She flew across the kitchen and into the wall.

"I am as ancient as the earth, but even my patience has its limits." Babs clawed the last bits of soil from her face, pulling off bits of skin, revealing the slimy green muscles beneath. She was on Troy in a moment. Her hot hand burned around his throat. She twisted the oven's dial. Orange-and-red flames crackled to life like a portal to a hellish underworld.

"Eat her," gasped Troy.

Babs cackled. "I intend to."

"I wasn't talking"—he struggled for his last breath, squeezing the amulet in his hand—"to you."

The oven sprang. It snapped Babs up in its jaws and devoured her. She got stuck halfway, fighting and shrieking. Her hand squeezed tighter around his throat, and everything blurred. He smelled burning flesh. Swords and clubs might not hurt the ancient hag, but judging by her terrible screeching, fire seemed to do the trick. The oven struggled to slurp her down, threatening to drag him in with her. On the verge of unconsciousness, he saw only the red haze of the hungry flames.

Helen yanked him free. Babs's hand refused to release him, and the smoldering limb broke off. The oven snapped shut and slid back into its proper place. Smoke billowed from its edges as its occupant pounded and roared.

Helen pulled the severed forearm from his throat. The still-living limb flailed. Deciding not to take any chances, she pinned it between her leg and the linoleum. It continued to squirm.

She put her hand on his chest to feel the steady rise and fall of his breath. Achilles licked his face, and he groaned.

"Dumb magic dog."

"Thank the gods." She threw her arms around him. The tight hug dredged up some phlegm, sending him into a coughing fit.

"The gods got us into this mess in the first place." He smiled with that boyish charm. Even half-conscious and with the bruises left by Babs's fingers, he was just short of adorable. All his coughing and retching did cause her to worry he'd throw up on her.

Babs's screams died down. The pounding faded. The stench of roasting witch remained just as strong. The disembodied hand drummed its fingers.

"Are you OK?" Helen asked.

"Are you?"

She helped him to his feet. The hand scurried away, taking shelter in a cupboard.

"We should probably get out of here," said Troy. "Who knows if that really killed her? She said she couldn't die."

Helen thought of the hand. Maybe it'd grow into another

witch given enough time. Or maybe it would just go on living forever. Either way, she considered it harmless for the moment.

They hurried to their rooms. Helen plucked the shield from the wall without much effort. They expected to be attacked, but nothing popped out at them as they gathered their luggage and made their way to the exit. At the threshold Troy stopped.

"Hold on. I almost forgot something."

He ran all the way back to Babs's hidden kitchen and grabbed the helmet. Metal screamed as the old witch punched her way free of the oven. The house trembled and shuddered.

Troy bolted toward the front door without looking back. He imagined Babs scrambling right behind him, but he didn't dare look.

Achilles barked.

"Troy, we gotta go!" shouted Helen from the porch.

With each step the rattling grew stronger. He vaulted over a tipped end table and narrowly missed being hit by a falling portrait of a foxhunt. They stepped off the porch just as the house rose into the air. The Mystery Cottage ascended, borne aloft by a pair of giant chicken legs. The monstrous structure took a step toward them. It knocked over several trees while shaking the earth with its stride.

The helmet flew out of Troy's hands and hovered above them. Its rust fell away, revealing a gleaming silver finish. Two pinpoints of yellow light appeared in its empty eyes, and thunder cracked in the clear night sky.

Somewhere the Lost God chuckled. The helmet fell at Troy's feet. The parking lot pavement cracked, and a dozen tall, proud trees withered and died in seconds.

Then there was only the quiet whistling of the wind through

the forest, sounding very much like the far-off screams of damned, demented souls.

The familiar cackle of Babs frightened the dead into silence.

She smiled down at Troy and Helen from her front porch. The hunched hag rubbed her hands together. "I'm afraid I can't step foot outside this old home, children. Oh, I suppose I could have my house step on you, but I'm not malicious. And since one of you didn't eat my food, I'm not so certain I'm allowed. Silly of me to think I could break the rules. Can't win them all. You've earned your lives. And your prize." She bowed, complete with a sweeping gesture of her long, gnarled arms. "Let's hope your world isn't made worse for it."

Her cabin mansion turned and stomped its way into the forest. Even after its footfalls ceased to shake the earth, the deathless witch's laughter echoed through the chilly night.

26

Helen and Troy drove until they found a truck stop with a restaurant where they found a booth, ordered some food they didn't want, and sat there, not talking, studying the silver helmet they'd won for not getting eaten.

Neither said much of anything. Both were too busy listening to the din of thoughts in their own heads.

"Hey, Troy," said Helen. "Thanks for not leaving me there. In the oven."

He pushed his cold eggs around with his fork. "Did you think I even considered it?"

"No, but it doesn't mean I can't say thanks."

"You're welcome."

They shared a smile.

"Hel..." He started but trailed off.

"Yes?"

"I just wanted to say that I like you."

She leaned back in the booth, took a bite of dry toast. Not because she was hungry, but it was something to do. "I like you too, Troy."

He said, "No, I mean, I really like you. Like, a lot."

Helen narrowed her eyes in a way that struck him as suspicious.

"I'm just trying to—" He waited for her to smile or nod. Or scowl. Or lean over and kiss him. Or throw the table in the air and storm out. Something. Anything. She only sat there.

"What I'm trying to say is that maybe we should, I don't know, like go see a movie or something sometime. After all of this is over."

"Wow." Her expression and body language remained unreadable. "You are really bad at this."

"Yeah. I guess I am. See, I've never actually asked anyone out before."

"What are you talking about? I've seen you with women."

"Oh, I've dated plenty," he said. "I've just never had to ask them out. Either they ask me, or we end up dating over time, like a natural progression. Never had to do the official 'Want to grab dinner sometime?' thing."

She smiled. Very slightly.

"So how about it?" he asked.

"No."

"What?"

"I said no."

Troy lost all interest in pretending to eat his eggs. "Don't you like me?"

"I'd rather not talk about it."

"Oh, OK."

He slouched in his chair. It was the first time she'd seen him slouch.

She picked up the helmet. "What do you think this does?"

"What did I do wrong?" he asked.

Helen set the helmet back down. "I really don't want to talk about it."

His hangdog expression confirmed he wasn't going to drop the subject.

"You didn't do anything wrong, Troy."

"Don't you like hanging out with me?"

She nodded.

"Don't you find me attractive?" he asked.

"That's a stupid question. Who doesn't find you attractive?"

"Then what's the problem? I'm not saying this has to be serious, but can it hurt anything to see what happens?"

It could hurt a lot of things, she thought.

"OK. You want to talk about this. Let's talk about it. Let's talk about the minotaur in the room. Let's talk about the horns and the tail and the fur. What about those things?"

"I don't think they matter to me," he said.

"You don't *think* they matter?"

Troy set down his fork and pushed away his plate, having lost even his fake appetite. "I won't lie to you. They could matter. But I don't think they will. I won't know, though, until we try."

She matched his slumped posture. "No, Troy, they won't matter. Not to you. Because you're so damn wonderful all the damn time. Everyone else sees Helen Nicolaides, cursed girl with horns. But not you. You see more than that."

"And how is that a bad thing?"

"It's bad because, for better or worse, this isn't about you and me. If we started dating, you have no idea what you'd be in store for. People would wonder why you were with me. People like us, we don't date. The world doesn't want us to. Because I'm what I am, and you're Wyatt Wingfoot."

"You lost me."

"She-Hulk can't date Wyatt Wingfoot."

She hoped the sentence would discourage him but wasn't surprised when it didn't.

"Wyatt Wingfoot is this amazing guy," she said. "Like you. He's good-looking and smart. He kicks ass. Hangs out with the Fantastic Four. Fights robots and saves the Earth. He's all kinds of awesome. And he sometimes dates She-Hulk, who is the Hulk's smarter cousin. But, despite the fact that Wyatt is amazing, he never gets serious with her because nobody wants to write that story."

"You're saying you don't want to go out with me because of a comic book character?"

"No, I'm saying we can't go out because of what that character represents. We don't live in a culture where regular guys, even amazing ones, have seven-foot monster girlfriends."

"You're not a monster."

"I look like one standing next to you. It'd be different with the genders reversed. Everybody gets beauty and the beast. But this thing between us, it'd be weird to most people."

"So you admit there's something here."

"Maybe. It could just be the excitement of the quest, though, a romantic fling brought up by all the dragon fighting. And as long as we're doing that, it might work, but what happens after the quest? Assuming we survive and don't destroy the world."

She leaned forward, almost put her hand on his, but folded them under her chin instead.

"You don't know what it will be like, Troy."

"I'm just talking about a date."

"Then what? What happens if it's more than that? What happens when you want to introduce me to your parents? What happens when your friends start making cow jokes or the tenth time some hot babe hits on you right in front of me because she assumes it'd be easy to steal you away? Or you start losing friends because they're not sure how to deal with your girlfriend? Do you think you're ready for that? Are you ready for people to start disliking you, being uncomfortable around you, just because your girlfriend has fur?

"You don't know what you'd be getting into. I'm not saying my life is bad. It isn't. But I'm reminded of what I am every day, and if we dated, you'd be reminded too. And you have the option of walking away from it. And I couldn't blame you if you did because there are days, lots of them, when I wish I could."

He wanted to tell her he wouldn't feel that way, but it would have been an empty promise. His own ethnic heritage came with baggage. People assumed things about him based on nothing more than a glance. He got around most of those by being personable and popular, but they were still there, popping up to annoy him on occasion.

He couldn't imagine what Helen dealt with. At school he'd heard the whispered jokes, the cruel jabs some of the other students could make. He didn't hear many because he was the cool popular kid, and he set the rules for his crowd. But he couldn't pretend that they weren't said or that many of his friends didn't say them when he wasn't around to disapprove.

He reached for her hands.

She pulled them away and hid them under the table.

"You're great," she said softly. "You have no idea how wonderful it is that you even asked. But you and me, we don't work together."

"Hel..."

She looked away. "Drop it, Troy."

He didn't want to, but he didn't see the point in arguing with her right now. There would be time to discuss it later. He hadn't given up, but he didn't press the issue.

She knew every thought running through his head. Troy wasn't easily discouraged. But he'd realize she was right sooner or later.

Helen excused herself to use the restroom. She locked herself in the small room that stank of cheap pine and that indefinable musty public bathroom smell. People knocked on the door. She ignored them until they went away.

She stared at the minotaur in the mirror, and as much as she wanted to hate her curse, this wasn't about horns or hooves. It went deeper, all the way to the place where a little girl wanted to believe a handsome prince could rescue her.

That girl wasn't there anymore.

"You suck."

Troy waited patiently for Helen to get back. After five minutes he resisted the urge to check on her. After eight he got out of the booth, walked halfway to the bathrooms, then changed his mind and turned back. After ten he found himself worrying, but he was determined to give her the space she needed.

He paid the bill and went outside to grab some air. He stood awkwardly in the parking lot. It was a new experience, this uncertainty. Helen was the first thing he had been unsure of in a long, long time. So long, he couldn't remember the last. Although he was positive there had to be at least one forgotten moment in his past.

He was wrong. This was the first.

A lunch wagon pulled into the parking lot. Lost in his own thoughts, he didn't pay it much mind. Not until the short, hairy man stepped out of it. Pollux Castor, the lunch wagon oracle, had found them again. Troy ran over.

"Am I glad to see you," he said.

Pollux glanced at Troy. "Something I can do for you, kid?"

"You can tell me what to do next. Isn't that why you're here?"

Pollux patted his belly. "I'm here for dinner. Now, if you'll excuse me..."

He pushed past Troy and walked toward the restaurant. Troy walked by his side.

"Don't you remember me?"

"Should I?"

"You helped me on my quest," said Troy.

"I've helped a lot of people on their quests. You'll have to be more specific."

"I was the guy with the...tall girl."

"Not ringing any bells."

Troy struggled to not say it. Pollux reached for the handle of the diner's door.

"The minotaur girl," said Troy softly.

Pollux stopped. "Oh, yes. I remember you two."

Troy hated himself for saying it, and he hated the world for making it such a big deal in the first place. It only proved Helen's point. She would always be the girl with fur.

Pollux said, "You're still alive. I wasn't certain you'd pass the first challenge, but you seem to be doing all right. You don't need my help. And if I'm not in Colorado by tomorrow night to show an unassuming middle manager how to get his hands on some golden fleece, you can kiss the Atlantic Ocean goodbye. The oracle business keeps me on a tight schedule. I just want to grab some steak and eggs and be on my way. Just follow the road you're on. It'll always lead you where you're going. Trust in yourself. Beware of Greeks bearing gifts. Other sagely advice. Et cetera, et cetera, et cetera."

"Can you at least tell me if I'm going to unleash a disaster?"

"I could, but why ruin the surprise?"

Troy was too tired to have this conversation. "Sorry. I shouldn't have bothered you."

"Don't worry about it."

Pollux went inside, leaving Troy with his thoughts. The short oracle came back a moment later.

"All right, all right. You seem like a good kid. I can spare a few minutes, but let's make this quick. What's bugging you?"

"It's Helen."

"Who?"

"The...tall woman I was with."

"Right, right. The *tall* one." Pollux rubbed his round chin. "Got a thing for her, do you?"

"How'd you know?"

"Just part of the oracle biz. Just like I know your next question. How do you win her over? Short answer: you don't. The way to another's heart, that isn't something I can help you with. It was different in days of yore. You met a woman, you slew a monster or fetched an enchanted rose from a frozen mountaintop, you get married. And sometimes it worked out. Sometimes the wife cooked her children in a stew and served them to her husband. Overall it was a simple system.

"Today it's a bit more complicated. I can tell you where to find a tree that grows golden apples that will make you immortal. I can tell you where to find a bottle holding the first ray of light ever to touch this world. I can tell you how to reach the kingdom of the gods above with a sailboat and a good sextant. But how to convince someone to trust you with their heart, that's not my department."

Pollux slapped Troy on the back.

"I wish I could tell you the right thing to say and the right way to say it. If I could slip you a love potion, I would. The only thing you can do is give her the time to figure it out on her own and be there when she's ready. And if she's never ready, be ready to move on. Unrequited love is bullshit. And it always ends up hurting everyone involved."

"You can't tell me if she changes her mind?"

"Everybody thinks they want to know the future," said Pollux. "But nobody does. Not really."

Troy said, "What are you hiding?"

"Oh, nothing important. Have a good life, kid."

He turned, but Troy grabbed Pollux by the arm.

"Ow. Just a word of advice. Manhandling an oracle is a good way to meet an ironic end."

"What is it?"

The look in Troy's eye told Pollux everything he needed to know. He'd seen it in the eyes of a hundred heroes more brave than wise. There was no reasoning with that type.

"By the end of this quest, one of you will have to die."

"What? How?"

"Don't know. Just know it has to happen. If you make it to the end of this journey, which I can't guarantee. But if you do, when the time comes, one or both of you is going to have to die because the gods love melodrama. And a story where two mixed-up kids conquer the world and become better for it, it might put a smile on your face, but it isn't going to be the stuff of legends.

"Sorry to break it to you like that, son. It's a hard pill to swallow, but you aren't the first hero screwed by the gods. You won't be the last. My advice is to try not to think about it and enjoy the journey."

He waited for Troy to release him. It took a few seconds.

"Best of luck to you," mumbled Pollux as he went into the diner.

Troy unfolded their map of destiny and stared at the big black question mark at the end.

Helen came out of the diner, and he quickly shoved the map back in his pocket.

"Was that the oracle?" she asked.

Troy nodded.

"Well...?" She paused, waiting for Troy to fill in the blank, but he didn't reply.

"Troy..."

"Nothing's wrong, Hel. He said we should keep on the road we're on."

He smiled. It was boyish and charming. It would've fooled anyone else, but Helen knew him better than that.

"What's wrong?" she asked. "What did he tell you?"

"Nothing. He told me nothing. We should get going. Should check on Achilles before he pees on my seats."

He walked away.

She glanced through the diner's dirty windows at Pollux, sitting at a booth. He noticed her looking at him and hid his face behind a menu.

Oracles hadn't been much help on this quest so far. She didn't give a damn about the future or the cryptic clues Pollux was sure to give her. She chalked up Troy's strange behavior to her rejection of him, and it wasn't surprising. The poor guy had probably never been turned down before. He'd get over it.

She hoped this stupid quest would be over with soon. The dragons and the monsters she could live with. She was even sort of enjoying them. But another week in the Chimera with Troy, and she might be tempted to say yes to his idiotic proposal. That scared the hell out of her, more than any cyclops or immortal witch ever could.

They hadn't gotten any sleep at the Mystery Cottage, and with the adrenaline wearing off and a lot on their minds, the road seemed long and dark and lonely. They found a motel. It wasn't a weird motel staffed by monsters. There were no legendary beasts in its parking lot. The most unusual thing about it was a fat guy enjoying a few midnight laps in the swimming pool, and that was more unsettling than otherwordly.

They got separate rooms. The clerk apologized because he couldn't put them beside each other, but Helen decided it was better that way. The more distance the better, and while it was only a matter of a few dozen extra feet, it all added up.

"See you in the morning, Hel," said Troy.

"Uh-huh."

She wished he'd never brought that date up. She'd been thinking it too, but she'd had the sense to leave it unspoken. That way they could've pretended they were just friends. Now the notion that they could be something more stood between them like a malicious spirit, grabbing their words and twisting them with all manner of horrible subtext and awkward implications.

She closed the door and locked it. Achilles had followed her in. He hopped on the bed, but she shooed him off.

"Don't get too comfortable. We've got to make sure this place is on the up-and-up."

She stripped off the blankets and sheets to be sure the bed wasn't some sort of vicious monster in disguise. She went through the drawers, found some stationery, a pen, a worn copy of the druidic tomes, revised edition. No goblins hid under the bed. The bathtub, as far as she could tell, was not some evil artifact waiting to devour her soul. And the television, while it did have a grainy image, wasn't especially menacing. After checking behind the paintings on the walls, she decided she was being paranoid. After double-checking that the closet wasn't a portal to some nameless dimension of horror, she sat on the unmade bed and dared to relax.

Achilles put his head on her lap.

"All clear, I guess." She picked him up and looked into his brown eyes. "Troy thinks you're magic. I'm beginning to think he's right. I know it's probably against the rules to admit it to us, but if you are magic, can you at least give me a sign?"

He licked her nose.

She smiled and set him beside her. "Close enough."

She unfolded her oracle map and crossed out the house on chicken legs. That left only the giant question mark at the end of their journey. One way or another, things were ending soon.

She was tired but couldn't sleep, so she decided a quick shower was in order. It was always better to shower at night so she wouldn't have to waste the forty-five minutes with a blow-dryer in the morning.

She stripped down, and while part of her wanted to avoid looking in the mirror, she forced herself to as she gave herself a quick brush-down from head to toe. Halfway through she noticed the fur on the carpet, but there seemed little point in stopping. She took her shower, standing under the hot water for longer than she really should've, but when she turned off the water she almost felt human again.

She was plugging in her extra-strength hair dryer when someone knocked on the door. She grabbed the cheap motel robe off the wall and wrapped it around herself. It was too tight in the shoulders and too short, showing most of her thighs.

"Go away. It's late," Helen shouted, before reaching the door. She had no interest in conversation right now. Not with oracles. Not with Troy. She only wanted to dry off and go to bed. She changed her mind after glancing through the peephole.

Agent Waechter's smiling face appeared to her.

She threw open the door and punched him in the stomach. He doubled over and fell to his knees.

"You son of a bitch—"

The two black-suited agents beside him drew their swords, and Helen balled her hands into fists.

"It's OK," gasped Waechter. "It's OK. Miss Nicolaides isn't dangerous. She certainly could've killed me with that blow if she'd wished."

Helen grinned. "Damn right."

The agents lowered their weapons.

"You set us up," said Helen. "You sent us into that witch's house blind."

"I did. But you must understand there are—"

"Rules," she said. "Everybody keeps telling us there are rules, but nobody seems to have the rule book handy."

She helped him up, though part of her wanted to pound him into a bloody mess. The agents couldn't have stopped her from doing so. She felt the power in her muscles. It was more than enough to flatten all three. The idea frightened and thrilled her. She had been more violent lately. She didn't know if it was the absence of her bracelet or the frustration of tonight or a little bit of both, but she found herself eager to hurt things.

Waechter was as good a target as any.

"You have every right to be upset," he said.

"I'm so glad to have your permission."

He stood, though still bent at a slight angle. "Miss Nico-laides...Helen..."

She glared down at him. He wasn't a small man, but he was still eminently crushable.

"Miss Nicolaides, I'm no happier about the path we've been forced on than anyone else. I'm only doing my job."

"Your job is to get me fed to a witch?"

"My job is to see if you're the right person for the job. These tests might not seem like it, but they're important. There are milestones on the road you walk, and it's essential that you pass them."

"Peachy. So it's your job to throw us into the dragon's lair and hope we don't get killed."

"More or less. Believe it or not, we are on your side."

"How am I supposed to believe anything you say?"

"I never lied to you. I never told you to trust the old woman."

Helen was tempted to punch him so hard that his head popped off like a cork. She imagined it sailing away, spinning end over end. She smiled.

"I don't trust you, Waechter, but I don't see how I have a choice. So tell me where to go and what to do, and I'll do it. As we've nearly reached the end of my patience and the only thing preventing me from beating the crap out of you is that I just want to get some sleep, I suggest you spit it out without any cryptic comments or long-winded philosophizing."

"Perfectly reasonable," he agreed as he handed her two tickets to an amusement park called Lands of Adventure.

"Let me guess. This place is cursed by an old wizard. The haunted house is actually haunted. If we eat the cotton candy, we turn into donkeys. But of course you couldn't tell me because that's against the rules."

She started to close the door.

"Don't you want directions?" he asked.

"Don't need them," she replied. "If I'm meant to find the place, I'm sure I'll find the place just fine on my own."

She shut the door with a displeased smile.

* * *

Troy was dreaming. It wasn't his own dream, though.

Helen stood beside his bed. She began to unbutton her shirt, and as she did so her fur disappeared. Her horns melted away. She transformed into a beautiful dark-haired woman, and she bent down and caressed his cheek.

"You've freed me from my curse with your love, Troy. I'm yours to have, forever."

Troy laughed. A puzzled expression on her face, Helen pulled away.

"What's wrong?"

"Seriously? This is the best you've got?" He swung his legs over the edge of the bed. "This is the fantasy you think I want?"

Helen, or her dream equivalent, said, "I don't understand."

"It's a bit simplistic, isn't it? I kiss the monster, and she becomes a beautiful girl. Then we ride into the sunset in my custom rocket car and get to eat all the ice cream we want. Do you think I'm five?"

"But this is your heart's desire. It's everything you want."

"It's not everything I want. It's everything I desire. There's a difference."

"Not for most people."

"I'm not most people."

"I don't get it. It's been a while since I've done this, but tempting mortals in their dreams has never been hard."

"I taught myself how to lucid dream." Troy went to the window and parted the curtains. His rocket car was parked just outside. "I was joking about that."

Helen waved her hand, and the vehicle vanished. "Very well. What do you want?"

"I want you to stop pretending to be her. The human form is fine," said Troy. "It's not her."

"But what if I told you it could be?" she asked.

"I'd say there's nothing wrong with how she is now and tell you to screw yourself."

The temptress flopped on the bed. "You're not doing this right. I'm here to offer you your wildest dreams. All you need do is ask." She expanded into Helen's minotaur form, naked on the bed. "Is this more to your liking?"

He closed his eyes. It felt wrong to look, like violating a sacred trust with Helen even if only in a dream.

"Stop it."

"As you wish."

The temptress transformed with a loud slurp. Troy opened his eyes to see the Lost God, in the form of a talking mound of raw hamburger, on his bed.

"Not my true form, but one you should have no problem recognizing."

"What do you want?"

The god said, "Why, to reward you for your excellent services. You've collected so many of the relics of power that I can now manifest, with some difficulty, in the astral realm. And that's quite an accomplishment."

"You're welcome." Troy threw open the door to his room. "Now go away."

The god slithered off the bed like a giant greasy slug. "Not quite yet. You've done a great job so far, but if all goes as I hope, there will come a moment when I'll have to ask one last thing from you."

"You've already asked for a hell of a lot."

The god formed shoulders to shrug with. "Yet I will ask for much more when the time comes."

Troy pointed to the mark on his hand. "Why ask at all? We don't have any choice."

"Yes, the curse I've placed upon you has been a fine motivator so far, but the final favor I ask demands more than your life. It demands your willing cooperation."

"You're wasting your time here because that's something I can't give you. I'll admit I like the adventure. It's been fun. But it doesn't change the facts. You're a banished god who could do a lot of damage to this world."

"Guilty as charged," said the god. "Though I'm not out to hurt anyone. You misjudge me. I only want to help you reach your full potential. I'm like Prometheus. He wanted to help you rise above your simple cave-dwelling existence, and what did he get for it? Strapped to a rock, having his liver pecked out for eternity. All because he cared for you in a way no other god did. I'm just like that. Except instead of giving you a gift to make you softer, I want to push you to become stronger. Prometheus was soft. I'm here for some tough love.

"I'm not evil. I have no desire to destroy. Only to enhance. You mortals can accomplish so much, but only when it is demanded of you. Only in pain and suffering, in endless disaster, can you find your true potential. The other gods are too weak to offer you the opportunity I bring. They fear what you might become. I only want you to become more than you are. Or perish as unworthy of my time so we can start over. Either way."

"You're crazy."

The Lost God shook his head. "I can see you're a stubborn boy. Nevertheless, I can offer you something you can't resist."

"No you can't. Now get the hell out of my dreams."

"If you insist." The god slunk out the door. "But are you certain I can't tempt you? Not even with your friend's life?"

Troy didn't answer, but the look on his face said more than enough. The god smiled.

"It's simple. When the time comes, and you'll know when that time is, I need you to put on that helmet you found."

"Why?"

"The metaphysics are a bit complicated, but when I rise into this world, I'll need a temporary host. Only for a day or two. Since you're a healthy young specimen, you're the best candidate. If you're fortunate you'll even survive the experience, though I make no promises."

"Why me? Why not Helen?"

"If only I could use her. She's perfect. So strong. So powerful. But the helmet won't fit her. Her head's the wrong shape, and those horns..." The god shuddered, raining flecks of meat. "They're a great look, but completely unworkable. I do hope you're not offended by being my second choice."

"You son of a bitch," said Troy. "The deal was we find your items of power, and you release us from the curse."

The god chuckled. "The deal is what I say it is. But you really haven't completed the quest until I am made manifest. And once I am, I'll undo the curse. I promise. With a little luck you'll survive. But at the very least, I can promise you that Helen will. It's a very generous offer. I'd suggest you take me up on it.

"There's no need to decide right now. Think about it. I'll get back to you."

The god sizzled, dissolving into a rancid mound of rotten flesh. It was only a dream, and the hamburger god didn't have to leave anything behind. But it was a subtle reminder that, even in this place, the dark god was watching. And waiting. The stench filled Troy's dreamscape.

It stayed with him, even after he'd taken the rocket car for a spin.

28

The next morning Helen was hoping they wouldn't have to talk about anything, but she expected Troy wouldn't let it drop so easily. He hadn't gotten this far in life by being easily discouraged. He did bring it up after they'd packed everything in the Chimera. It was, thankfully, a brief exchange.

He settled into the driver's seat and spoke without looking at her. "Hel, I want you to know that I think you're wrong, but I respect your decision. I won't push it."

"Thanks, Troy. I appreciate that."

A twinge of disappointment hit her. She didn't want him to press the issue, but she realized she'd been hoping deep down inside that he'd be more persistent. It was unfair to both of them. If he didn't take no for an answer, then he was a jerk. If he backed off, then he probably lacked the necessary commitment to make any kind of relationship work.

If this was dating, she was glad she had so little experience with it.

"Troy, I just want you to know that in a different world, I'd have been thrilled. And I'm glad you're my friend."

"There's no one I'd rather quest with."

Achilles whimpered from the backseat.

"I guess you're all right too, dog." Troy reached back and scratched Achilles behind the ears.

"We haven't made you into a dog person, have we?" she asked.

"They have their good points."

He started the Chimera and they resumed their travels. The Lands of Adventure wasn't difficult to find. Only two hours down the road, just off the interstate.

The billboards had made it clear the Lands of Adventure was an amusement park. They hadn't prepared Troy and Helen for the size of it. It looked to be almost as big as Disneyland, and judging by the crowded parking lot there was no shortage of customers. They had to take a shuttle to get to the front gates, modeled after a castle's.

Costumed characters and mascots were stationed to greet arrivals. Half appeared to be ordinary people dressed in kitschy getups. The other half were genuine enchanteds and thaumaturgicals though dressed a bit garishly. A family posed for a photo with a pair of harpies. A six-armed giant danced cheerfully for several giggling children.

A gorgon, her face hidden behind a veil, stopped Helen.

"Cast members aren't supposed to enter through the front." The gorgon's serpent tail flicked.

Helen pulled the tickets from her pocket. "I'm a customer."

The gorgon's blood-red eyes widened. "Oh, I'm terribly sorry. My mistake." She directed them toward the ticket takers.

"This is going to be a long day," muttered Helen.

"Lighten up, Hel. We're here to have fun."

"No, we're here to fight something or do something dangerous to get a new relic."

"Yes, but while we're here we might as well have some fun."

He grinned at her. It struck her as odd. It wasn't strange to see him smile. Nor was it strange for him to be positive. But there was something different about this grin. Something forced. For the first time, he looked as if he was trying too hard.

They asked the ticket taker, a sixteen-year-old boy in chain mail, about the park's policy on dogs.

"You can bring in anything you want," said the boy.

Helen considered going back to grab her wand from the Chimera's trunk. Troy talked her out of it.

"It doesn't make any sense to go in unarmed," she said.

"I'm not going to lug around a sword and shield all day, Hel."

"I'm pretty sure there's going to be a monster or something in there."

"Not necessarily," said Troy. "It can't be that dangerous. They're letting children go in."

"Are there monsters in there?" asked Helen of the ticket taker.

"Yes, ma'am. Lots of them. Most of them aren't dangerous, though."

"Most?"

The ticket taker shrugged, adjusted his collar to scratch underneath it. "We have incidents, but if you pay attention to the signs, stay out of the off-limit areas, you should be fine. Oh, and if you go to the Sea Serpent Super Spectacular, I recommend avoiding the tentacle zone. The giant squid is well fed, but she is still very grabby."

"I'm getting my wand."

They rode the shuttle all the way to the car and collected their items of power. She took the amulet. He took the sword and shield. She suggested he wear the helmet, but he made an excuse about how uncomfortable it looked. It covered its wearer's entire face, save for two slits for the eyes. He thought he glimpsed something in those slits. The helmet caused his curse mark to burn with a prickly heat. The pain was strangely compelling. Comforting in a way.

Helen snapped her fingers at him, drawing him from his distraction.

"Hey, you OK in there?" she asked.

He tucked the helmet under his arm and pretended he couldn't hear it whispering to him. "You better be right about this."

"You'll thank me when some beast of legend leaps from the shadows. If there's one thing I've learned from this quest, it's that relics don't just drop into our laps. There's always something we've got to overcome. Unless you think we'll find the next one as a prize at the dunking booth."

"No. You're probably right." He adjusted all the gear slung across his back. "You better be, because this is going to be hell to take on the roller coasters."

They returned to the gate, where the ticket taker didn't say a word about Troy's sword.

"This is a real magic sword," he said. "Not a replica."

"I'm aware, sir."

"Aren't you worried about me hurting people?"

"Should I be, sir?"

Troy admitted defeat. Helen laughed. It was good to hear her laugh.

On the other side of the gates, the Lands of Adventure was a wonderland of amusement park design. To get to the park proper they had to walk down a quaint cobblestone road lined on either side with gift shops in the shapes of cottages. Whoever was in charge of signs had gone a tad overboard with the phrase *Ye Olde*, and everything, from the stuffed dragons to the baseball caps and collectible crystal figures, was overpriced. But it was charming in a prepackaged, family-friendly, inoffensive way.

Troy bought a backpack with a cartoon kraken on it and shoved the helmet into it. It didn't quiet the whispers.

A mishmash of costumed characters and monsters walked among the tourists. The park spread its theme as far as it could, and while it was a bit weird to see a bare-chested Hercules only a few feet from a fully armored knight and a capering Monkey King, it all made sense in an eclectic way. The greatest hits of legend.

Troy pointed to a handsome young man juggling balls of string. "Hey, they have a Theseus."

"Great," said Helen. "Maybe I can punch his face in as payback for my great-great-great-great-great-great-grandfather."

"I didn't know you were related to the original minotaur."

"I have no idea if I am, but I still could do without meeting that guy."

But Troy was already getting Theseus's attention. Smiling, the curly-haired performer came over, never stopping his juggling.

"Excuse me," said Troy, "but would you mind terribly if we got a photo of you with my friend here?"

Theseus was all too happy to cooperate. Eager even. And when Troy suggested they get a photo with Theseus in a headlock, he didn't hesitate. Maybe it wasn't the real Theseus, but it was close enough to bring a smile to Helen's face.

Troy unfolded the park map and pointed out areas of interest. "Too bad. It says here that Castle Adventure is under repair."

The castle, a construct of faux stone, stood on a tall hill at the center of the park.

He said, "Hey, they have a labyrinth."

"Think I'll pass on that."

"OK, how about we check out Underworld Land? Says here the Cerberus roller coaster is the third-tallest in the world. Also, you can get your soul weighed beside a feather."

Her voice fell flat. "Sounds like fun."

"Hel, we're here. We might as well enjoy ourselves."

He was right, but she was in a sour mood. There was something in the air. Something that made her fur bristle. Her muscles were tight. Her nerves were frayed. She blamed it on her minotaurism. She unconsciously rubbed her arm where her bracelet should have been. Troy noticed, but said nothing.

She also wanted very much to avoid having a good time with Troy. She needed to put a wall between them because whenever he smiled at her, whenever he made her laugh, whenever she made him laugh, she found herself forgetting the impossibility of anything more between them. She couldn't count on Troy to be sensible about this, so she had to be the one who kept things in check. Having too much fun with Troy made that harder to do.

He put his hand on her arm. She wanted to pull away, but couldn't make herself do it.

She smiled at him. "Sorry, just not feeling like myself today. But you're right. Let's have some fun. Eat, drink, ride roller coasters. For tomorrow we die."

He pulled her down the street. "That's the spirit."

* * *

The Wild Hunt pulled into the Lands of Adventure without much joy. Their wounds from the dragon fight had healed enough that their orc blood allowed them to ignore the pain, but twenty hours of solid revelry had taken their toll.

Nigel ran his tongue around his dry mouth. He chugged his fourth bottle of water of the day. It helped, but he wasn't as young as he used to be. If he was honest with himself, he'd never been much of a drinker, even in college, and he'd gotten a bit carried away after their fight with the dragon.

His body was in good shape. Surprisingly good. He knew he had a genetic advantage when it came to pushing through pain, but all the ache that should've been in his bones was noticeably absent. The other club members had healed up as well, and it was no mystery why. The dragon blood and vomit had enchanted them. They didn't need the spirits to tell them that.

Nigel and Franklin, having been most thoroughly doused by the dragon's supernatural bile, were blessed with speedy regeneration that kept them going. The others healed slower, based on the amount of dried goop still sticking to their skin and clothes.

Dragon blood. There wasn't much it couldn't do.

Unfortunately, one of those things was cure a hangover, and while the Wild Hunt had healed up nicely from their wounds, they all struggled against the alcohol-fueled imps throttling their brains.

Their binge had taken more casualties than the dragon itself. Carl Heartchewer, Travis Bladebiter, and Susan Scalphack were too nauseous to ride, and no one had been able to wake Bob Earripper. The best they'd been able to do was roll him out of the puddle of his own vomit and throw a blanket over him so that he could sleep it off.

Only Franklin had been spared the bulk of the hangover because his pathetic constitution had forced him to switch to ginger ale early in the revelry. There were advantages to being an orc in a human body.

Peggy, paler than normal, which meant you could practically see the bones under her skin, pointed to the amusement park gates. "They're in there."

The club parked their motorcycles in a spot by the front gates. A knight tried to tell them it was a tow-away zone, but right now no one could give a damn. Harold Marrowmaw wrapped the knight in a headlock, but Nigel ordered the guy released. He was just doing his job.

"Tow the damn things then," said Nigel.

The knight clomped away.

The orcs approached the ticket booth. A disinterested teenager charged them admission, and Nigel paid for everyone with a credit card just barely under its limit.

"Before we kill these two," said Franklin, "can we maybe ride a roller coaster or two?"

The other club members groaned. No one felt much like being jerked and thrust around in a little cart.

"I hope they have snow cones."

Franklin ran ahead, and Nigel recalled his family vacation to Disneyland. The screaming, the crowds, the horrible little creatures that kept calling him "Dad" dragging him around the park like sadistic slave masters until he seriously considered abandoning them on the teacup ride and driving to Mexico.

Today couldn't be any worse than that.

Franklin bought a churro from a cart and devoured the sugary treat while sporting an idiotic grin.

"Can we kill him today?" asked James Eyestabber.

Nigel pushed his sunglasses up his crooked nose. The late-afternoon sun was still too damn bright.

The grumbling orcs trailed after their human brother.

* * *

Despite her best effort, Helen started having fun. She could pinpoint the exact moment it started. It was on Odysseus's Wild Voyage. As they were trapped between Scylla and Charybdis, the boat guide instructed them in the art of frightening away the animatronic terror and calming the whirlpool via cheering and clapping. It might not have been a historically accurate way to overcome the obstacle, but it was impossible not to be swept along with the energy of the other passengers. When Scylla lowered its six heads in herky-jerky defeat, the boat's passengers let out a cheer. Helen high-fived the ten-year-old girl next to her, and lost the will to fight the good time.

Together Troy and Helen tamed the Cerberus coaster twice. They proved themselves worthy of the blessings of the Qilin (earning some souvenir T-shirts), and routed a group of surly bullies at the bumper cars.

Park visitors mistook her for an employee now and then. She stopped getting annoyed and started rolling with it, posing for photos, letting children touch her fur and horns (as long as they asked politely). It reminded her she was different, but that being different wasn't always a problem.

She most enjoyed the Siege of the Mad Necromancer Interactive Stunt Show, where the audience took on the roles of heroes against impossible odds. The magic animating the skeletons caused them to fall apart at the slightest touch. It didn't matter. It somehow still felt heroic to "save" the villagers, even if she did so with a foam rubber sword. While the maintenance crews swept up the piles of bones, Troy stood by a fountain. Two huts filtered the late-afternoon light so that a golden beam shone down on him like a spotlight, as if the heavens smiled down on him for his glorious triumph and foreshadowed all the glorious triumphs to come.

On their stroll down the midway, she thought of how to tell him that she'd changed her mind. She didn't believe they had a future together. There were too many obstacles in the way of that. But a date wasn't a lifetime, and a few weeks with Troy were worth all the heartache that was bound to come afterward. She was mentally rehearsing her speech, both simple and profound, when it dawned on her none of it was necessary.

She said it all when she took his hand in hers.

He looked into her eyes and smiled.

She smiled back, nodded.

His gaze moved to her left. He pulled her toward a midway game called Dunk the Ga-gorib. A weird, lumpy creature sat at the edge of a tank of water. The monster perked up at their approach.

"Hello, sir," said the chubby attendant. "Care to take your shot?"

"Troy, these games are scams."

He pointed to the wall of prizes. "Hel, check out the dagger."

There was a knife sitting among the potential rewards. It was ordinary except for the symbol of the Lost God engraved on its handle.

"This can't be this easy," she said.

"I never knew you were so pessimistic. How's this work?"

"You get three balls," explained the attendant. "You hit the target, the ga-gorib goes in the tank, you get to pick your prize. Easy as that."

"What's the catch?" asked Helen.

"If you fail, the ga-gorib gets to dunk you. And he tends to hold you under a long time."

The ga-gorib, smiling wickedly, rubbed his hands together.

"Three balls, please," said Troy.

"The game has to be rigged," said Helen.

"Hel, we're here to get that dagger. This is the way to do it."

"Or we could just give this guy a couple of bucks to look the other way and give it to us."

"We can't ask him to compromise his ethics like that. And I'm pretty sure there are some rules against it. Right?"

The attendant said, "I get paid minimum wage to watch people get drowned. Ethics aren't my thing."

They slipped the attendant one hundred dollars, and he gave them the dagger. The ga-gorib was terribly disappointed by the deal.

"Feels like cheating," said Troy.

"It worked, didn't it? Legends are full of heroes breaking the rules and getting away with it. Who says all tests have to be about physical prowess? Maybe that was a test of our problem-solving skills."

He took the dagger from her. Their hands touched, and a jolt passed between them. It wasn't only the curse they shared, though the way their marks burned made it clear that was a big part of it.

The fur on her neck stood on edge. She smoothed it down with her hand.

"Hel..."

She waited for him to finish the thought, but he couldn't tell her what he knew. One of them had to die. He didn't feel right keeping it from her, but he couldn't think of a reason to let her know. It would only burden her. She had enough burdens already.

She saw the concern in his face. "Troy, is something wrong?"

"Nothing. It's not important. You want to get some ice cream?"

"I don't eat ice cream."

He grinned. "I knew that."

The ground rumbled. Dark clouds appeared overhead. Shadows slithered around them. Neither of them paid much attention. It was all very standard at this point, and they were distracted by their own concerns. The thundering temper tantrum of the gods above paled in comparison to their more personal dilemmas, insignificant as they might have been on a cosmic scale. The shadows, seeing this, slunk away, grumbling to themselves. The clouds dissolved, and the last crack of thunder wasn't so much ominous as apologetic.

Achilles growled.

The Wild Hunt stood before Helen and Troy.

"I told you they'd be here," said Peggy.

29

Nigel slurped down the last of his soda and tossed it in a nearby trash can. "Hate to interrupt such a private moment, but we're here to kill you. You seem like good people, so I'll give you a choice. You can make this quick and easy. Or you can put up a fight. Either way."

"I hope they put up a fight," said Franklin.

"You handle the dog," said Nigel.

"But I don't want to hurt a dog."

"Then just grab the damn thing."

Helen said, "Who the hell are you?"

"Believe it or not, we're the good guys," said Nigel.

The orcs all laughed.

"Weird, I know." He unslung his dragonblood ax. "It still sounds weird to say that."

"You can't be serious," said Troy. "You aren't going to start a fight here, now, with all these people around."

"What people?" asked Franklin.

The harsh clack of steel shutters being drawn drew Troy's attention. The Midway of Heroes was empty of both employees and visitors, all very quietly and efficiently evacuated. Calliope music played in the distance accompanied the roars of the nearby roller-coaster passengers. Just over a tall hedge, the Ferris wheel kept turning.

A hot wind blew across the midway, and a discarded hot dog wrapper tumbled not unlike a lonely tumbleweed.

Helen grabbed her wand.

"You were right," said Troy. "I am glad I brought these." He drew his sword and readied his shield.

Peggy bit into her blueberry snow cone. "The spirits say enough talk. It's time to throw down."

"Shazam!" shouted Helen.

The pavement around the orcs rose up in four great slabs, imprisoning them. She twirled her wand. "There. Problem solved."

Magic frost spread across the slabs. The ice crystallized in thick sheets, and with a mighty blow from Nigel's ax the walls shattered.

"That really shouldn't have worked," said James Eyestabber.

"It's magic," said Nigel. "It doesn't have to make sense."

"Shazam!" proclaimed Helen.

A new cage thrust itself around the orcs. She didn't expect it to hold them for long, but it bought her and Troy some time.

"Are we really going to have to fight these guys?" she asked. "I don't want to do that."

"I don't think we have a choice, Hel."

Achilles's lip curled to show his teeth.

Nigel's ax destroyed the prison. "Do we need to—"

"Shazam!"

The slabs popped up.

"How many charges does your wand have in it?" asked Troy.

She tapped the jewel at its tip. Its glow dimmed. "I have no idea."

The prison shattered, and the orcs wisely dispersed. Helen threw another prison around the bulk of them, but a half dozen escaped. Bellowing savagely, they charged forth with such speed that they were on Helen and Troy in a moment. Or they would've been if she hadn't pointed the wand at her feet.

"Shazam!"

The stone walls sprang up around Troy, Helen, and Achilles. Their attackers pounded at the barricade.

"This hardly seems like a better solution," said Troy.

She grunted. "If it's a fight they want"—she cracked her knuckles—"I guess we can give it to them."

"Maybe you should take the shield, Hel."

Icicles formed across the stone and when she spoke, her breath came out as frost. "You keep it. I can handle these guys."

Achilles's ears flattened, and his fur bristled.

The wall shattered, and the orcish gang was on her in one massive heap of flailing limbs and gnashing teeth. Before Troy could defend her, he was attacked by four others. A short sword and a mace were swung in his direction. Troy blocked them with his shield, and its magic teleported him safely out of harm's way just before contact was made.

It took the orcs a few moments to find him. It took Troy almost as long to get his bearings. The shield's magic had a disorienting effect. An attacker hurled a hatchet. The shield moved Troy out of its path to avoid a split skull, but suddenly finding him three feet to the left didn't do his strained perceptions any good.

His blurred senses focused on Helen and her personal horde. He ran to her side, but a pouncing attacker activated the shield again. Troy blinked to farther away than where he'd started.

Helen screamed. Whether with rage or pain, he couldn't tell. He saw her face for only a moment before it was obscured by a clawing green hand.

The orcs closed in on him. Peggy sat on the sidelines, watching with a profound disinterest while Franklin hopped around with Achilles latched onto his ankle.

Troy tossed the enchanted shield aside. It was more of a hindrance than an asset. He only needed his sword of invincibility to handle this problem. An orc struck with a sword. Troy parried, slicing through his opponent's steel with supernatural sharpness.

"That's cheating!" said the orc.

Troy slammed his fist into his opponent's throat, followed it by kicking the orc's ankle, causing him to drop to one knee.

"I thought you said he didn't know kung fu," said James.

"It's not karate," replied Troy. "It's Jeet Kune Do."

"The spirits do delight in being technical," said Peggy by way of apology.

James Eyestabber and Jenny Gutspitter made their moves. Troy was invulnerable as long as he stood his ground, but he met their strikes. He punched James in the breadbasket and smashed Jenny's nose with his forearm. He didn't pause to admire his perfect form; he ran toward Helen.

The ground quaked as roots sprouted, wrapping around his legs. Peggy paused in her mumbling to say, "The spirits tell me you can't be hurt while holding that sword and touching the ground. Let's see what we can do about that."

Troy hacked at the roots, but the tendrils overwhelmed him, coiling around his limbs, hoisting him in the air. He struggled, twisting and turning, trying to angle his sword to slice himself free.

Gaunt, pale Peggy drew her dagger. "If you stop squirming, I'll do my best to make this quick."

Achilles came out of nowhere to snap his jaws around her arm. She dropped the dagger.

"Damn it, Franklin! You had one job! One job!"

The roots loosened, and Troy started cutting them away while Franklin tugged at Achilles, who was latched onto Peggy.

"Forget the dog, you idiot!" said Peggy. "Kill the kid before he—"

Troy stood on solid ground. Jenny came up from behind and bashed his invulnerable head with a heavy stone. He turned on her with a frown. She threw a punch that he didn't bother blocking, then he smacked her with the hilt of his sword.

"You have to get him off his feet," said Peggy. She struggled to incant to the nature spirits, but Achilles proved distracting.

Franklin threw himself at Troy and got a punch to the face. The other orcs attempted to wrestle Troy to the ground or get his sword away from him, but he was faster. He slashed James across the chest and nearly sliced off Denise Spinecracker's arm.

Survival instincts buried Troy's reaction to the blood coating his blade. This was no game, no fun challenge, no goofing off with dragons. This situation was serious in a way that even the Mystery Cottage had not been. Because these weren't monsters to be overcome. They were people trying very hard to kill them.

The pavement rumbled in that familiar way. Franklin had pried Achilles off Peggy, and she stared at Troy with her milky-white eyes, summoning forth more entangling roots.

Troy tapped his sword against the ground. The massive earth elemental erupted with a howl.

"What is it you—"

Troy pointed to Peggy. "Get her."

The asphalt monster moved toward her with steady steps. Thorny roots entangled it, but the elemental snapped them without breaking its pace.

"Damn it!" Peggy turned and ran with the elemental in slow pursuit.

Helen roared. She'd beaten half the orcs, but blood soaked patches in her fur. He couldn't tell if it was hers or the attackers'. He noticed a sword sticking out of her back, though it didn't seem to be slowing her down.

"Helen!"

She paused, turned her head in his direction. He saw nothing but rage in her eyes. A sneer twisted her face. He was afraid, not of the orcs or dark gods, but of something deep down inside her that had found its way to the surface.

She saw his fear, and it broke her bloodlust.

"Troy, I—"

She was buried under a renewed assault.

He took a step toward her, but Nigel stood in his way. Nigel clutched his ax, frost dripping from its blade.

"We're all the playthings of the gods," he said. "Let's try to give them a good show."

Their weapons clashed with a shower of sparks and snow. Over and over again the weapons struck. They danced back and forth. Troy was faster, and he managed to work around the edges of Nigel's defense, nicking his flesh here and there. Also putting holes in Nigel's leather jacket, and that pissed him off even more.

Nigel got in his own hits, but most bounced off invulnerable Troy. Once he caught Troy off balance, with one foot off the ground, and managed to gash a wound across his thigh.

Their weapons locked together. Ice ran down Troy's blade and covered his hands. The cold numbed his fingers.

"You don't have to do this," said Troy.

Nigel said, "I can't defy my god. Even if I could, I can't let you loose havoc on this world. You don't know what you're doing, kid."

"I know it doesn't have to be this way. I don't know what the gods told you, but we don't have to do this their way."

Nigel eased the pressure. He snarled, not at Troy but at the Fates for putting him in this situation. "I'm not any happier with this than you. Now shut up and fight."

Ice formed on Troy's sword hilt. The weapons slipped as Nigel applied more pressure.

"I'm not going to kill you," said Troy.

"Then you'll die."

Nigel spoke the words like a true orc, but they sounded hollow. A thousand years ago he'd have cheerfully slaughtered this boy on the field of battle. It didn't seem right today. It wasn't only the corruption of civilization that made it so. It was Troy himself, who showed neither fear nor weakness.

Troy kicked Nigel's knee. The joint popped, but Nigel didn't fall. He gritted his teeth. It was only pain.

"We can work this out," said Troy. "We can find a solution."

Nigel squared his shoulders, pushing harder. "This is the solution."

With a final shove he dislodged Troy's magic sword. The weapon clattered to rest a few feet away. Troy punched Nigel in the jaw. Nigel spat, wiped his mouth.

"You're a fighter, but this ends here."

Troy held up his hands. "OK, OK. You got me. But I don't think you have it in you to kill an unarmed man in cold blood. I don't see that in your eyes."

"It doesn't matter what you think you see," said Nigel. "In the end, it's always blood. Blood spilled in the name of the gods because they don't want to get off their asses. Violence isn't optional. It's the way this world works. It sucks, but it's the way it is. The way it always will be."

He raised his ax.

Troy made no move to defend himself. He pointed to Helen, wrestling with the four or five orcs still standing. "Call off your horde. We don't have to fight just because the gods get off on it."

Nigel groaned. "Damn it, you aren't going to make this easy, are you?"

"It is easy. Just stop. And we'll talk this out."

Nigel lowered his weapon. A chill ran through his bones. No doubt it was the disapproval of his gods, but his gods could go to hell.

A blade pierced Troy from behind. The short sword thrust through his belly. Both Troy and Nigel stared at the bloodied blade in abject surprise.

"We can still work this out," said Troy before dropping to the ground.

Franklin stared at his handiwork. His blank expression conveyed no emotion other than shock. "I did it."

Achilles stopped chewing on Franklin's ankle and whined, sniffing Troy's crumpled form.

"Yeah." Nigel grumbled a curse to the gods for their cruelty and to himself for believing there had been any other choice. "You did it."

"Troy!" screamed Helen.

She threw off her attackers and, more beast than woman, glowered at Nigel.

Nigel pointed to Franklin.

"He did it."

30

Helen had never feared becoming a monster. She had a recurring dream where she grew to Godzilla proportions and stomped her way across innocent cityscapes, but that wasn't an especially terrifying proposition. If her condition transformed her into a mindless beast, she always figured it wouldn't matter because who she was, deep down inside, would be gone, replaced by some primal creature no more malicious than a rabid dog.

She feared more the idea that there would be something left inside her, some small piece of herself that could only watch from a tormented prison while her bestial self killed and maimed. Seeing Troy bleeding on the ground triggered her inner monster, but the beast wasn't the rage-filled terror she'd always assumed it would be. It was cold. Hollow. An emptiness. She'd always assumed she was wrestling with the Hulk. But she wasn't filled with unbound rage. Rage could be tamed. Rage could be mastered.

This emptiness was different. She wasn't enraged. She wasn't out of control. She knew exactly what she was doing.

She just didn't see any reason to stop herself.

Her first target was Franklin. She trampled him beneath her hooves. Seven stomps shattered his bones, pulped his organs, and reduced him to a gurgling lump of flesh. The enchanted dragon blood kept him alive. She picked him up and stared into his broken face. One eye had burst out of his skull. He twitched. His lips moved, though only blood and teeth spilled from his mouth.

He poked her with his sword, but his twisted arm didn't have the strength to pierce her skin. The weapon slipped from the two remaining fingers on his right hand.

She tossed him aside. He fell beside Troy. Blood spilled across the pavement. Troy's blood. Franklin's blood. It coated her hands and hooves. Some of it was hers. Most of it wasn't. She rubbed it between her fingers.

The Wild Hunt, those who could still stand, circled around her as she stared at the sticky red liquid.

Nigel held up his hand to stop the orcs from renewing the attack.

"I don't know your name," he said to her.

She kept staring at her hands. "Helen."

"Helen, I'm sorry. This has gotten out of hand. We need to take a—"

She looked at Troy, unmoving, on the ground. "He was the greatest guy ever, and you killed him."

"Not me," said Nigel. "Franklin did it. And you killed Franklin. We're even now. We don't need to—"

"Even."

The calmness in her voice frightened him.

"We can never be even."

"No, we can't." He dropped his battle-ax and motioned for the others to do the same. They clattered on the ground. The muscles under her bristling fur tensed. "But you killed Franklin. You avenged your friend. And now—"

She whirled, grabbing him by the jacket, hoisting him in the air. There was nothing in her face, no hint of anger.

"His name was Troy. You killed him, and you didn't even know his name."

Nigel smiled, though he recalled that an orc smile was a sharp-toothed, innately malevolent expression.

"Not me. Franklin. And you killed Franklin, so—"

"It's not enough."

She dropped him, noticed the pain of the short sword in her shoulder. She yanked it out, stared at the blood running down the blade. Her blood.

"Even when I kill you all, it won't be enough."

"Now let's talk about—"

Alan Spleenspearer snatched up a club and with a mighty shout smashed Helen across the back of the head. The mighty blow broke the weapon in half. Helen barely moved.

"Goddamn it," yelled Nigel. "Why the hell does everyone keep doing that?"

Alan shrugged.

Helen punched Alan hard enough to launch him across the midway. He crashed into a ring toss booth, causing it to collapse in a heap.

The orcs piled onto Helen, and the battle renewed. Nigel stepped back to a safe distance. He retrieved his ax, held it in tight fingers. He would wait his turn. If he was going to do something stupid, he was going to do it right.

Helen made short work of her opponents. Nigel was reminded of their fight with the dragon, but whereas the dragon was only a wild beast, she was a brutal, efficient killer. She broke bones and smashed skulls with her bare hands. While orcs could be stubborn foes, even they had their limits. They fell to the wayside. Helen snorted, stepping over her defeated foes and moving toward Nigel.

He raised his ax and unleashed his war cry.

She didn't make a sound.

They launched into one another. He would only get one strike, and he swung for her head. The magic blade sliced through her left horn, sheared away a few locks of hair. She punched him in the solar plexus. He gritted his teeth, stifling a shriek as every rib broke and his right lung collapsed. Whether because of his own stubbornness or the enchanted blood encrusting him, his crushed heart continued to beat.

He made a second clumsy attack. She caught his hand and squeezed. The bones ground together, though he was beyond pain. He felt only heat running through his arm. She twisted it to an impossible angle. His ax dropped to the ground.

Nigel staggered but didn't fall. He wiped the blood and drool dribbling from his mouth.

"For what it's worth"—he punched her in the chest, doing far more damage to his hand than to her—"I'm sorry."

Helen pushed him to the ground. She fell to her knees and proceeded to punch him in the face, over and over and over again, until his head was little more than a stain on the concrete. She didn't stop until several members of the Wild Hunt, running on the dwindling reserves of enchantment, dragged her away.

* * *

The great god Grog stood beside Nigel, who stood beside his own corpse.

"You had one job," said Grog. "And you screwed it up."

Nigel's spirit body wasn't in much better shape than his corporeal one. It hurt when he drew breath, and every move was agony. The only thing that made it tolerable was the knowledge that he was already dead so he couldn't end up hurting himself any more.

He pointed at Helen. She wrestled with the orcs, but she wasn't that into it anymore. It was the only reason they weren't all dead or dying.

"Have you seen her? How were we supposed to stand up to that?"

Grog's five heads glowered. "Don't give me that. You have that battle-ax, enchanted with dragon blood. You could've killed her. You pulled your strike at the last second. You were one clean stroke from beheading her before you lost your nerve."

Nigel grunted as he straightened his spirit fingers. "You can't prove that."

Franklin, a disembodied spirit, lurched into view. He mumbled unintelligibly with his broken jaw.

"This pathetic human is more orc than you could ever hope to be," said Grog.

Nigel willed away the hunch in his broken back and pushed his knee back into place. "If being an orc is killing two innocent kids, then I'll pass."

"Innocent?" Grog chuckled. "She killed the both of you."

"Doesn't mean they're killers. Come to think of it, not sure I'm really one either. The more I think about it, the less I see myself as a killer who happens to be an accountant and the more as an accountant drafted into doing your dirty work."

"You shame your ancestors."

Nigel twisted his foot into its proper position. It was his spirit body. He saw no reason it should be bent and broken.

"My ancestors can kiss my ass. They were a bunch of un-civilized dumbasses. They formed massive armies over and over again, and every time, no matter the size of their legions, no matter the promised glories of mad wizards or crazed gods, they always lost. It's what we orcs do. We lose. We always get beat. If we're lucky, we grab a little glory on our way to oblivion. I don't think I need to hear any crap from you about it because you picked us for the job. This was the only way it could go.

"And even if I did pull the deathblow—and I'm not saying I did—then I'd be content with the results. If I could've won but didn't, then it puts me ahead of every other damn orc that's ever been. And I don't have to be a killer to have that."

Franklin mumbled with his broken spirit body.

"I'm not judging you, Franklin. You did us proud. And when I'm added to the bones of the unworthy, I'd be honored and priv-ileged if you lay beside me."

Franklin smiled. Or tried to, but the sinews of his spirit flesh only managed to pull the left side of his jaw up.

"This is all very touching," said Grog, "and maybe you're right that orcs always lose. I was hoping that, since this time you were the good guys, you'd break that particular habit. Yet there's still time."

"We're dead," replied Nigel.

"Not quite."

"I don't know if you've been paying attention, but that slab of bloody meat in a leather jacket is what's left of me. Considering that there are bits of my brain scattered across the pavement, I think it's safe to say my time is up."

Grog said, "No, you're not. You can't die as long as the dragon puke covers you."

"Glad I didn't rush to take a shower after that. But I'm a living slab of immortal mush. I'm still not doing much good to anyone."

"Your body will recover. Given time. Time we don't have."

Three of Grog's heads nodded toward Troy's body. A gray shadow, another astral body, crouched beside him.

"The boy isn't dead. Not yet. And the Lost God whispers in his ear, telling him it is time to don the helmet, to take on the mantle of power."

Franklin stammered and grumbled.

"Yes, if he's there right now, you take care of it," agreed Nigel. "You're the great and terrible Grog. You can't put this guy in his place?"

"There are rules," said Grog.

"Screw the rules. Just kick his astral ass."

"There's no way to harm anyone or any god on this plane."

Grog and the gray shadow locked glares. The shadow flashed a wicked smile before returning to its corrupting whispers.

Nigel grunted. "Awfully convenient how you can't do a damn thing on your own."

His god roared, and the lighting of the astral plane shifted to a crackling crimson. He pounded his fists at Nigel and Franklin, and Grog's bloodshot eyes stared them down. Neither mortal soul blinked, though Franklin would've if he'd had eyelids on his good eye.

"You've become a pain in my ass, Nigel." Two of Grog's heads smiled. "I can respect that. But if you truly aren't a killer, then you must stop the boy from—"

"His name is Troy," said Nigel.

One of Grog's smiles dropped, though the remaining head nodded its approval. "Troy must not put that helmet on. Death and destruction will be the inevitable result, and if you choose not to act, then you are surely as responsible as we useless gods."

Franklin mumbled his agreement.

Nigel said, "I don't remember asking you."

And then he was in his body. Searing flesh and powdered bones made every move agony. Even with the magic of dragon vomit, he wondered how he could move at all. He crawled, inch by inch, toward Troy. His eyes had grown back but could see the world only as a blur. Whooshing filled his ears, but he could hear Helen fighting the few remaining club members. He hoped they could keep her occupied long enough.

He reached out and grabbed Troy's shoe. With his hazy vision he glimpsed Troy struggling to free the helmet from a backpack.

"Don't do it," gasped Nigel. The words came out as a squeak pushing past a crushed throat.

He tugged at Troy's pants, using them to inch forward. With his other hand, Nigel grabbed the helmet. They wrestled. Troy had lost a lot of blood. He was dying. But his body was mostly whole, and Nigel wasn't much of a match. Troy planted his free hand on Nigel's face and attempted to push him away.

Helen grabbed Nigel by the arm and yanked him into the air.

"Why aren't you dead?" she asked.

"Stop. Helmet," he croaked.

Noticing Troy moving, she threw Nigel aside. "Oh gods! You're alive. You're alive!"

Troy donned the helmet.

Nigel cursed the heavens. It was the way of orcs to always lose. Troy stood.

"You're OK?" she asked. "But how?"

"It's fine now, Hel. It's all fine. It was the only way. Now you're safe. I'll take care of everything."

He smiled, though it was impossible to tell with the helmet covering everything but his eyes. The curse mark on Helen's hand vanished.

"You're the best. Never forget that."

He doubled over. His body tensed as the Lost God overwhelmed him. Helen reached for him, but a decorative fiberglass gryphon tore loose from the concrete. It pushed her aside with a screech. Troy, but not Troy, climbed on the creature's back. It spread its shiny wings and launched itself into the sky. It shot toward Castle Adventure at the center of the park.

The magic sword, her wand, the shield, and the dagger flew after him. The amulet ripped free of her pocket, but she slapped it tight against her leg. It punished her with agony, a wicked fire burning across her nerves. Not just figuratively. Smoke sizzled on her fur.

Maybe it was the adrenaline or her monstrous curse or pure force of will, but she refused to let go. When the amulet seared its way out of her jeans and then tried to do the same to her hands, she only squeezed harder. With one last determined burst of magic, it yanked her off the ground. It spun around like a top. Her fingers loosened. Her grip failed. The amulet flung her away and she slid across the asphalt with such force, the fur and flesh of her right shoulder and arm peeled away in a bloody red scrape.

She sat up, only to watch helplessly as the relic sailed off toward Castle Adventure.

Peggy and the earth elemental, having reached an understanding, surveyed the carnage. Beaten orcs. A slithering pile of goop that was Franklin slowly pulling itself together. Nigel, looking more dead than alive. And Helen, wounded and bloodied, standing there silently.

"What the hell happened?" asked Peggy.

Not even the spirits had a good answer for her.

31

The gate to the midway rolled up. Agent Waechter, flanked by several other NQB agents in gray suits, strode onto the scene of carnage.

"OK, everyone," said Waechter. "That's a wrap on this operation."

Nigel's throat had healed enough to allow him to speak. "Who the hell are you?"

"I could ask the same thing of you, sir," replied Waechter. "You very nearly gummed up the works. How did you get involved in any of this?"

"We were sent by the gods," said Peggy.

"Ah, that explains it." Waechter loosened his tie. "Gods always do love mucking about in our affairs. I do wish they'd learn to leave this business to the professionals. In any case, everything worked out well enough, so no harm done."

"No harm done?" Helen growled like a beast. "No harm done?"

The earth elemental stepped back. "If you don't need me anymore, I should probably get going."

"Nobody goes anywhere until we straighten this out," she said.

Though the elemental could've returned to its plane of origin, where she could never follow, it decided to stay. Just in case she was determined enough to find a way.

Waechter smiled in a manner meant to relax her. It only pissed her off.

"Helen..."

Scowling, she towered over him. He held his ground but gestured at his agents, who drew their swords. Except for Agent Campbell, who stood ramrod-straight with her standard unreadable expression.

Waechter said, "Miss Nicolaides, you have every right to be upset. This isn't the ideal resolution, but this isn't an ideal world. We take the victories we can get, and are thankful they aren't the defeats they could've been."

"What happened to Troy?"

"He donned the helmet, taking on the hosting duties for a banished god. He did so of his own free will, and by doing so he satisfied the conditions of your curse. You're free to return to your own life now."

"And Troy? What about him?"

"He's gone. Or he soon will be. But I can assure you his noble sacrifice won't be in vain. It's regrettable, but—"

Helen grabbed him by his lapel and pulled him close to her. She snorted in his face.

The agents moved to his defense, but the Wild Hunt, battered as they were, readied their own weapons. Agent Campbell stood to one side. She smiled, amused by thoughts she didn't feel like sharing.

"I thought you were the assassins of the gods," said Waechter.

Nigel used his ax to steady his broken legs. "The young lady asked you a question. I suggest you answer it."

Waechter sized up Nigel's band. None of them were in prime fighting shape. That only made them more dangerous. Their fearsome, bloody grins showed they were less concerned with avoiding death than with dragging as many souls into oblivion with them as possible.

"There is a cycle to these things," said Waechter. "The Lost God attempts to break from his exile every three hundred years or so. He drafts two innocent souls. They gather the relics of power. One sacrifices him- or herself. The god gains physical form for a few hours and then returns to exile again. That is the way it always goes."

"What's the point?" she asked.

"Point? There's no point. It's just a cycle. There are thousands of them, invisible gears turning, keeping the universe running as it must."

"Says who?"

"The Fates. The gods. Some implacable, nameless thing beyond even them. I don't know. I only know that it's the way it works."

Helen dropped him. "And there's no way to change it?"

He stayed sitting on the ground. "No cycle is unbreakable. They can change. They *must* change eventually. But they're like time bombs. They must be disarmed or reset. Remember when I told you that my job is to see that some quests are never completed? This is one of those quests. The Lost God can't escape his banishment, but if the other gods are forced to take a direct hand in shoving him back into exile, the resulting tiff of the gods would be a national disaster. Hundreds of thousands of deaths. Billions in property damage. Environmental shifts that would take decades to recover from.

"But now this god has found a mortal body, and because he's a god and easily distracted, he'll spend the next few hours indulging himself, and then, because gods also lose track of time, his window of opportunity will pass him by. His host will burn out, and he will return to banishment until the next cycle."

"But he has all the relics," said Helen.

"All of the relics, yes, but he's missing the final element to unlock his prison."

"What?"

"It's not important. All you need to know is that we have things in hand."

She said, "You knew this was the way it would turn out?"

"Knew? No, I didn't know. We can never truly know. We can only predict based on previous patterns, but there are always exceptions. Things don't always unfold by the numbers. Your friends here, for example. We didn't see them coming, though we should've." He nodded to an agent. "Make a note of that, Campbell. Intelligence dropped the ball there."

Campbell pulled out a notepad and jotted down a reminder.

"So it doesn't have to end like this?" Helen asked.

"No, but this time this *is* how it ends." Waechter stood. "Go home, Miss Nicolaides. Go back to your life, and leave the rest to us."

"You don't expect me to abandon Troy."

"You can't save him. If you try, you'll only make things worse. The best thing you can do is trust us to do our job."

Helen stuck her hand in her pocket, felt the old key. It had to be the final relic. It was the only thing that made sense, and Waechter had practically said so in a roundabout way.

The fates had given it to her, and saving Troy had to be the reason. Destiny might be impossible to decipher, but she refused to believe it was outright cruel.

Waechter and the NQB agents must have read her thoughts on her face.

"Miss Nicolaides..."

She turned to the elemental. "Kick their asses for me."

The elemental scratched its head. "Technically, I only follow the orders of the sword bearer."

Peggy said, "I'm a shaman, so by the powers given to me by the spirits of nature, I suggest you follow the young lady's orders."

The elemental locked stares with the pale orcess. Her skull-like face and milky-white eyes proved disconcerting to the monster.

"All right already." It shrugged. "If you insist."

He tapped a nearby agent. It was enough to send her flying across the midway. The agents' swords clanged harmlessly against its stone body. Within moments it'd knocked them all away and held Waechter in an inescapable bear hug.

"Keep him here," Helen ordered.

The elemental saluted. "Yes, ma'am."

She took the measure of Agent Campbell, standing inscrutably to the side. "You aren't going to try and stop us?"

Campbell smiled. "Doesn't seem like an option at this point."

Helen walked away. Waechter shouted at her back.

"You can't do this! You don't know what horrors you could unleash!"

He was right. She didn't know. Nor did she care.

The Wild Hunt, those in walking shape, trailed her. Nigel,

Peggy, and James struggled to keep up. It wasn't easy for any of them. Franklin, wincing with every step of his twisted body, brought up the rear.

Helen kept walking. "Why are you following me? Can't wait to finish what you started?"

"You're going to need our help," said Nigel.

"Didn't you try to kill me? Didn't you almost kill Troy?"

Peggy shoved Franklin forward.

"I'm sorry about stabbing your friend," he said. "I was…we all were following the will of the gods."

"Yes, sorry about trying to assassinate you earlier," said Peggy. She slowed. "And now?"

Nigel said, "And now we'd like to believe there's another choice, that we don't have to blindly follow, that we can make our own decisions. If our gods don't like it, they can go ahead and smite us now."

Thunder rumbled in the clear sky.

"Ignore them," he said. "They're all talk."

A bolt of lightning struck the ground beside him.

"And they can't aim worth a damn."

He chuckled.

"Ever since the first cursed orc stepped onto a world that hated him—"

"Or her," said Peggy.

"A world that hated him or her," he said, "we have been deemed nothing but an inconvenience, minions and savages. Even when times changed, even when the world became civilized, we were still monsters. When the hordes of the steppes crushed the armies of warlord Napoleon, no one thanked us. When my ancestors devastated Alexander of Macedonia's forces, did the Arabians even give us an ounce of credit? When my grandfather won the day on the beaches of Normandy, they didn't even give him a medal. Just told him to shove off and not make trouble.

"We've always been the whipping boys of destiny—"

"And girls," added Peggy.

He glared at her. "After a while, you start seeing yourself the way the rest of the world does. You wouldn't be in this mess if not for us falling into that trap, and so we pledge our strength and our honor to help you save Troy. Give us a chance to make it right."

He paused to catch his breath. Immortal or not, he was fairly certain one of his lungs had yet to regenerate.

"Give us a chance to show we're more than murderous thugs. Please."

Helen stopped. She glanced over her shoulder.

The Wild Hunt raised their weapons and roared. It wasn't much of a roar, but something about its pitiful nature moved her.

"You aren't going to be much use to me as you are."

Nigel said, "We are temporarily immortal, and Peggy here's a shaman."

Now that she was no longer moving, Helen felt the ache in her flesh, the sting of every cut. It was only supernatural endurance that kept her on her feet, but there had to be limits.

She said, "Waechter is right. Troy's just one person, and I'm being reckless and irresponsible by even considering this. I don't know if there's even a way to save Troy now. I don't know what's going to happen, but if even part of it's true, then I am very likely about to get myself and a whole bunch of innocent people killed. I could have nothing to show for it and we could be caught in the middle of a full-fledged scuffle of the gods, and I honestly don't see how it can turn out any other way."

They smiled.

"Getting stepped on by the gods is a good way to die," said Franklin.

Achilles went over and sat by the orcs. It was a good-enough endorsement for her.

32

The Lost God's fiberglass mount landed on the tower of Castle Adventure. Three dozen worshippers bowed before him. Some were park employees who had quietly awaited his return. Others were tourists, drawn to this place of power by omens. There was tension between the two groups. The employees saw their years of putting up with cranky customers, sprinkling sawdust on vomit, and capering sweatily in mascot suits as proof of their true devotion, whereas any idiot could read an omen. Plus the tourists had a hard time respecting anyone wearing an "I Love Churros" apron.

Rather than fight about it, the two groups had appointed their own leaders. A woman in a foam gargoyle costume and a man sporting a trilby hat, wearing black socks and sandals, approached the Lost God.

"You return to us as you have promised," said the woman.

"As revealed in signs," added the man.

They exchanged glares.

"All has been made ready," added the gargoyle woman. "All that's required is the relics of power that we may complete the ritual."

The relics orbited the Lost God's head. He snapped his fingers, and they fell to the floor. His followers fought among themselves for the right to gather them up. They scurried around, preparing the ancient magics. He didn't pay attention to the details. Those were mortal concerns.

"Have anything to drink?" he asked. "I'm parched."

A soda, borne aloft on a golden platter by a pair of attractive young women, was brought to him. The can was too large to fit in the helmet's face opening. He tapped it several times against the helmet.

"You wouldn't happen to have a straw on you?"

A straw was found, and the Lost God was led to his throne room, where he sat while the followers did their jobs.

The sacred slab had been seamlessly integrated into Castle Adventure. He didn't know how it had gotten there. He didn't care. The rune-scarred slab always found its way to him. Or he to it. It made no difference where the gods above hid it. It was always found by the right silly mortals who would read whatever promises they wanted to see in its writings.

He wasn't responsible for any of it. It just sort of happened on its own. He suspected the gods above had made it that way on purpose. They could've dropped the slab in the deepest ocean, buried it in impenetrable magma. There were dozens of places where no mortal might reach it, but that would have been boring. If there was one thing the gods despised, it was boredom.

A twenty-year-old woman in a tank top, no bra, and short shorts asked, "Is it true you're going to help all the animals?"

The Lost God sipped his soda. "Of course."

"And do something about the Man?" asked a second youth, draped in loose-fitting jeans and a lopsided baseball cap.

The Lost God, his gaze trained on the woman's ample bosom, nodded. "Yes, I'll get right on that."

A fat man in a Hawaiian shirt said, "Beg your pardon, Lord, but there's this guy at work who keeps using my reserved parking space—"

"Consider him smote."

His followers surrounded him. They assailed him with their petty requests. He pretended to listen for a moment. He didn't give a damn about their dreams of power. Mortals were such silly little things. While the gods above sometimes chose their favorites, the Lost God saw the lot of the creatures as pathetic, weak things. Amusing at times, and with so much potential, though he was convinced they would be able to realize that potential only after he'd burned their world to cinders.

Yet still mortals looked to him to offer them aid and comfort. If not him, then something else. Given the brief and disorienting nature of their existence, he didn't blame them. He listened to their prattling and nodded wisely, and they misread his condescending smile as sympathetic. In the end, it was the limit of any relief he would deliver them.

He grew bored and snapped his fingers. Thunder shook Castle Adventure.

"All your enemies will die horribly. All your desires will be satisfied. This world will be remade in a shape pleasing to you, and I shall reign, forever and ever and ever, with you, my loyal believers, at my side. Ice cream and cake for all. For those who dare stand in our way, only death, suffering, and the poorest parking spaces."

He eyed the buxom neo-hippie. "And every kitten shall have a loving home."

He motioned for her to approach. She knelt before him.

He took her hand, cupped her chin, and lifted her face to his. "Stand, not as my subject, but as a flower of the cosmos, a goddess in your own right."

She smiled. Mortals ate that nonsense up.

The gargoyle woman and trilby-hatted man approached again.

"My lord, there seems to be a problem." He fell and prostrated himself before the Lost God. "We're missing the final element. Without it, we can't complete the ritual to make permanent your ascension."

"I wouldn't worry about that. It should turn up soon."

"But..."

"Do you not trust in your benevolent god?" he asked.

"Your wisdom and power are beyond measure," said the gargoyle woman.

"Then believe me. The final object will turn up in time. Now prepare things while I acquaint myself with this lovely young creature." He ran his fingers through the young woman's long hair, and she smiled coyly.

They returned to their work.

He removed his helmet.

"Wow, you're even more gorgeous than I expected," said the neo-hippie.

"Aren't I, though?" He studied his reflection in the gleaming helmet. As host bodies went, Troy's was one of the best he'd worn.

"Can I try on your helmet?" she asked.

"Nobody tries on the helmet," he replied. "Tell me, child. What is your name?"

"Chandra."

"Nice to meet you, lovely Chandra. I am your god."

Since the dawn of time, he'd yet to need a better pickup line.

There were three obstacles to entering Castle Adventure.

The first was a velvet rope, and a sign reading CLOSED FOR RE-PAIRS. SORRY FOR THE INCONVENIENCE.

Helen undid the clasp and marched onward.

The second obstacle was a locked gate. She tried her key, but it didn't fit.

"Should we climb it?" asked Franklin.

Helen grabbed the wrought-iron gate and yanked. It snapped off its hinges with hardly any effort, and she tossed it aside.

"Remind me to stay on her good side," said James.

"You're already on my bad side," she said, and marched onward.

The last obstacle was a trio of sentries. Two wore knight costumes. The third was a blue-skinned ogre in khaki shorts and a Che Guevara T-shirt. Though the knights' armor was plastic, their swords were real enough. The ogre, though unarmed, was bigger than Helen.

The Wild Hunt and Achilles girded themselves for battle, but Helen calmed them with a gesture. She expected a fight, but in her current shape she was hoping to avoid it for as long as possible.

"We should have a signal for when it's time to attack," said Nigel.

"We'll probably know when that time is," replied Helen.

"Can't hurt to have something ready, just in case," said Franklin. "How about *grapefruit?*"

"Why *grapefruit?*" asked James.

"Why not?" answered Franklin. "It's an easy word to remember, but not so common it's likely to pop up randomly in the conversation."

The Wild Hunt agreed it made sense. They briefly debated other possibilities, like *honeydew* and *cantaloupe.* They moved on to non-melon possibilities, with Peggy suggesting *pineapple* because it didn't sound so tough, but it at least had a tough outer shell, and James offered *attack pattern alpha omega* because it sounded more badass, though it was a mouthful. They were still working on a consensus when Helen silenced them as they approached the guards.

"We're here to see your boss," she said. "I have something he needs."

A knight stepped forward and removed his oversized foam helmet. "You've been expected."

The guards allowed them entry through the great wooden doors. Helen and the Wild Hunt entered the castle and the guards followed close behind as an escort. Under normal circumstances the castle would've been a wonderland for tourists, full of interactive exhibits. Everything was switched off today. Half the lights were dimmed. Animatronic monsters stared at them as they passed, but they were too cartoonish to be frightening. The most sinister thing in the whole place was a sign warning against flash photography.

They were led up several flights of stairs and to the throne room, where the Lost God sat on his seat with Chandra on his lap.

Helen hated that. This wasn't Troy, but the Lost God wore Troy's body. Her first instinct was to pull Chandra from the throne and break her every bone. Helen attributed it to her bristling monstrous urges.

The Lost God smirked at her. He had Troy's face, but all the easy confidence Troy had exuded was gone, and arrogance had taken its place. She tried to see if any of Troy was buried under there, some influence she could play upon. If he was still in there, the god smothered him completely.

"You came? I must confess I'm a bit surprised. They don't always come."

Helen held up the old key. "Release Troy and you can have this."

A puzzled expression fell across the Lost God's face. "Why would I want that?"

"It's the key. The last thing you need to unlock your prison."

The Lost God gestured to one of his followers. They had a quick whispered conversation.

"You must be thinking of another banished god," he said. "I have all the relics I need."

"But the fates gave this to me," said Helen. "It's a key. It must have some symbolism, right?"

He looked genuinely puzzled by her confusion. "Don't ask me. I think the fates mostly make it up as they go along and then swoop in and take credit whenever the opportunity presents itself. Regardless, I have all the relics I need. I had the heroic sacrifice, thanks to Troy."

He stood suddenly, letting Chandra fall unceremoniously to the faux cobblestones in a way that made Helen smile.

"But the final ingredient for my freedom is the arrival of the headstrong fool, entering of his—or her—own free will, rendering the sacrifice meaningless. And here you are."

She squeezed the key tighter and cursed the gods. "Shit."

The Lost God put his helmet on. She was grateful for that.

"Getting the relics is the easy part," he said. "The sacrifice is a bit trickier. It happens maybe half the time. But the fool..."

She couldn't see his arrogant grin beneath the helmet, but she could imagine it.

"That's the part that so rarely lines up. To think that you're probably only here because of that useless key in your hand. I must remember to thank the Fates the next time I see them."

"Is that it then?" she asked. "You're free?"

"Oh, there's some incidental chanting, some dancing, maybe some wanton sexual depravity." He nodded toward Chandra. "A blood sacrifice, if we get around to it, though I understand that thing isn't quite as fashionable as it once was. But all the hard work is done, thanks to you, and this is mostly dotting the *i*'s and crossing the *t*'s. Nevertheless, you're welcome to stick around for it. In fact, I insist."

The followers formed a circle around Helen and the orcs.

"But it's all but done now, and there's nothing the gods above can do to stop it."

"Why do you even need Troy's body?" she asked. "I'm sure any of these people would be happy to serve as your host."

The cultists murmured and nodded among themselves.

"Have you seen this body?" The Lost God unbuttoned his shirt to reveal his bare chest. "Have you seen these abs, this muscle definition? This is the Cadillac of mortal flesh. Anything else would be a trade-down."

The cultists murmured and nodded among themselves.

Helen resorted to her last hope.

"I think I love him."

The Lost God walked up to her. "Of course you do. Why else would you be here? But if mortal life is fleeting, mortal affection is even less substantial. You'll get over it. Or you'll die horribly when the gods above try to stuff me back into my prison."

Thunder rumbled.

"What a bunch of killjoys. Banishment is almost preferable to having to deal with those idiots on a regular basis. Almost. You're quite lovely in a way. If you'd like to take a tumble with this mortal's fleshy shell after this is all said and done, let me know."

He put a hand on her face, and she shuddered. It wasn't Troy. He wasn't in there anymore. And if she'd lost him, she was sure as hell not going to let the Lost God keep what was left.

She put her hand on his, smiled.

"Grapefruit."

She unleashed a jackhammer punch right to his helmeted head. The Lost God flew across the throne room. He shattered his plywood throne and embedded into the fiberglass stone wall.

The Wild Hunt joined the battle, pouncing on the followers with every ounce of orcish fervor at their disposal. It was only half of what they had available under normal circumstances, but it was more than enough for their poorly trained and off-guard opponents. They might have been overwhelmed still, but a third of the cultists turned tail and ran, discovering they valued their lives more than their god's favor.

The ogre moved toward Helen. She punched him in the face, breaking his forty-dollar sunglasses. Blood dribbled down his nose and onto his Che Guevara T-shirt. The look on his face showed his surprise. Like her, he'd probably spent most of his life avoiding fights simply by being bigger and stronger than everyone. Unlike her, he hadn't spent the past few days fighting dragons.

She laid him out with a single mighty uppercut.

The Wild Hunt stared incredulously at the fallen giant. Helen smiled, slammed her fist into her knuckles.

The Lost God extracted himself from the wall. He adjusted his helmet and sighed. "So this is your army. These pathetic souls are all you bring to this fight."

"Seems like we beat the hell out of your army," said James Eyestabber.

The god nodded. "True enough."

He pointed at James, whose bones transformed into gelatin. The orc fell in a loosey-goosey pile of grumbling flesh.

"I suppose if you want anything done right, you simply must do it yourself. Shall we have at it then? Sometimes the gods are moved by entertaining displays of mortal courage. Perhaps they'll even give you a hand. I'll even give you first strike, but fair warning—"

Nigel threw his battle-ax. The dragonblood blade spun through the air, leaving a trail of frost behind it. The weapon sailed on target to strike the god, and in that moment Helen wondered if it could kill a god currently in a mortal body. If it could do that, then it could certainly kill the body as well.

The Lost God held up his hand, and the ax stopped in midair, dropped to the ground.

"You didn't let me finish. Fair warning, I cheat."

The Wild Hunt heedlessly joined a battle they had no chance

of winning. Their weapons bounced harmlessly off their foe, and he snapped his fingers, knocking friend and foe away. The entire fight lasted all of two seconds. Only Helen and Achilles managed to stay on their feet.

"If you really are a god in disguise," said Helen to the three-legged mutt, "now would be the time to show it."

Achilles pounced.

The Lost God swatted the dog away. Whimpering, Achilles limped to one side.

Helen grunted. "Terrific."

He pointed at her, and an invisible sledgehammer hit her in the stomach. She staggered but didn't fall. The hammer smashed her across the face, sending a couple of teeth flying from her jaw. It dropped on her shoulders, and she fell to one knee.

"You have spirit," he said, "even for the heedless fool. If you could wear the helmet, I'd be sorely tempted to change hosts."

"You can't have him," she grumbled through her shattered jaw.

He squeezed her hand, shattering its bones. She would've screamed, but she was already in so much pain she barely noticed that this added to it.

The amulet, the sword, the shield, the wand, and the dagger floated off the ground to orbit the Lost God. The ancient runes on the unholy slab glowed to life. The cloudless sky rumbled with the displeasure of the gods.

"Hey, don't get mad at me," he said. "You're the ones who chose such lousy champions."

Helen stood.

"You can't have him!" she shouted, though it mostly came out as an unintelligible roar.

"Oh, really? If you insist on dying, then so—"

In the heavens, the gods above would tell the story of Helen's mighty haymaker, the strike that would define mortal defiance in the face of a cruel universe. A blow that broke her other hand and staggered a living god in a way that caught even the Fates by surprise.

The strike knocked the Lost God's helmet off. The cursed object bounced to a rolling stop at Franklin's feet.

Why the gods above decided to act then, Helen didn't know. Perhaps they were inspired by her act of suicidal bravery. Or perhaps seeing the Lost God swayed by sheer determination, they could no longer sit on the sidelines. Or maybe they were just waiting for the opportunity, the momentary distraction.

Helen's fur stood on end as the air crackled with static electricity.

The Lost God snarled at the sky. "Oh, now you're really starting to piss me off."

She found the strength to jump out of the way as a bolt of cosmic power lanced through Castle Adventure's roof. The Lost God exploded.

Dust choked the air. Helen lay there, ignoring her pain, drawing ragged breaths. When the dust cleared a few minutes later, the Lost God lay not too far from her. His mortal body, Troy's body, was barely marred, but he wasn't moving. He'd been hurt at least.

She dragged herself over to him and looked into his eyes. There was no trace of Troy in there. Only the Lost God, who was quickly shaking off his daze.

Nigel threw the dagger. It landed beside her.

"You have to do it," he said. "One life against thousands. It sucks, but if the gods won't clean up their own messes, it's up to us."

She picked up the dagger in a hand barely able to hold it. The Lost God fixed her with his eyes and put a hand on her face. She saw Troy again. Perhaps he was closer to the surface because of the weakened state of the Lost God. Or the god had allowed him loose to play on her sympathies, to make her hesitate.

If so, it worked. She threw the blade away.

She couldn't do it.

The Lost God pushed her away and stood. "Sentimentality is a weakness I look forward to breeding out of you mortals. But enough of the previews. Let's get on with the main attraction, the headline act, the—"

Troy's features softened, and he was himself. Just like that.

"Hel? What…what's happening?"

Franklin, now wearing the Lost God's helmet, chuckled coldly. "Well, it's not as good as the old one, but it'll do in a pinch."

His body bulged with muscles. The light filtering through the hole in the ceiling cast a dim spotlight on him. In the twilight the indefinable, impossibly giant form of the gods above streaked toward Earth to begin, if not a war, then at least a divine bar brawl.

Nigel planted his battle-ax in Franklin's back.

The Lost God fell silent. He stumbled a few steps before falling on his face. Without saying so much as a dying curse, both the god and his mortal host perished.

The gods above veered away. The sun lit up a dusk that seemed bright and hopeful.

Troy ran to Helen. She fell into his arms, knocking them both to the ground, pinning him under her limp body. James and Peggy rolled her to one side.

"Helen!" Troy took her hand, and she didn't care that it hurt like hell. "Hel, stay with me!"

She smiled up at him. All her pain vanished as she squeezed his hand tighter.

"I'm not going anywhere."

33

Waechter supervised a small battalion of NQB agents in the midst of the cleanup operation. Agent Campbell handed him a clipboard as he exited the car. He flipped through the report.

"Is this true, Campbell?"

"As far as we can tell, sir."

"Imagine that. Gather up the artifacts anyway, just in case. Take a jackhammer to that stone. Maybe it'll take this time." He gave her the report. "How are our two renegade agents doing?"

"Miss Nicolaides was in bad shape when we arrived, but we gave her and the others some wine and they're recovering. Except for one Franklin Rodriguez, who was pronounced dead on scene."

"Only one casualty? That's something of a miracle, given the situation."

"Yes, sir. This operation did go off the rails at the end, didn't it?"

Waechter undid his tie. He'd always hated the damn thing. "Indeed it did, Campbell, but if this job were easy, they'd pay us less."

She went off to continue supervising, and he found Helen and Troy sitting by an ambulance. Achilles sat in Troy's lap.

"How are you?" asked Waechter. "Feeling better?"

"Still sore," said Helen, "but I can move. What was in that wine?"

"Enchanted grapes. Should fix you up, good as new, not even leave a scar behind."

"Thank you," said Troy.

She mumbled. He nudged her.

"Yeah, thanks," she said.

"No problem. So you very nearly made quite a mess of things, Miss Nicolaides."

"Sorry."

She didn't sound sorry.

"What happens to all the stuff we gathered?" she asked.

"We'll take them back for study, but they're all disenchanted as far as we can tell. They're just MacGuffins anyway, magical bric-a-brac. They have no importance of themselves. It's the act of collecting them that gives them their real power. Now that they've served their purpose, they're harmless.

"It's the same with that stone these idiots dug up. It was indestructible, but now it's just fifteen tons of granite. We'll destroy it now. We always do. It always comes back when the time is right. Though perhaps not this time."

"What happens to us now?" asked Helen.

Waechter bent down and scratched Achilles. "You go home."

"But didn't we break the law?"

"It's a funny thing, Miss Nicolaides. You defied logic and good sense and risked everything. In the process, you nearly ended up unleashing untold disaster that could've killed thousands. Hundreds of thousands. You did so for a prize no greater than the life of a friend.

"It could've gone horribly wrong, but it didn't. By some quirk of fate, you even managed to break a cycle that has gone on for eons. The Lost God is dead. He won't be back, and while there are still a thousand other quests out there we have to keep an eye on, there's one less. You might have done something stupid for a stupid reason, but we at the bureau can't argue with the results. If we threw every defiant, headstrong fool in prison, the NQB would be out of agents very quickly."

Waechter shook their hands.

"Take care of yourselves."

He walked away, but Troy stopped him. "Agent Waechter, not that I'm complaining, but someone told me that either Helen or I was fated to die because that's how legends go."

Waechter smiled. "Who says it was your legend?"

The Wild Hunt sat on the sidelines. Nigel spent the majority of that time staring at Franklin's corpse and running his fingers along the blade of his magic ax. The dragonblood steel was cold to the touch, but there was something new. A static charge caused the hair on his knuckles to curl.

Peggy put a hand on his shoulder. "You did what you had to do."

He grunted.

"What I don't get is how I killed him at all? He was a god."

"Avatar of a god," corrected Peggy.

"Close enough. He was also still affected by the dragon blood. Shouldn't he have regenerated like he did earlier? I mean, I had to try it, but I didn't think it would actually work."

"Blood against blood," said Peggy. "Like against like. Dragon blood is powerful stuff, but there's always a loophole with magic. No ordinary weapon could kill him, but your ax isn't ordinary. There's a lot of mojo running through it. Even more now that it has tasted the blood of a near-immortal. Something like that, in the right hands, can destroy anything. Even a god."

Nigel recalled the words of Thuzia, orc goddess of wisdom. "The hand of a mortal, chosen not by the gods or the Fates, but by his or her own will," he said.

"Something like that," said Peggy. "Think of that ax as your Excalibur. A power that builds kingdoms. Or destroys them. Usually both."

"It's an incredible amount of power for a mortal to have," said James.

The clear sky rumbled as the gods above voiced their agreement.

"Well then," said Nigel with a sly grin. "I'll just have to be careful with it, won't I?"

Thunder cracked.

Nigel nodded to the sky. "Oh, shut up."

The gods above quieted, though they could still be heard rumbling softly from their lofty perch.

"I wonder why Franklin put on the helmet," Peggy said. "Did it mesmerize him, take control of his weak mind?"

"He put it on because he was an idiot. He was always an idiot." Nigel scowled at the corpse. "He lived like an idiot. He died like an idiot."

"Oh, I don't know about that," said James. "Come on, guys. We all know why he did it. He had incredible power in his hands. He had to try it on. Best-case scenario, he would become a living god. Worst case, he gets a snazzy new helmet. Can you honestly say any of us would've done any differently?"

They shared a grin.

Peggy held up her plastic cup with a few drops of enchanted wine left in it. "To Franklin. He might have been an idiot, but he was a hell of an orc, all things considered. May his bones find a place of honor on the heap."

Nigel and James laughed.

"I'll drink to that." Nigel nodded to the stars twinkling in the heavens. "Take good care of the little guy." He tapped his god-killing ax with his knuckles. "Or you'll be hearing from me."

"Nigel Godkiller isn't someone to be trifled with," added James.

It was of the old ways for an orc of special achievement to earn a new name, though it wasn't practiced anymore.

"He wasn't a full god," said Nigel. "And it was a cheap shot."

"Still counts," said Peggy.

The agents threw Franklin's body on a stretcher and carried it away. Agent Waechter approached.

"Our research indicates that you're the closest thing he has to family. What do you want us to do with the body?"

"He's an orc, isn't he?" replied Nigel. "Burn it, feed it to wolves, donate it to science. We don't care."

"That's quite an ax you've got there," said Waechter. "Dipped in the blood of a dragon and now a mortal god."

"Two dragons," corrected Nigel. "It gets the job done." He

wrapped his fingers around the grip. "I suppose you'll want to take it from me."

"I'll admit the thought occurred to me, but we both know you won't surrender it easily. There's been enough violence today already."

"More than enough." Nigel slung the weapon over his shoulder.

"You'll be happy to know most of your friends are recovering from their injuries."

"Thanks." Nigel climbed on his motorcycle, started the engine.

"Oh, one more thing, Mr. Skullgnasher," shouted Waechter. "The South American division has been having a hell of a time with a snake monster prowling the jungles of Bolivia. They tell me it's prophesied to swallow the world. Probably an exaggeration, but the damn thing just won't die. I'm thinking that an ax that has killed a god might be up to the task."

"The wife's going to kill me if I don't come home soon," said Nigel.

"The firm has been sending me nasty e-mails," added Peggy Truthstalker.

"Too bad," said James Eyestabber. "I've always wanted to see Brazil. We could have stopped along the way."

"Beautiful country," said Waechter. "But you have obligations."

"Maybe we can move some things around," said Nigel. "We'll get back to you."

"You do that, Mr. Skullgnasher." Waechter handed Nigel a card. "We'll be in touch."

Nigel tucked the card in his jacket pocket. "The name's Godkiller."

34

Franklin sat in the shadow of the Gray Mountain, beside the Mound of Unworthy Bones, beneath the Cruel Skies. He'd been there a while, though time was meaningless with no days or nights to measure it, no hunger in his spirit body, nothing to do but sit by a cooler of cheap beers and drink.

Fortunately the cooler never seemed to empty, and the beer was cold enough. He was technically allowed only one, but he found he didn't care so much about rules now that he was dead. While the endless day had given him a bit of a sunburn, he was in no hurry. He was happy to relish the moment.

He'd made it.

The ground rumbled as Grog came burning down the Gray Mountain on his roaring motorcycle. The five-headed god revved the engine a few times before killing it. Silence swept the planes.

"Hi." Franklin smiled. He'd been smiling for what felt like weeks now. "Want a beer?"

Grog waved it away. "Sorry, but I'm in a bit of a hurry. I kept putting off getting to you until a convenient time came along. Then I forgot about you. Then I remembered, but...long story. Shall we get this over with?"

"So I did it?" asked Franklin. "I'm an orc now? All the way?"

Grog nodded. "All the way. Some of the other gods fought me over your soul, but I convinced them to back off. We don't often come across jurisdiction conflict such as yourself, but I said you'd earned this through deed and spirit. It took some arguing, but at the end of the day, I explained that you were on the verge of living godhood when you were stabbed in the back by your best friend. If that isn't an orc-worthy death, I don't know what is." A giant ax materialized in his hands. "Are you ready to take your place upon the mound?"

Franklin tossed away his beer and raised his fists. He still couldn't stop grinning.

The orc god lowered his weapon. "Some of the other gods did have a question, though. Me too."

It pleased Franklin to think of gods talking about him. In the cosmic scheme, he knew he amounted to little more than a speck. But at least he was a speck the gods had noticed, if only for a moment. It was more than he could've reasonably expected.

"Why'd you put on the helmet?" asked Grog.

Franklin lowered his fists. "Funny. I'm not really sure. I guess it just came down to having to try it."

"But how did you know it would work?"

"I didn't. But I figured, best-case scenario, I get to be a living god for a little while. Worst case, I get a snazzy new helmet."

"So you weren't trying to sacrifice yourself for the greater good?"

Franklin shrugged. "Nope. Just couldn't resist the opportunity."

Grog threw back his heads and laughed. The terrible din darkened the Cruel Skies. Four of his heads continued to chuckle as the fifth appraised Franklin.

"You're all right."

"Thanks."

Grog raised his mighty ax. Franklin couldn't escape the strike, but he thought if he timed a forward roll just right, the blood spatter from his corpse might stain Grog's boots. It was worth a shot. He leaped forward, but the ax blow never came.

He found himself staring up at the massive god, who was still holding his ax as if to strike.

"Is there a problem?" asked Franklin.

Grog propped his weapon over his shoulder. "Do you play bridge?"

"I used to, though I'm a bit rusty."

"Can you teach me?"

"Sure. If you need me to. Why?"

Grog said, "The other gods have a regular tournament. They always invite me, but they know I don't know how to play."

"Why don't you ask them to teach you?"

"Oh, they'd love that, a chance to teach the savage orc god how to play cards. Smug bastards, every last one of them."

It was Franklin's turn to laugh.

"What?"

"I just didn't expect you to be so insecure."

Grog ground his teeth together. "Let me tell you, it's not easy being a god of the orcs."

"I can imagine. Yes, I can teach you, but isn't it against the rules to not obliterate me and throw my bones on the pile?"

"I make the rules, so who is going to argue? Also, you're friends with Nigel Godkiller, and I'm not so sure I want to mess with that guy. I can always pencil you in tomorrow, though that's shuffleboard Tuesday. Ever play?"

"I won a tournament on a cruise. I'd show you my trophy, but it's back on the material plane."

"I'll take your word for it."

Grog climbed on his terrifying cycle. He revved the engine until Franklin thought his entire body would disintegrate. He noticed his own motorcycle, or at least the spirit equivalent, sitting beside Grog's own.

Franklin mounted his own iron steed. Its familiar rumble vibrated comfortingly. His soul and the god roared up the Gray Mountain. Franklin inhaled deeply, choking on the thick clouds of exhaust belched from Grog's terrible machine.

It smelled good.

35

Helen had worn a dress maybe three times in her life. She had nothing against them, but jeans were just so much easier. She twirled in front of her mirror. The red skirt swirled, and she had to admit she liked the way it looked. She was still a jeans girl, but sometimes it was nice to just feel pretty.

She turned to Achilles, sitting on her bed.

"What do you think?"

He wagged his tail. It'd been a week since they'd completed their quest, and if he was a god or helpful spirit in disguise, he had shown no signs of dropping the act. She doubted she'd ever be completely convinced there wasn't something supernatural about the dog, but it didn't matter. He'd earned his kibble and then some.

Her brother stuck his head in the doorway. "Hey, they're waiting."

"It's polite to knock," she said.

Will rapped on the door with his knuckles. "Everybody's waiting."

"Thanks. I'll be right down."

He looked her up and down.

"That's your cue to leave, squirt," she said, feeling self-conscious.

"You look good, Helen," he said.

"Thanks."

He pursed his lips and made kissing noises. "You're welcome."

She threw a brush at him, but he ducked behind the door.

She did look good. She might be taller than other girls. Hairier. But the benefit to all that fur was that she didn't have to worry about makeup, and shaving her legs would've been kind of weird. Not that it wasn't kind of weird already, when she thought about it.

She might not be the petite flower the world expected her to be, but that was the world's problem. She adjusted her breasts, ran a brush through her hair one last time, and drew in a deep breath. She'd battled a dragon, a cyclops, and a cannibal witch. She'd fought a god for the fate of Utah, Wyoming, and greater Idaho.

But tonight, things were getting serious.

She and Achilles walked downstairs. She'd imagined everyone gazing up at her as she descended, but they were all in the living room, talking. Helen paused to listen.

She heard Troy. "—Then, and I swear to the gods above, I was positive she was going to drive that dagger right through my heart."

Her mom and dad laughed.

"She almost killed you?" asked Will. "And now you're going out on a date with her?"

Troy said, "Guess you had to be there."

Helen glanced at him from the alcove. She didn't know how it was possible, but he was even more handsome than before. He wore a button-up shirt, black slacks, green-and-blue sneakers that would've looked hipster on anyone else. But damned if he didn't make it work.

"Sounds like you had quite an adventure," said Roxanne.

"I'm not going to lie," he replied. "There were some dark moments, but it all worked out in the end. I never would've discovered how wonderful your daughter is without this trip. She's very special."

Helen suddenly felt guilty for eavesdropping. She stepped into view and cleared her throat. All heads turned toward her.

"Oh, Helen." Roxanne wrapped Helen in a tight hug. "You look beautiful."

"Thanks, Mom."

Troy looked at her and smiled. Smiling wasn't unusual for him, but this one seemed special. As if it was one he'd been saving just for her.

She dreaded the conversation that was bound to happen now. She loved her family, but she wanted this over with. Troy came to her rescue.

He scratched Achilles behind the ears. "We better get going if we want to make the movie."

They bid hasty good-byes, though Roxanne insisted on several more hugs. She started crying too, though she did her best to keep it under control.

"You take good care of my little girl," she told Troy.

He promised he would. She insisted he call her Roxanne. Then demanded a few quick photographs. It took them five more minutes to finally walk out the front door. Helen's family watched them walk away until her dad, mercifully, shooed them back inside and shut the door.

"Well, that was awkward," said Helen.

"They're cute. I can see why you turned out so great." Troy took her hand. "You do look beautiful, y'know."

"Thanks."

"You're supposed to tell me I look good," he added.

"You always look good."

"Doesn't mean I don't like to hear it every so often."

She tousled his hair. "I had no idea you were so insecure."

"I have my moments."

She caught Roxanne watching them from slightly parted curtains.

"What movie are we seeing?" asked Helen.

"I made that up. I figured you'd want to end the awkward family-meeting-your-boyfriend stage as quickly as possible."

"My hero. Though I think it's a bit premature to say you're my boyfriend. This is our first date."

He winked at her and smiled. He could get away with anything with that smile.

"Hel, I forgot to ask you. Did you ever find a use for that key the fates gave you?"

She opened her handbag and showed him the old key. "I think getting me to walk into that castle was its purpose. Or maybe not. Maybe it was something they gave me with no purpose other than what I'd make of it. I'm not so sure the fates know what the hell they're doing, but nobody dares call them on it because they don't want to take the chance."

"It's a thought," he said.

"But they never said when it would come in handy. Maybe there's a door somewhere down the road waiting to be opened. For now, I think of it as my good-luck charm."

They leaned in and kissed, softly. Nothing very passionate, but sweet and wonderful.

"Thanks for almost destroying three states for me, Hel."

"Don't mention it, Troy."

She tossed the key away, where it was lost in the grass of the next lawn over. He raised an eyebrow.

"Who needs the fates?" she said. "I'll make my own luck from now on."

The next day she'd spend the better part of an afternoon looking for it. Optimism was great, but it never hurt to have a little help from the universe now and then.

Troy grinned at her.

"I think I love you, Hel."

She winked.

"I bet you say that to all the girls with tails."

extras

orbit

meet the author

Sally Hamilton

A. LEE MARTINEZ was born in El Paso, Texas. At the age of eighteen, for no apparent reason, he started writing novels. Thirteen short years (and a little over a dozen manuscripts) later, his first novel, *Gil's All Fright Diner*, was published. His hobbies include juggling, games of all sorts, and astral projecting. Also, he likes to sing along with the radio when he's in the car by himself. For more information on the author, check out www.aleemartinez.com or follow @aleemartinez on Twitter.

introducing

If you enjoyed
HELEN AND TROY'S EPIC ROAD QUEST,
look out for

THE EMPEROR MOLLUSK VERSUS THE SINISTER BRAIN

by A. Lee Martinez

Emperor Mollusk.

Intergalactic Menace. Destroyer of Worlds. Conqueror of Other Worlds. Mad Genius. Ex-Warlord of Earth.

Not bad for a guy without a spine.

But what's a villain to do after he's done... everything. With no new ambitions, he's happy to pitch in and solve the energy crisis or repel alien invaders should the need arise, but if he had his way, he'd prefer to be left alone to explore the boundaries of dangerous science. Just as a hobby, of course.

Retirement isn't easy though. If the boredom doesn't get him, there's always the Venusians. Or the Saturnites. Or the Mercurials.

345

*Or... well, you get the idea. If that wasn't bad enough, there are also
the assassins of a legendary death cult and an up-and-coming mega-
lomaniac (as brilliant as he is bodiless) who have marked Emperor
for their own nefarious purposes. But Mollusk isn't about to let the
Earth slip out of his own tentacles and into the less capable clutches of
another. So it's time to dust off the old death ray and come out of retirement. Except this time, he's not out to rule the world. He's out to
save it from the peril of THE SINISTER BRAIN!*

There's no sound in space, but my saucer cannons simulated
a shriek with every blast. A swoosh followed every barrel roll.
And when my autogunner scored a hit, a sophisticated program supplied the appropriate level of response, ranging from
a simple ping to a full-fledged explosion. I could have pro-
grammed it to provide an explosion every time, but that
would've cheapened the experience.

The atmosphere burst with color as the cannons belched
their staccato rhythm. My ship blasted the enemy fighters to
scrap, but an impressive fleet stood between my target and me.
The shields were holding, but I had only a few moments before
I was disabled.

I'd gone over my exo options before mission. Neptunons
might have been the smartest race in the galaxy, but outside of
our exoskeletons, we couldn't do much more than flop around.
We could drag ourselves across the floor, a means of mobility
both embarrassing and ineffective. Our brains had grown too
fast, and we just hadn't possessed the patience to wait around
for nature to bestow what we could give ourselves. Over the
centuries, we'd only grown smarter and squishier.

The obvious choice for an exo on this mission would've been

a big, burly combative model. But I'd opted for stealth, taking a modified Ninja-3 prototype. It stood barely five feet tall and space limitations meant it didn't pack much weaponry. But I wasn't planning on fighting every soldier on the station. It sounded like a laugh, but time was a factor. Terra was a little over six minutes from total subjugation.

I slipped into my exo, loaded myself into the launch tube, and prepared to fire.

"It was a pleasure serving with you, sir," said the craft's computer.

"Likewise."

I ejected, rocketing through space in a jet-black torpedo that was practically invisible in the darkness of space. A stray plasma blast could've gotten lucky and struck the torpedo. If it didn't destroy me outright, it would knock the torpedo off course, either sending me spinning into the void of space or plummeting to Terra. But I'd done the math and decided to take my chances.

The torpedo breached the station's hull. I kicked open the torpedo's door and exited. There were no guards. Only a couple of technicians gasping for air. The artificial gravity held them in place, but the decompression had taken all the oxygen.

A security team stormed the room. I vaulted over their heads before they got off a shot. A few punches from my exo's four arms knocked them all senseless before they could even realize I was behind them. The Ninja-3 had several built-in blades, but I tried not to kill people just for annoying me.

I took a second to grab the emergency oxygen masks off the wall and toss them to the technicians.

Then I was on my way. My exo's camouflage feature allowed me to avoid guards. I slipped through the security net without much trouble, though it took a few minutes. By the time I reached the device, I was running short on time.

The immense orb hovered in a containment field. Hundreds of lights, purely ornamental, blinked across its surface. Its ultrasonic hum filled the chamber. Only a Neptunon could hear the sound without having their brain melt.

I blasted the device. It shattered into a thousand little pieces. There was nothing inside. Just a ceramic mock-up of a doomsday weapon.

A door opened, and a Neptunon in a hulking exoskeleton marched into the chamber. He banged his hands together. Their metallic clapping echoed.

"You didn't think it would be that easy, did you?" he asked.

All Neptunons look alike. We even have trouble telling each other apart. It wasn't surprising that this one looked like me, but the resemblance went deeper.

The clone had been a mistake. I don't often make mistakes, but I own up to them when they happen.

"A decoy," I said.

Emperor Mollusk, Mark Two, laughed maniacally. Had I really sounded like that? The clone carried a set of memories minus a few years of experience and the personality to match. Looking at yourself, at who you used to be, wasn't pretty.

"You should see the look on your face," he said. "How does it feel to be outwitted?"

"Someone was going to do it eventually," I replied. "At least I can take some small comfort that I outmaneuvered myself."

"Yes, if anyone could do it..." He raised an eye ridge in a pompous, self-satisfied manner. We don't have eyebrows.

"The fleet, the personnel, the space station," I said. "This must have cost you a small fortune."

"Ah, but it was necessary, wasn't it? I knew that only one being in this system had the knowledge and ability to pose any significant risk to my plan. I couldn't hide an operation like this without something to distract you. So I devised a small game for your amusement. Little clues leading to a fun diversion then a full-blown operation that was every bit as involved and complex as the real thing. But at the heart of it . . . nothing."

I said, "Meanwhile, you build your weapon somewhere else, somewhere unimportant, somewhere unnoticed. It was exactly what I would've done."

"And now nothing can stop me. In three minutes, Terra shall be mine."

"You don't want it."

He chuckled, but one look at my face told him I was serious. Neptunons might not have the most expressive features, but we get by.

"Having billions of dominated souls chant your name in unison can be great for the self-esteem. Although, really, self-esteem was never our problem, was it?" I asked.

Mark Two studied me skeptically. He suspected a trap, trying to figure out my angle. There was no angle. Just a lesson learned.

"Once you're crowned Warlord of Terra, you'll see that it's a lot more responsibility than I . . . we . . . planned."

He scanned for any sign of deception. I had never been a very good liar. Strange, considering my hobby as a world conqueror, but it was a conscious choice. Being a skilled liar might have made the job easier, but telling the truth, with the occasional lie by omission, increased the difficulty level.

"Let me tell you how everything will go if you succeed," I

said. "You'll become ruler of this world. You'll hold it in your hands like a beautiful blue pearl. That'll be enough at first. Just to have it.

"But then you'll start tinkering. Oh, you'll have the best of intentions. You'll fix those little pestering problems the Terrans themselves never could. Hunger. War. Poverty. Those will be easy, a long weekend.

"After that, you'll struggle against the relentless urges that drive you. You'll realize, intellectually, that there's little left to do. But you won't be able to help yourself. Terra will become your own personal science project until your inevitable nature nearly destroys the world. Several times.

"Now, providing you manage to prevent this, you'll learn some restraint. But it'll always be there. That insistent desire, that nagging need. You'll never be able to suppress it. Not completely. And you'll find yourself wondering if tomorrow is the day you destroy it, most probably by accident."

Mark Two said, "I'll learn from your mistakes."

"Or you'll just make slightly different variations of the same ones. Regardless, the Terrans have been through enough under one warlord. They don't need another."

A klaxon blared, signaling the final countdown. I pushed a button on my exo, and the station blast shields lowered. Mark Two frowned, realizing that I'd hacked his systems.

Mark Two shook off his confusion and resumed his laughter. "I don't know what happened to you in the time since you were me, but it doesn't matter. Terra will be mine, and there's not a thing you can—"

"I already stopped it. You didn't think you could hide your operation in Minneapolis from me, did you?"

He smiled. "No, that was merely another decoy."

"Of course, it was," I replied. "As were your machinations in Lisbon, St. Petersburg, and Busan."

His smile dropped.

"I'll admit you almost had me with Melbourne," I said. "But the decoy in Geneva was sloppy work, if I may be so bold as to offer some criticism."

He wasn't angered. He was curious. He was me, after all. And I was rarely frustrated by my failures. I preferred using them as learning opportunities.

I pressed another button. I kept the gravity and lights on for convenience, but everything else in the station went dead. The countdown ended. The doomsday device, the *real* device hidden aboard this station, wound down.

Mark Two glared. "How did you—"

"I'm you, remember. Just you with a few more years' experience. Everything you've done, I've already thought of. Every contingency plan, every possibility, I already did five years ago before you were even hatched from your tank."

He hid his incredulity behind a scowl, but I sensed it. If the situation were reversed, I'd have been the same. I hadn't been one hundred percent certain that I would foil his plans. But I was a humbler guy now than I was when I had been him.

His mottled flesh darkened with rage. I could see where he was coming from. I'd failed before, but I'd never been outwitted. But I'd never had to face off against myself. Now it'd all gone freshwater for Mark Two, as the old Neptunon saying went.

His hulking exoskeleton lumbered forward. "You may have stopped me this time, but you won't be around to stop me the next."

He threw a clumsy punch that would've pulverized the

Ninja-3 if I hadn't sidestepped the blow. He followed that with a haymaker that I danced under. I glided behind him and used a microfilament blade to slice open the hydraulics behind the exo's right knee. It wobbled but didn't fall.

He hadn't even bothered to change the specs. Perhaps he wasn't a perfect clone after all.

Mark Two teetered on his damaged leg as he struggled to line me up in his sights, but it was a simple thing for me to scamper up his back. I stabbed a few vital systems along the way. The last thing I hit was the stabilizer. His powerful exo tumbled over, ten tons of scrap metal.

A hatch opened, and he ejected in a smaller exo. The clear, fluid-filled dome that held his head bubbled with his frustration. I'd never lost my temper like that, but then again, I'd never been foiled so effortlessly. Or maybe the cloning process had simply been incapable of re-creating every bit of my pragmatic genius. He must've known his backup was no match for my Ninja, but in his anger, he didn't care. I dodged the blasts he sent my way and dismantled his exo with three efficient cuts. It clattered to the floor in pieces.

He flopped around, glaring daggers. Neptunons could survive out of water for extended periods, but it wasn't comfortable.

"You can't stop me," he gurgled. "I'll be back."

"No, you won't."

I activated the station's self-destruct countdown. Just a little something I'd slipped into his blueprints when he wasn't looking.

"So that's it?" he asked. "You're just going to leave me here to die?"

"I'm afraid so. No hard feelings."

Mark Two undulated in a shrug. "No, I suppose not. I'd do the same to you if the situation were reversed."

"I guess I haven't changed so much after all," I replied.

We shared a laugh.

"Just tell me something. It would've worked, right?"

"It would have worked," I said.

He grinned. "That's something at least."

"Yeah, it's something."

I made my escape without incident, boarding my automated rendezvous craft, and watched the station explode from a safe distance.

It was quite beautiful.

Then I pondered the small world below, oblivious to its own fragility.